Spellbound

Also by Hilary Norman:

In Love & Friendship
Chateau Ella
Shattered Stars
Fascination

HILARY NORMAN

Spellbound

A DUTTON BOOK

DUTTON
Published by the Penguin Group
Penguin Books USA Inc., 375 Hudson Street,
New York, New York 10014, U.S.A.
Penguin Books Ltd, 27 Wrights Lane,
London W8 5TZ, England
Penguin Books Australia Ltd, Ringwood,
Victoria, Australia
Penguin Books Canada Ltd, 10 Alcorn Avenue,
Toronto, Ontario, Canada M4V 3B2
Penguin Books (N.Z.) Ltd, 182–190 Wairau Road,
Auckland 10, New Zealand

Penguin Books Ltd, Registered Offices:
Harmondsworth, Middlesex, England

First published by Dutton, an imprint of New American Library, a division of Penguin
Books USA Inc.

First Printing, July, 1993
10 9 8 7 6 5 4 3 2 1

Quote on page xi is from *The Prophet* by Kalil Gibran. Copyright 1923 by Kalil Gibran and
renewed 1951 by Administrators C.T.A. of Kalil Gibran estate and Mary G. Gibran.
Reprinted by permission of Alfred A. Knopf, Inc.

 REGISTERED TRADEMARK—MARCA REGISTRADA

LIBRARY OF CONGRESS CATALOGING IN PUBLICATION DATA
Norman, Hilary.
    Spellbound / Hilary Norman.
      p. cm.
    ISBN 0-525-93621-1
    I. Title.
    PR6064.O743S64   1993
    823'.914—dc20   93–11993
                                       CIP

Printed in the United States of America
Set in Garamond Light
Designed by Leonard Telesca

For my nephew, David

ACKNOWLEDGMENTS

A number of kind people and organizations gave me their valuable assistance and time during the research and writing of this novel, but I owe special thanks to the following (in alphabetical order):

Jon, Barbara, and David Ash; Howard Barmad; Andrea Blackwell; Officer Frank Bogucki, NYPD; Clare Bristow; Carolyn Caughey; Sara Fisher; John Hawkins; Liz and Ray Hopwood, The King's Arms Hotel, Askrigg; Dr. Anthony Isaacs; Sarah Kilgarriff; Elaine Koster; Audrey LaFehr; Agnes and Ole Licht; Burlington Bookshop, NYC; Mrs. H. Norman; Helen Rose; Neal Rose; Susan Sheldon; Dr. Jonathan Tarlow; Michael Thomas; Joyce Thorp. And extra special thanks to Anthony Cornish, for his patience, expertise and generosity.

AUTHOR'S NOTE

Since this is a work of total fiction, much of which is located in the very real world of theater, I have mixed truth with make-believe in a number of places. The productions I have written about are wholly fictitious, whereas most of the theaters are not. For instance, neither Diana Lancaster nor any real actress could have played Titania at Stratford-upon-Avon in October 1944, since out of the six productions that did play the Shakespeare Memorial Theatre during that month, not one was of a Shakespeare play. With regard to my fictitious 1954 production of *Hedda Gabler*, I do feel compelled to pay my respects to Dame Peggy Ashcroft's hugely acclaimed portrayal of Hedda which opened at the Lyric Hammersmith in September of that year.

I hope that all the participants in the productions actually playing in the theaters at the times about which I've written, will forgive me.

You may give your children your love but not your thoughts,
For they have their own thoughts.
You may house their bodies but not their souls,
For their souls dwell in the house of tomorrow, which
you cannot visit, not even in your dreams.

—Kahlil Gibran, "On Children," *The Prophet*

Extract from his statement to the police, given by Jeremy James Adam Mariner at St. George's Hospital, London, on Friday, December 31, 1976

What can I tell you? Sebastian Locke's my best friend, as well as my business partner. He's one of the finest artist's agents in the country. He's sharp, he has brilliant instincts and he cares—he's never stopped caring. But so far as his private life goes, I think he's been wretched for years, though he never really admitted it, at least not to me. I think he hardly admitted it to himself.

I've known Seb since we were both five. I met Katharine, briefly, when she was the same age, but I didn't really get to know her until she was in her mid-twenties. Just over two years ago. It's strange, you know, but I think I know almost as much about her background as his. Seb's been my best friend for about as long as I can remember, but he's always been a bit of a closed book, but Kate—well, Kate's an honest, open girl.

I don't think she really wanted to be an actress at all. She just wanted to do anything that would make Seb happy. Katharine's like that. I'm afraid she's always believed, in her heart, that I resent her—perhaps even that I hate her. Actually, I like Kate. I admire her.

But I love Sebastian.

We were all there together, you know, when it began—all the stuff that's ended up here tonight. Such a stupid, tragic, fucking waste.

It was May 1954. We were in The Oaks—Seb's family's house—he still lives there. It was warm for May, I remember.

Just coincidence, I suppose, our all being there—unless you believe in predestination. And for Katharine and me, it wasn't really all that much more than an incident—we didn't understand, and our parents got us out of the house before it got too heavy. I felt sorry for Seb, later, of course, but at the time, I'm sure I just felt bloody relieved to be able to escape. Kate and I thought we came away from The Oaks unscathed. But we didn't.

We both know that now.

PART

One

c h a p t e r

1

The last time Sebastian saw his mother, she had just shot herself, through the head.

She lay, sprawled on the couch, limp and dead, but still beautiful, her face pale and still, her dark, wavy hair a little unpinned. Sebastian sat bolt upright in his seat, his hands clenched, his heart pounding, unable to move, and his eyes were trained, through his opera glasses, with ferocious urgency, on her chest, exactly as she, just a few hours ago, had directed him.

There. It rose, scarcely perceptible, fell, then rose again.

Sebastian sank back against his velvet seat, tore his eyes away from the stage for just an instant, stared up at his father's rapt face, and grinned, shakily.

It had been the most exciting moment of his life.

He was only seven years old, but he already knew all about theater, had been steeped in it almost from the day of his birth. Their house was a theatrical home, its walls decked with photographs, posters and playbills, its bookshelves laden with plays and scripts and cuttings albums, its handsome cabinets crammed with awards. Most of his parents' friends were actors or writers, or directors or producers, and all his mother's many superstitions had their roots in the dressing room.

Until today, however, although Sebastian had watched and heard his mother rehearsing many more times than he was able to count, he had never seen her on a real stage. He had seen her on a cinema screen, in the single film she had made when he was five, but this was only the second part to have enticed her out of the house and out of his nursery. This was the role that Diana Lancaster had wanted to play all through her illustrious career, the role that had, until now, eluded her. And although Sebastian knew that she had been unwell, that his father, Andrew Locke, had been concerned about her, that sometimes, during the course of rehearsals, their doctor had come and gone with unsettling frequency, Diana had made it absolutely plain that she was not prepared to be cheated, even by her own ill health, out of this, of all parts.

Sebastian had heard his parents, who seldom quarreled about anything, arguing heatedly behind their closed bedroom door, and although he knew that eavesdropping was strictly forbidden, he had listened for long enough to realize that his father had wanted his mother to rest, but that she had no intention of giving way.

"No one else is going to play Hedda," he had heard her voice ring out one morning, clearly, passionately, unequivocally. "No one, do you hear?"

He had visited her, before the dress rehearsal, in her dressing room backstage, had been permitted to stay with her while she applied the heavy makeup that had transformed her from his familiar, beloved mother into someone else, a charismatic, bewitching stranger of whom he felt in awe. But he had known her kiss, had known her scent, her rich voice and the loving gentleness of her arms as she had embraced him, before Rose, her dresser, had claimed her from him. And he had listened intently as she had cautioned him to pay attention to the play, to allow himself to be immersed in the magic of theater, if it captivated him as it had her at his age. And then she had reminded him that everything he was about to see was, no matter how real or terrible it might seem, make-believe.

"You will even see me die, my darling," she had told him gently and carefully. "Right at the very end of the play. And it may even, for just a moment or two, seem quite real to you."

"But it won't be." His own voice had trembled a little.

"Of course it won't. If you watch me very, very carefully, through your opera glasses—Daddy will see that you have a pair—you'll see that I'm still quite alive. Keep your eyes here"—Diana had laid one hand on her chest to show him—"and you'll be able to see me breathing, and you'll know that Hedda Gabler may be dead, but your Mummy will be home later on as usual."

"Will you come and kiss me good night?" he had asked, still just a tiny bit anxious.

"Certainly I will, darling. But I may be late, so you're to go to bed and go right to sleep."

"But you'll still come in?"

"Just you try and stop me." And she had embraced him again, and he had closed his eyes and inhaled her wonderful, special fragrance, and he had felt an intense and rare excitement.

There were scenes in the play that he had not really understood at all, some that had felt disturbing, others that had so bored him that he had almost fallen asleep. But his father's touch on his arm, and his occasional whispers of explanation and encouragement had bolstered him, and Sebastian *had* felt the magic, had, after a time, come to believe in what he saw and heard on the stage. And he had felt entranced by the theater itself, by its sounds and smells, by the rows of plush, mostly empty seats, by the handsome pillars and columns, by the dark, empty boxes that loomed above either side of the stage, by the spotlights and the curious way in which specks of dust danced, trapped in their beams . . .

It had been the first time. Already, he longed for the next.

He wanted to go backstage again afterward, to see her again as that fascinating, spellbinding half-stranger, to experience once more that moment of high excitement, that prickle of tension, when the stranger touched him, spoke to him, kissed him and became, again, his mother. But that wasn't possible today, Daddy said, though it might be on other days, after the show had opened to the public, after matinees, perhaps. This afternoon, however, Diana would have to stay behind with the other actors to receive the director's notes, while Andrew and Sebastian went off onto the next stage of these days of celebration.

These, Mummy had explained to Sebastian, were special, rare days. There was nothing like the last week of rehearsal, she had told him, nothing like the dress rehearsal and, beyond that, *nothing* like opening night itself. There would be a party after the first night, she told him, and if the play had gone well, they would be ecstatic, though everybody involved with the show—everyone from the cast right down to the people who sold the tickets in the box office—would be gnawing nervously at their knuckles until the reviews were in.

"On the morning after the show," Diana had warned Sebastian, "you may find me gloriously happy or terribly miserable. But even if it's all gone horribly wrong and I'm in the absolute doldrums, you have to understand that it's still worthwhile, because even if it's hard for you—for anyone who isn't in the theater—to understand, there is nothing on earth as thrilling as putting on a show."

And then, he remembered, she had given him one of her extra-special hugs, adding that he, of course, was the exception to that rule. That having Sebastian had put even the finest play, the most glowing reviews and the fullest houses, in the shade.

Because these few days were, inevitably, "grown-up" days, where seven-year-old boys, however well mannered, could not participate, Andrew and Diana had arranged a little house party for Sebastian. Jeremy Mariner—his best friend from the preparatory school in Hampstead that they both attended even though the Mariners' London home was in Regent's Park—was to stay at The Oaks, the Lockes' house in the Vale of Health near Hampstead Heath, for three nights; and a girl neither of them knew, the five-year-old daughter of American friends of Diana's and Andrew's, a girl called Katharine Andersen, was to stay for two. The boys did not exactly approve; she was, after all, unknown, foreign, younger than they were and, worst of all, a girl. But the Andersens were staying at the Savoy, where the opening night party was to be held, and Diana and Andrew had thought that it would be much more fun for Katharine to come to Hampstead and be with other children.

Andrew drove Sebastian from the theater first to pick up Jeremy, and then on to the Savoy, where Andrew left the boys in the Rover and went into the hotel to fetch Katharine, and then, after a short, but awkwardly silent drive to Fortnum & Mason in Piccadilly, they filed into the Fountain Restaurant for high tea.

"What would you like, Katharine?" Andrew smiled sympathetically at the pretty blond child as the boys, Sebastian flaxen-haired and Jeremy very dark, sat rather straighter than usual, not quite hostile, but far from welcoming. "It's all delicious, isn't it, boys?"

"Absolutely scrumptious." Sebastian looked at Katharine. "We've just been to the theater," he said.

"I know." She smiled. "Your mother's an actress, isn't she?"

"A great actress," Sebastian said, not exactly bragging, but intensely proud and wanting everyone to know it.

"I love the theater," Jeremy told her.

"I've never been," Katharine said.

"I've been heaps of times," Jeremy said loftily, though he had, in fact, been twice, both times to pantomimes at Christmas.

"Katharine's mother is an actress, too," Andrew told the boys.

"But she's not in *Hedda Gabler*, is she?" Sebastian asked.

"She's in the hotel," Katharine said.

"That's the name of a play, silly," Jeremy said, and sniggered.

"Oh." Katharine's cheeks turned a touch pink, and she wriggled in her seat.

"You never heard of *Hedda Gabler* before I told you about it," Sebastian reminded Jeremy, and turned to Katharine. "I like your accent. It's American, isn't it?"

"I like yours too," she said, and smiled at him gratefully. She had dimples in both cheeks, Sebastian noticed, and her eyes were a color he'd never seen before, a sort of golden brown.

It was almost six o'clock before they left Fortnum's, after steak-and-kidney pies and waffles with maple syrup, and headed north toward Hampstead. Andrew Locke was not an actor, nor had anything to do with the theater at all; he was, in fact, a barrister with a substantial practice near Lincoln's Inn Fields, but since his wife had returned to acting, Andrew often took time off to help out with Sebastian, or to ferry Diana to and from the theater, and he never complained, never had any desire to complain, for he had known that she was an actress when he had first fallen in love with her, and he understood one of the basic tenets of theater folk: that the play was, almost always, more important than anything else, and certainly infinitely more important than a drab old law practice, however lucrative.

Back at The Oaks, the Lockes' house, Katharine was shown to her bedroom, and the usual argument arose between Sebastian and his father about the rule, laid down by Annabel Mariner, Jeremy's mother, that her son was only permitted to stay over if the boys did not share a room. Jeremy was asthmatic, and the first time he had slept at The Oaks the boys had, inevitably, stayed up most of the night, and

Annabel Mariner had blamed the severe attack her son had suffered the next day on high jinks. From then on, whether the boys were staying in Hampstead, or at the Mariners' flat in Regent's Park, or at their estate in Yorkshire, Sebastian and Jeremy slept in separate bedrooms.

"I can't see any point in arguing about it," Andrew reasoned with his son in the wood-paneled hall. "Rules are rules, and besides, we both know perfectly well that it's never stopped you from having as much fun as you like."

"Are you going back to the theater now, Daddy?"

"Of course, and I've no idea when we'll be back, so Ellie's in charge, and you'll do as she tells you, right?"

"Right."

"And you boys be nice to Katharine—remember, she's younger than you are, and a guest."

"It's going to be a bit difficult."

"I don't see why."

"She's a girl," Sebastian said, as if that explained everything.

"Girls are people, too, Seb, you know," Andrew reminded him gently.

"I know that, Daddy."

"Make sure that Jeremy does, too, okay?"

"Okay."

Katharine Andersen was certainly only five years old, but within moments of meeting Sebastian Locke and Jeremy Mariner, she had already come to understand that five-year-old girls were not in the least bit inferior to seven-year-old boys. Boys did not scare her, anyway. She didn't have any brothers, just her three-year-old sister, Annie, but she'd met plenty of boys in her kindergarten in Washington, D.C., and whenever Mommy or Nanny Cooper took her to the playground in the park, Katharine liked playing with Bobby and Gary Fisher, who were twins, and seven and a half years old, far better than she liked playing with their kid sister, Babs.

These English boys didn't scare her two hoots, but she wasn't quite so sure about being left all alone in a strange room in a great big strange house in a strange country, miles and miles away from her parents. She'd liked the Savoy, loved their beautiful suite, comfortingly scattered, within moments of their arrival, with her father's belongings. Mommy was always complaining that Daddy was untidy, but Daddy said that he had to spend most of his life being so neat and clean that he liked nothing better when he got home than getting what he called "comfortable." Katharine loved spending time with her parents, and would certainly have preferred to stay at the hotel with them; but Mommy had arranged this for her before they came to London, had decided it would be a special treat for her, and Katharine knew that arrangements had already been made and that it would be considered discourteous to change them. *Discourteous* meant the same as *rude*, and Mommy had talked to her on the airplane about British good manners and how important it was to be polite in London, even more than it was back home, though of course it was important there too.

Katharine looked around the room in which she had been left "to get comfortable." It was a grown-up's bedroom, with everything at adult height. She could see that she would have to stand on something to reach the handbasin on the far wall, and the bed was so high that she'd have to remember to lie right in the middle so as not to fall out. The wardrobes were all wood, exactly the same kind of wood as the dressing table and the bedside tables on either side of the bed, and there was a big rug on the floor that had a warm red background color, with a sort of painting woven into its tufts in all kinds of rich shades.

There was a knock at the door, and Ellie Wilkins, the gently spoken Welsh-born housekeeper to whom Katharine had been introduced downstairs, came in carrying a vase of daffodils and tulips, and three pink towels draped over her left arm.

"To brighten things up for you, my dear," she said, putting the vase on the dressing table and hanging the towels over the rail by the basin. "Did anyone show you where the bathroom is?"

"Yes, thank you," Katharine said, trying to be extra polite. "I like the flowers."

"They're from our garden." Ellie walked over to the window. "You can't see it from this room, but you've a lovely view of the Heath."

Katharine had seen the wonderful, sprawling expanse of heathland on the drive up to the house, and Sebastian had told her that he and his father often walked their dogs, Jasper and Rufus, on the Heath on Sunday mornings. She hadn't seen the dogs yet, since their greetings tended to be exuberant and Ellie had taken the precaution of shutting them out in the back garden in case they overwhelmed the little girl.

"Are you ready?" Sebastian appeared in the doorway. He had changed out of his smart, theater and Fortnum & Mason clothes into a pair of corduroy trousers and a blue cotton pullover that made his blue eyes seem even bluer. "Aren't you going to change, Katharine? We're going to be playing in the garden."

"Did you bring something else with you, my dear?" Ellie asked, wanting to give Katharine the opportunity to escape, in case the prospect of games in the garden with two bigger boys was too daunting for her.

"I think so." Katharine was already delving into the small overnight case that her mother had packed for her. "Is this okay?" She pulled out a tartan skirt and red sweater that Mommy had said would do if she needed something more sporty.

"They look awfully nice," Sebastian said doubtfully. "What if they get mud on them?"

"It won't matter."

"Are you sure?"

"Yes, thank you."

"Okay. See you downstairs in five minutes." Sebastian remembered his manners. "Or however long it takes you to change."

It took her less than five minutes, keen as she was to let the boys know she was a match for them, and when she told them that they should call her "Kate," Sebastian felt suddenly certain that having her around was going to be fun, though it was pretty clear that Jeremy still resented her being there.

"What would you like to do?" he asked her.

"It doesn't matter," she answered.

"We were going to play Explorers," Jeremy said.

"That sounds good," Katharine said.

"It sometimes gets a bit rough," Sebastian counseled.

"I don't mind," she said.

The game was fine, as they pretended to be intrepid explorers in South America, climbing a planted rockery that was transformed, in their minds, into a mountain, and having to leap a small pond that was, Sebastian declared, an alligator-infested swamp. Her legs being shorter than the boys', Katharine didn't quite make the jump, and fell into the pond, but it was shallow, and though she did experience a moment's anxiety over what her mother would have to say about her sodden shoes, she suppressed the thought and giggled as the dogs barked wildly and Sebastian and Jeremy took one arm each to rescue her. And in the end, it was Jeremy who began coughing, so that Sebastian, warned to be alert for signs of his friend's asthma, went to fetch Ellie, who terminated the game and brought them inside to play gentler, if far-less-satisfying, games of Snakes and Ladders and pick-up-sticks, until it was time for milk and biscuits, when Katharine endeared herself to both boys by telling them a series of ghost stories with such relish that they forgot completely that she was either five years old, or a girl.

And then, at last, it was bedtime.

They all slept well, tired out from excitement, fresh air and exercise. Jeremy, his breathing quiet now and even, lay sprawled on the top of his covers, as he usually did, his narrow features, always a little taut in wakefulness, softened by sleep. Katharine, tucked securely into the center of her great high bed, dreamed of her parents and her sister and home, and of waffles with maple syrup and of two big golden dogs who licked her face and wagged their tails and made her laugh.

Sebastian, too, was sleeping peacefully, the nursery in which he had slept since infancy bathed in soft moonlight, a gentle breeze from the slightly opened windows making the tassels on the overhead lampshade dance. It was a perfect room. A place for sleeping and for playing, full of warmth and security and love, every detail designed with utmost care, flawlessly calculated to keep the child safe from harm but carefree nonetheless—even the steel bars at the windows had been wrought in teddy bear shapes. And at the foot of the bed, the toys, stuffed animals, miniature trains and cars and airplanes, a skipping rope, a football and a cricket bat, spilling over the top of the big hamper, waiting for morning. Nothing too neat. Nothing too tidy. All normal.

It was pitch-dark when he awoke, startled out of sleep, he thought for a moment, by an alien sound of distress. There were no heavy curtains at the windows, but the moon had disappeared behind black clouds, and a strong wind was whistling and cracking through the branches of the great oaks in their garden and beyond, on the Heath. Sebastian lay very still, listening to the storm, watching the eerie shadows being thrown back and forth across the room, and his head ached a little, his scalp felt tight, and he felt unaccountably afraid.

He wondered if Jeremy and Katharine were awake, too, but the fear chained him to his bed, prevented him from getting up and leaving the safety of his room. Fear was a quite unfamiliar sensation, yet suddenly it was tangible and terrible, and the fact that he knew that it was groundless did little to comfort him.

Dawn consoled him, calmed him. The nursery lightened, the shapeless blurs came into sharper focus, and, relieved, Sebastian rested back more comfortably on his pillow, closed his eyes and knew that in just a few hours it would be time to get up, and then he would see his mother and father, and Ellie would make breakfast for him and for Jeremy and Kate. And he remembered the previous day, remembered his mother on stage. The greatest actress in England, maybe even the world. And the fears drifted away, and he slept again.

Ellie woke him at nine o'clock.

"Come on, sleepyhead."

"Good morning, Ellie." Sebastian stretched and yawned widely.

"Good morning, my sweet."

"Where's Mummy?"

"Gone to an early rehearsal, and your father's gone to the office, and it's high time you were up and about. Your friends are both wide awake and hungry for their breakfast, but I told them they'd have to wait for you."

"Why didn't Mummy and Daddy come in to see me before they went?" he asked, and just a little of the night's disquiet came back to him. "Mummy promised she'd come in when she got back last night, but she didn't."

"I hope you didn't stay awake on purpose, waiting." Ellie pulled the eiderdown off him, and tugged him to her for a quick hug, and she was as jolly as she was every morning, but her eyes seemed especially bright, and Sebastian could not help feeling, in the pit of his stomach, that something was wrong, something was bad, though he could not tell what it was.

"Is everything all right, Ellie?" he asked her, and his voice sounded strained.

"Of course, my love." She opened one of the windows wide. "Now hurry yourself up, or it'll be lunchtime."

He forgot all about the feeling, again, when he saw Jeremy and Katharine, who looked quite shiny and pretty, her hair gleaming as if it had been freshly shampooed, and they ate porridge and bacon and eggs and toast and honey, and Jasper and Rufus lay under the kitchen table waiting to catch the crumbs of bacon and buttered toast that Sebastian let fall from his plate accidentally on purpose. And then they flung themselves out into the garden, and the sun was shining again, and they played energetically at another game of Explorers, and Katharine impressed Sebastian and Jeremy again by trying to climb an oak tree as fearlessly as any boy.

And it was only when, just before lunchtime, Annabel Mariner and Jake Andersen, Katharine's father, arrived at the house, without warning, to collect their children—when, suddenly, all the adult faces around Sebastian seemed grim and pale, their smiles forced—that the fear came back, hit him roughly, rudely, like a punch to his stomach.

"But *why* do we have to go, Daddy?" Katharine was asking her father for the second time.

"I told you, honey, something important came up," he said quietly, "and we have to get back to the hotel."

"Is Mommy okay?"

"Of course she is, I told you. And Annie's okay too, but now we have to go." He smiled again, but with his mouth, not with his eyes. "Say good-bye to Sebastian and Mrs. Wilkins, honey, and say a big thank you for letting you stay."

"Thank you very much," Katharine said to Ellie, who bent down and kissed her on the cheek. Katharine turned to face Sebastian. "I'm sorry I have to leave," she said softly.

"Me too," he said.

Jeremy had no intention of giving in without a fight. He planted both his feet firmly on the parquet floor of the front hall and glared at his mother. "I don't see why I have to go."

Annabel Mariner, statuesque and blond, glared back at her son. "Because I say so. Now stop being difficult and come on."

Jeremy's dark eyes were thoughtful. "Is it mumps or something like that?" he asked.

"Of course not." His mother gave an embarrassed smile.

"Only I remember one day at school we all had to leave in the middle of the morning, didn't we, Seb? When Jeffrey Beamish had mumps."

"Measles," Sebastian said, tightly. He didn't believe that this was anything to do with mumps or measles, but he knew enough to realize that no one was going to tell them what was going on, because they were children, and this was grown-up stuff.

He tried asking Ellie again, after Jeremy and Katharine had gone, where his parents were, but Ellie put him off, evaded every one of his questions. She gave him his lunch, which he did not eat, and then took him out for a walk up to Whitestone Pond, letting him sail his toy boat and feed the ducks, and the knot in his stomach loosened a little while they were up there. And when they were walking back, and were turning the corner into the Vale of Health, and Sebastian saw that his father's car was parked in the drive, he gave a whoop of joy and ran into the house.

Andrew was standing in the drawing room in front of the empty fireplace, beneath Diana's portrait, his back to the door.

"Daddy!" Sebastian ran to him and tugged at his sleeve. "Daddy, the *strangest* thing happened! Jeremy and Kate had to go home— both of them! Jeremy's mother came, and Kate's father, and they made them go, and we hadn't even had lunch, and I thought they were going to stay here for days!"

His father turned around then, and quickly, soundlessly, he bent and embraced Sebastian with a fierceness that was both painful and alarming in its unaccustomed passion, and when he drew back again, Sebastian saw that his face was almost as white as blackboard chalk, and that his eyes were red, as if he had been crying.

"Daddy?" he said. "What's the matter?"

Andrew opened his mouth, but he seemed unable to speak, and suddenly Sebastian no longer wanted to ask any more questions, for he was too frightened to ask, for a deep, inexplicable instinct was warning him that if he did ask, he might be answered, and that then he might find out that the feeling in his stomach—as if everything inside him had been ripped rawly apart—might never go away.

It was a little later in the afternoon, while Sebastian was playing disconsolate, solitary games in his bedroom, that he heard the solid thump of the front door, and then the sounds of his father in conversation with another man. And he knew that it was wrong to eavesdrop, and he wasn't even certain that he wanted to hear, but he felt compelled, drawn like a pin to a magnet, and he slipped silently out of his room and, hearing that they had gone into his father's study, he went down the staircase and listened at the door.

His father's voice was dull and strange.

"So the understudy goes on, after all," he said.

"You know Diana wouldn't have it any other way," the other man said, gently, and Sebastian realized that it was Dickie Forbes, his mother's agent.

"You're wrong," Andrew said. "Oh, I know Diana was the absolute professional, the *consummate* professional—we all know that, I better than anyone." Now he sounded bitter and terribly angry. "But she didn't want another actress to have this part, not this one. She'd played most of the great roles, God knows, but Hedda was the one she longed for." His voice was choked. "I *begged* her to give it up, I knew it was too much for her, but she wouldn't. She couldn't. And it killed her."

"It might have happened anyway," Forbes said.

"No."

"Of course it might. The doctor thought—"

"Heart attack, coronary, stroke. They can label it whichever way they choose." Andrew Locke's voice was very clear now, and filled with hate. "But it was Hedda that killed her."

Killed.

Behind the door, in the darkening corridor, the boy listened. He heard the word. But it was his father's voice, not the words he had spoken, though they were, in themselves, terrible enough. It wasn't even the tone, though that, too, was awful enough. It was the sound itself, the timbre of what lay underneath the words, of what was happening inside his father. Sebastian was only seven, just a child, with no experience of life except his own, with its secure boundaries, with no experience of death except for a year-old tortoise that had died in hibernation the previous winter. Yet he heard and felt, in Andrew Locke's voice, what some adults might not have heard. It was primitive and it was terrifying. The sound of a human soul in torment.

And the sense of tearing, ripping, searing agony in Sebastian's own stomach spread all the way through him like a burning ink blot, grasping at his heart and at his mind.

Consuming him.

c h a p t e r
2

The nation's capital was one of the most remarkable cities in the world, Katharine Andersen's mother, Louise, used to write in her letters home to her mother in Minneapolis, but it was certainly not an ideal city for an actress to thrive in. But then neither was an eminent orthopedic surgeon an ideal husband for an actress. Especially when he lived and worked in, and would refuse, probably until death, to be parted from, Washington, D.C.

Louise Grahame Andersen had wanted to be a great actress almost as soon as she had learned to read and write. She wanted to be a star, and she wanted to live in New York City. Those twin ambitions went hand in hand, after all, since everyone knew that the Great White Way was the theater center of America and, probably, the world. Louise had met Jake Andersen on her very first trip to New York, when she was just nineteen years old, had met him during the intermission of Lillian Hellman's new play at the Fulton Theatre, and had fallen head over heels in love.

Born Jacob Andersen in Copenhagen, Jake was lanky and blond, with the keenest blue eyes and the most exquisite hands Louise had ever seen on a man, and he was ten years older than she was, and a hundred years wiser. He and his widowed mother, Karen, had emigrated from Denmark when he was sixteen, settling in Great Neck,

Long Island, and Jacob, transformed swiftly to Jake, had set about making his mother proud of him; he had excelled at school, had been accepted by Harvard Medical School and had, ultimately, gone on to specialize in orthopedics. When Louise met him, Jake was assistant resident at New York Hospital, and the petite, dark-eyed, dimpled brunette had scarcely believed her magnificent good fortune.

"It means so much more than fixing broken bones," Jake told her at their first dinner date. "It's helping children born with misshapen spines or club feet, or giving patients who've lost arms and legs the means to walk and be independent again."

"It sounds miraculous," Louise said, already misty-eyed.

"Not a bit," Jake corrected. "What it is mostly is me getting the technical stuff right, and then damned hard work and courage from the patients."

They had married before her twentieth birthday, but only a month later, Jake had announced that an excellent position had opened up for him at the Georgetown University Hospital in Washington.

"Jacob's going to the top, you mark my words," Karen, his mother, told Louise. "In Washington, the sky's the limit—who knows, one day if the president breaks his leg, my son may be the one to fix it."

"I don't think Jake wants to stop helping real people," Louise ventured to her mother-in-law.

"The president's a real person, wouldn't you say?" Karen said crisply, ending the conversation.

Louise was happy for Jake, but the move represented the end of her own dreams of acting success, since Washington's only theater, the National, had recently been closed down by the actors' union because of racial prejudice. But Louise knew that she had no real choice, for she would have flown to the moon if her new husband had asked her to. From the day she met Jake, Louise's life revolved around him, around their beautiful townhouse in Georgetown and, after the spring of 1949, around their baby daughter.

Even as a small child, everyone agreed that Katharine was a rare beauty. The color of her hair defied description in a single word. It was dark blond and streaked with natural golden highlights, so that it glittered and shimmered in every light. Her eyes, too, were an exceptional color, amber and brilliant—

"The color of fine old cognac and firelight," Jake said in one of his lyrical moods, swinging his beloved daughter high in the air. And when her sister, Annie, was born a little over two years after Katharine, he was equally rapturous, for the new baby was dark-haired, like Louise, with pale skin and huge, brown eyes—"Chocolate and cream," he said, this time, kissing her arms and legs, "and good enough to eat." Everyone loved Annie, who had the sweetest, most infectious smile that tugged at the heart each time one saw it.

Louise was utterly content. Jake was an almost perfect husband, gifted, respected, loving, and even if the nature of his profession meant that there were never enough hours free to spend with his family, he never disapproved when, after the reopening of the National and the opening of a second theater, an occasional career opportunity presented itself to his wife. The children had a nanny, after all, and if Louise had a part in a play or, as had become more usual, was participating in some fund-raising event for the Red Cross or the Gray Ladies, one of Washington's elite charitable groups, then Mrs. Murray, their cook, saw to it that Jake ate well no matter what time of day or night he found his way to the dining table. Early in 1953, Louise's career hit a modest high spot when her agent arranged a screen test for her on the West Coast and she won a part in a British film titled *Lieutenant Rose*. The picture starred Gregory Peck as an air force pilot and the charismatic English actress Diana Lancaster in the title role. Louise played Peck's younger sister, and filmed in England for just three weeks, but in that short time, she and Diana Lancaster struck up a friendship that endured, within the limits of correspondence, long after the film was completed.

It seemed to Louise, after that experience, that she had accomplished something respectable in her acting life, had been a part of a real critical and commercial success in America and Europe, and she felt happier than ever about relaxing back into comparative domesticity. She adored being able to entertain for Jake, to host cocktail parties and to be seen out and about with him, even if they were often interrupted by emergencies. And their house, too, occupied her and gave her pleasure; the detached redbrick house on the corner plot of 28th and Q streets in Georgetown was admired by many of their acquaintances, though most of them had lovely homes of their own, and Louise thought it was heaven on earth, with its charming brick exterior, its curving stone steps with wrought-iron handrails ascending to the front door, and its tall, narrow windows. Inside, too, it was a house of delights, with plentiful rooms, many of them impressive but none daunting. In addition to all the usual living rooms, there was a small library, a music room in which Louise took piano lessons at the Bechstein and in which she hoped the children would follow suit, a charming, but rarely used sewing room and the family's favorite: an enchanting and bright breakfast room, which opened directly onto their small garden with its wisteria-covered arbor, rose-bushes and flowering cherry trees.

And then, of course, Louise had the girls, her greatest pride and joy, her beautiful and intelligent Katharine, her ever-laughing little Annie. It seemed to Louise that after *Lieutenant Rose*, her ambition vanished in a puff of joy, forgotten along with her other long-abandoned desire, to live in New York. And after the whole family traveled to Europe in the spring of 1954, partly to attend Diana Lancaster's opening in *Hedda Gabler*, and after tragedy struck the British actress, leaving her husband and young son grief-stricken by their loss, it seemed more foolish than ever for Louise to want any-thing more than to surround herself with her loved ones.

When Annie fell gravely ill the following spring, and the doctors diagnosed leukemia, all the joy and contentment disintegrated. She was just four years old, her courage was inspirational and, all through her illness, almost to the very end, sometimes in the Children's Hospital, mostly at home, she still smiled her magical smile. But then little Annie died, after only six years of life, and the Andersens crum-bled. It ought, perhaps, to have brought Louise and Jake even closer together, but bereavement drove them apart. Jake buried his grief in his work, took his consolation from his ability to help others, to save his patients and their families from suffering. Louise, he reasoned, had Katharine and her friends and charities to comfort her, to keep her busy, to pull her through the anguish. Jake never intended to be cruel; he was struggling to survive in the only way he knew. But Louise felt that she had nothing and that, with shocking suddenness, she *was* nothing, just a bleak, drained, pain-wracked soul in a black, gaping void.

Katharine was eight when Annie died. She knew a little bit about death, because Daddy often told them when one of his patients had died, and she knew that it always made him sad; and she had been with Sebastian Locke in England when his mother had died, though her Mommy hadn't explained that to her until she and Daddy had left the Lockes' big, old house and gone back to their hotel. Katharine had written a letter to Sebastian, because Mommy had said it was a nice thing to do, and she'd told him that she was very sorry and could imagine what he must be feeling. But she knew now that she hadn't understood anything about the real sadness, about the awful, inexplicable finality of death, or about the way the English boy had felt about losing his mother. Now that she had lost Annie, her beloved baby sister, now that she had seen her in death, so silent, so mysterious—so absent—Katharine found that she thought about death a great deal. Thought about Annie in the ground, and imagined—always battling against the imagining—her Mommy dying, her Daddy, too, and even herself.

The quarrels began about seven months after Annie's death. Louise and Jake, though unable to help each other through the first half-year of mourning, had nevertheless maintained a careful barrier of respect for their separate, but mutual grief, but once the initial piercings of anguish had passed, and after that the numb dullness of endurance, the first signs of real anger and bitterness began to show. They tried to shield their daughter from the worst of it, tried not to fight in front of her, but it wasn't always possible.

Katharine overheard them, one evening, after she'd woken from a bad dream and was on her way to their room, seeking comfort.

"You're never here." Her mother's voice, accusing, kept her from tapping on the door.

"I'm here as much as I've ever been," her father replied.

"That isn't true, and you know it."

There were tears in Louise's voice. Katharine knew that Mommy often cried. She always locked herself into their bedroom and never, ever wept in front of her, but Katharine could tell because her eyes were pink.

"I don't mind so much for myself," Mommy went on, "but Katharine needs both of us more than ever."

"She has us both," Daddy said, wearily.

"Does she?"

"Sure she does."

"You tell her that, Jake—if you're ever around long enough to do more than give her a kiss on the cheek. Kisses are cheap, Jake, even hugs."

"Is that why you never let me near you anymore?"

"That isn't true."

"It is from where I'm sitting. God knows I've tried enough times."

"To get me back into bed, maybe. Sex is cheap, too, Jake."

"I still think of it as lovemaking, you know, Louise. Maybe that's my mistake."

"You make a lot of mistakes."

"And you're Eleanor Roosevelt, I suppose."

Katharine didn't really understand why they were fighting. She didn't understand why her mother was telling her father he made a lot of mistakes, when Mommy was always telling Katharine that Daddy was the most brilliant doctor in the world. She could hear the hurt in both their voices, and it was hard to resist the impulse to push open the door and beg them to stop, but then they'd know she'd been listening, and that might just make everything worse.

"I'm a human being," she heard her mother say. "I'm a mother who's lost a child."

"I lost Annie, too, remember?"

"But I feel as if I lost my husband at the same time."

"That's funny," Jake said sadly. "I feel the same way about my wife."

Katharine was eleven years old when her parents' marriage finally died. It felt almost as bad to her as the loss of her sister, for she had witnessed at close quarters the crumbling away of their relationship, and had felt herself powerless to do anything to stop it. Mommy and Daddy had begun to act almost like strangers in the last few months, acting really unkindly to each other and, worst of all, fighting endlessly over her.

They told her, together, one night, in her bedroom, that they were going to file for divorce, told her that it didn't mean they didn't love each other anymore, and certainly not that they didn't love her, but that they just couldn't live in the same house any longer.

Katharine, sitting on the edge of her pink, frilled, cozy bed, stared at them both, standing in front of her so uncomfortably, so miserably, and she recognized, without a glimmer of hope, that there was nothing she could do about this either. That they had made up their minds.

"I guessed," she said, quietly.

"Did you, honey?" Jake's voice was husky.

"Not before, I mean. Not really. Just now, when you came in together like that." Katharine's amber eyes looked steadily from one to the other. "You haven't both come into my room at the same time since my last birthday."

Shame colored her parents' cheeks. She was right, she was so right, they both knew, but there was nothing to be done. It was too late.

"We're so sorry, sweetheart," Louise said. She sat down on the bed beside Katharine and began to weep again.

"Then don't get divorced," Katharine said. "Please."

"I wish it weren't necessary," Jake said. "But we're making each other unhappy, and that's no good. And if we don't stop it now, we'll end up making you unhappy too."

"I'm unhappy already, Daddy."

"Oh, God." Louise put one hand over her mouth.

The divorce was not the end of it. Driven by lawyers, Jake and Louise went to court to argue over which of them should have custody of their daughter. Out of earshot of Katharine, Jake claimed that because Louise had thrown herself into her acting career after Annie's death, and because nowadays she immersed herself as completely as possible in her work and in her charities or, when they failed her, in shopping binges at Garfinckel's, she was too frequently out of the house to be a really stable mother. And besides, he said, throwing it all in because his lawyer told him he had no choice, Louise slept with other men now, and though Jake hadn't claimed adultery in the divorce for her sake, and for Katharine's, when it came to custody he felt bound to raise it. Louise, fighting like a tigress, brought a set of diaries into court that helped to prove that whatever her husband said, Jake was and had always been, out of the family home markedly more often than she had ever been. And Louise won the case.

"What does it mean?" Katharine asked her next morning, in the breakfast room. It was early winter, and the flowers in the pretty little garden outside were all dead.

"It doesn't change anything, my darling," Louise said, putting down her coffee cup and taking Katharine's hand. "That's the main thing."

Katharine stared at her untouched orange juice and felt sick. "Can I still go and stay with Daddy sometimes?" Since Louise and Jake had separated, Katharine had spent a few weekends at her father's new house in Chevy Chase. It wasn't nearly as nice as their own house, but Katharine missed Daddy so much that she'd gladly have spent weekends in a hole in the ground if it meant being with him.

"Of course you can," Louise tried to reassure her. "And things will be better now that this is all over."

"Really?"

"I promise."

"Will Daddy come home again?"

"Not that much better, sweetheart. I'm sorry."

Katharine looked at her mother intently. "Do you wish he would, Mommy? Come back, I mean."

Louise answered unhesitatingly. "Of course," she said.

Katharine thought about it almost all the time, just the way she'd thought about death after losing Annie. She still loved them desperately, but she was aware that, for the first time in her life, she also felt true anger at her parents for the continued pain that they were causing each other and her. If she ever married, Katharine vowed passionately, she wouldn't allow anything on earth to blow her family apart the way that they had.

"If I get married," Katharine said, out loud in the privacy of her bedroom, "it will be for life, no matter what."

Throughout the rest of her childhood years and all through her teens, Katharine maintained her unshakable conviction that Jake and Louise were still in love, and as she grew older, she became increasingly adept at thinking up events at which they would feel obliged to come together under one roof for her sake. Even in 1964, four years after the divorce, when Louise married a Broadway actor named Sam Raphael, Katharine still experienced shafts of painful pleasure whenever she saw Jake and Louise together.

At thirty-nine, just three years older than Louise, Sam Raphael was fair-haired, but not as blond as Jake, gray-eyed and handsome in an agreeable way. He was, in fact, an affable man, talented and intelligent and modest, for an actor. He was in love with Louise, and he cared enough about Katharine to have understood when Louise had told him—when they had just finished making love in his room at the Willard a few hours after his marriage proposal—that it was vital to her daughter's stability to keep the Georgetown house, even if it meant frequent separations for herself and Sam when he was acting in New York City.

"It won't be so bad," Louise told him, snuggling against his naked back. "Katharine's fifteen now, and I'll be able to be up there with you a lot of the time. As long as we have Mrs. Murray, I know I can leave Washington without worrying too much."

"And Jake's here, too," Sam reminded her.

"I guess so." Louise hated talking about Jake, even with her new fiancé.

"Katharine can always stay at his place if she likes, can't she?"

"Naturally."

Sam rolled over and looked at her. "So how about next week?"

"What's next week?"

"I have that big audition, remember? I'd love you to be in Manhattan with me for moral support—among other things."

"I can't."

"Why not?"

"Katharine's school play." Louise saw Sam's face fall and winced a little. "I'm sorry, darling, but I can't miss it. She's playing the lead."

"I suppose her father will be there, too," Sam said, evenly.

"I suppose so. If Katharine's asked him to come."

"Do you doubt it?" Sam had been around long enough to know how his future stepdaughter felt about her parents.

"Jake'll be there," Louise admitted. "Do you mind?"

"Not if it's Katharine who wants him there, and not you."

"I want him there for her sake, Sam, not mine. Okay?"

"Okay."

For the duration of her school years at National Cathedral, it was almost always a school play to which Jake and Louise were drawn to see their lovely, amber-eyed daughter, who, like her mother before her, was often cast in leading roles, though sometimes they came because Katharine had designed the set. She was, indisputably, a talented actress, but as she matured, she found herself resisting the natural urge to follow in her mother's footsteps. Katharine loved acting, loved the thrill of winning a new part, enjoyed the burrowing into a new character, the way she found herself able to become that separate person, and she went to the theater as often as possible. But unlike Louise, who, at Katharine's age, would have been content to set up camp inside a theater, Katharine was just as happy in Constitution Hall listening to a concert, or wandering through the Corcoran or National Gallery, gazing at American and European art.

When she told them that she had decided to apply to Carnegie Mellon University in Pittsburgh to study scene design, Louise, Jake and Sam were all equally surprised and impressed. Jake had never fostered any false illusions that his daughter might take after him, but Louise was forced to admit that she had indulged in dreams that Katharine might fulfill her own thwarted ambitions.

She tried to express her disappointment to Sam. "She acts better than she paints," she said.

"Do you believe that, or do you just want her to act?"

"I want her to do what's going to make her happy."

"Looks like, for the moment at least, that's going to be studying scene design—if she gets her place." Sam smiled. "Have you seen those miniature sets she's made for *As You Like It*? They're wonderful."

"I know they are." Louise paused. "But why Pittsburgh, of all places? All that iron and steel and coal." She shuddered. "Why not New York? We could all be together in New York."

"Carnegie Mellon is why, Louise, you know that. Carnegie Mellon is it. *The* place. The one you pull out all the stops to try to break into."

"And then torture yourself for three or four years making sure you're too good to get thrown out." She looked anxious. "Do you think she's tough enough, Sam?"

"Acting is tougher, honey."

"But I still can't help feeling that acting is what Katharine's made for." Louise flushed a little. "And it isn't because that's what I wanted for her—I'll be prouder than you could imagine if she gets into that place. I just hope she's doing the right thing."

"I'd trust her instincts if I were you," Sam said.

He did not tell Louise what he believed to be Katharine's real, deep-down reason for turning her back on an acting career. Sam had come to know his stepdaughter fairly well over the past few years. Katharine was, on the whole, an open, candid girl. She had never resented Sam, was quite aware that her parents' marriage had ended long before he came on the scene, and though her loyalties, had they been called upon, would have remained firmly with Jake, Katharine liked Sam, regarded him as a friend. They talked, occasionally, about the past. She liked to remember Annie and the blissfully happy days of her early childhood, liked keeping those memories fresh, and once in a while, she allowed herself to talk about the bad times, too, and it had become apparent to Sam that whether Katharine recognized it or not, she blamed her parents' ultimate breakup on her mother's return to acting.

"Of course I know it had nothing to do with the divorce," she had said to Sam when he had challenged her. "My mother needed something of her own after we lost Annie. Acting made her happy—I wouldn't have wanted to deprive her of that."

"But from what I've heard about the divorce and that crazy custody fight that they had over you," Sam had persisted, "Louise's return to the theater, and the freedoms that came with that, were a big part of your father's problem."

Katharine hadn't wanted to continue the conversation after that, and Sam had let it go, feeling that he had, at least, prodded her into giving her decision some more thought. And she had forced herself to confront it all again, when she was alone, and she did acknowledge, in her heart, that she might have become a fine actress, and that it was possible that, needing to pin the blame on something, she had made acting her scapegoat. But she was lucky enough to have a second talent; she was enormously fascinated by all the many facets that went into a successful stage set. And if she was going to stand any kind of chance at all of being accepted at Carnegie Mellon, she realized that she would have to finalize her decision now, and then be prepared to stick to it through thick and thin, and hard work and disappointments and nervous breakdowns. Carnegie Mellon wasn't for vacillating schoolgirls. It was for winners.

c h a p t e r

3

Sebastian Locke had been born a few minutes before midnight on the twenty-first day of April in 1947, in an exclusive private nursing home in St. John's Wood, London. The new mother had wept tears of joy and exhaustion for more than a half hour after they first placed him in her arms, and a bulletin had been swiftly issued to the reporters waiting outside in the rain, confirming that both mother and son were in perfect condition. The presence of the new father was no more than incidental to them, his personal pride and happiness no less than what was expected of so fortunate a man.

The press were there in force because Diana Lancaster Locke was, at the age of thirty-nine, and after almost twenty years in the business, one of Britain's most distinguished and best-loved actresses. Her professional career had started in high style and with great good fortune with Sir Barry Jackson's Birmingham Repertory Theatre Company alongside the then equally unknown Laurence Olivier. In a comparatively short time, she had established herself in London's West End, playing a succession of substantial supporting roles, and at twenty-five, having played her first Juliet at the Old Vic, swiftly followed by her first Ophelia, she found great popularity in Shaw's *Pygmalion* at the Savoy.

Diana never considered herself pretty, but she was aware that her looks were powerful and malleable enough to be an asset to her career. She had an oval-shaped face of great strength, with pronounced cheekbones, a patrician nose, a wide mobile mouth, forceful jaw and a superb neck. Her dark brown eyes flashed or sparkled or were grave, according to her mood, beneath arched eyebrows just a hint darker than her wavy, thick auburn-brown hair. She had known, by the time she was nine, that she had been born to act, and the fact that all through her school days she had been cast as the male lead in every end-of-year play only served to boost her confidence in her ability to take on any role she was given. She was an only child, living in comfort with her headmaster father, William Lancaster, and her mother, Phyllis, a former nursing sister at a hospital not far from their home near Tunbridge Wells. It was a measure of Diana's compelling personality and persuasiveness that William and Phyllis gave their consent to her move to London, after only a fairly brief battle of wills, so that she could take up the place offered her by the Royal Academy of Dramatic Art. Diana shared a flat in Belsize Park near the Underground station, with two other girls, also students, and was blissfully happy, aware that she was now well on her way. As a teenage girl, she had awed the boys a little, but now that she was a young woman, men of various ages began to pursue her vigorously. Diana fell in love quite frequently, but neither deeply nor lastingly. Her personal craft, the theater itself, and that blessed life came before everything else. There would be ample time, she reasoned, for true love and marriage, and children, perhaps, once she had succeeded in establishing a solid foothold in the West End.

Having built on her early dramatic successes, Diana had begun to capitalize on her good singing voice and, to a lesser extent, her dancing ability, working in musical comedies and revues, thriving on the variety and grueling hard work, and when the shadow of war began to loom, she flung herself even more wholeheartedly into her work, determined that nothing on earth would interrupt the life she so adored. She had bought an ivy-clad white cottage on a steep hill in Hampstead, with the Village and the Heath almost on her doorstep; she had a most wonderful circle of friends, actors mostly, but also writers and artists and musicians. It was all fine and solid, quintessentially English and secure. But when war was declared, the theaters of London were closed and the whole profession was suddenly, shockingly, unemployed. The total ban did not last long; within a few weeks, daylight performances were permitted, and swiftly, most willing and able artists found themselves performing for the troops and the Red Cross all over the country.

For months, Diana struggled with her conscience, trying to decide what war work she could most easily bear to do and what she could do sufficiently well to be of use, guiltily aware that her attitude was much too selfish for the times. The problem was that there were simply no branches of the services to which she was naturally suited; she disliked airplanes, could become seasick in a rowing boat on the Serpentine in August, hated the sight of blood and found rising before ten in the morning a genuine penance.

"I must do something," she said to Dickie Forbes, her agent.

"But you are doing something, darling."

"Singing and dancing, and spouting speeches." Diana's self-disgust was reflected in her voice. "Useless."

"Hardly."

"I can't do shorthand," she went on. "I can't type. I don't even know how to drive a car, let alone an ambulance. Useless," she said again.

As the phony war ended, and the very real war began, it became clear that ENSA—the Entertainments National Service Association—would provide Diana's war effort. By 1944, she had sung and performed monologues in every part of the country, and had traveled, often in intense physical and emotional discomfort, all over the Mediterranean, into the Middle East and through much of India. She returned to Hampstead, to her thankfully still-unbombed cottage, humbled, grateful to be alive and home, with her parents both still unscathed, most of her priorities much altered, but with her popularity not only intact, but greatly enhanced.

Andrew Locke entered Diana's life seven months before the war ended in Europe. She was thirty-six years old, and he was a forty-two-year-old barrister and former army captain who had received an honorable discharge from the service in 1943 after being seriously wounded. Now fully recovered, with only the slightest of limps to remind him of his injuries, Andrew was an attractive man, tall, slender and strong, with fair hair, blue eyes, thick, shaggy blond eyebrows and a cleft chin. Women found him glamorous, though his appeal was entirely effortless and unself-conscious; whether beautifully turned out in a Savile Row suit, Jermyn Street shirt and tie, or wearing one of his guernsey pullovers and corduroy trousers, Andrew always looked, in their eyes, simply marvelous. Nevertheless, he was a bachelor, a quiet, reserved man, stimulated by his work, fond of music and theater, of reading and golden retrievers—a man who would never, in a hundred years, have dreamed that he might, one autumn night in 1944, find himself waiting, like an adolescent fan, outside a stage door, longing for a glimpse of an actress.

Diana Lancaster was playing Titania in *A Midsummer Night's Dream* at Stratford-upon-Avon, at the same time that Andrew was undertaking some research for a case in nearby Warwick. On his third evening there, needing a break, he drove to Stratford and attended a performance. Never having seen Diana Lancaster act before, Andrew was entirely unprepared to be so startlingly captivated by her that, after the final curtain call, he found himself standing outside the stage door with a cluster of autograph hunters, scarcely knowing how he had arrived there, waiting with an acute sense of excitement.

She emerged, dressed in a chocolate brown turtleneck sweater and trousers, her face scrubbed clean and even lovelier than she had appeared in full makeup beneath the spotlights, her dark hair tied back in a thick ponytail. She looked a little tired, but the gathering seemed to delight her nonetheless, and she smiled and signed each book and program, speaking for a moment to each person.

Andrew stood back, content just to watch. And then, as she began to press forward toward her waiting car and driver, Diana noticed him, saw how out-of-place he looked beside the duffel-coated students, in his immaculate suit, with his raincoat over his arm and his hat in his hand. She paused, momentarily, as their eyes met. Andrew's smile was tentative, Diana's unhesitating. And then she moved away to the car and, in another moment, she was gone.

Two nights later, Andrew sat through the play again, sitting forward in his seat each time she entered, watching her every move and gesture, hearing every lilt and nuance in her voice, fascinated by the extraordinary mobility of her unusual face. This time, there were flowers in his arms and there was no hesitation at all in the manner in which he left his aisle seat the instant the play ended, arriving before anyone else at the stage door. When she came out, she recognized him instantly, took the flowers with obvious pleasure and looked into his face with curiosity as he made a small, courteous bow and turned away. When, on her arrival at the theater the following afternoon, she found his note inviting her to lunch with him at The White Swan next day, her reply, delivered by taxi to his hotel in Warwick, was swift and unreservedly positive.

*   *   *

"I loved the flowers," Diana said, as soon as they had been seated at their window table in the restaurant.

"They weren't quite what I hoped for, I'm afraid," Andrew said. "I wanted roses, but there weren't any."

"I thought they were very beautiful." She smiled. "I liked the note, too."

"I didn't think you'd come."

"Why ever not?" She sounded surprised.

The lunch was perfect. The food was unsensational, the restaurant as hampered as most by shortages, but the maître d'hôtel, a great admirer of Diana's, found them a rare bottle of claret and lavished his most discreet attention upon them. Andrew, self-assured, experienced barrister, was, to begin with, almost inarticulate with pleasure, enjoying each swiftly passing second, certain that there would be no second meeting, since this ravishing, famous, talented woman would surely find no common ground with—or more than the most fleeting interest in—a man so wholly different from herself as he was. And yet, almost instantaneously, the often cautious, trained legal brain and the artistic, necessarily flamboyant mind reached out to touch, delved eagerly, probed deeply and found that the lawyer and the actress shared far more than the intense physical attraction that had brought them to this lunch table. They also shared a strong sense of fun and of humor, a gentleness, intuitive sensitivity and acute intelligence.

Since neither had been married, they both understood independence, and they were both aware that a liking for one's own company at times did not equate either to loneliness or to aloofness.

"I find I need to get away from people now and again," Diana told Andrew. "I'm a gregarious person on the whole, but it's such a hectic life that if I didn't have my quiet times it would all be too much."

"I suppose our lives are quite similar in some ways," Andrew said. "Worlds apart, of course, superficially, yet we're both performers in a sense." He smiled into her eyes. "I don't suppose you suffer from stage fright, do you?"

"I feel sick as a dog before every show." She pulled a grimace. "Does it happen to barristers too?"

"Before every court appearance. Though once things are under way, I settle down."

Diana drank some wine. "Are you aware when you've performed particularly well?" she asked, curiously.

Andrew nodded. "And when I've done badly. Though in my case, of course, if that happens, chances are I've wrecked things for my client."

"That must be terrible for you," she said sympathetically. "Even worse than letting down a whole cast of actors. At least we usually get to do it all over again next day—in your case, your client could go to jail, or even get hanged!"

Andrew laughed. "That hasn't happened yet, thank God." He tapped the side of his chair. "Touch wood."

"Actors are dreadfully superstitious, too, you know," Diana said with pleasure.

The common ground spread on and on. They both loved dogs, liked long walks, enjoyed all kinds of people, were fascinated by their uniqueness and idiosyncrasies. Their favorite restaurant was the Savoy Grill, they both liked to dance, both detested caviar, were fascinated by history, found air raid shelters almost too claustrophobic to bear. And then, of course, there *was* that undeniable physical attraction.

They both felt changed overnight. Diana had enjoyed living alone in her cottage, and Andrew had liked his solitary life with only his part-time housekeeper and two golden retrievers for company in his compact, cream-colored townhouse on the border of Camden Town and Regent's Park. From the moment he met Diana, however, his joy in that old existence was at an end. He no longer wanted to be alone; he wanted to be with Diana at every possible moment, and his greatest delight was in the knowledge that she felt precisely the same way. They were married within three months, Diana moving into his house until they could find something larger, and for Andrew, more than for his wife, life was altered beyond recognition. Exultant and tireless, he hurried back and forth between his offices, the law courts, the Camden Town house and whichever theater Diana was rehearsing or playing in. She never questioned the importance of his work, and he thrived on hers, happy to do everything he could to make her comfortable and content.

Life with Diana was thrilling, her friends varied, interesting and hugely entertaining. The Lockes gave regular dinner or luncheon parties on Sundays—the only day on which so many of Diana's acquaintances were free—and they met friends for late suppers at the Savoy or Claridge's or the Ritz. His wife knew everyone, it seemed to Andrew—the Oliviers, Noël Coward, the Redgraves, Binkie Beau-

mont, of course—even the Mountbattens. Diana was naturally hospitable, delighted to entertain anyone she liked, from her dressers
to the postman. At times, the little house felt as if it were bulging at
the seams, and at others, when it was just the two of them, it was
serene and blissful. Diana studying scripts and learning lines, Andrew
ploughing through paperwork and briefs, with Mozart on the gram-
ophone and the dogs lazing by the fireplace; Andrew mowing the
small rectangle of grass in the back garden, Diana sunbathing; Andrew
watching his wife at her dressing table, brushing her hair, and Diana
turning to see his eyes on her, and rising and coming to him; Andrew
and Diana in bed on Sunday mornings, birdsong from the garden
floating in through the open window, accompanying their lovemaking . . .

They found The Oaks, their house, one month after VE Day. It
stood in semi-seclusion, sheltered from the winds that sometimes
blew off the Heath, in Hampstead's Vale of Health, a small, steep
road bordering the east side of the great, sloping heathland. It was
a large, Tudor-style, half-timbered house, handsomely oak-paneled
and beamed, with ornately molded ceilings and big fireplaces.

"It's perfect," Diana said instantly, clutching at Andrew's hand as
they walked around for the first time on their own.

"Nothing is this perfect," he said, forcing himself to be cautious,
though in truth he felt no caution at all, felt only a bubbling excitement and pleasure.

"This is," she insisted. "Not a single room the same—all shapes
and sizes. That wonderful hall, and that beautiful drawing room—"

"The library is charming," Andrew allowed.

"And that lovely, intimate little room at the front would make an
ideal study for you, wouldn't it, darling? Or would you want something larger?"

"No, you're right." He smiled. "It would suit me well."

"This is my absolute favorite, of course." They were standing in
the master bedroom, a spacious, bright and airy room overlooking
the garden at the rear and beyond that the Heath. "It needs a four-
poster, don't you think, my love?"

"Definitely a four-poster."

"And a chaise longue, I think."

"Perhaps."

"And somewhere comfy for the dogs."

It was a house both imposing and intimate, a house to be hung with great paintings and tapestries, and a house for living in, for laughter and love and everyday existence. Rufus and Jasper, Andrew's retrievers, were transformed back almost to puppyhood by the size and scope of their new home and the wonders that lay just beyond the back garden, and Diana adored being back in the delightful north London village that had always been her favorite part of the great metropolitan sprawl. In between acting roles, Diana lavished love and care on the house, spending hours with their decorator, poring over wallpaper samples and choosing curtain materials and, often with Andrew, attending auctions at Sotheby's and Christie's, buying antique furniture and other irresistible items.

Now married, secure and settled, Diana had become aware that she did, after all, want to have children. The passing of years and youth had never really worried her, nor the effect on her childbearing capacity, and had she not met her husband, she might have continued unperturbed, her creative life sufficiently satisfying to fend off thoughts of motherhood. But she had found Andrew, and now they had The Oaks, and it seemed to her to cry out for babies, for children, for young people, to fulfill its potential and to make it a complete home.

Andrew had misgivings, for Diana was in her late thirties, and he had heard warnings of the problems that sometimes arose in women of her age having first children. And besides, he was in his mid-forties—if they did have a baby now, by the time he or she was a teenager, he would be an old man. Diana scoffed fondly at all his concerns; just because they had found each other later than most couples did not mean that they had to forfeit their right to be parents.

Her resolve was unwavering, but she did not conceive, and although no physical cause could be found, they were starting to admit defeat when, more than eighteen months later, Diana found that she was, finally, pregnant. She suffered severe morning sickness and frequent migraines during the pregnancy, and the birth, in April of 1947, was exceptionally long and difficult, giving both Andrew and her obstetrician several hours of grave concern; but being given Sebastian, their son, to hold in her arms, swept away all the pain and fear that had gone before.

"He's perfect, isn't he?" she whispered to Andrew, cradling him on his third day of life.

"Absolutely," Andrew agreed readily. Looking at the infant in his wife's arms, his heart had never been more full of emotion and pride.

"Really perfect, I mean," Diana breathed, stroking the wispy, silken golden hair and studying the tiny nose and rosebud mouth. "And he's so exactly like you."

"Poor little thing."

Diana laughed. "No false modesty, please. You know very well how handsome you are, and Sebastian is the most beautiful baby I've ever set eyes on, don't you think?"

Andrew put his right index finger into his son's tiny palm, and the little fingers curled around it in reflex. "I think I'd feel he was the most beautiful baby in the world even if he was quite ugly," he mused softly. "If you see what I mean."

Diana smiled at him. "Of course I do."

"Not that it matters, in this instance, since Sebastian *is* absolutely beautiful."

"Perfect," she said again.

Sebastian was not only golden-haired and blue-eyed like his father, but he was also good-natured. His proud, adoring parents put aside their natural roles as performers and became his audience, constantly, intently focused upon their son's every stage of development through infancy, early childhood and on. He had brought them, they agreed, total contentment; Andrew found it difficult to tear himself away during the week, and Diana could not begin to contemplate a time when she would be willing to work again. At her husband's insistence, they had employed a nanny, but Diana's determination to do almost everything for her child created friction between the two women; and after Sebastian, recovering from measles, had a convulsion while Diana was out for a rare lunch with a girlfriend, she fired the nanny on the spur of the moment.

"Was that really fair, darling?" Andrew asked her gently when he got home later that afternoon. "I mean it was hardly the poor girl's fault."

"Of course it was. She let him get too warm—she knew he still had a temperature."

"I thought it had come down."

"Well, obviously it must have gone up again, and a trained nanny ought to have known that immediately."

"But Michael says that Sebastian's going to be fine, doesn't he?" By the time Diana had arrived home, Michael Adler, their family doctor, had already made an examination and pronounced any danger over.

"Thank God, yes." Diana was still pale and jittery from her fright. "So there's no real harm done."

"No *harm*?" Diana seldom lost her temper with Andrew, but now she was outraged. "Have you ever seen a convulsion? No, I thought not. Well, I have—a girl at school had one while she was sitting right next to me at lunch." Diana shuddered at the memory. "It was horrible, Andrew. She completely lost control, her eyes rolled right back and she twitched all over—we were all terrified."

"I'm sorry, darling," Andrew said gently, putting his arm around her comfortingly. "I'm sure I'd have felt exactly the same way if I'd been the one here."

"That's the real thing, of course," Diana said quietly. "I wasn't here, was I? I was out having lunch with a friend."

"You can't be with him all the time."

"Yes, I can, and I should be. And from now on, I shall be."

From that day, Diana's attention became almost obsessive, her fear that something terrible might happen to Sebastian becoming irrational and disproportionate, and when the morning came, shortly after his fifth birthday, for him to go to the kindergarten she and Andrew had chosen near Regent's Park, she was distraught.

"He'll be home with you for lunch every day," Andrew pointed out, trying to calm her. "And you know it's important for him to start making friends of his own age."

"I know, I know," she said. And she did, of course, but it didn't make her feel any better about it. "But I'm already dreading next year."

Sebastian would be attending a preparatory school in Hampstead from the following September, and that, Diana realized full well, would be the start of her child's growing away from her, and though she was thankful that her husband wasn't one of those men who believed in sending six-year-old boys away to boarding school, she knew that once Sebastian was out of the house for most of each day, her life would feel empty and miserable until he was home.

"I do try not to let him know how I feel, Andrew," she said now, anxiously. "Do you think I succeed? I couldn't bear to give him some kind of complex."

"You succeed admirably," Andrew said, meaning it. "But then you are one of the finest actresses in the country."

Diana bristled. "I've never been an actress with you or Sebastian."

"I know that. I just meant that you've managed to keep your fears from him, that's all."

His wife sighed. "I'm sorry, darling. I knew perfectly well what you meant. I'm afraid I'm getting absurdly touchy—quite ridiculous, really."

"You could never be ridiculous, my love."

Sebastian loved school, just as he loved home. He was a happy child who made friends as easily as breathing, and he enjoyed learning, found the world a wonderful, ever expanding adventure. He had made a best friend at kindergarten, a boy called Jeremy Mariner, whose family had a big, grand flat overlooking Regent's Park, and a big house and farm in the Yorkshire Dales, and both children had been ecstatic when Jeremy's mother and father had allowed him to attend the same preparatory school as Sebastian.

Jeremy and Sebastian were opposites. Whereas Sebastian was fair, Jeremy was dark-haired, with deep brown eyes. Both boys were slender, but Jeremy's features were narrow and pointed, bordering on angularity. Even with their unbroken children's voices, their styles of speech were markedly different; Sebastian, though as capable as the next boy of exuberant, excitable behavior, spoke calmly on the whole, his tone even and pleasant to the ear, while Jeremy alternated between slow, lazy speech, which irritated his parents and teachers because it made him sound disinterested and even sullen, and rapid, sharp outbursts that seemed rude, aggressive and opinionated. It was not Jeremy's intention to appear that way, it was simply his manner, but there were only two people who had ever understood him. The first was his brother, Thomas, two years his junior but already blessed with more social grace than his older brother. The second was Sebastian.

"How come you like me?" Jeremy asked Sebastian one day in the playground at school.

"I don't know."

"You do like me, don't you?" Jeremy felt almost obliged to ask the question, though he felt confident about the answer.

"Of course I do."

"But why?"

"Why not?"

"No one else does."

"Don't talk rot."

"It's not rot. It's a fact. The only two people in the whole world who like me are Thomas and you."

"What about your parents?" Sebastian asked.

"My father doesn't mind me too much, I suppose," Jeremy admitted, "but Mother doesn't like me at all."

"She must do." Sebastian was appalled.

"No." Jeremy's tone was matter-of-fact. "She's told me quite often. She loves me, she says—though I'm not sure about that either—but she doesn't like me. She says that when I'm being awful, but I think she feels that way most of the time."

"Well, I like you," Sebastian said staunchly.

"You haven't said why, though."

"Because you're my best friend."

"That's not an answer."

Sebastian frowned. "I don't know what else to say. I liked you right away, that first day at kindergarten, remember? I came in a bit late, and I sat down next to you."

"That's because there was a space," Jeremy said. "Maybe if there hadn't been a space, we wouldn't have made friends."

"I think we would." Sebastian thought about it. "You seemed a bit different from the others. More fun. And I thought you liked me."

"I did." Jeremy smiled. That was another difference between them; Sebastian smiled freely and easily, an open, natural smile that crinkled up his eyes, while Jeremy's smile was much rarer and slighter, with a guarded quality as if he thought he might be told to stop at any moment. "I do like you," he said, confirming it.

"That's all right then."

When Andrew had suggested to Diana, early in 1953, while Sebastian was still in the kindergarten, that she might want to return to work, she was outraged. The theater was out of the question, she said. She and Sebastian had little enough time together already, and within a few months they would have even less, and if she went back to the West End, he would soon forget that he had a mother at all. It was their first major battle, and Diana felt confident that she had won it, but Andrew, sure in his own mind that this way of life was not good for his wife, paid a secret visit to Dickie Forbes, her agent.

Andrew came straight to the point. "Dickie, do you think you could find Diana a film?"

"She's never made a film."

"I know that—I just think perhaps she should."

"Diana loves the theater, Andrew. She's never harbored fantasies about Hollywood or the cinema in general. What's changed her mind?"

"Not a thing," Andrew said. "This is my idea. Diana doesn't know I've come to see you, and if she finds out she'll skin me alive."

"Then why, if you don't mind my asking, are you here?" The agent was irritated by the barrister's presumptuousness, but his eagerness to have Diana Lancaster back at work—any kind of work—prevented him from being as rude as he would have liked to be.

"Because I believe that Diana misses the theater—"

"It misses her," Forbes said pleasantly.

"But she refuses even to consider taking on a play while our son is still so young—she feels that he needs her at home."

"I can understand that." Forbes paused. "I'm only surprised that as her husband you're not only too delighted by her attitude."

"So far as I'm concerned, my wife should do whatever makes her happy," Andrew said, a little stiffly. "And she's made it perfectly plain that a theater engagement, with the prospect of a long run, is out of the question for the time being."

"But if a film script were to find its way to her," Forbes said, "it might be considered."

"Exactly." Andrew paused. "The right script, of course."

Dickie Forbes smiled genuinely for the first time.

"Of course," he said.

It was over two months before the script fell onto their doormat at The Oaks. Lieutenant Rose was the perfect role for Diana, and it was the ideal film for the times. It was not a war picture, but the story of a lieutenant in the Women's Royal Naval Service who, at the end of hostilities, collected a group of war orphans and set up a home for them in Devon. Approaches had been made to Gregory Peck for the part of the American hero, and there was no doubt that the part of the compassionate, daring heroine was perfect for Diana.

Refusing, at first, even to read the script, Diana was furious with Andrew for his connivance with Dickie Forbes, but having looked it over and having been forced to recognize its potential, she found herself tempted. She told herself that it was impossible, but knew that it was not, that it was merely a question of adjustment. She told Andrew that she hated him for going behind her back, but in truth she knew that she loved him all the more for recognizing that her old vital spark had lately been diminished by her increasingly ob-sessive behavior. And aware that she was close to giving in, she repeatedly questioned her own motives. But at the end of the day, the only things that seemed quite clear were that Sebastian would not suffer in any way, that their marriage would only benefit from an injection of optimism and energy. And that it was a good part.

Having capitulated and won the role with flattering ease, Diana reveled in the filming process—even having to rise before dawn became almost worthwhile once she was in makeup and the transformation had begun. It was a brand-new learning experience, and Diana Lancaster Locke was still a keen student, aware that professionalism on a film set at Shepperton Studios was, if anything, of even more paramount importance than on a stage, if only because every moment wasted cost vast sums of money. Gregarious and warm as she had always been, Diana made new friends easily, in particular the pretty young American named Louise Grahame Andersen, playing Gregory Peck's character's younger sister. Louise had two young children and a professional husband she clearly adored, and Diana felt they had much in common.

The cast and crew all sensed a box-office winner and, in the event, they were not to be disappointed as *Lieutenant Rose* was given the thumbs up by the major critics, and the audiences came in droves to what was being called the biggest British picture since *Brief Encounter*. Sebastian was ecstatic at having a film star for a mother, and Andrew sat through it seven times in the cinema, his eyes unashamedly moist each time, while Diana sat beside him, loving him more than ever.

Her headaches began toward the end of November, headaches even more excruciating than the migraines she had suffered during pregnancy. Normally a healthy woman, seldom catching anything more serious than a cold, she consulted Michael Adler, but though the doctor was concerned by her distress, he could find nothing specifically wrong with her. The pains continued for a month and then, just before Christmas and just before Diana had agreed to see a specialist, they receded, making the holidays even more magical than usual for the whole Locke family. Sebastian, now six, was ecstatic, for both his parents were at home for several days, his mother was feeling better and the house itself was magnificent, its oak-paneled walls warmer than ever under the weight of all the holly and berries and mistletoe, and its fireplaces almost constantly ablaze.

Diana did not feel well for long. Almost as soon as the festive season was over, the headaches returned, bringing with them dizzy spells that alarmed her. This time, however, she chose to ignore the symptoms completely, telling herself that she was being a neurotic, perhaps even a hypochondriac. Michael had found nothing wrong with her before, and she was determined not to play the part of a chronic invalid. Andrew worked much too hard to be burdened, and Sebastian had been clearly distressed when she'd taken to her bed before Christmas. And besides, professionally she was in the grip of an excitement she had never felt before, for the fulfillment of a long-cherished ambition was hovering temptingly on the horizon.

She had been the most fortunate of actresses. She had played most of the young Shakespearean heroines, she had played major roles by Sheridan, Chekhov, Shaw and Oscar Wilde, and she had appeared in two of Ibsen's works, once as Mrs. Elvsted in *Hedda Gabler*. But that title role, which Diana had for many years longed to play above all others, for its fascinating monstrousness, its extraordinary, contrasting iciness and passion, had eluded her. But now she had learned that Leonard Beauchamp, an old friend and one of the producers Diana respected most highly, was planning a new production of the play and, knowing that she was still hungry for Hedda, Beauchamp had spoken to Diana early on. The part was finally hers, and she was determined that nothing—certainly not her own weakness—should stand in her way.

She took herself in hand, trying to maintain a sensibly low dosage of aspirin to control the worst of the pain she was now suffering most days; she took long, gentle walks on the Heath with the dogs, spent as much time as possible with Sebastian, since her hours with her beloved son were, to her, the best therapy she knew, and avoided too much time alone with Andrew, for her husband, knowing her better than anyone else, invariably knew when she was feeling unwell. Rehearsals began in April, and Diana found the work more grueling than any she had previously experienced, but her sense of professionalism and responsibility and desire kept her going through the hours before and after rehearsals, when she was at her lowest ebb. And onstage, as always, adrenaline and the sheer magic of playing Hedda, at last, helped her to forget, almost completely, how ill she had been feeling.

Andrew saw through the mask, through the makeup and courage.

"You have to give it up, darling," he said to Diana on more than one occasion.

"Give up Hedda? Never."

"But it's making you ill."

"Nonsense, I'm all right, just a little tired."

"You're more than tired, your head's bad again, isn't it?"

"It would take more than a few headaches for me to give up a part, any part, and you know how I feel about this one, Andrew."

"At least let Michael take another look at you."

"He's looked at me," Diana argued.

"And suggested you see a specialist."

"A neurologist—I don't need a neurologist poking around inside my head, and certainly not in the middle of rehearsals."

Andrew knew that it was hopeless, understood that this was the woman he had fallen in love with, knew that she would keep going, keep performing, until the final curtain, that nothing and no one would make her give in.

Diana did not survive until opening night. She played Hedda brilliantly at three dress rehearsals, watched at the third and final one by her spellbound son, and by her husband, lost, as always, in admiration. But within three hours of the play's end, while Andrew, having delivered Sebastian, Jeremy and Katharine—Louise Andersen's little daughter—to The Oaks, was driving back into the West End to meet her, Diana had collapsed in her dressing room. By the time Andrew reached her, she was dead.

Andrew was completely shattered. Through all his warnings and pleas to his wife, in spite of all his very real anxieties about her health, he had never dreamed for a single instant, even in his worst nightmare scenarios, that he might lose Diana.

That playing Hedda Gabler, that one elusive role, would kill her. Leaving him. And Sebastian.

chapter
4

Andrew had warned Diana that he was too old to become a father. Now he was fifty-two years old and a widower with a seven-year-old son whose entire future depended upon him. At first, he found every moment spent in their home intolerable. Without Diana by his side, The Oaks was, to him, stark and cold and indifferent. Sebastian, he found, seemed a little soothed by the memories that seeped from its walls, but although Andrew sensed that the child longed to talk about his mother, he could not respond to that need. He could not bear to hear her name spoken.

Until a bleak afternoon that October, when Andrew came across Sebastian standing all alone in the drawing room, staring up at the great portrait of Diana painted by Nathan Smith that had been her personal favorite. She had posed for Smith in a dressing room at the Globe Theatre before the war, and the fact that she had worn a fine black wool sweater and a string of pearls with a tweed skirt—normal, everyday clothes—and yet her face had been fully, dramatically made up for performance, had given the portrait a strangely haunting and unique quality. Sebastian had always been fascinated by the painting, and now, seeing the terrible desolation in the blue eyes that were so like his own, Andrew understood with a pang that was almost a body blow how utterly lost his son had become, and he realized that he had indulged his own grief for long enough.

"Sebastian?" he said softly.

The boy turned slowly away from the painting. "Hello, Daddy."

"Have you been here long?"

"Not very." Sebastian hesitated. "I'm sorry."

"Whatever for?"

He shrugged. "I'm not sure. I thought—"

"What did you think?" Andrew asked gently, and he felt a flush of shame heat his own cheeks, for he knew the answer. "That I'd mind you looking at your mummy?"

There was a brief silence, and he knew that Sebastian had registered what had occurred. That Andrew had, at last, volunteered to speak of Diana out loud.

"I often look at this painting," Sebastian said. "It's my favorite."

"It was hers, too."

"What about you, Daddy?"

Andrew kept his eyes on his son's upturned face. "I find it hard, very, very hard to look at it."

"Why?"

"Because it hurts me too much."

"Because you miss her."

"Yes. That's right."

Sebastian shifted a little closer to his father and put out a hand to take his. "I feel a bit better, sometimes, when I come in here."

Andrew's throat was tight. "You're braver than I am, I think."

"I'm not," Sebastian said definitely, and then, sharing a confidence, he said, "I cry a lot."

"So do I."

"Do you, Daddy?" Sebastian looked surprised.

"Of course I do." Andrew heard his own voice shaking. "Every night, when I go to bed."

There was another pause.

"If you're lonely," Sebastian said, "you can always come into my room."

"Can I?" Andrew was smiling through his tears. "I'd like that."

"Me, too." Sebastian hesitated again. "If we can't sleep, we can talk about Mummy." His eyes, too, were wet, yet at the same time they seemed brighter, filled with hope. "If you don't mind, that is."

Andrew got down on his knees and held him close.

"No, Sebastian," he said. "I don't think I'd mind that at all."

* * *

As time went on, Andrew found it immensely difficult to maintain a well-balanced stability in Sebastian's life. If the child had been his pride and joy before, now he was the center of Andrew's universe. If Sebastian woke from a nightmare, crying, Andrew was at his side before Ellie had even heard him. If Sebastian fell over, or caught a cold, or had a problem at school, his father blamed himself. Had Andrew returned to full-time work at his practice, the situation might have steadied more easily, but instead, for months on end, he canceled appointments and delegated cases in order to spend as much time as possible with the boy. He realized that he was behaving almost as obsessively as Diana had during Sebastian's first few years, yet he could not stop himself. Colleagues and friends peered in from the sidelines, troubled and apprehensive about the long-term effects that Andrew's coddling and overprotectiveness might have on the child, but it seemed that their concerns were, if not unfounded, exaggerated. Sebastian missed his mother keenly but openly, and as time progressed and he slowly became more able to come to terms with his loss, he developed, too, an intuitive compassion for his father's more slowly healing grief that was remarkable for his age.

In spite of Andrew and Ellie, his best friend, Jeremy, and Rufus and Jasper, the elderly retrievers, Sebastian still felt very much alone. In the early days after Diana's death, once he had been persuaded to go back to school, he had found that, apart from Jeremy, most of his friends had kept their distance, as if embarrassed, somehow, by Sebastian's loss, and resentful, too, because their own parents suddenly seemed shockingly mortal. They were all over it now, of course, death and grief buried and forgotten. But for Sebastian it was not so simple.

Nighttime was the hardest for him, for on the occasions when sleep did not come easily, he lay rigidly in bed, his eyes tightly shut against the darkness of which, since the night of his mother's death, he had become increasingly afraid. Sometimes, when it was very bad, he switched on his bedside lamp and relief would steal slowly over him as all those black, nameless shapes became familiar and unthreatening again. Often, however, when his light was on, either his father or Ellie, concerned and kindly, would come in to check on him, and Sebastian would feel guilty because he had worried them and would turn the light out again.

"You can keep the lamp on, you know, if you like," Andrew told him late one evening, his tone gentle but matter-of-fact.

"No," Sebastian said. "It's all right. I just forgot to switch it off, that's all."

"Because if you're more comfy with a bit of light, there's nothing wrong with that."

"I'm not afraid of the dark," Sebastian said stoutly.

"I used to be, when I was your age," Andrew said, although in truth that had never been one of his fears.

"Really, Daddy?"

"Lots of children are—grown-ups, too, sometimes."

Sebastian reflected for a moment.

"Well, I'm not," he said, for his father, he thought, had enough troubles without his adding to them. "I'm all right, Daddy, really."

"And you'd tell me if anything was wrong, wouldn't you?"

"Of course, Daddy."

On those nights, after Andrew or Ellie had looked in on him, if the fears returned too fiercely, Sebastian waited until he could be sure that they were asleep, and then he left his bedroom and tiptoed to his mother's dressing room, where her clothes still hung in the walnut wardrobes. More comforting even than light, more soothing than anything in the world was his mother's scent. A grown woman would have been able to identify it as a blend of Mitsouko perfume, Roger et Gallet soap and Johnson's baby powder, with the added touch, if a garment had been hung in a theater dressing room, of Leichner makeup; to Sebastian it was, simply and uniquely, his mother's fragrance.

If he opened the wardrobe doors, knelt down and buried his face in the fabrics that had formerly touched Diana's skin, had been smoothed by her soft hands, Sebastian could imagine, for a while at least, that she was there with him, embracing him, caressing him, and the fears would recede. Sometimes, he even crept up to the attic, where his father had put some of her costumes and stage things into a big trunk, and once, he actually fell asleep up there, on the attic floorboards, with one of her dresses clutched in his fingers, but neither Andrew nor Ellie found him, and his secret remained undiscovered.

And by the time his father felt able, almost two years after Diana's death, to sort through her belongings and to clear her wardrobes, Sebastian no longer needed to touch her things physically in order to conjure his mother up, for he had long since learned how to summon the strong and almost tangible memory of her scent, at will.

*   *   *

The last week of the long summer holidays of 1959, most of which Sebastian and Jeremy had spent apart because the Lockes had gone abroad to France while the Mariners had stayed in Yorkshire, brought the two boys closer together, emotionally, than they had ever been before.

Jeremy had never really felt that either he or the rest of his family truly fitted into the environment into which he and Thomas, his brother, had been born. It had been his great-great-grandfather, Adam Mariner, who, having lost two sons and two brothers to the Atlantic Ocean, had sold his cottage and boats and abandoned the Cornish fishing village in which he had been raised. Adam had taken his wife, Leonie, and his surviving unwed brother, John, and had embarked upon a journey north, determined to find his own solid piece of England, vowing to settle only where they might spend the rest of their days wrapped in land and sky and removed from the sight, smell and savagery of the sea.

Adam Mariner had found his land and house in the North Riding of Yorkshire, in the incomparably beautiful, often inhospitably hard heart of the Dales. The house—built a hundred and fifty years earlier and, for over a decade prior to their arrival, uninhabited following a major fire—was absurdly large for their modest needs, as well as being bone-chillingly cold and damp, depressingly dark and all but derelict in many parts. But Adam and John, both strong, gritty Cornishmen accustomed to hard labor and adversity, had set immediately to work, and within three years, Leonie had had a home of tolerable comfort in which to bring up her new baby son.

The Mariners had kept sheep and chickens in those days and, in time, cattle, and life inside the house had revolved almost entirely around the kitchen, with its flagstoned floor, stone sink and cast-iron range. Leonie and Mary, her new sister-in-law, a young girl from Aysgarth quickly snapped up by John only months after their arrival in the district, spent much of their time here, baking oat cakes, boiling hams, curing salt beef, washing clothes, blackleading the range, polishing the implements, pots and pans, and scrubbing the hearth, around which the whole family sat each night, when the day's labors were at an end, by the fire's warmth and glow, and the light of a single lamp.

Four generations later, Annabel Mariner had ripped the heart and soul and the worst of the remaining discomfort out of the kitchen, had installed an electric stove and refrigerator and had sealed off the ancient beef loft—the compartment over the fireplace in which sides of bacon had, in the past, been hung, and which had projected up into the master bedroom. And since those early days of her marriage to James Mariner, that same kitchen had been remodeled again, sporting by the late 1950s Italian ceramic tiles brought home by Annabel from Milan, a freezer and an automatic washing machine, and her housekeeper and a maid took care of all the domestic chores. But Annabel was from London, and although she had loved James deeply at the time of their marriage in 1946, and had continued to love him, she had always disliked the Dales and had always rather despised Mariner Hall, her husband's isolated, inconvenient and hopelessly unglamorous heritage.

The house stood on a hill between the little village of Thoralby and the larger village of Aysgarth, overlooking Bishopdale and in reach of a handful of picturesque, old stone villages, but it was about ten miles in either direction from Hawes to the west and Leyburn to the east—the closest towns of any substance in the area—and an hour's drive from Ripon, the only town that was, to Annabel, worth a personal visit. The views from Mariner Hall were panoramic and magnificent, sweeping down into the valley and up beyond into the gentle, lush, soft green fells; a wonderful, random jigsaw of fields and grazing meadows all divided by dry-stone walls, hand-built out of loose limestone, and dotted by the aged field barns built of the same stone. It was handsome, glorious land that had changed miraculously little since the time that Adam Mariner had set his hopes on it, and yet nature provided enough ceaselessly changing variety in shape and color through the seasons—the young, vigorous green of spring and the waving yellow buttercups of June; the sleepy pastoral warmth of a showery English summer; the fiery colors of the woods in autumn and the silent blanket of snow in winter. And always the livestock, the cattle, nowadays mostly black-and-white Friesian, and the sheep, with their black faces and magnificent wool coats, forever grazing, only brought off the fell by the dalesmen and their dogs for shearing, dipping, tupping, lambing, feeding in deep, harsh winter and, finally, for their last journey to market.

The blood in James Mariner's veins was still, after several generations, not entirely pure Yorkshire, and his devotion to the farming lifestyle—already not as strong as it might have been—had been even further diluted the day he had succumbed to the beauty and city charms of his wife. His parents had sent James away to school in York, and he had been infected then by a liking for town life; Annabel's longing to remain in London had given him the excuse he had long sought to take a city flat, but in spite of the fact that, as he grew older, his increasingly poor circulation and arthritis made the inherent hardships of the land ever more acutely painful, James still had an abiding loyalty to his heritage and a genuine love of Mariner Hall itself.

Jeremy would never know if he might have shared his father's love or loyalty had his young life been differently shaped. As it was, Annabel had seen to it that even his primary education had taken place as far away from Bishopdale as possible, and consequently Mariner Hall and the Dales were, to Jeremy, his second home and a magical, extended playground for himself and his younger brother.

Thomas looked up to Jeremy in the fashion that only a young boy can to his big brother. Jeremy was his leader and his hero. If Jeremy wanted to get up at midnight to forage in the larder, Thomas followed his lead. If Jeremy wanted to steal birds' eggs from their nests, Thomas was his accomplice; if Jeremy wanted to temporarily remove all Cook's enormous brassieres from her underwear drawer, Thomas thought it as hilarious a prank as his brother did. And in the summer of 1959, when Jeremy was twelve years old and Thomas was ten, when the older boy suggested that they cycle down to Aysgarth and play Explorers, Jeremy's old favorite game, the younger boy, of course, readily agreed.

"Are we going to the wood?" Thomas called, as he cycled downhill a little way behind his brother.

"Of course," Jeremy called back. "If there aren't too many people around."

They often played in Freeholders' Wood on the northern bank of the River Ure. They climbed trees, fought with snapped-off branches, picked bluebells, threw nuts at squirrels and watched out for deer, none of which they were permitted to do. But then, if their mother had anything to do with it, they would never be allowed to do *anything*—and in any case, she was usually down in London, even during the holidays, and James was much too busy on the estate to keep an eye on them.

If Freeholders' Wood was out of bounds, then Aysgarth Falls were certainly taboo, although the boys, and Jeremy in particular, could not understand why. The Falls, after all, were not awesome like Niagara, nor even obviously dangerous like Hardraw Force near

Hawes, where the water dropped ninety feet down sheer rock face. Aysgarth Falls were divided into three sections, and the ledges over which the River Ure fell were nowhere more than about twenty feet high. It was easy enough to clamber down to the water's edge, especially at the Middle Falls, and to walk right out onto the broad, sharp-edged ledge on the north bank. This ledge was perfectly safe, a great slab of flat rock scarcely covered by the swiftly flowing water, and on gentle, fine weather days, this part of the Falls was almost too tame for Jeremy to fancy bothering with. But when the river was full, and if the rainfall had been heavy, then the waterfall was more aggressive, the air filled with roar and bluster and clouds of spray.

It had been raining off and on for the best part of a week when the Mariner boys came to the Falls that August afternoon, great deluges of summer rain interrupted by brief drenchings of warm sunshine.

"Great," Jeremy said, pausing for a moment to stare through the trees down to the river. "It's really full."

They left the narrow road that divided Freeholders' Wood from the Ure, pushed their bicycles through the gate and along the rough, unmade track, and let them fall to the ground, wheels spinning, at the top of the broad steps that led down to the viewing platform from which visitors could safely look down onto the Middle Falls.

"I can't see any people," Thomas said, craning his neck.

"Super." Jeremy moved his bicycle to the side of the track and pushed it under a bush. "Hide yours, too, in case."

"In case what, Jerry?" Their mother detested the shortening of what she called "perfectly good names" to Tom and Jerry, but it made Jeremy laugh, so Thomas called him "Jerry" whenever Annabel wasn't around.

"In case the natives come, of course." Jeremy watched to make sure that Thomas did a good job. "Okay, now, we're taking on the Amazon—"

"Again?" Thomas asked.

"It's a bloody long river, and this time we're much further south, and there are cannibals and tigers and snakes in the jungle, so we need to get right down to the water before we make our plans."

They took off their shoes and socks, rolled up their trousers and leapt down the steps, bypassing the viewing platform and creeping up the bank, where they could crouch and survey, concealed by the bushes. The sun was shining warmly now, creating tiny rainbows in the spray that rose over the Falls, and, except for the central section, where the water turned an ugly rusty yellow as it tumbled, the whole setting was at the peak of loveliness.

"What's the plan, Chief?" Thomas, used to taking orders, waited, his cheeks already pink with eagerness. He was much fairer than Jeremy, just as slim, but softer-featured with sparky blue eyes.

"Hold on, let me think." Jeremy scanned the river. "Right, this is it. We've smashed our canoe on rocks upriver, and all our supplies went with it, so we're absolutely reliant on our wits, got it?"

"Got it." Thomas fished in his trouser pocket. "I saved this from the water." He brought out a half-eaten Mars bar.

"Excellent," Jeremy said. "But we may need it later, if all else fails, and we get stranded on this side. See those berries?" He pointed up at an overhanging tree. "Poisonous. Everything on this side of the river is poisonous, Tom. Which is why we have to cross over."

"To the other side?"

"Of course. That's the goal."

"But how?" Thomas asked. "We don't have a boat—"

"And it's much too dangerous to swim," Jeremy said, "because of the rapids and the sharks—"

"Sharks?"

"Deadly sharks, and strangling octopi and poisonous jellyfish."

"Great," Thomas said, and grinned, showing very white teeth against his suntanned face.

"I'll bear the brunt of the danger, obviously, since I'm the leader."

"How?"

"I'll try to get out onto that ledge, to get a better idea of what we're up against."

"You can send me, if you like, Chief," Thomas volunteered. "They often send scouts, don't they?"

"Sometimes," Jeremy agreed. "But when they're really up against it, Tom, the leaders, the really good ones, never ask their men to do anything they're not prepared to do themselves."

If Jeremy had not removed his shoes and socks, and if the coldness of the water, when he stepped barefoot out onto the ledge, had not startled him so severely, shocking his body into the unmistakable beginnings of an asthmatic attack, the afternoon would probably have ended just as innocently as it had begun. But Jeremy, whose attacks recently had been mild and infrequent, felt the tightening in his chest and throat, heard his own sudden wheezing as he tried to get a deep breath, and, panicking, he fell onto his knees on the ledge.

"Chief!" Thomas called out to him.

Jeremy, concentrating on trying to breathe, didn't answer.

"Chief, are you all right?" Thomas asked, raising his voice over the sound of the water.

"No," Jeremy managed, still on his knees.

Thomas saw his white face then, and his open, gasping mouth, and he understood what was happening, had seen the attacks before. "Is it your asthma?" Not waiting for an answer, Thomas jumped to his feet and scrambled down the bank to the river's edge. "I'm coming!" he called, the game forgotten. "Can you stand up, Jerry?"

Still struggling for breath, Jeremy tried, but failed.

"Don't worry, I'll help you."

Thomas stepped out onto the ledge, gasping as the icy water swept across his bare feet and ankles. "Golly, it's freezing, isn't it?" It had looked so shallow and harmless, yet it moved far more rapidly and with far greater force than he had anticipated. "Coming," he said again, stoically, but Jeremy didn't say a word, seemed unable to speak.

"Give me your hand," Thomas said, but Jeremy was wheezing so badly now that Thomas was not sure he heard him. "Come on, Jerry." He stooped, put out a hand and touched his brother's heaving back—

"Don't!" Jeremy gasped, panicking again, and lashed out unexpectedly with his right hand, catching Thomas on the chest. Off-balance, the younger boy slipped on the wet limestone, cried out again, just once, a high, thin cry of sheer surprise, hardly fearful at all, and then he fell backward, his head striking the sharp corner of the ledge, and tumbled down into the water.

For a long, seemingly infinite moment, Jeremy's breath stopped altogether. And then he crawled over to the edge, gasping, his whole body trembling violently.

"Tom?" He hardly knew his own voice. "Tom?"

He stared down and saw Thomas, saw his brother, clearly visible in the rushing, foaming water, almost motionless except for his hair, waving in the current. His leather belt had caught on a sharp snag of rock, which was holding him still, preventing him from being carried on down the river.

"Tom," Jeremy said again, softly.

Thomas's face was still surprised, his eyes were open, and his mouth, and Jeremy knew that he was dead, that he had been dead even before he had gone into the water, that the jagged edge of the ledge had killed him. And as Jeremy stared down, seeing the pale fringes of pink blood eddying around his brother's head, all his own breath came back into his body and, filling his lungs with damp, fresh air, he began at last to scream.

And the sound of his screaming seemed, to him, to blend into the furious voice of the river and the Falls, but in reality it rose, hauntingly, terrifyingly, up into the air. And a white-breasted dipper soared, startled, up into the blue sky, and the nuthatches and warblers and chaffinches in Freeholders' Wood flapped out of the trees, rustling branches. And a little further up the riverbank, a white-haired lady, leaning on her walking stick, stood bolt upright, and felt her flesh prickling with alarm.

Jeremy knew that his parents blamed him for the accident, and that was terrible enough, but he blamed himself, too, and that was infinitely harder to bear. His father was kind enough, once the trauma of Thomas's funeral was over, seeking specialist help for the asthma which afflicted him more severely than it had ever done before his brother's death, and his mother saw to it that he was well cared for and lacked nothing. But Jeremy knew that Annabel had always loved Thomas better than him, and he knew now, whatever anyone else might say to comfort him, that she hated him. He, in turn, hated Mariner Hall after the accident, and his hatred spread swiftly, like a sickness, to cover the estate and Bishopdale and the whole North Riding.

"I hate everything at home now," Jeremy told Sebastian, when they spent the weekend together at The Oaks at the end of the holidays. "It reminds me of Tom, and I can't stand it." Dinner was over, and they were in Sebastian's room, supposedly getting ready for bed, though the old rules still applied, and Jeremy would be sleeping in his own bedroom.

"But surely it's good thinking about him, isn't it?"

Jeremy shook his head. "Not for me." His eyes looked darker than ever in his pale, gaunt face. "Besides, they're there."

"Your parents."

"Staring at me when they think I'm not looking, blaming me."

"I'm sure you're wrong about that," Sebastian tried to reassure him, not for the first time. "It was an accident. They know that."

"I don't mean they think I murdered him, or anything like that," Jeremy said morosely. "But it comes to the same thing."

"Of course it doesn't." Sebastian remembered that his father had told him it might be best to try to keep Jeremy's mind off the accident if he could. "Anyway, what shall we do tomorrow? We could take our bikes on the Heath."

"I'm never going to ride a bike again," Jeremy said, and his voice was very hard. "And I shan't ever play Explorers again, with anyone, and I shan't go near any rivers or—"

"Jeremy," Sebastian said, gently. "Don't."

"And I wish I didn't ever have to go back to Yorkshire again." The harshness began to waver, and his eyes grew hot with unshed tears. "I wish I could just stay here in London, and not see my parents anymore."

"You don't mean that."

"Yes, I do, because they hate me—"

"They don't hate you, Jerry."

"He called me that, and I called him Tom, and Mother hated it because of the cartoons, so we did it all the more." The tears were falling now, and he had hardly cried since it had happened, and was scarcely aware that he was weeping now. "I miss him so much," he cried, "and I'd do anything—*anything*—if it would bring him back—"

"I know you would," Sebastian said, shaken by the intensity of his friend's grief. Jeremy always put on such an impassive, tough front, and he never, ever cried.

"How can you know?" Jeremy said, roughly. "You don't have a brother."

"I felt like that when my mother died." Sebastian was still gentle. "I don't remember that much about it anymore, but I know I used to daydream that she had come back again, and then it would be more terrible than ever when she didn't." He paused. "But it did get better, after a long time."

"You didn't kill your mother," Jeremy said.

"And you didn't kill Thomas," Sebastian said, distressed. "You know you didn't, you mustn't keep saying that."

"Why, when it's true?" And the scalding tears continued to spill.

They broke Annabel Mariner's rule that night about sleeping in separate rooms, and when Ellie looked in, an hour later, and saw them curled up together in Sebastian's bed, she decided against disturbing them.

"Poor boy," she said to Andrew, when he came home from a dinner meeting a little later. "I could see he'd been crying, and I couldn't see any harm in leaving them."

"On the contrary," Andrew said. "I should think Jeremy needs some comforting, and Sebastian would be the right one for the job."

"It'll take him some time to get over it, wouldn't you say?" Ellie said sadly.

"Some things," Andrew said, "you never really get over."

In 1960, when Sebastian was thirteen, Andrew sent him to Marchmont School in Buckinghamshire. They had discussed alternatives together at great length and had, ultimately, chosen Marchmont partly because it was one of the most aesthetically lovely boys' schools in England, with a strong reputation as a relaxed and happy home as well as a fine educational establishment, and partly because Jeremy Mariner had been enrolled at Marchmont by his parents.

Andrew was aware that Diana would never have agreed to have sent their son to boarding school, but he had become convinced in his own mind that it was the right thing for Sebastian under the circumstances they now found themselves in. Marchmont provided a liberal education, encouraging individualism and initiative, tempered by a common-sense approach to discipline, and though Andrew had been educated perfectly contentedly at Rugby, he knew several men who had grown up at Marchmont, and their recollections had always seemed quite enviable to him.

The school's motto was *Omnem Movere Lapidem*—"Leave No Stone Unturned." Its main house was handsome, ivy-clad Tudor, its smaller houses and dormitories pleasantly furnished and friendly, and its grounds a well-balanced blend of playing fields, tennis courts, beautifully landscaped flower gardens and vegetable patches. Sebastian had never really known ugliness, but on the morning of his interview with the headmaster, when he stood at the top of the stone steps outside the main house, taking his first long look at the lovely lawns rolling gently away toward Marchmont's lake, used, in summer, for swimming, Sebastian felt a rush of pleasure and anticipation.

That September, as Andrew drove silently through the tall iron gates, and the first broad expanse of green stretched before them again, he glanced sideways at Sebastian, his private emotional turmoil intensified by his son's heavy silence.

"All right?" he asked.

"Would you mind stopping for a second, Dad?"

Andrew braked sharply. "What's wrong?"

Sebastian smiled. "Nothing's wrong, Dad. I'm fine." He paused. "It was just that I had the feeling that once we cross that—" He looked at the attractive little bridge just ahead of them that broke up the long drive to the main house, making it less imposing.

"Last-minute doubts?" Andrew's heart was racing painfully.

"Of course not," Sebastian said. "I just wanted another minute alone with you, that's all." He paused. "Listen, Dad, I know you've been really worried about sending me away, but you don't have to think I'm upset, because I'm not. I'm a bit nervous, but I'm excited, too."

The lump of anxiety that had wedged itself in Andrew's throat, making it hard for him to speak, shifted a little, and he was filled with gratitude, yet again, for his son's sensitivity.

"Promise me something," he said.

"Of course."

"Any problems—and you're bound to have some problems at some point, everyone does—try to solve them yourself if you can." Andrew grasped Sebastian's hand. "But if they're too tough, if you need advice, promise you'll remember I'm there for you at any time of day or night."

"I promise, Dad."

"I can always be here in a couple of hours, don't forget that."

"The same goes for you," Sebastian said softly. "You've got to promise to tell me if there's anything wrong at home."

"Don't you start worrying about me," Andrew said.

"It works both ways, Dad."

Though he did, of course, miss his father and Ellie, Sebastian was almost blissfully happy at Marchmont. He enjoyed learning, liked most sports, made friends easily. With each passing year, he became more attractive but remained unaware of the appeal of his abundant wheat-colored hair, his keen blue eyes, his strong, clean features and slim build. The teaching staff appreciated him because he was a good, conscientious student, and the other boys liked him because he was not overly bookish. His sense of humor and his consideration, the two characteristics which had been apparent even in his early years, had strengthened, and as time passed his classmates tended to flock around him. Sebastian was especially popular because, with his natural ability to combine mischief with common sense, he often saved other boys from trouble because he knew instinctively when to stop, and although he never sought leadership, from the outset of his time at Marchmont, it became his natural role.

The boy who turned most often, and most urgently, to Sebastian was Jeremy. Though more than three years had passed since his brother's death, Jeremy had never really come to terms either with Thomas's loss or with the manner of that loss, and the old spark of dynamism and vitality that Sebastian had always observed in his friend, the old capacity for fun, had, for the moment at least, been extinguished.

Though their friendship had endured, the two boys were still opposites in almost every way. Where Sebastian was naturally kind, Jeremy could be sharp to the point of cruelty. Whereas Sebastian found Marchmont's grounds and the surrounding countryside beautiful, Jeremy hankered for the city. When it came to preparing for examinations, Sebastian strove to make his father proud, while Jeremy, though innately intelligent, made only the most minimal efforts to pass, and that only because failure and possible expulsion would mean that he might have to go home to Mariner Hall. One of the few interests Sebastian and Jeremy had in common was their mutual passion for the theater and cinema; the only times Sebastian ever saw a glint of the old Jeremy these days was when they were talking about a film they had seen or a Dramatic Society production, and on those occasions Sebastian, too, was in his element for, unsurprisingly, considering his heritage, he had discovered in himself an intense interest in the theater and films.

During a half-term break in the spring of 1962, while Jeremy and his mother were staying at their Regent's Park flat, Annabel took her son to the theater for a birthday treat. When they emerged after the show into Shaftesbury Avenue, it was raining heavily, and when Jeremy volunteered to find them a taxi, Annabel accepted.

"I'll wait in the foyer," she said. "Try not to be long, darling."

"Back before you know it," Jeremy said.

It was after one in the morning when Annabel next saw him, when he strolled, quite casually, into the flat.

"Where the *hell* have you been?"

"I got lost."

"For two and a half hours?" She was white with anger. "I've been out of my mind worrying about you."

"There was no need," Jeremy said.

"No need? No *need?*"

"I was perfectly all right, just lost, that's all."

"How could you have been lost when we were slap bang in the middle of Shaftesbury Avenue?"

Jeremy remained unruffled. "I stood on the corner for ages, and there weren't any free cabs anywhere, so I went up a side street—"

"Which one?"

"I don't know, that was the problem, and then I turned into another road and spotted a taxi with its light on, and I chased it around a corner and after that I seemed to be lost."

Annabel glared at him. "I don't believe you."

"Where do you imagine I was, Mother?"

"I couldn't begin to imagine. I only know that you abandoned me, and that I was terrified that something might have happened to you." Her eyes were cold. "But you wouldn't let that worry you, would you, since you've always been the most insensitive, selfish boy."

Had Annabel known that Jeremy had passed the missing hours with a Soho prostitute, and that he had spent the rest of his birthday money on cannabis, she would have been, justifiably, infinitely more appalled. Had Jeremy not tried to sell the drugs to another boy at school, a boy on whom he had, the previous term, played an unkind practical joke, he would not have been reported to his housemaster.

"In my locker," Jeremy whispered in Sebastian's ear the instant he knew he had been summoned. "Get it out, for God's sake."

"Get what out?"

"Just do it, please. If they find it, I'm finished."

"You *idiot*."

"*Please*, Seb."

Sebastian did as his friend had asked, swiftly, not allowing himself to consider the risk he was taking. If drugs were found in their dormitory, Jeremy would certainly be expelled, but if Sebastian were discovered aiding and abetting him, he'd be fortunate not to meet the same fate. In the event, by the time a search had been ordered, not a trace of cannabis remained. Both Jeremy and the boy who had reported him spent more than an hour in the headmaster's study, but without evidence and in the face of Jeremy's fervent denial, the matter was laid to rest. If Jeremy had felt close to Sebastian before, after that incident, despite his friend's very real anger at having been placed in such a compromising situation, Jeremy idolized him.

Sebastian's own anxiety over the affair caused him more than one sleepless night, and although lying awake in the dark did not panic him as it had done years before, he still suffered acute unease. Night noises in the dormitory were distasteful to him, the hush filled with snuffles and snores and occasional groans, but there was nothing to be done but to grit his teeth and wait until morning.

And then, on his third sleepless night in a row, it came to him, unbidden. Wafting toward him, in the darkness, coming closer until it was all around him in the air, comforting and warming—a gentle, soft fragrance hovering over him, a blend of Mitsouko perfume and Roger et Gallet soap and Leichner makeup, reminding him so intensely of his mother that tears of surprise and pleasure pricked at his eyes. And though he had not experienced it for many years, and though he was almost fifteen years old now, almost adult, the sensation was so sweet and languorous that Sebastian welcomed it back, almost as an old friend, and allowed it to soothe him, and to rock him gently into sleep.

The following June, when he was sixteen, old ghosts came back to haunt Sebastian, when the Dramatic Society staged a production of *Hedda Gabler*. Heavily preoccupied with examinations, he had no direct personal involvement with the play, but on the day of the group's dress rehearsal, curiosity drew him into the main hall to observe. It was nine years since Sebastian had witnessed his mother's final performance, but although he still remembered that it had been the first great thrill of his life, what had happened afterward had wiped away all but the most dreamlike and insubstantial memories of the play itself.

He was sitting in the fourth row, over to the right-hand side, watching the opening scene, amused, as all the boys were at the outset of every school production, by the spectacle of male students in female roles, when, just after the actor playing George Tesman had made his first entrance, Sebastian was jolted from his seat by a piercing scream.

"What the hell—?"

The action, onstage, stopped. Dan Jacobs, the director, in the front row, held his hands up in the air, palms forward, waiting, listening.

"Shall we start again?" the boy playing Juliana Tesman asked, hesitantly, in his natural, male voice.

The scream came again, a clear scream of agony. They all ran, the play abandoned, Sebastian running with the others, back to the communal dressing room, seeking the source of the terrible sound.

Charlie Grenville lay writhing on the floor, grotesque in Hedda's wig and long dress.

"Help me!" He tore at his face with his hands, his heavily made up eyes wide with shock and pain. "My face—*help* me—"

"Charlie, what happened?" Dan Jacobs fell to his knees and forced the clawed hands away so that he could see. "Oh, my God." He tried, but failed to conceal his revulsion. The young actor's skin, from his nostrils down to his chin, was red—with streaked, smeared lipstick, with blood from where he had tried to bite and scratch away the agony—and with the burn itself.

"Someone get help," Dan Jacobs said, his voice urgent and shrill. One boy rushed out of the room to vomit outside. On the floor, Charlie Grenville moaned and tried to pull at his face.

"For God's sake, *do* something!" the director shouted, and two other boys ran.

There was a fierce black pounding in Sebastian's head, and his heart was racing wildly. He could hardly move, knew that he was standing by uselessly, and was shocked by his own impotence.

"Seb, get some cold water," Dan Jacobs said.

For another moment, Sebastian still stood motionless.

"Locke!"

He came back to life. "Water, right." And he ran to one of the basins, found a towel, drenched it with cold water and ran back. And as the awful dark hammering in his head began to subside, he, too, knelt by Charlie Grenville's side and tried to help him, to do something, to hold his hand and to speak soothingly, gently, until they came to take him away.

It had been caused, Sebastian wrote to Andrew, a few days later, by acid in Charlie's lipstick.

The damage looked much worse than it really was, thank heaven, and the Doc doesn't seem to think there'll be any scar or anything. But the whole school's in an uproar, and the police were called in because Mr. Giles (the chemistry master) reported some hydrochloric acid missing from the lab. All the dangerous stuff gets locked away every evening, so I suppose they reckon someone must have pinched it during class.

It's been pretty ghastly, Dad. Every single boy in the Lower, Middle and Upper Schools has been interviewed at length, but so far they haven't found either the culprit or any kind of motive. One of the masters told us on the second day after it happened, that they thought it might have been a practical joke that went wrong, and Jeremy says that, during his interview, they kept going on at him about the jokes he's played on boys in the past. As if Jerry could ever do anything so despicable. You and I both know him better than that—I've known him to hurt people with words, but he'd never in a thousand years deliberately cause anyone physical pain.

Mind you, it's almost impossible to conceive of anyone being capable of such wickedness, don't you agree? Most of us would prefer to think it was just an accident, though I'll admit it's hard to see how it could have happened.

Oh, well, Dad, summer holidays soon. I'm looking forward to seeing you, and Ellie, of course—and I can't wait for Greece.

All my love.

Your Sebastian.

At the beginning of the long summer holidays that same year, with the unsolved horrors of the school play already fading into memory, a few days before Sebastian and Andrew were due to leave for a month's stay at a friend's villa in the hills of Rhodes, Sebastian made love to a girl for the first time.

Her name was Vanessa Mills, she lived not far from the Lockes in her parents' house in Church Street, and she and Sebastian had met in The Coffee Cup in Haverstock Hill. Vanessa was red-haired and green-eyed, with freckles; she was attractive, funny and bright and by far the most flirtatious girl Sebastian had ever met. He had dated occasionally since his fifteenth birthday, and he had French-kissed and, twice, petted in the Everyman Cinema, but over dinner with Vanessa at La Gaffe, a romantic restaurant in Heath Street, he began to realize that she was not only willing, but also eager to go further.

"Would you like to come back to my house for coffee?" she asked.

"I'd love to. Won't your parents mind?"

"They won't know."

"How come?"

Vanessa smiled, showing small, white teeth. "They're out of town for the night, staying over with friends after a dinner party. We'll have the whole house to ourselves."

"Great," Sebastian said.

It was the first time he had been in a young girl's bedroom, and the light femininity of the flowery wallpaper and peachy chintzes, all quilting and flounces, intoxicated him almost as much as the vision of Vanessa slipping uninhibitedly out of her clothes. She was a pretty enough girl when fully dressed, but naked, Sebastian found her breathtakingly lovely—her legs were long and shapely, her shoulders were broad, her waist was slender and her breasts were high and full, with rosy nipples.

"Like what you see?" she asked, standing close to him.

He felt desperately nervous. "You're beautiful."

"Truly?"

He was finding it hard to breathe. "You're the most beautiful girl I've ever seen."

"Kiss me then."

He pulled her to him and kissed her as well and thoroughly as he knew how, and the sensation of her nakedness, all softness and curves, against him, made his head spin.

"Why don't you get undressed?" Vanessa murmured against his mouth. "You've got a marvelous erection, I can feel it." To prove it, she wriggled even closer. "Mm, marvelous," she said again.

He undressed quickly, embarrassed when he ripped a button off his shirt and blushing scarlet when she unbuckled his belt and slipped her right hand down inside his trousers.

"Lovely," she said. "You really should let it out, you know."

"Christ," Sebastian said, and dropped his trousers.

He kissed her again in a fever of unbearable excitement and then tumbled with her onto her bed, making love to her clumsily, but in a state of joyous abandon, shooting his sperm into her open, avid body much sooner than he might have wished.

"Sorry," he mumbled, when he was able to speak again.

"Nothing to be sorry about," Vanessa whispered. "It was lovely."

"But it was too—" He stopped, too embarrassed to go on.

"Too quick? Never mind, there's plenty of time." She reached for his right hand and guided his fingers into her damp pubic hair. "Do you like my bush, darling?" It was golden red, like her hair. "There, that's the way to touch me." He groaned, and his fingers quickened. "That's it exactly, darling."

It was only afterward, after the lovemaking, that Sebastian tasted his first disappointment. Of all his expectations, the only one of which he had been certain was that after it was all over, he would want to hold Vanessa, to cuddle close to her, to enjoy the snugness of her body after all their passion was spent. But curiously, he felt no warmth for her at all, and that dismayed him a little.

He questioned himself, silently, still lying beside her under the rumpled sheets. Surely he wasn't such a hypocrite as to disapprove of her in some self-righteous way? But no, that couldn't be it, for he found Vanessa admirable, a free and glorious spirit he'd been fantastically lucky to meet. Did he perhaps feel guilty for using her? But there wasn't any need for guilt, for she had instigated the sex, and she seemed as strong as a horse and completely undemanding.

He couldn't understand why he felt so emotionally chilled, and later that night, in his own bed at home, he still found himself unable to put it out of his mind. He tried to recapture the exquisitely pleasurable sensations he had enjoyed earlier, but his mind seemed to be playing tricks on him and he couldn't remember them at all. Instead, he found himself lost in curious, blurry recollections of a much more distant past, of the shadowy yet indelible memories of his mother's embraces and caresses, and suddenly Sebastian became angry with himself and even more dismayed than before by the connotations of Oedipal love that those thoughts suggested to him.

"You're overreacting," he told himself, getting out of bed and going to the open window. "For God's sake, calm down."

He was just suffering from anticlimax, he rationalized. It was quite a natural reaction. Of course it was normal not to feel emotionally bound to Vanessa—why should he? After all, if he was going to fall in love every time he had sex with a girl, he was going to be in for a hell of a time.

c h a p t e r
5

There was so much for Katharine to learn. No member of any audience could possibly conceive of how much went into a stage set of any complexity. And there was an entire world to discover, a massive history to pore over before a student could begin to understand that world as it was in the late 1960s. Katharine learnt about the first "flying machines" used in Greek dramas, about the extraordinary ambitiousness of Roman theatrical architecture, and about the construction of the first Globe Theatre in London, whose thatched gallery roof was set ablaze by the firing of a cannon during a performance of *Henry VIII*, resulting in the theater's destruction. She learnt about the fantastic and complicated special effects that became popular in the Middle Ages, when sometimes huge crews of people were employed to help with the trapdoors and pulleys, and great lengths were gone to to create authentic sounds and smells, when even a dummy being used in a scene where a man was being burned at the stake was packed with entrails to make the odor more realistic.

"It makes modern American stagecraft seem almost tame," Howard Hart, a fellow student and Katharine's current boyfriend, commented.

"I don't know," Katharine said. "Look at what Norman Bel Geddes did in the twenties and thirties—"

"I'm not talking about then," Howard interrupted her. "I mean contemporary."

"Was there something wrong with *West Side Story*?" Katharine inquired. "Or if that's too old-hat for you, how about *Fiddler*? Those sets were so gorgeous I drooled. And what about *Cabaret*?"

"All musicals."

"I love musicals."

"I noticed," Howard said wryly. He disapproved of musicals because they were always more expensive to go to than straight plays. The fact that they were vastly more costly to produce ought, by rights, to have made him more understanding, but so far as Howard was concerned, if he was buying the tickets, that made him a regular customer, not a designer.

Most of the students went to the theater as often as humanly possible, in Pittsburgh itself, but if time allowed—and even when it did not—they went to Philadelphia and, of course, to New York City. Katharine thanked her stars that she was blessed with boundless energy, for her life, since coming to Carnegie Mellon, was crammed with activity. She put everything into her studies and more, yet she was still conscious of wanting to maintain an even balance in her life and in her relationships. She went home to Washington, D.C., every vacation and break, to the house that she still regarded as her ultimate sanctuary, the place where she felt she truly belonged, or sometimes she stayed with Jake at his house. Louise came down from New York when she could, but quite frequently Katharine combined her theater visits to Manhattan with overnight stays with her mother and Sam, and occasionally—though fitting it all in was a permanent struggle —she went out to Long Island to see Karen Andersen, her grandmother, who had moved, a few years earlier, into a beautiful new house in Easthampton, and who considered herself, these days, something of a *grande dame*.

In spite of the hectic quality of her life, Katharine was conscious of living an encapsulated, almost protected existence. She and her fellow students were living through the era of peace and love, through the period when other students all over the world had been making their voices heard, through times of revolt and riot and of Vietnam. Yet Katharine's personal world felt, to her, smaller and gentler, consumed as it was by theater. If you were hard at work hunched over your drawing board or at your easel, or wholly absorbed in discussing your designs with carpenters or painters in a huge scenic shop, or trying to calculate the effects of lighting and space on a fabric that you wanted to use, or the consequent effects of that fabric on the faces or costumes of the actors; or if you were sitting in the Kresge Theatre, trying to analyze every ingredient that had gone into making a particular set a success or a failure—it was hard, almost impossible, to remember what else was happening on the outside, in the real world.

Halfway through Katharine's second year at Carnegie Mellon, Louise arrived on an unexpected visit to Pittsburgh. She looked tired and drained, and Katharine was terrified when she saw her that her mother might be seriously ill. But on the first evening of her visit, as they were eating pasta in a small, family-run trattoria, Louise told Katharine that she was perfectly well; it was her marriage to Sam that was unhealthy.

"I thought you were happy," Katharine said, shocked.

"We used to be," Louise said, then sighed. "But not for some time now, I'm afraid." There were shadows under her lovely brown eyes, and a new scattering of fine lines around her eyes and mouth.

"What happened?" Katharine picked up their carafe of chianti and poured another glass for her mother.

"Nothing dramatic. No adulterous affairs, no cruelty." Louise smiled wanly. "Sam's a decent man, you know that. And I've been faithful to him."

"But?" Katharine waited.

"He says that he's never felt as if I was truly his wife."

"What does that mean?"

"I think it means that Sam wanted more than I've been able to give him. More of myself, the core of me, you know?" Louise bit her lip. "He told me, a couple of weeks ago, that he sometimes feels as if I'm still married to Jake—that Jake's my real husband, and that he's just an understudy."

An old, half-suppressed hope flickered inside Katharine, but she didn't let it show. "Is he right?"

"Of course not," Louise said. "It's not as if I jumped into marriage to Sam right after the divorce. It was never a rebound love affair— but it was a love affair, and a wonderful one. While it lasted."

"You really think it's over?"

"I'm afraid it may be. Sam thinks it is."

"But you've been married for six years. You have a good marriage. Don't you want to fight, Mom?"

"I've been fighting, sweetheart. This hasn't just happened—I didn't just have an argument with Sam and jump on a plane to Pittsburgh to cry on your shoulder."

Katharine had to ask, couldn't hold back the question. "What about Daddy?" Jake had never remarried, though there had never been any shortage of women in his life.

"What about him?" Louise answered. It was a rhetorical question, inviting no further discussion.

There was a moment's silence.

"I'm so fond of Sam," Katharine said. "If you guys can't work it out, I'll be really sad."

Louise's eyes were somber. "So will I, my darling."

During that summer of 1969, Katharine's own social life was brimful and happy. She had dated fairly regularly in high school, but going to Carnegie Mellon, breaking away from the inevitable constraints of home, had broadened her horizons in many ways. Though modest by nature, she knew that she was pretty—it was hard not to when young men and, even more convincingly, her girlfriends, were always telling her she was—and she knew that people found her good company, and it was the latter fact that increased her self-confidence more than anything, and the more her confidence grew, so did her beauty and her appeal.

Howard Hart had long since faded from the picture, and taking his place had been Rob Newman, a third-year student playwright, and after Rob had come Joe Maretti, a talented young actor who found it hard to understand why Katharine had chosen design over acting.

"You're nuts," he told her one evening, after she'd helped him out by working through a new script with him. "You're a natural."

"No, I'm not," she said.

"Sure you are. So how come?"

Katharine shrugged. "I loved acting and design—I had to choose."

"I don't get it," Joe said. "I mean, your designs are great, but to me you feel like one of us."

Katharine liked Joe, but he disturbed her equilibrium, and she stopped dating him after a few weeks. She liked all her boyfriends, made it a rule never to date anyone she didn't instantly like and respect, but her relationships never lasted more than a couple of months at most, because Katharine was still—some thought miraculously—a virgin, and although she had no outmoded notions about sex before marriage, she did have an idea that she'd like to be in love with the first man she slept with—or at the very least, that she'd like to *think* she was in love with him.

She met Saul Stone, a student director, when her car broke down one morning in early September on her way back from buying groceries before her first lecture of the day. He stopped to help; Katharine took one look at his black hair, green eyes and his quirky, exciting mouth, and decided that he was the one. Her legs turned to jelly and the lecture flew out of her head, and her heart sang with happiness because he kept lifting his head from under the hood of her car to stare at her. When he asked for her phone number, she gave it without hesitation. When he called her that evening to invite her to dinner, she accepted. When he did no more than kiss her gently on the lips after he'd driven her home, Katharine was torn between pleasure at his restraint, and fear that he didn't want her as much as she wanted him. But after the second date, when he brought her back to the apartment that she shared with two other students —both of them out that evening—she knew that this fear had been misplaced.

"I've been waiting for this a long time." Saul leaned against the refrigerator in the tiny kitchen, watching her.

"Really?" Katharine went on making coffee, commending herself on the calmness of her reactions.

"You bet." Saul stepped closer, and his voice was so marvelously husky she thought she'd melt. "You're the most gorgeous girl on campus, Katharine."

She flushed, and grinned. "We both know that isn't true."

He reached out and stroked her hair. "Accepting a compliment isn't a sin, you know. Anyway, I meant it."

They took the coffee into her room, poster-lined and cluttered with books and her own designs, and Katharine was glad that she had taken the time to turn her bed back into a sofa before going out.

Saul crouched down to get a better look at one of her model sets. "I like that," he said, straightening up. "Perhaps we'll work together some day."

"I'd love that," she said, pleased.

"First things first." Saul took Katharine's hand, drew her down onto the sofa and kissed her. It was a long and thorough kiss, and Katharine felt her whole body glowing with heat before she drew away.

"Are you hesitating because you didn't like it?" Saul asked. "Or because you did?" He didn't wait for her answer. "Either way, I have to warn you that if you don't let me make love to you soon, I may become incapable of coherent thought, and you'll be responsible for depriving the world of a great director."

Katharine laughed.

"It's not funny," Saul scolded her, and took her in his arms again.

Katharine began taking the pill that week, and Saul waited, impatient as a prowling lion, until she said she was ready, but when the evening came, he was properly considerate and romantic, bringing her a single red rose and insisting on taking her out for a more expensive dinner than he could afford before, glowing with good food and red wine, they stumbled back to his apartment.

Katharine was not disappointed. Saul's lovemaking was just as wonderful as she had fantasized, and the pain, the first time, was not nearly as bad as some girls made it out to be; but a tiny part of her was infuriatingly amused by Saul, because she could not help but be aware that he was directing her through the actions.

"Now, Katharine," he commanded her. "Open your legs for me." And a little later, after the first shock of pain had passed and she had found herself beginning to enjoy the mass of brand-new and intense sensations: "Don't be afraid to move, baby—that's it, great, oh that's so *good*."

The trouble was that all three times that they made love that night, every time Katharine was close to coming to orgasm, Saul's directions made her feel as if she were performing for him.

"Yes, baby, give it to me—keep it coming—oh Christ, you look so great—no, don't hold back, it's perfect, this is perfect—you're the best, baby, the absolute *best!*"

And after that, Katharine found that her orgasms had deserted her, and she was conscious of acute disappointment because she realized now that she was not, after all, in love with Saul Stone, but there was no regret, for she had been ripe and ready for sex, and if it hadn't been perfect, it had certainly been enjoyable. Katharine knew that Saul was hell-bent on having a career in the theater, but she felt absolutely certain, after that night, that his destiny lay in the movies.

They continued to date for a few weeks after that, though they were both now aware that this was not, as they'd first believed, going to be the great passion, but they liked and respected each other, and they had fun together, and that, Katharine supposed, for the time being at least, was more than enough. When it ended, on a gratuitously theatrical note, after Katharine wandered onto the stage of the Kresge Theatre to take a close look at the set for *La Belle Hélène*, and discovered Saul in the process of entering Queen Helena on Menelaus's couch, complete with directorial instructions far more graphic than any he'd given her, Katharine felt an infinitely greater desire to laugh than to weep.

When Louise's marriage to Sam ended in divorce in January of 1970, Katharine did her utmost, as time allowed, to comfort her mother, but this being her final year at Carnegie Mellon, there were great limitations on her ability to help. As it turned out, this was a blessing in disguise, since the only other person Louise felt close enough to turn to was her first ex-husband. She and Jake had been divorced for over a decade, but during the last five of those years their friendship, limited as it was by distance and by Sam, had strengthened. When the second marriage failed, and Louise came back, full time, to Washington, she and Jake began seeing each other once a week for dinner, and Louise started to realize that maybe Sam hadn't been as crazy as she'd believed about her relationship with Jake.

When, on the occasion of Katharine's twenty-first birthday, during the spring break of that year, Jake and Louise threw a party for her at the Shoreham Hotel, it was blazingly apparent to Katharine almost from the beginning of the evening that her parents were contemplating a reconciliation.

It was the happiest night of her life. Dancing snugly close to Ted Lowell, her boyfriend of several months, as the band played "People"—Ted was an architect from Philadelphia, and although Katharine knew that she was not in love with Ted, she had long since decided that she was very much in "like"—Katharine found it impossible to keep her eyes off Jake and Louise.

"Don't they look wonderful together?" she said to Ted, watching her parents dancing cheek-to-cheek.

"They're a great-looking couple," Ted said, and started to hum.

"I wonder," Katharine murmured.

"What are you wondering?"

"Nothing."

She tried to be realistic, to remind herself that it was simply a special night for them all, that it was probably little more than a case of good friendship, old times' sake and quite a few drops too many

of Dom Pérignon, but nevertheless Katharine felt her heart surging
with hope and joy.

A little after one o'clock in the morning Louise, glowing in her
honey-colored crêpe-de-Chine Dior gown, drew her to one side.

"Darling, would you mind very much if we left now?"

"We?"

There was a blush, Katharine noted, a definite heightening of color.

"You and Dad?" She waited. "Together?"

Louise laughed. "There's no need to say it like that."

"How's that?" Katharine teased.

"With such innuendo."

"Is it so very misplaced?" Katharine asked.

"Not so very," Louise said, and blushed again, just as Jake arrived
at her side, carrying both their coats.

"We're leaving you young people to party for as long as you want,
did your mother tell you?" he said to Katharine. "Do you mind,
honey?"

"Of course I don't mind, Daddy," she said, and kissed him on the
cheek. "And thank you, both of you, for tonight. It's been wonderful,
the best party ever."

"God bless you," Jake said, and his eyes were very tender.

"Will you see us out, darling?" Louise asked.

At the front door of the hotel, Katharine saw that they were both
leaving in her father's Lincoln convertible, even though she and her
mother had come in Louise's car. And she watched the way Jake was
holding Louise's arm as he helped her in, and the way Louise smiled
up into his eyes, and Katharine was reeling with romance as she ran
back to Ted's side and agreed, as he'd asked her earlier, to spend
the night with him at the hotel. It wasn't so much that she wanted
to, but just in case Jake and Louise took it into their heads to go back
to the old house, she wanted to be certain that they would, apart
from the diplomatic Mrs. Murray, have the place to themselves.

The very idea made Katharine dewy-eyed with optimism.

It was five minutes before six in the morning when the telephone
in the hotel bedroom began ringing and Katharine, waking before
Ted, startled and fuzzy, reached to pick it up to stop the jarring sound.

"Hello?" she said, still half asleep.

"Katharine, is that you?"

"Who is that?" The room was still dark, the early morning light not penetrating the heavy curtains. Katharine fumbled for the light switch. "Hello?"

"Oh, Kate—"

It took Katharine another moment to recognize that the voice at the other end of the line was Mrs. Murray, and still another second or two to realize that she was weeping.

"Mrs. Murray, what is it?" She sat bolt upright in bed, and Ted, beside her, stirred for the first time. "What's happened?"

"Oh, my dear—"

"Mrs. Murray, tell me what's happened, please."

"I've been trying to find you for hours. Katharine, you have to come home."

"Why?"

"Now, right away. You have to come *home*."

"What's up?" Ted asked, awake now, too, and seeing her face. "Who's on the phone?"

Katharine could not answer him. She felt the creeping horror, starting all the way down at her icy toes, crawling higher and higher, clutching at her stomach, at her throat, at her face and eyes. As Mrs. Murray's sobbing voice told her that her father's car had been forced off the Potomac Parkway by a drunk driver. And that both Jake and Louise had been killed outright.

chapter

6

When, six years later, Sebastian glanced back over his shoulder at all the years of his education, from kindergarten through to his three years at the University of Edinburgh, he found it hard to judge which period had been the happiest. Marchmont had, of course, been wonderful, but the sublime experience of university life was something which, from the outset and, toward the end, with the sorrow of parting, he realized was unique. The gleaning of knowledge, the broadening of horizons, new friendships forged—Jeremy Mariner and he had been separated for the first time in thirteen years—problems overcome, chances taken and achievements recognized; all these ran like a strong, common thread through the years from the first school term to the last stroll from Edinburgh Castle down the Royal Mile to Holyrood Palace. But university's greatest gift to him, he thought, was freedom.

Despite the comparative liberty and ease of Marchmont, any closed community life inevitably encouraged a team spirit, thereby inadvertently thwarting individualism. Sebastian's first year at Edinburgh was the time when he became conscious of his right to establish a singular identity. His brain felt like resilient elastic, capable, it seemed, of limitless absorption—this was his license to the life of his choice. And that life, Sebastian was certain, lay in the theater.

He was no actor; it was the love of theater in general that Diana had passed on to him. But his father, too, with his acute legal brain and finely tuned business instincts, had provided an important counterbalance. As the years passed, and his university life began hurtling inexorably toward its close, the small part of Sebastian's mind not bound up with study began to focus with increasing concentration on the area which most strongly fascinated him. The theatrical agency business.

"Even the most brilliant actor can achieve nothing without the right agent," Diana had once said.

Sebastian was not certain whether he remembered his mother saying those words, or whether Andrew had repeated them at some point after her death, but there had been more: "A really fine agent has to do much more than keep his clients in work," Diana had gone on. "He has to care about them. He has to understand their talents more thoroughly than they do themselves, so that they reach their full potential."

With an Honors degree in English accomplished, he resisted friends' invitations to share exotic wanderings through America, India and the Far East, and settled down instead to lay the foundations for his future. While Andrew holidayed in Cap d'Antibes, Sebastian remained in London working at his father's desk in The Oaks, developing his ideas until they began to take on flesh, plotting one strategy after another until he was satisfied he was on the right track.

His first move was to investigate the business in general as thoroughly and swiftly as possible. Selecting carefully, he enlisted the services of a market research organization, giving them one month to deliver their report. He required a detailed study of a number of agencies he had identified as being most closely related to the operation he hoped to set up. He wanted to know their backgrounds, their personnel, their aims and their potential, their strengths and their weaknesses, and he asked for absolute anonymity. It was an expensive exercise, but a sound investment. He had considered his own assets and limitations. He realized that it might be more usual to start out by looking for a job with an existing agency; there would certainly be those who would suggest that the rich man's route might qualify him less. But by buying the experience of others and by studying that information painstakingly, Sebastian knew that he could achieve several years' work in a few months; besides which, any talent or flair he might personally possess would benefit his own clients and himself, not his employer.

He came with strong ideals, convinced that he would prosper. He saw a wide and almost uncharted gap between the "monster" agencies and the small companies, tough and tightly run at their best, sloppy and struggling at the lower end of the scale. Sebastian's personal vision was of a compact organization, managed by a handful of gifted, dedicated people, with a small, handpicked client list that would consist exclusively of artists of unique value to the agency. On his perfect list, there would be no more than one individual in each category: one strong, established leading film actor, one actress and so on, each one a secure, profitable unit inside the agency, unthreatened by conflicting interests or professional jealousies, since their functions would never be duplicated.

And then there was his desire to seek out new talent, to support and nurture it, to watch it grow and become established. And Sebastian's dreams did not stop there; he had more plans, hazy still, for stretching the confines of an agency to accommodate fine production skills so that, in time, he might be in a position to sell exclusive, versatile packages of talent.

His idea grew and became an obsession. Already it was impossible to contemplate any other future. With each passing day, he found the whole industry that surrounded and supported the acting profession more and more fascinating. The agent was a vital part of that industry, blending talents into the machinery, strengthening the industry, helping it to thrive. Sebastian was keenly aware of what a legacy of contacts his mother had bequeathed to him. That, combined with their family's prosperity, put him in an advantageous position. If some other graduate, without his advantages, were to assemble the identical plans, he might be accused of fantasy. No one, Sebastian felt, would laugh at the son of Andrew Locke and Diana Lancaster, or if they did, he was determined that they would not laugh for long.

He began to involve himself with people in the profession. He spoke to actors, to casting directors and directors; he created opportunities for conversations with theater managements, chatted to their assistants and secretaries, lunched with their accountants and lawyers. He would have liked to have spoken to a wide cross section of agents, too, but he had to content himself with talking, at length, to Dickie Forbes, his mother's agent, now retired.

"One recurring headache for many perfectly efficient operations,"

Forbes told him, "is a failure to hold on to successful artists for the duration of their careers. Many agencies make their reputations either by building up, or by maintaining, or sometimes by resurrecting careers, but very few manage all three."

The "builders" were often the small, hungry outfits, ferociously doing battle for their clients from morning to night. But when the first, albeit often quite prolonged, glow of success had passed, gratitude sometimes petered out; and then artists would allow themselves to be snapped up by the big-time wizards who had little choice but to measure triumph in turnover, and who often withdrew their vigorous, high-powered management as soon as a career was on the wane. Sebastian felt sure that there was space and real need for a new kind of agency. It had to combine competence and, ideally, virtuosity, with zealousness and enthusiasm, financial stability with integrity. It had to be capable of nursing star names and of creating new successes, and of establishing a manageable level in the "bread and butter" areas such as television advertising. But the most decisive factor of all, he felt, was a determined policy of restricted growth. This child of Sebastian's was to be a small, but perfect creation.

He had come down from Edinburgh in late June of 1969, armed with little more than a handful of ideas. It was the last morning of September when he took up the worn pigskin briefcase that held the final, much-revised draft of his proposal, and took a taxi to Heathrow, where his father's flight from Nice was due to land. Andrew having left his Bentley at a garage near the airport, they drove together into London, where Sebastian had reserved a table for lunch at Scott's. After almost eight weeks of leisure, Andrew felt fit and relaxed, and more than a little intrigued to know what was inside the folder that now lay between them on the table, beside their coffee cups and cognac glasses.

Sebastian waited in painful silence while his father, with spectacles perched on the end of his nose, read the long document, eyes turned inscrutably downward, face impassive. But finally, as he laid the folder back on the cloth and removed his spectacles, his blue eyes contained such intense pleasure that his son realized, with a thrill, that he was well pleased.

"I'm impressed," Andrew said, quietly.

Sebastian remained silent.

"And I'm proud, and I'm more excited than I have been about

anything for years." He paused. "But—and you knew there had to be some reservations, didn't you?"

"Of course." Sebastian lit a cigarette and steeled himself.

"But I do have several major concerns." Andrew took a sip of his cognac. "Knowing you as well as I think I do, I'm aware that if you've put this much time and care and expense into anything, you have decided to commit yourself."

"You're right," Sebastian said.

"This is a very impressive proposal, Sebastian, but how can I be sure that it isn't just an extension of your academic training? Your ability to prepare convincing propositions for debate or to twist the written word to suit your meaning and needs will never be more finely tuned than it is right now."

"I believe it's a lot more than that."

Andrew nodded. "Then let's move on a step. Your proposal reads as the work of a professional, but there is obviously an idealist at its root, at its core. Only a consummate realist could make it actually happen."

"I agree with you, Dad."

"I haven't finished," Andrew said, and smiled. "I've barely begun. To start any kind of new business and make it a success takes dogged hard work, but to get this particular business off the ground will take a special type of flair, humility, aggression and diplomacy. I've never been an agent, of course, but I was married to your mother for ten years, and I've acted for any number of people in the business."

"That's why I need to know what you think, Dad." Sebastian grinned. "One of the reasons, anyway."

"It takes unshakable self-confidence to be a good agent," Andrew went on, "and enormous charm. It takes an infallible eye for talent and for knowing where that talent should be placed, and it takes a swift readiness to admit mistakes."

"It also," Sebastian took over, "means meeting requirements for licenses, finding the right location and employing the right staff. It means building a sufficiently credible, sufficiently arresting foundation in order to legitimately win artists." He paused, looking his father in the eye. "And it also, of course, more than anything, means a major investment."

Andrew looked back into his son's earnest face.

"Nothing is impossible," he said.

chapter 7

A fter the death of her parents, Katharine Andersen's loneliness had overwhelmed her. Even after their divorce, even when she, Louise and Jake had all lived in separate cities, she had always known that her mother and father were there for her, either in the background or, if they needed one another, just a few hours away. Now the only family Katharine had left in the world were Jake's mother, Karen, Louise's mother, Lilian Grahame in Minneapolis, and Jake's uncle, Henrik Andersen, in Copenhagen.

Katharine knew neither of her grandmothers well. Before this new tragedy, she had met Lilian Grahame only on major family anniversaries and at Annie's funeral; and Karen Andersen had lately grown remote and sad and, when Katharine had last visited her, her Danish-born nursing companion, one Gudrun Nielsen, had told Katharine, with polite regret, that Mrs. Andersen seemed more at ease these days when she was not faced with reminders of a past she was no longer able to come to terms with.

"Are you saying that you think I shouldn't visit my grandmother?"

"Of course not," Mrs. Nielsen, not uniformed but nonetheless starchy, said hastily. "I'm sure Mrs. Andersen will very much enjoy an occasional visit."

Katharine managed a smile. "But I shouldn't make a habit of it."

She had never met her great-uncle in her life, for Henrik Andersen, her father had once told her, never traveled abroad. Yet after hearing of her parents' death, although he had not made it to Washington for the double funeral, Great-Uncle Henrik had written to Katharine more movingly than anyone else, inviting her, with unmistakable sincerity, to come to him. *"Any time,"* Henrik wrote, *"you are welcome to stay with me. For one night, for one year. For ever."*

Katharine had not felt up to traveling to Denmark, but neither could she face staying in Washington or even going back to Pittsburgh to finish her studies at Carnegie Mellon. All she could think of was selling the house in Georgetown, sorting through Jake and Louise's belongings and her own remembrances, getting the agonies out of the way, and escaping from the past.

"This is not a wise move," Sam Raphael, deeply concerned for her, told her on a visit to Washington that first summer. "I can understand you selling this house, but not going back to Carnegie Mellon is crazy, Katharine."

"Maybe it is," she assented, "but I'm not going back."

"But you have friends there, you have a life there—a life you never shared with Louise or Jake. You'll feel better once you're up there."

They were sitting in the little Georgetown garden, side by side on the old canopied swing seat that Louise had installed when Annie had been one year old, and in which she'd loved to sit with both her daughters. The wisteria on the arbor was in full bloom, the roses were rich and heavy and gently buzzing with bees, and Mrs. Murray had brought them a jug of iced lemonade and freshly baked almond cookies.

"No," Katharine said, "I don't think I would feel better." She offered Sam a cookie and nibbled one herself. "Part of the joy of being away from home, till now, was looking forward to *coming* home, to seeing my mother and my father, or having them come up there to see me. Carnegie Mellon would just remind me that they're not here anymore, Sam. That they're not anywhere."

"You're going to feel that way wherever you go, for a while, at least." Sam understood her feelings very well, had been grief-stricken by Louise's death, had never stopped loving her even after their divorce.

"I'm sure you're right." Katharine sighed. "But if I start something new, brand new, then at least I may not be reminded every minute of every day." She paused. "And it hasn't been easy for me at Carnegie Mellon—"

"It isn't supposed to be easy. Only the best survive, remember?"

"Maybe I'm not the best." Katharine waved away a wasp.

"That's crap."

"It isn't, Sam. We both know that it was a miracle I was ever admitted to Carnegie Mellon."

"You're very talented."

"There's no shortage of talent, Sam. But most of my fellow students—maybe all of them—have known almost from birth what they wanted to do, had their sights set on Carnegie Mellon from the moment they heard about it, were prepared to do *anything* to get in. And then there was me, sailing through school always presuming I was going to be an actress."

"So you changed your mind," Sam said. "Big deal."

He drained the last of his lemonade, and Katharine poured him another glass.

"You always suspected my reasons for changing my mind," she said, "didn't you? You thought that deep down I was giving up on acting because I blamed it for my parents' breakup, and maybe you were right."

"But you've proved that *you* were right, haven't you—you did get into Carnegie Mellon, and you've hung in there while others flunked out. And your designs are good, in fact they're terrific."

"My work isn't bad," she allowed. "It's probably good enough, in fact, to get me started in New York even without my degree."

"But the degree would let you in at a different level," Sam argued.

"Not necessarily. It's tough breaking in whichever way you start." Katharine paused. "And frankly I don't care anymore, Sam. Nothing seems to mean what it did before."

"It takes time," he said gently.

"But I'm too much of a coward to face it. If there's a way to make it just a little easier for myself, then I want to find that way."

Sam smiled. "You've made up your mind, haven't you? You're not going back."

"I have."

"And you're moving to New York?"

"It seems the obvious decision, if I'm ever going to find an opening for my designs." She took his hand. "Besides, my favorite stepfather's in New York, one of my few surviving relatives."

Sam's gray eyes reflected his pleasure. "I guess I'll have to be grateful for that."

"You may regret it—I'll be looking to you for help, Sam."

"All the help you need, sweetheart. Depend on it."

New York was the obvious answer, Katharine felt, the only answer. Although Manhattan, too, held memories, it also contained Broadway, and she did at least know the city, understood, approximately anyway, its shape and structure.

She closed the house, completed the formalities, loaded Mrs. Murray with possessions, and moved into the most secure apartment in the least hazardous area she could find in Manhattan. The Upper East Side, with its imposing residential buildings, its elegant hotels and its wildly expensive art galleries did not touch her, and though her apartment was spacious and beautifully furnished, and the solid redbrick building, on Eighty-seventh Street between Madison and Fifth avenues, was immaculately managed, with a twenty-four-hour doorman, Katharine couldn't imagine it ever feeling like home.

"Is this quite you?" Sam Raphael asked her, the first time he came to visit, standing in her cool and perfect entrance hall. "I mean it's lovely, but—"

"It's perfect," Katharine said firmly. "Exactly what I want. I can stroll to the Met and the Frick and the Whitney, and the Guggenheim's just a little walk away, and—"

"And it's safe," Sam finished for her.

She had been going to add that she could wander, without effort, into Central Park, but the truth was—not that she would share it with Sam—that she couldn't see herself having the courage to walk alone in the park, for she had discovered that along with her parents' death and the end of her life as she had known it, had gone her confidence, her boldness, her sense of invulnerability. She remembered that Annie's death, so long ago, had shaken her similarly, but she had only been eight years old then, and she had always felt safe in Washington, though she had known perfectly well that there were plentiful dangers there too. But New York City scared her. As life now scared her.

I can call it my "Yellow Period," she told herself, wryly, as she set up her new apartment, *and just hope it doesn't last too long.*

Work, of course, proved her salvation. She had a sizable portfolio, consisting of sketches, folded-down models of sets and photographs of the work she had done at Carnegie Mellon, and she began to make contact with some of the people Sam had talked to about her, as well as visiting all the production managements in the city who would see her. Early on one producer, in particular, seemed very taken with her work and her ideas, but Katharine was aware that he liked her gold-streaked mane of hair and her full breasts and long legs even more, and so she thanked him for his interest and went on looking.

She was frequently told that she lived too prosperously and dressed too expensively to convince anyone that she was struggling to make it as a theater designer. But what Katharine was really struggling to do was to regain the sense of identity that she felt had been smashed up on the Potomac Parkway on the night of her twenty-first birthday, and she felt a strong conviction that if she gave way to the pushings and proddings of strangers who were, possibly, jealous of what she possessed, she might never find herself again. She went into the homes of these people, periodically, these people who seemed so anxious to change her, and sometimes their tiny studio apartments were snug and homely and clean, but often their beds were unmade and their socks lay on the floor and unwashed dishes stood around gathering penicillin. And then Katharine would make her polite ex- cuses and escape, back to Eighty-seventh Street and the uniformed doorman who would doff his cap, and greet her by name, and press the elevator button for her.

It was all part of her Yellow Period.

Her first job was to design the single set for a two-act play in an off-off-Broadway production by a new writer. Katharine threw herself into it, but when the play opened, the acting was worse than the script, and if her set had been carved out of Carrara marble, she doubted if anyone would have noticed. But Sam Raphael, who had lately found himself thrust into television stardom and was currently playing the lead in a prime-time Western riding high in the ratings, talked his agent and two directors into coming along just to look at her work, so Katharine knew it had not been a waste of time.

She graduated to off-Broadway, designing two sets for a comedy, then working as an assistant on trial for Burt Brice, an established and gifted designer, but they clashed frequently, Brice blasting her vigorously and openly, Katharine bristling and shutting herself down like a clam instead of expressing her wounded pride and anger, and after that nothing came up for many months. Sam took her out to dinner one evening in January of 1971, found her depressed and even lonelier than ever, and he called one week later to say that Laszlo Eles, one of the great names of the last ten years, was ready to meet her with a view to using her on his forthcoming show at the Kennedy Center in Washington.

Katharine took the train instead of flying down, needing to take her time, afraid of going back, afraid of going home. Yet in the end, after the interview with Eles and with the job promised to her, she knew that the trip was a positive turning point, for she had forced herself to confront her fears. She had visited Jake's and Louise's graves, and Annie's, had walked past the old house on 28th and Q, and had gone to her father's hospital, had stood inside his old department, breathing the antiseptic odor he'd so often brought home with him—and though she had felt a vast, penetrating sorrow, she recognized that she had, nevertheless, moved on, had survived.

By the early spring of 1973, Katharine was feeling fine. Better than fine, for she was working as an assistant to Laszlo Eles on a new play at the Morosco Theater, and she and Eles were getting along famously and she was beginning to feel almost a New Yorker, at one with the city, almost at home. Almost safe. She had friends these days, she threw dinner parties and lunched out, and enjoyed shopping, and sometimes she rented a car and drove out of the city for weekends, exploring the state or heading up to New England.

She was alive and, if not as invulnerable as in the old days, she supposed she was in no imminent danger of dying. And she had to admit that she looked good—perhaps even better than good—for she was often aware of heads turning when she walked down the street or into a store or restaurant or theater, and she had eyes, after all, and more than one mirror. It wasn't just her rare coloring, for she'd always had her amber firelight eyes and her lion's mane streaked hair, and it wasn't just that her body was in good shape or that her skin was good. It was a sparkle, and it was composure returning, and it was fear diminishing.

She walked, these days, in the streets, even after dark, and in Central Park—though not at night there, of course, nor after the first sign of dusk—but early in the morning, often before buying a newspaper or having breakfast, when young men and women jogged, and old men walked their dogs, and the squirrels and birds hustled greedily around potential providers, and the air was as fresh as it ever could be in New York City. Katharine did not jog, took no organized exercise except forty to fifty lengths of the pool at her health club and a little tennis in summer, but she walked briskly into the park entrance near Eighty-fifth Street, striding out toward the reservoir in a tracksuit or pullover and jeans, swinging her arms and looking keenly at everything and everyone, taking in colors and hues, and shapes and clothes, and faces and expressions.

It was a perfect morning in late March, crisp and sunny and sweet-smelling, when Katharine, beginning to think of hot coffee and scrambled eggs, turned back from her walk, heading for home, and saw the man on the footpath ahead of her.

He wore a purple tracksuit and black running shoes, and he was bent over and grimacing. Katharine assumed, for a moment, that he was simply out of breath and taking time out, but then she realized that he was in serious pain. She stopped.

"Excuse me? Are you okay?"

His head came up a fraction. His hair was dark and shiny with sweat or grease, and he groaned.

"Are you sick?" Katharine asked. "Can I help you?"

"Sit down," he muttered, speaking with difficulty. He nodded his head, his face still half down, toward a bench a few yards ahead.

"All right," Katharine said.

She put one arm around his waist, steadying herself to take his weight. "Carefully," she said, and the man jerked suddenly upright, his right arm came up sharply, the fist clenched, swinging, and punched her hard on the nose.

Katharine screamed, too late, felt the agony, felt her blood spurting, and the man hit her again, on her body this time, punching her viciously in the stomach.

"No!" she screamed again. *"Please!"*

He pushed her backward and she fell onto the path, moaning, trying to cover her face with her hands, curling her body into a ball as well as she could, to protect herself from more. And she felt rather than saw him kneel down beside her, felt his hand slip inside the pockets of her jeans, one at a time, as if he had all the time in the world.

"Fuck you, bitch," she heard him snarl, and she knew it was because she only had ten dollars on her, and she whimpered and braced herself for another onslaught, and as he straightened up he kicked her, once, in the buttocks, and Katharine was aware, even in that painful instant, that a few inches over or higher and he might have injured her spine.

"Please," she cried out, still covering her face. And then she heard his footsteps, running away, over the footpath for a few yards and then away, lightly, over the grass. And she knew it was over.

Two young men, out for a stroll with their cocker spaniels, found her a few moments later, trying to get herself up off the ground, and one of them sat with her and held her hand and spoke kindly to her, while the other went to a telephone. And soon the police came, and they helped her to an ambulance and took her to Metropolitan Hospital at Ninety-eighth and First, and Katharine tried to tell them in the emergency room that she was fine and that she wanted to go home, but they told her that her nose was broken, and that since her assailant had punched her in the stomach, it would be sensible to be sure that she wasn't bleeding internally, and did she have insurance?

And Katharine tried to sit up, but she was dizzy and trembling, and she began to cry, and a nurse asked if there was anyone they could call for her, but Katharine couldn't think of anyone, and she kept on crying even though she despised herself for her weakness, for she knew that, after all, it could have been so much worse, she could have been raped, or even killed.

"The lousy bastard!"
"The son of a whore!"
"If I could just get my hands on him—"
"*Allat!*"

Sam Raphael had come to the hospital as soon as he was telephoned, and within a half hour, Laszlo Eles, too, had arrived. Both men were horrified and paternal, and Eles, a short, slim, white-haired and immensely elegant man, who only broke into his native Hungarian when he was tremendously aroused, had seen to it that Katharine was transferred to New York Hospital, while Sam made a string of calls until he had arranged for one of the finest plastic surgeons in the city to fix her nose.

"You don't have to do too much," Eles told the surgeon, having snatched the telephone in Katharine's room from Sam. "Miss Andersen's nose has always been perfect—straight and fine, exactly the way a nose ought to be."

"Jake's nose," Sam added, and Katharine, deeply touched, began to cry again.

* * *

The surgeon's name was David Rothman, and if he felt in any way irritated by the two men telling him his job, he didn't show it, just listened patiently until they'd finished.

"Photographs," he said, and turned his attention to Katharine. "Do you have some photographs that show your nose from different angles?"

She nodded painfully. "They're a few years old, though."

"Doesn't matter as long as they're adult."

"They are."

"Then do you think that one of these gentlemen could go fetch them and bring them here?"

"I'll go," Sam said.

"Aren't you supposed to be at the studios?" Eles asked him.

"Christ, yes," Sam said, looking at his watch for the first time in hours.

"I can go," the Hungarian said, "if Katharine doesn't mind."

"Of course I don't." She tried to smile. "I'd be so grateful, Laszlo."

"Anything for my beautiful assistant," he beamed.

"That's fine," Rothman said. "And if you could try to find a selection—something that shows Miss Andersen face on and both profiles, if possible?"

He waited until both men had gone, before he took another, very gentle look at her nose, and took some measurements.

"Are you in a lot of pain?"

"Not too much," Katharine said, though every part of her hurt in such a variety of ways that it was hard to say what felt the worst.

"I'll give you something to help you rest." He smiled at her. "Your friends seem certain that your nose was perfect—you feel the same way? This is your chance to have whatever you want. You may as well get something out of all this misery."

Katharine shrugged weakly. "Will you think I'm vain if I say that I liked my nose, too?"

Rothman smiled again. "On the contrary, I'll just assume you're honest and intelligent, and probably very beautiful."

"Though it's hard to tell right now?" she said wryly.

He patted her hand. "We'll have you back to normal in next to no time."

Katharine lay back against the hospital pillows.

"I can hardly wait."

* * *

The aftereffects, both immediate and long-term, of Katharine's mugging, were various and profound. The pain and discomfort, especially in the first few days following the surgery on her nose, were quite acute, and catching her first glimpse of herself in a mirror, Katharine was more than a little dismayed. But Dr. Rothman assured her that the rhinoplasty had been a minimal procedure and that she would see her old self again in just a few weeks, and Katharine believed him.

David Rothman was, for such a young and successful surgeon, wholly lacking in arrogance, and possessed of a marvelously comforting, no-fuss bedside manner. He was also, Katharine could not help but notice, a good-looking man, with thick, wavy dark hair, keen, gentle brown eyes and fine fingers that reminded her strongly of her father's hands. Katharine enjoyed his visits and felt a little regretful whenever he left, and she was aware that she had seldom, if ever, trusted a stranger as she did him. She was not alone in her admiration; many of the nurses, it was plain to see, were more than a little in love with him.

"If Dr. Rothman told me I needed surgery anywhere from my scalp to my behind," one of them confided in Katharine one afternoon, "I think I'd just follow him down to the OR and lie down on the operating table."

"I don't think I'd go that far," Katharine laughed. "But he does seem like a nice man."

"Brilliant, rich, gorgeous, and nice, too." The nurse winked at her. "All that, and still single."

They sent a counselor to her room to talk over her feelings following the assault, but Katharine felt so strangely confident in herself that, courteously but firmly, she sent the woman away. It seemed to her as if the traumatic event, or at least the aftermath of the attack, had been therapeutic in some strange way.

"How the hell do you mean, 'therapeutic'?" Sam asked her, when he came to visit. "You liked getting your face smashed up?"

"Hardly." Katharine tried to explain her feelings. "But for one thing, I've often thought of myself as a coward, and I guess something like this, by rights, ought to have made me feel more scared, not less."

"But it hasn't?"

She shook her head. "I think it's because the worst has happened, or almost the worst, and I'm still here, more or less in one piece."

She paused. "And something else. This last week has proven to me that I'm not nearly as alone as I'd thought I was."

"I could have told you that if you'd asked," Sam said. "It would have been a lot less painful than getting mugged."

"I don't know that I'd have believed you though." Katharine looked somber for a moment, remembering. "When I was in the emergency room, just after it happened, someone asked me who they could call, and for a little while I couldn't think of anyone."

"You didn't think of me right away?" Sam asked.

"Of course I thought of you, Sam. But my mind was sort of wild, and I was confused. I was going to give them your name, and then I thought, no, they want a blood relative or a husband or something, and I don't have anyone—except my grandmothers, and I certainly didn't want either of them getting another call from a hospital."

"And now?"

"Now I've realized—really realized—for the first time, that even without Louise or my father, I'm not alone at all. I have you, and Laszlo, of course—he's been wonderful."

"Eles is very fond of you."

"Is he?" She smiled. "And all kinds of people have been dropping by to visit. My grandmother came in from Long Island—I thought I'd better let her know, once I was able to make the call myself. Karen's a very grand old lady, she left her chauffeur waiting on the curb outside all through her visit, and let everyone know about it."

There had been other visitors, too: Rosy Krantz, a woman Katharine had met in Gristede's and with whom she lunched once in a while, some of the actors and stagehands she'd worked with, and even the doorman from her apartment building, Ike Sherman, had come by. Her room was filled with flowers and cards, and even while her nose was still in plaster and her stomach was still bruised and sore, Katharine felt herself beginning to glow within.

Going home was more difficult. Sam picked her up and drove her back, and he had fully stocked her refrigerator, and Laszlo had hand-painted a magnificent sheet of silk which he said she could either put on her bed or wear as a sarong around the apartment. But the moment came, nonetheless, when she was alone, and for the first time since the mugging, Katharine felt some of her old insecurities returning. She checked the locks on her front door three times, drew her curtains the instant dusk fell, and turned on the television sets in her bedroom and the living room just for company.

David Rothman arrived just after ten that evening.

"I know I should have called first," he apologized, after the night doorman had allowed him up.

"You never did in the hospital." Katharine had never been so glad to see anyone on her doorstep.

"I brought a little something." He was carrying his doctor's case and a large brown paper shopping bag.

"What is it? Bandages?" She flushed a little, suddenly unsure of how to speak to him.

"Chinese takeout, and something to wash it down." He hesitated. "You've probably eaten, but I haven't had time, so I thought I'd just pick something up before I made my last house call of the day."

"Do surgeons make house calls?"

"Sometimes, and I'm really starved. I hope you don't mind."

Katharine didn't believe him about the house calls, but she didn't mind in the least. They sat on the rug near the gas log fireplace, since it was a chilly evening, and spread the dishes out over the low coffee table, and Katharine had eaten nothing earlier because she hadn't felt hungry, but suddenly she was ravenous, and the spare ribs and egg rolls and duck-filled pancakes tasted better than anything she'd ever eaten.

And David Rothman was the best company she'd ever had.

He waited until Katharine had paid her last visit to his office, until after he had discharged her formally as his patient, before he told her how he felt about her as a woman. David Rothman was accustomed to broken bones and shocked, tearful eyes; had grown proficient at seeing through traumatized faces and picking through emotional debris to find what lay beneath. It had not taken him any time at all to discover that Katharine Andersen was special, not least because of the fervent, touching concern of Sam Raphael and Laszlo Eles, both busy, distinguished men, neither of them her lover.

He invited Katharine to lunch at La Côte Basque two days after their last appointment.

"If I tell you how unreasonably, unprofessionally relieved I was the first day I saw you," he said after they had been seated, side by side, on one of the comfortable red banquettes, "that you had no husband or fiancé—not even, apparently, a significant boyfriend—will you hate me forever?"

"I don't think I'll hate you." Katharine, perfectly, happily confident of her appearance for the first time in many weeks, looked unconvinced. "But I'm not sure I'll believe you, since I remember being bloody and battered at the time?"

"You were, but that's still how I felt."

Katharine had known for some time that Rothman cared for her in a way that was more than professional. That first Chinese dinner he'd brought to her apartment had not been the last. He had come by numerous times—"just passing"—since then, usually bearing bagels or croissants if it was early in the day, or Chinese or even a flask of home-made soup if it was late. He had always checked her nose, inspected her face, asked if she was experiencing any discomfort or suffering any other ill-effects, but otherwise he had never once touched her, nor had he asked her a single personal, let alone intimate question. He had expressed keen interest, even fascination, in her work. He had known a number of performers, directors and writers, he told her, but he had never before met a stage designer. He had looked long and thoughtfully at her models, at the meticulous, miniaturized rooms and gardens and street scenes, some with exquisite, tiny suspended figures for added authenticity, most of which would never be used in production. And he had listened attentively, the keen brown eyes unmistakably tender as Katharine had described how it felt when she was permitted to help bring one of those models to life, how energizing it was to work with real carpenters and painters, how much fun it was to talk over the furniture for a drawing room set with a propman—and how utterly magnificent and terrifying it was to stand back from the completed work and allow it to be taken over and used, exactly as it was intended to be used, by the cast on opening night.

"At the risk of scaring you off completely," David Rothman said to her now, in the restaurant, "I'm going to make a full confession, and tell you that I think I fell in love with you that very first day."

"Oh," Katharine said, staring into her martini.

"What does 'Oh' mean? Does it mean 'Oh God, no'?"

"No," she said. She was suddenly acutely aware that they were sitting very close to one another, yet that Rothman had not, since brushing her arm when they had been shown to their table, touched her. "It means I don't know what else to say right now."

"That's okay," he said. "It gives me more time to explain how I feel, how I felt then." He looked into her eyes. "If I swear to you that it's never happened to me before—that I've never fallen in love with a patient before, in the emergency room or anywhere else for that matter, will you believe me?"

"Yes," Katharine said, realizing how much she wanted him to touch her.

"I didn't exactly recognize it as love right there and then," Rothman went on, plainly flustered for the first time. "For one thing, I was your doctor—I was there to treat you, and getting you fixed up and out of pain was a hell of a lot more important to me than anything else."

"Thank you."

Katharine knew it was an inadequate response, but they were the first words that came into her head that she felt bold enough to say out loud. There were a whole bunch of other thoughts flying around in her mind, of course—like the thought that what he had just said had made her feel crazily happy, and another thought that he was the very best thing that had ever happened to her—but somehow they seemed too forward, too impulsive, and so she held on tightly to them, kept them unsaid.

"It was all right while you were in the hospital," Rothman said. He lowered his voice, as a party of four arrived at the next table. "It wasn't too hard remembering our doctor-patient roles. But once you were home, I'll admit it was a lot more difficult."

"You managed pretty well," Katharine said.

Rothman winced. "That makes me sound like some hopeful would-be seducer, just biding my time—oh, Lord, I guess in a way that's exactly what I was."

"No," she said, gently. "I wouldn't say that." She smiled. "Though I have to say I've never known any doctor bring so much food with him on his house calls."

David Rothman smiled. "I'm a very hungry surgeon."

Although she'd thought he felt something for her, it had not occurred to Katharine, until then, that David might actually be in love with her. Neither had she considered that she might have fallen for him. She knew that she was attracted to him, but she had often heard about women—even the most mature women—becoming infatuated with their doctors, and with surgeons in particular; something to do, presumably, with their power and skill, and the remarkable self-confidence that made it possible to slice into a human body without terror or panic or revulsion. Cosmetic surgeons, most of all, were bound to arouse feelings of gratitude so intense that they could easily be misconstrued as love. But surely she, the daughter of a surgeon, ought to know better than that?

Now that their professional relationship had ended, David swept her off her feet. He worked harder than anyone Katharine had ever known, except, perhaps, for Jake, but he still managed to make time for her. He took her out at every available opportunity, and with as much variety as he could muster. They both enjoyed food, and they ate a great deal. They breakfasted at the Plaza, the Stanhope, in Chinatown, in Central Park, and in bed. They lunched at the Four Seasons, the Russian Tea Room, the Tavern on the Green, the Stage Delicatessen, on hot dogs and pretzels at the Central Park Zoo, and in bed. They dined at Sardi's, in the Rainbow Room, at The Bitter End in the Village, at La Grenouille, at The Palm and Elaine's, in his dining room, on Katharine's living room floor, and in bed. They went to the theater at least one evening a week, went to museums and galleries, went shopping together and swimming and, so long as David felt confident of hearing his beeper in an emergency, to discotheques.

He proposed to Katharine after six weeks of dating. The city was miserably hot and humid, and David had suggested they take one of the dinner cruises that sailed around Manhattan each evening. It was a fun night, the food indifferent but the atmosphere festive, and between courses, David and Katharine danced for a while, and then wandered up to the outer deck to enjoy the cool breeze and to gaze at the city.

"It's so beautiful," Katharine murmured, leaning against him, her hair blowing wildly around her head.

"Just right," David said, and fell silent.

"What's up?" Katharine asked after a few moments, looking up at him. "You don't seem with me."

"I'm very much with you." He paused. "More than you understand, I think."

"Go on," she urged, softly.

David nodded slowly. "Okay," he said. "Here it is. I'm thirty-two years old. I've never been married, though I lived with a girlfriend for more than three years while we were both in med school."

"You told me," Katharine said. "Joanne."

"We had some great times, and we cared for each other, but we both knew it wasn't for keeps, and we were both too ambitious to settle down."

He paused again, while a party of about a dozen Swedish men and women squeezed past them, laughing and chattering loudly.

"The thing is," David went on, "I don't just want to live with you, Katharine. The thing is, I want to marry you. But I have no idea on earth how you feel about that." He took a breath. "I don't know how you feel about me, period."

Startled, Katharine did not speak. He had taken her entirely by surprise, and suddenly her mind was whirring with reactions and thoughts and emotions, and she felt quite dizzy. Looking up, she noticed that they were sailing parallel with the Empire State Building, and she was conscious that she would never receive a more romantic, or more heartfelt, proposal of marriage.

"I don't know what to say," she began, knowing that she had to say something before David thought she had been struck dumb with horror.

"Start with how you feel," David said, gently.

"That's easy. I love you."

"Thank God." David took her hand and feeling it cold, squeezed it. "So what isn't easy?"

"The marriage part."

"Oh." David kept hold of her hand. "Okay."

"No," Katharine said, quickly. "It's not okay. It's not as simple as that."

"Tell me how it is."

A cigarette, tossed carelessly over the side of the boat, flew past Katharine's right cheek, and David, swifter than her, pulled her smartly back.

"Damn fools," he said, angrily.

"It didn't touch me," Katharine said.

"It might have got you in the eye," David said, and drew her closer.

"I've never lived with a man," Katharine said, and suddenly she had the words, knew exactly how she felt, and wanted, needed, to be completely honest with him. "I do love you—and we have such wonderful times together I can hardly believe my luck. But I"—she faltered, briefly—"I'm afraid of marriage."

"To me, or to anyone?"

"Anyone." Katharine paused. "Truly."

"Is this something to do with your parents, do you think?"

"I know it," she answered readily. "I guess I'm a little wary of commitment altogether. Afraid of the pain."

"I won't hurt you." Abruptly, David shook his head. "That's foolish, isn't it? I can't be sure I'll never cause you pain."

Katharine smiled. "I'm sure you'd never hurt me if you could help it," she said. "My father didn't mean to hurt my mother, and I know she didn't intend to hurt either him or Sam. But that's what happened."

"Isn't it a risk worth taking?" David asked, still hopeful.

"I'm sure it is," Katharine replied. "When you know. When you really, absolutely *know*, without a doubt." She looked into his eyes, saw how warm they were, how safe. "Or maybe when you know you can't survive without the other person."

"We all survive, ultimately," David said, and he strove to keep the hurt out of his voice and face. "I think we'd better stick with waiting until you know. Otherwise I'll never stand a chance." He lifted her hand and kissed it. "Do I stand one, do you think?"

Katharine managed a smile. "Well, if you don't, I can't imagine that anyone else ever could."

Still cautious, but knowing that she had to make some commitment or risk losing him, she moved into David's place in the middle of July. He had a penthouse apartment near Gracie Mansion, with huge windows, superb views of the East River and beyond, and a wealth of modern American art on the walls. David was a sensitive man, instinctively attuned to the needs of women, but his apartment was, nevertheless, a man's home, with stark lines, clean, straight surfaces and sharp edges.

"I wish you'd redecorate," he told Katharine.

"I couldn't possibly," she said.

"Of course you could. This is your home now, as much as mine." He was aware that Katharine was reluctant to tamper with his possessions, had too much respect for his taste to change things. "The only room I feel any strong attachment to is my study—the rest of it could do with remodeling. I wish you'd do it."

"I'll think about it," Katharine said, but the one room she allowed herself to touch was their bedroom, and even there she simply ordered new drapes, a bedspread and new wall-to-wall carpeting. David asked her if she would rather that they moved to a new place, one that would be her own from the outset, and Katharine was touched, as she constantly was, by his love and care and his efforts to make her happy, but a move of that nature would be almost as much of a commitment as marriage, and she was not ready yet for either.

* * *

Their wonderful times continued. Aware that Katharine needed a studio in which to work, and knowing that she would never presume to dismantle one of his impeccable rooms for her purposes, David called in workmen while Katharine was away for a few weeks working on a two-act comedy in Philadelphia and had the two spare bedrooms gutted and knocked into one so that she would have no choice, when she returned, but to have it designed to her own specifications. Once she had her own workspace, Katharine felt much more at ease, but instead of encouraging her to plunge more wholeheartedly into work, her gratitude just increased the desire she already felt to enhance David's own home life. Katharine knew exactly how a busy, committed surgeon needed to be looked after. She remembered the early, happy days in Georgetown, before Annie's illness, when her mother had still been blissfully content to be a good wife and partner to Jake, and she remembered, much more vividly, how her father had suffered during the sad, grim years that had followed, when Louise had withdrawn, had stopped giving, stopped loving.

"Being a surgeon's important," Katharine tried to explain to Laszlo, when he came to see her new studio and to try to bully her into spending more time on her own designing, rather than looking after David. "Much more important than being a stage designer."

"That's crap, *kedves*," Laszlo said.

"How can you say that?"

"Easily. Many more people visit the theater than they visit a plastic surgeon, wouldn't you agree?"

"That's irrelevant."

"It's far from irrelevant," Laszlo argued. "We care for the human spirit, help to keep it healthy, and we, too, have studied, have learned our skills, our craft. All this mystique about the greatness of surgeons—it's crap, Katharine, whatever you say."

"But David isn't like that," she argued back. "He doesn't claim to be superior at all—he thinks my work is very important."

"So why don't you?"

"I do."

"Then why do you spend half your life cooking for Rothman, shopping for Rothman, picking up his dry cleaning?" Laszlo tossed his white hair in exasperation. "Instead of working in this beautiful studio."

"Because he doesn't have the time."

"And you do." Laszlo glared at her. "Exactly."

* * *

David rarely took vacations, but once Katharine moved in with him, he insisted they rent a house in Sag Harbor so that she could escape from the gasping city through the summer whenever she felt like it, and he could join her whenever possible.

"Do you like it?" he asked her the first time he showed it to her.

"I love it." Katharine looked at the big verandah with its pale blue awning, and at the creamy walls and rugs that were repeated throughout the house, and at the floral chintz fabrics and early American furniture. "It's beautiful. It feels as if no one else ever lived here."

"I hoped you'd be pleased," David said. "But I don't want you to think it's a fait accompli—if you'd rather see some other houses before we sign the lease, I don't mind."

Katharine smiled at his consideration. "How could I possibly not like this, darling? Besides, it's only for the summer—right now, I feel I could stay here forever."

"If you like it that much, we could sign up for next year too."

She laughed. "Let's take it one step at a time. You never know, there may be hidden problems. Maybe they painted it so beautifully to cover over the cracks."

There were no cracks, no problems at all, Katharine soon came to realize. It was fine having the hideaway, fine having the ocean at her feet and fresh air to breathe. It was nice having her grandmother, now ailing, close enough for easy visits. It was good making friends with the people who lived around them and going out sailing and, sometimes, fishing with them. It was heavenly having David there at weekends so that they could barbecue in their own backyard, and swim together in the ocean or in their pool, and rub suntan oil into each other's backs and make love for hours with the telephones turned off.

Through August, Katharine stayed out on the Island almost the entire time, grateful not to have to drag herself back to the steaming swamp that was Manhattan during that worst month of the year, and they became like many of the married couples in the Hamptons, with David trekking back in on Sunday evenings and ploughing back through the traffic again on Friday nights.

Too much like marriage, Katharine realized, stirring herself out of what she thought was complacency, and come September, she was back in the fray again, trying to be what David needed and wanted, and trying, at the same time, to be herself.

That was the trouble really, if she admitted it. Trying. Life with David was immeasurably worthwhile, and no sane woman could honestly ask for more. But it was an effort, and although Katharine knew that everyone always said that you had to work hard to get the best out of any relationship, she couldn't help wondering if it ought to feel like such a *conscious* effort.

Yet David didn't seem to feel that way at all; as far as he was concerned, life was just about perfect. His skills as a surgeon were still improving, his reputation still growing, and he had never been happier to come home.

If Katharine would only agree to become his wife, and perhaps, in time, if they were to have the children he longed for, David thought he might be in danger of becoming almost smug.

"Not yet," she said, whenever he dared to broach the subject. "This is all so wonderful, I don't want to do anything to change it. Do you mind so very much, my darling?"

"Of course I don't mind," he answered, and forced himself to leave well enough alone.

After all, as Katharine often reminded him, she was only twenty-four years old, and there was plenty of time.

c h a p t e r

8

Five lines on William Hickey's page in the *Daily Express* and an article in *The Stage* announced the first official working day at Locke Artists on the fifth of January 1970. Sebastian had rented a suite of offices with three rooms on the first floor of an exclusive building in Albemarle Street, a few doors from the back entrance of Asprey. He had a three-line telephone switchboard, a temporary secretary named Caroline, and lunch dates booked every day for the next two weeks. He did not have a single client.

By half past ten, the lights on the switchboard were flashing at one call per minute with inquiries from artists ranging from the unemployable to the inexperienced, down to amateurs willing to do anything—and they meant anything—to obtain an Equity card. The other calls were from companies hoping to sell Sebastian stationery, office equipment, insurance and advertising space. When, at noon, Caroline told him that Jeremy Mariner was on the line for him, Sebastian was surprised and delighted.

"For heaven's sake, where are you?" They had not seen one another for three years, for Jeremy had been in New York since 1967.

"I'm in London."

"When did you get in? Is this a visit or are you back?"

"I'm back."

"For good?"

"That depends on you."

"Why?" Sebastian saw two lights flicking on his telephone. "Could I get back to you later, Jerry? I've two calls waiting, but I really want to talk to you."

"I have to see you."

"And I'm longing to see you, but we'll have to work it out later."

"It can't wait, Seb."

"How come?"

"Can you meet me tonight?"

"I'm snowed under—this is our first day."

"This really shouldn't wait—I need to talk to you."

Sebastian heard the urgency in his old friend's voice. "Of course," he said. "When and where?"

They met at the Ritz at ten o'clock. Jeremy had a corner table in the Palm Court. He rose as he saw Sebastian walking up the steps, saw how much and yet how little he had changed, and realized that he had not been so glad to see anyone in years.

"God," he said, "it's good to see you."

"Same here."

They shook hands, then smiled and embraced before sitting down and ordering champagne. Sebastian watched Jeremy speaking to the waiter, and thought that New York had completed the transformation, long since begun, from interesting boy to fascinating-looking man. Jeremy had been a thin youngster; now he looked lean, his narrow features eager and alert, his straight dark hair quite long, but immaculately cut, his suit elegant and sober.

"My father died two weeks ago," Jeremy said, suddenly.

Sebastian was startled. "I'm sorry—I didn't know."

"How could you?"

"What happened? Was he ill?"

"Heart. Mother called me an hour after he'd been admitted to hospital. She knew it was very bad, suggested I might feel like flying over, so I left that night. He died shortly after I arrived."

"I wish you'd told me sooner," Sebastian said quietly. "I mean I'd have understood if you wanted me to stay away, but there might have been something I could have done for you."

Jeremy gave a small shrug. "There was nothing. The funeral and all that jazz was over in a few days, and then there was my mother to contend with."

"How's she doing?"

"She seems okay, considering." He paused. "She's going to South America."

"You're kidding."

Jeremy smiled. "I couldn't believe it myself. But it's true. Annabel Mariner, the most English of roses, is packing up, thorns and all, and swanning off to Buenos Aires."

"Who with?"

"She has friends, apparently." He shrugged again. "I just think it's a measure of how much she's always hated the countryside—she wants to get as far away as possible."

"But she always loved London, didn't she?"

"While she had my father. But now she says she doesn't want the memories. She really loved the old man, I'll give her that. And she says that Buenos Aires is supposed to be one of the most glamorous places on earth, so she's off."

"What about the estate?" Sebastian asked.

"All to be sold off," Jeremy replied. "Which brings me back to the reason for this meeting." He picked up his champagne glass. "I didn't get in touch with you earlier, I suppose, because I wanted it all to be settled before I saw you. Then this morning, I saw William Hickey's piece, and fate just stabbed me between the eyes."

Sebastian said nothing, just waited, intrigued.

"I'm going to put a proposition to you, Seb, and I want you to take your time before you respond, because no matter how unexpected it may seem to you, I've never been so positive about anything in my entire life."

"All right," Sebastian said.

Jeremy took another swallow of champagne and put down his glass.

"I want to come into the business," he said. "I want to be your partner."

For the longest time after his brother's death, more than a decade earlier, anything and everything had seemed to remind Jeremy of Thomas's life and death. Most of all, his own reflection in the mirror, and the wheeze in his chest whenever he felt his asthma coming on. Even Marchmont, with all its gentle energy and the kindness of its masters, and even the comforting, supportive presence of Sebastian had not healed the isolation, bitterness and self-loathing that he had continued to feel for years after the accident. It was certainly far better to be there than at Mariner Hall, but Jeremy would sooner have been in a city, any city, protected by concrete and noise and indifference.

He had stayed on after his O levels, mostly because Sebastian was staying, and partly because he was buying time before having to make up his mind about what he planned to do with his life. Jeremy was idle at heart, without burning ambition or motivation. He still loved the theater, but not as an actor, nor as a director or writer. He still loved the cinema, but as a filmgoer, without the need to turn a picture inside out and to try to understand every tiny ingredient that went into it that the aspiring filmmaker generally felt. And then, before he knew how it had all passed so swiftly, time was almost up, and Sebastian was going up to Edinburgh, and for the first time since they were five years old they were going to be separated, and Jeremy had been forced to make a decision. His father wanted him to take over the running of the Mariner estate, but Jeremy knew that he could not bear it, and when, in the spring of 1965, a friend suggested to him that a career in broadcasting might suit him as well as any other, Jeremy decided to hell with procrastination and wrote to the BBC.

His first job had been as a clerk in the reference library in Broadcasting House in Portland Place. Jeremy had grown monstrously bored within a fortnight, and, as swiftly as was considered decent, he had applied for the only position available that would place him in sniffing distance of drama: another clerical job, but this time in the radio play library. At least now he had access to scripts and to the people who turned them into programs. He was well aware, already, that he had made a fatal error in not going on to university, for there were no good trainee production jobs open to men and women without degrees. This, therefore, he determined, was a temporary situation, one that he would only put up with so that he could accumulate as much variety of experience as possible before moving on. There was a system within the BBC of "attaching" employees to new positions on a short-term basis, giving them on-the-job training and the opportunity to display their talents for a few months before returning them to their own jobs, which had been kept secure for them. Jeremy became a reader in the drama script unit first for three months, and then again for six, finding at the end of both attachments that he was expected to relinquish the duties he had so enjoyed, and to return, docile as a lamb, to being a clerk.

When he won his attachment as a special assistant on a major drama serialization that would take six months to produce, Jeremy threw himself into his task with a fervor he had never known before. In all his years of schooling, he had never enjoyed the learning process as he did now; he immersed himself in every aspect of production, watched and listened to the producers and studio managers—who did everything from creating the most perfect sound quality possible to playing in the wealth of effects from the sound effects library and opening and closing squeaky doors in the studio itself—and to the production secretaries, who were the extra eyes, ears and minds of the producers for whom they worked, and who frequently knew as much as their bosses did.

Jeremy had learned when to assert himself, and when to slip discreetly into the background, absorbing useful information and the experience of others as efficiently as an amoeba. Given the opportunity to codirect two episodes, he was perfectly aware that the fine cast and the studio team were, by that time, such a well-oiled machine of talent that it might have been a substantial achievement to ruin an episode. Even so, he knew that he had acquitted himself well, that he had fitted smoothly into a working team for the first time in his career, and that he had the makings of a good director. And yet again, when it was over, he was sent back to the play library. He had been warned, but he had not believed it. To have been given his creative head for just long enough to gain a degree of confidence, competence and a touch of personal flair, and then to be expected to sink back into the same old rut. It was intolerable.

Jeremy had resigned from the BBC early in 1967, but he recognized that his time there had not been wasted, had taught him a great amount, not least that casting was the aspect of production for which he had most personal talent. He had an unfailing memory for excellent performances, however small, and during his last months in the drama department, some of the younger producers had begun to pick his brain for casting ideas. Jeremy took to playing casting games for his own pleasure, imagining, as he listened to radio plays and watched television dramas and sat in the theater, alternative artists in the roles being played; he spent hours on end poring through the Spotlight casting directories, and he made a friend of one of the bookers, habitually dropping in for a visit with coffee and staying for long, gossipy chats during which he pumped her about her own job and about her connections outside the BBC. It was chiefly through her, and the telephone conversations that she allowed him to listen to when he wished, that Jeremy had discovered the inestimable value of a good agent to an actor.

"That was when I made up my mind," he told Sebastian now, as their waiter opened a second bottle of champagne for them. "I set my sights on joining an agency."

"You never told me."

"Because I failed. I had no practical experience as an agent, but I was overqualified to make the tea or be an errand boy. If I'd been a woman, I could have started out as a secretary, but as it was, there was nothing they were willing to trust me with."

Frustration had mounted inside him, soon dissipating to the lethargy he had often known in the old days, but it was during the week of his father's fiftieth birthday celebrations, when both James and Annabel had made a concerted effort to persuade him to return to Mariner Hall and learn the family business while his father was still young enough to teach him, that Jeremy had made up his mind to leave the country.

"Surely," James had said, over his birthday lunch in the grill room at the Connaught Hotel, "you must see by now that it's sheer folly to turn your back on such a fine inheritance."

"Surely," Annabel had added, "you must have learned by now that the world owes you neither amusement nor a living."

"I see all those things," Jeremy had told them.

"Thank God," James said.

"Which is why I'm going to New York."

"I don't believe it." Annabel had grown pale with anger. "I don't believe that even you could be so irresponsible."

Jeremy had, for once, tried to be gentle. "I can't come back to Yorkshire, Mother."

"Why can't you?"

"Because of Thomas," he said, softly. "I can't stand it."

"That happened eight years ago," James said. "You have to try to get over it, old man."

"Do you suppose it's been any easier for us?" Annabel said harshly. "You've had long enough to hide yourself away. We had no choice but to face it."

"No, Mother, I don't think it's been easy for you."

"Then why don't you stop being so damnably selfish for once in your life and do as we ask of you?"

"Because I can't." Jeremy had paused. "And at least if I'm out of the country, you don't have to keep seeing me and being reminded whose fault it is that Thomas isn't here. He would have taken over the estate in a flash—he adored our house, loved the land."

"You loved it too, in those days," James had said, sadly.

"Did I? I can't remember."

He had bought a ticket, had a visa stamped in his passport and had gone up to Edinburgh for a few days to see Sebastian.

"I'm here to say good-bye," he told him. "I'm off to New York."

"How long for?" Sebastian was dismayed.

"Who knows?" Jeremy shrugged. "I have to get away, Seb. My folks are going to drive me crazy if I stay in England and don't knuckle down in Yorkshire. My mother thinks I'm selfish and ungrateful."

"And your dad?"

"He just looks unhappy. I can't stand it, to be candid—I've never been good at facing guilt."

The festival was on in Edinburgh, and they spent a week together, sampling plays, concerts and street performances. On one single day, they saw Shakespeare at the Lyceum, heard Mozart at the Usher Hall, saw a new Fringe play at the Traverse Theatre Club and Ibsen at a converted house in Tollcross, a production so poor that when Sebastian developed a headache and wanted to leave, during the first act, Jeremy was delighted.

"Where to now?" he asked, outside.

"Back to the flat for me," Sebastian said, rubbing the back of his neck to try to ease the tension.

"Come and have a drink first," Jeremy said. "Then maybe we can find a film worth seeing."

Sebastian shook his head. He had felt under par for much of the afternoon, but within minutes of sitting down on the hard, narrow bench in the last, makeshift theater, the pain in his temples had increased, and a strange sense of detachment had begun to overwhelm him, until, at last, he'd had to get out into the fresh air.

"You go on without me, Jerry."

"You do look a bit seedy," Jeremy said. "Sure you're okay to get back by yourself?"

"Quite sure." He managed a smile. "Go on. I'll see you later."

"Don't wait up." Jeremy grinned.

Sebastian felt relieved to see Jeremy go. He wanted to be on his own, as he always did when the headaches came on. The pain, often accompanied by a woolly-headed sensation, made him feel isolated, made it difficult to behave or speak normally. Tonight, it seemed worse than ever.

He thought about finding a bus to take him home, but suddenly the effort seemed too great.

A drink, perhaps, he thought, vaguely. *And a cigarette.*

He felt in his jacket pocket, then remembered he'd smoked his last one before the start of the play.

A pub, he decided. *And then I'll go home.*

He began walking.

At two in the morning, Sebastian stood in the street surrounded by other spectators, some of them from neighboring houses and flats, some wearing dressing gowns, even pajamas, their feet slippered or bare on the pavement.

Across the street, several hundred yards away, three fire engines stood, nose to tail, their lights flashing, while the men from the Edinburgh Fire Brigade fought the blaze in the old, derelict Tollcross house.

He could feel the heat, even from that distance. It was hotter than anything he had ever felt, meltingly hot, and the glow was dazzling and almost stunningly beautiful.

He closed his eyes and listened to the sounds. The thunder of the fire, the cracking of glass, the whoosh and roar of the hoses, the raised voices of the men at work, and the excited, fearful chatter of the crowd of onlookers surrounding him. He smelled the smoke, bitter and acrid, tasted it in his mouth and throat, and his heart pounded in rhythm with the blood in his ears.

"Move along now," one of the firemen said, his voice loud and firm, penetrating the rest of the sounds, and Sebastian opened his eyes again, and saw that most of the people had moved back, further up the road. "You don't want to get in the way, now, do you, lad?"

Sebastian moved along.

"Where did you get to last night?" Jeremy asked, over coffee next morning. "I got back after one, sure you'd be tucked up asleep, and no sign of you."

"I watched a fire," Sebastian said.

"What do you mean?"

Sebastian shrugged. "What I said. I watched a house burn down.

Not quite down, in fact—they put it out quite quickly. Here." He passed the *Scotsman* over to Jeremy. "It was that Fringe place we walked out of."

Jeremy took the newspaper.

"Christ," he said, reading. "Bit of a coincidence." He put the paper down and buttered some toast. "No one hurt, at least."

"Pass the marmalade," Sebastian said.

"How come you were still there?" Jeremy asked.

"I went for a drink," Sebastian said.

"Thought your head was too bad?"

"It was, but I couldn't face waiting for a bus, so I found a pub."

"Any good?"

"I don't remember," Sebastian said.

Jeremy had flown to New York three days later. He had a handful of contacts given to him by James and by Andrew Locke, but nevertheless it was a leap into the unknown, and it had enthralled him. As Manhattan did, for the city was everything Jeremy had ever dreamed of and more, the authentic concrete jungle exploded into light and life and action. He felt as if he were living out a film script. He took advantage of every contact and made new ones of his own, accepted American hospitality shamelessly and quickly discovered that he had struck New York at a time when almost any personable British man or woman could expect a warm welcome.

He even landed a job with a small agency operating out of a seedy two-roomed office suite near Times Square, run by a gruff but warmhearted old man by the name of Louis R. Schwartz, who drank shots of bourbon at least a dozen times a day from a silver hip flask, and whose eyes all but vanished into his deeply lined face whenever he smiled, which was often.

Jeremy appealed to Schwartz, with his dark, interesting, sexy looks and his impeccable British manners and accent. The boy was ambitious, full of untapped energies and an innate shrewdness that the old New Yorker felt were worth taking a chance on. Jeremy liked Schwartz, too, for he was wily as any fox but honest at the same time.

"You willing to get kicked around," Schwartz asked Jeremy at their first meeting, "and get paid fuck-all for the privilege?"

"Sounds fair to me," Jeremy answered, "on one condition."

"Try me."

"If I bring in new talent, you give me a chance to look after it."

The old man's eyes had crinkled up. "You planning to find me the next Paul Newman?"

"Could be."

It had taken Jeremy a year to learn the business, but by that time he had absorbed all there was to know, knew just about everything that was going on in New York and knew, too, how to find out, without fuss, what was going on in theater, television and the motion picture industry in every other city in the United States. His second year had brought him his first personal clients; his third had brought him the complete faith of his boss and job offers from two other, larger agencies, which he had turned down. The possibility of a partnership with Louis Schwartz had just been broached when the telephone call came from Annabel Mariner telling him that his father was gravely ill. By the time Jeremy had reached the Middlesex Hospital, James had been in a critical condition. He had spoken just once before he died, Jeremy's name, nothing more.

"The estate has come to me," Jeremy told Sebastian, "lock, stock, barrel, sheep and death duties."

"And your mother?"

"Well taken care of, don't worry about her. The lease on the London flat is hers, and that's the tiniest part of the holdings that Father wrote over to her years ago." Jeremy paused. "My father was a prudent man, Seb. I'm going to be a wealthy young man—distasteful to some, of course, but frankly true. Once Mariner Hall and the estate are sold, I shall be seeking investments." He poured more champagne into both their glasses. "And that's where you come in."

Sebastian waited.

"When I heard about the agency, as I told you, it just seemed such a stroke of fate, I had to call you there and then." Jeremy smiled. "There's no one in the world I'd rather invest in than you, Seb. No one I'd rather work with on a day-to-day basis. No one I'd rather have for a business partner."

Sebastian scarcely hesitated. He would need, he told Jeremy, to talk it over with Andrew, his silent partner and backer, and he realized that he needed to take a little time at least to mull it over, for this man, this forceful, compelling young man, seemed a million miles removed from the schoolboy friend who had been so devoid of motivation, so frankly lazy. And yet Sebastian had always cared for

Jeremy, had always trusted him, had understood and respected the differences between them. Those contrasts would still be there, of course, but so would the affection and the trust. This was, Sebastian had to agree with Jeremy, an extraordinary stroke of fate, and not to be ignored.

He spoke to Andrew when he got home that night, and within a half hour, both men knew that the decision was already as good as made.

"Jeremy's experience isn't exactly what you might have hoped to find in terms of the daily running of the agency," Andrew pointed out. "But I suppose that all that American expertise shouldn't be too hard to translate into British needs."

"I know what I want, ultimately, to achieve," Sebastian said, "but you and I both know that I haven't a grain of solid experience to sell. And then here, on day one, out of the blue, comes Jeremy Mariner, a real live agent with a track record and a whole bundle of contacts that are bound to be more than useful."

"You're very certain of him, aren't you?"

"More than I'd ever have believed possible," Sebastian said.

The three men met next morning in the Albermarle Street office, and Andrew saw for himself a young man who had found his way and knew exactly what he wanted. There was fire and energy in Jeremy's dark eyes, and stronger even than that, there was still the old and absolute willingness to follow Sebastian's lead that had been there when they'd been small boys. They talked business, shook hands and went to lunch at Brown's Hotel, drank toasts to the new partnership and laid plans late into the afternoon, agreeing, arguing and compromising.

"Only one day in business, and already changing the name of the company," Sebastian laughed. "At least they can't imagine it's because I failed on my own."

"There's no need to change anything," Jeremy said.

"Certainly there is, since you're going to be an equal partner."

"I agree," Andrew said.

"How do you feel about Locke Mariner?" Sebastian asked them both.

Jeremy said nothing.

"The Locke Mariner Agency," Andrew said, and repeated it, testing it and nodding. "It sounds strong. I like it."

"Jerry?"

Jeremy sat back in his chair, his eyes dark with emotion. "It sounds wonderful," he said.

chapter
9

I t was perfectly acceptable for beginnings to be modest, and some believed that a humble start was preferable to an instantaneous and, perhaps, untrustworthy success. But what Sebastian and Jeremy did in the case of Locke Mariner was to stretch a profoundly unremarkable first stage to boundaries that many people considered unwise and dangerous.

For several weeks they had not a single client, and when they did sign their first, he found himself out of work for longer than he had in years. Simon Kean was a fresh-faced actor in his late twenties who, after a promising beginning to his career, had fallen too comfortably into the category that Sebastian called "bread and butter." Kean had met Jeremy at the BBC, and since he had become disenchanted with his own agent, on hearing what Sebastian and Jeremy had to say, he made the decision to take a chance with them.

"You've appeared in a good dozen or more television plays and series," Jeremy told him bluntly, "yet I doubt if many viewers could put a name to your face."

"You have talent," Sebastian added, "and marvelous looks, and the kind of internal energy that we're both sure would translate into a real charisma on screen given the right opportunity."

"It's all a matter of strategy," Jeremy said.

Numerous small parts came up, but they refused to allow Kean to accept any of them. The actor grew unhappy and anxious and, finally, angry. Sebastian and Jeremy understood his feelings all too well, yet still their instincts told them to continue with their low-profile but intensive search for what might be Kean's crucial break.

"Just how long do you expect me to wait?"

"Bear with us a little longer," Sebastian said.

"That's all very well, but it won't pay the rent."

"Three more months," Jeremy said.

"That's too long."

"Give us three more months, and if nothing materializes we'll push you back on the old safe road," Sebastian said.

"In three months' time," Kean countered, "you won't be pushing me anywhere other than out of your agency."

One week later, Andrew learned from an old acquaintance who was a senior executive at Thames Television that a new drama series—based on the adventures of a young investigative journalist, to be aimed at an international market and to be scripted by the team behind *The Avengers*—was in the pipeline.

"Perfect," Sebastian said.

"Now what?" Kean asked.

"Now we snaffle a script, and we groom you for the part. We put you on a diet and exercise routine so that you'll be fit enough to deal with whatever they throw at you, and we do our damnedest to turn you into a mirror image of this character."

"Do you honestly believe it might work?" Kean looked dubious.

"We'll never know if we don't try it." Sebastian paused. "I know it sounds cold-blooded, but with a bit of luck, the casting director will see what we see."

It was prepackaging, and it was a gamble, but beginner's luck, albeit several months overdue, was with them, and with their first client locked into a sound contract with Thames, Sebastian and Jeremy, now steered by their new secretary, Elspeth Lehmann, began their search for a second.

It was Elspeth's choice to be known as their secretary, though it was clear from the start that she was to be a highly valued administrator. She was an immaculate, middle-aged woman with candid eyes, a low, cultured voice and a wealth of knowledge, having been in the business for almost twenty years. For ten of those years she had worked devotedly for one agent, but he had recently died, and Elspeth had considered premature retirement until the intriguing gossip she had heard about Locke Mariner had spurred her to make contact. She had adored Sebastian on sight and found Jeremy an interesting young man, and she was perfectly confident that, if she chose to help them, her assistance and experience could make all the difference between failure and success.

Elspeth was the answer to their prayers, a paragon of efficiency, prepared to set aside old attitudes if new ideas impressed her. Diplomatic and witty and warm, she set about creating the systems upon which the agency would need to run, organizing routines and methods, reminding them daily of the tedious chores that both young men might have dismissed as unproductive, but which were vital, in the long term, for the smooth running of any business.

With Elspeth in the office, Sebastian and Jeremy began to travel. For three days each week, they visited provincial theaters, as many agents had habitually done in the past when pressures had been lighter. After all, Sebastian reasoned, if the provinces had sheltered great talent in years gone by, there was no reason to assume that was no longer the case.

It was Jeremy who found Janet Johns, a young actress in Bolton who was ploughing every ounce of her considerable energies into a lackluster whodunit. Janet was deliciously feminine, she had fine, natural timing, and Jeremy peered through the dramatic intensity of her performance and felt sure he saw in her a strong streak of comic talent. He took her to dinner, learned that she loved comedy above all else, and, finding her ripe for persuasion, he signed her there and then. With a new Leonard haircut, carbohydrates sliced from her diet, two outfits chosen by Elspeth, a series of makeup lessons at Elizabeth Arden and a new first name, Judy Johns, was launched onto the London audition scene. Jeremy's instincts proved sound; at the end of September, the director of William Douglas Home's new comedy was smitten by Judy, and within weeks, the critics were hailing a new star.

Having begun on their own terms, Sebastian and Jeremy turned their attention to the voice-over business, bringing in one actor, dissatisfied with his representation, whose dark brown voice already encouraged thousands of television viewers and cinema goers to drink a particular vodka and to smoke a certain brand of cigarettes; and to maintain the balance they desired, they signed an actress who had been on Elspeth's late employer's books, and who was almost never out of work since, although she was unmemorable to look at, she was blessed with a voice of tremendous versatility, allowing her to play a huge range of radio roles, to narrate documentaries and to cover an age range between eight and eighty in the advertising voice-over field.

It was Andrew, once again, who brought about the signing of Locke Mariner's first distinguished artist. Barbara Stone was forty-two years old, with gleaming russet hair and warm brown eyes, an actress of powerful appearance, high intelligence and sensuality who had been compared, more than once, with the late Diana Lancaster—though neither Andrew nor Sebastian could find much similarity, for Diana had been pure, straight actress, and Barbara Stone was more playful, sometimes cat, sometimes kitten, sometimes a touch malicious, sometimes full of mischief. Andrew's law firm was representing her in a libel action against a newspaper, and after Barbara had made a play for Andrew and he had tactfully and charmingly rejected her, they had become friends.

"She hasn't worked for two years, you know," Andrew reminded Sebastian.

"Difficult to believe," Sebastian said, "since she's hardly ever out of the public eye."

Barbara Stone had costarred for three years in one of British television's best-sold series, which had thrust her into public consciousness far more forcefully than all the years of classic theatrical roles ever had, and on the heels of that fame had come a well-publicized love affair with the French film star Thierry Dupont, some ten years her junior. Finding herself pregnant, Barbara had been passionately, unreservedly overjoyed, but she had steadfastly refused to marry Dupont, and their relationship had barely survived the nine months of her pregnancy.

"I gave up work just before Patrick was born," Barbara told Andrew. "A little over two years ago, yet you'd imagine I'd been away for at least a decade and grown three double chins and snow-white hair."

Her agent, she complained, was pushing her to accept a part that all her instincts told her was wrong for her comeback.

"It's a character part, darling, a little cameo—a perfectly dear part for the right person, of course." Barbara leaned closer. "But do you think this is the appropriate moment for me to be so aged by makeup and padding as to be virtually unrecognizable?"

Andrew set up a meeting between Barbara and Sebastian in March of 1971 over dinner in the Terrace Room at the Dorchester. As usual, she attracted attention, especially since she was wearing an outrageous black midi dress that plunged dizzily at front and back. Sebastian thought that she looked more sensational than ever. Motherhood and two years off camera and stage had added a few fine lines around her eyes and mouth, but there was an extra radiance too. He steered their conversation cautiously, not about to criticize too openly another agency, especially one with which her relationship went back so many successful years, but he did wonder what lay behind such palpably poor advice. Instead of attacking the agent, he attacked the material; the film script in its entirety as well as the inappropriate role. She had been away for two years, and she had been sorely missed, he told Barbara. The greatest mistake was in hurrying her comeback; if the right vehicle could be found, the perfect film, her public would fall at her feet just as audiences had come in droves to see his mother in *Lieutenant Rose*.

Four months passed before Barbara Stone became a client of Locke Mariner, but her arrival took them into the lower ranks of the respected agencies, and Sebastian and Jeremy found that they were beginning to have their pick of more substantial artists. That autumn, Sebastian bought a little mews house in Mayfair, at the back of Park Lane, and though the leaving of Andrew and The Oaks was a great wrench, he was aware that the move was overdue and necessary. In many ways, living apart from his father forced them to spend more valuable hours together, for in busy times previously, they had often merely passed one another when one was leaving or coming home, whereas nowadays they met for lunches and dinners, as well as for their business meetings.

Sebastian enjoyed his little home, enjoyed the decorating of it and the furnishing and the finding of paintings to cover its walls, and he liked walking to the office, strolling to the theater and to restaurants and clubs. He loved the agency even more than he could have dreamed, for though it was hard, often relentless work, it was all coming his way, and when he had laid his plans in the early days, he had not anticipated having his best friend as his partner, nor having Andrew so happily involved, nor being so gently but capably guided by their wonderful Elspeth Lehmann.

With the start of 1972, Sebastian realized that, with his working life so stimulating and fulfilled, it was time to try to similarly elevate the quality of his personal existence.

He had never known a shortage of girlfriends, and Sebastian enjoyed a sex life that many young men might have envied, yet those relationships gave him no peace of mind. Where women were concerned, he seemed to lose all capacity for emotional involvement, and it troubled him. Whether he slept with a series of women or spent a longer period exclusively with one, the result was always the same: sexual pleasure and release came to him easily, but his mind remained frigid.

Love was a vital element of Sebastian's life; he loved his father deeply, had the greatest fondness for Jeremy, took his friendships seriously, regarded all human relationships as of the utmost importance. And yet, in the single area in which he longed to find warmth and closeness, Sebastian failed repeatedly. There was, by now, little doubt in his own mind that it was physical contact itself—the very thing that should have helped to cement a bond between a man and a woman—that suffocated all emotional feeling in him.

For some weeks now, he had been dating a young woman who organized the booking arrangements for one of the London sound studios at which many advertising agencies recorded voice-overs for their television commercials. Sabrina Bright was a twenty-three-year-old brunette, nymphlike in appearance and gregarious in temperament. She was lusty in bed and tender afterward, not seeming to mind that, if they were in her flat, Sebastian invariably left her by four in the morning, or that, if they were in his own bed in Mayfair, he would roll silently away from her once their lovemaking was over.

Despite his self-doubts, Sebastian felt a certain degree of peace with Sabrina. His daily life was rigorous and, sometimes, frenetic, and however much he thrived on it, it was good to be able to escape to a comfortable oasis where few demands were made on him. Perhaps, he thought, he was asking too much of himself. Maybe if he ceased worrying about his own responses and simply gave this relationship a real chance, it would grow into a stronger bond. On the other hand, instead of waiting passively for emotions to flood through him, perhaps he ought to work harder at producing them . . .

"Dinner tomorrow night?" he asked her, on the telephone, one brisk January morning.

"Love to," Sabrina said. "Where?" They both tended toward verbal shorthand during business hours, both understanding work pressures.

"My place. I'm cooking."

"Great. Need me to pick up something?"

"Thanks, no, I'll take care of it."

"Can't wait."

Sebastian took time out to plan a romantic meal *à deux*, went shopping in Soho at lunchtime the next day, then collected Sabrina from the studios after work and brought her home.

"Feel like helping me, or are you too tired?"

"It's not like you to let me help," Sabrina said, surprised.

She was right. Usually, when Sebastian cooked, he became rather too independent and protective of his kitchen, but this evening he encouraged Sabrina to participate, biting down his irritation when she used the wrong dishes and spilled vinegar over his pine breakfast counter, reminding himself that he would never be able to consider living with any woman if he allowed himself to become too meticulous. Routines and set methods were all right in the office, but not for the home—and they were certainly the kiss of death for any intimate relationship.

"Everything all right?" she asked, watching him light candles.

"Fine," he said. "Why shouldn't it be?"

"You seem—different."

He smiled. "How?"

"I'm not sure." Sabrina paused, while Sebastian tasted the Bordeaux he'd opened earlier. "Anyway," she said, "I like it."

"So do I. The wine, I mean."

Sebastian enjoyed the evening, as he generally did when he was with Sabrina. She was fun, she had energy, she was extremely pretty, and she seemed to care for him, and watching her across the table with increasing warmth, he determined that she was worth making a real effort for. He would not let himself reject her tonight, he vowed silently, however strong his desire to be alone.

As they undressed one another, later, in his bedroom, Sebastian was aware that he had not asked Sabrina to stay the night. He had intended to make an issue of it; she often did stay, but only because common courtesy stopped him from asking her to leave. Tonight, he wanted her to know that it was his choice, his wish, that he *needed* her to stay—but Sabrina's body was so warm and just as eager as his own, and words were soon forgotten as they tumbled onto his bed, desire mutual and energetic and wholly absorbing.

Afterward, lying sated in the dark, drowsiness engulfed Sebastian, and his eyelids began to close. Sabrina edged a little closer, and he sensed, rather than saw, her hand on the pillow hovering near his face, ready to stroke his cheek.

Unthinkingly, he rolled away, but then, remembering his earlier intentions, he winced.

"I'm sorry," he said, softly, and reached for her, tentatively.

"That's all right." Sabrina snuggled closer. "I'm used to it."

Sebastian waited another moment. "Will you stay with me tonight?" Even to his own ears, the words sounded forced and insincere, and he felt Sabrina stiffen in his arms.

"Will I stay?" She paused. "I always do, don't I?"

He said nothing, just lay silently, cursing himself.

Sabrina sat up. "Well?" she said.

"Yes, you do stay."

"Even though you've never done me the big favor of asking before." She reached over and switched on one of the bedside lamps. The sudden, unprecedented anger in her face and voice was startling. "And did you imagine I've never noticed that you get as far away from me as you can after we've done it—after you've finished—"

"Sabrina, don't." Sebastian, too, sat up, appalled.

"You act as if I had a disease."

"That isn't true." He reached for a cigarette and lit it.

"Isn't it?" She got out of bed, grabbing the bedspread to cover herself. "You're quite good company, Sebastian," she said harshly, "and damnably handsome, but I can tell you now I've never met a more cold-blooded man."

"Sabrina—"

"No, don't say anything." She was pulling on her clothes, not caring if she smeared makeup on her cashmere polo neck or snagged her tights. "I've tolerated it until now, because at least you never tried to pretend you felt anything for me—"

"Of course I feel—"

"Please!" She was close to tears, but her anger held them back. "But it's tonight I don't understand—tonight I almost believed, for just a little while, that you might care for me after all."

Sebastian got off the bed, wanting to go to her, to stop her, to hold her, but whether it was something in her face or something in himself that stopped him, he stayed his distance.

"I do care for you, Sabrina."

She softened just a little. "Maybe you do. Maybe that weird, uptight little invitation for me to stay meant something to you, I don't know. But I do know—and I suppose I've known it all along, but I just didn't want to admit it"—she ran a hand through her hair, not willing to take the time to find a brush—"I know now that you really are cold, where it counts, and that's no good to me."

Sebastian said nothing, and Sabrina went to the bedroom door and opened it.

"Thank you, but no," she said, softly. "I won't stay tonight, or any other night."

When Sabrina had gone, the house felt still and silent. Sebastian lay for a few moments on his bed before he went into the bathroom and turned the shower on full, and as he let the hard needles of cold water strike his face and body, he forced himself to acknowledge, painfully and wryly, that though he did regret, sincerely, having hurt Sabrina, he was, nevertheless, relieved that she had gone.

Chilled through by the shower, he wrapped a bathrobe around himself, went downstairs, adjusted the central heating thermostat and took a bottle of Glenfiddich malt out of the antique oak chest he used as a liquor cabinet. There was no need to switch on a light. The moon was full, and through the French windows he could see a light frost already silvering the winter-barren flowerbeds in his little town garden. It looked very cold. Silent and lonely and cold.

"Cheers," he said quietly, and drank his tumbler of whisky in one long swallow, and then he went back upstairs to bed. His relief at finding himself alone had already diminished, and depression was taking its place. Perhaps it was Sabrina's reproachful, angry voice echoing in his ears.

"Cold-blooded," he said, repeating her words.

She was right, of course, but it had been distressing to hear it from her lips, especially when he had hoped for something so different from their relationship. But when all was said and done, here he was, alone again. And worse than that, glad of it.

Sleep claimed him fitfully, drawing him down into its depths, then spitting him back again, so that he tossed and turned, growing more and more restless and unhappy. Until the comforting sentinel of his childhood and adolescence swept its gentle fragrance around him, that balm that he had seldom allowed himself to summon as a grown man, but which his subconscious mind brought back to him now.

And at last he slept, soundly, dreamlessly, till morning.

c h a p t e r

10

For almost a year, Andrew had been spending a good deal of his time with an old family friend, Virginia Hart. Sixty-one years old, Virginia had been married, until his death three years ago from cancer, to Matthew Hart, an eminent psychiatrist, who had known Andrew for more than a decade. Virginia was classically English, calm and elegant but vivacious, her hair was naturally wavy and brown, with neat streaks of white, and her clothes were predominantly Jaeger.

Sebastian had been aware that she and Andrew had been seeing each other and that they enjoyed one another's company, but it had never occurred to him that their relationship extended beyond close friendship. When his father told him, that April, that he had asked Virginia to marry him, and that she had agreed, Sebastian was stunned, but observing Andrew's expression, his reaction was one of unequivocal pleasure.

"You don't mind." Andrew's relief was boundless.

"Mind?" Sebastian clasped both his father's arms. "In all the years I can remember, I've never seen you look so happy. How could I mind?"

*   *   *

They planned a spring wedding at Caxton Hall, and Sebastian was touched by Andrew's determination that every last detail be impeccably arranged. They became officially engaged, with a notice in *The Times* and an emerald ring from Asprey and, with the exception of engagement gifts, which they made it known were being discouraged, each short stage of the romance proceeded as earnestly as if they had been in their twenties and marrying for the first time. Virginia was to move into The Oaks, and her fiancé plunged into an uncharacteristic shopping frenzy, wanting new linen, new kitchen equipment, new crockery—everything fresh and unused for his bride, who had more than enough to occupy her with the sorting out of her own flat in Cadogan Square, and her belongings.

In early June, two weeks before the wedding, Andrew and Sebastian, returning to Hampstead together after an extravagant excursion to Harrods and The White House in New Bond Street, decided to have dinner at Keats before going home. With Locke Mariner demanding so much of Sebastian's attention and time, it was rare these days for them to find time to enjoy a meal together, and they dined with great pleasure on lobster mousse and Chateaubriand, before driving back to the house along the quiet road that ran parallel to the Heath, just beginning to sink into lush purple shadow with the late sunset.

"Stay for a cognac," Andrew said.

"I think I may have had enough."

"Just a small one. I don't want you to leave just yet."

The house was silent, Ellie having gone to bed early, as usual. The two men wandered companionably into the drawing room, and while Andrew poured their cognac and lit a cigar for himself, Sebastian sank into one of the deep armchairs and gazed into the bare grate of the fireplace. Most people envied Andrew the position of The Oaks during the spring and summer months, with the tangle of heathland on their doorstep and the long hours of sunshine pouring through their windows, but Sebastian had always preferred the house in winter, when logs filled the fireplaces and the polished timber glowed and reflected the flickering of the flames. In summer, after dark, the drawing room had a cool, almost depressing feel to it. Perhaps, he thought, with a woman to run the house again, things might be different.

They went on talking, easily, as they had in the restaurant, about the agency, about Virginia, about the wedding.

"It's all changing," Sebastian said, softly.

"What do you mean, in particular?" Andrew asked.

"Mainly," Sebastian said, slowly, "that for most of our lives together, you and I have spent many of our quiet, reflective moments thinking about old times. Now, suddenly, we're looking ahead, into the future."

"Have I held you back, do you think, in those old times?"

"I don't think so. No more than I wanted to be held." Sebastian paused. "I can still remember the days, after she died, when you didn't want to talk about Diana. You couldn't, of course, I know that now, but then, one day, it changed. You began telling me how you felt, letting me in, and it made me feel so much better." He smiled. "I still like hearing you talk about her, I still love hearing about the old days, before I was born. It's a link to the past, to her."

"I remember the day I found I was able to speak about her, without breaking apart," Andrew said.

Sebastian rose from his chair, and looked up at the big Nathan Smith portrait of Diana hanging over the fireplace.

"That's right," Andrew said. "That's where you were standing, that very day. You told me that you often came in here just to look at the painting." The poignant memory swept over him of his small, flaxen-haired son standing in that same spot, solemn and alone, gazing up at his mother. "She would have been so very proud of you, Sebastian. Then, and now."

Sebastian did not speak.

"How much," Andrew asked, gently, "do you really remember about your mother? We have our collective memories, I know, but you were so young when we lost her, I'm never certain how much you accurately remember."

Sebastian walked over to the windows and looked out into the garden, now quite dark. Clouds had gathered in the past hour, and drops of rain were beginning to fall.

"The thing I remember most vividly," he said, "was her beauty."

He put out his right hand and, with one finger, followed the path of a droplet of water as it trickled down the other side of the glass. The window was starting to mist over—it was like looking at his reflection through gauze, his eyes seeming bigger, darker.

"Probably all mothers seem beautiful to their children," he said softly. "And, of course, in my case I always had all those hundreds of photographs and the paintings to prove that it wasn't just my bias."

"No," Andrew said. "It wasn't."

"Her eyes," Sebastian went on. "Her dark, wonderful eyes have never left me." He paused. "I always felt that I understood why the public loved her so much, even though I never saw her in performance—except in *Lieutenant Rose*."

Andrew looked up, surprised. "You did see her onstage. Once." An old sadness welled up inside him. "Don't you remember?"

Sebastian turned and leaned against the wall, one hand absently brushing back and forth across the heavy velvet curtains. "Yes." His eyes glittered. "I remember." He paused again. "The part she never played."

Andrew glanced at him, puzzled by the sudden, odd harshness in his tone. Sebastian's expression had become unreadable. He turned away again, back to the dark, rain-splashed windows.

"The part that killed her," he said.

"In a way," Andrew said. "Though I—"

"*Killed*," Sebastian repeated with a soft, curious violence.

Andrew stood up, unnerved by the curious transition that seemed to have taken place in his son. The cigar in his hand dropped onto the carpet, hot ash burning his fingers as it fell, and mechanically, Andrew picked it up and laid it in an ashtray.

"What do you mean by that?" he asked, gently.

Sebastian stood quite still, facing the garden, staring into his own misted reflection, his back stiff as a rigid shield, holding his father at bay. "That was what you said."

"What did I say?"

"That Hedda killed her."

It wasn't the words themselves, but the way they were spoken. Hollow and incongruous and bitter, bordering on savage. Had he not been less than a few feet away, Andrew might almost have disbelieved that the voice was his son's.

Sebastian turned slowly around to face him, and Andrew shivered. The room felt suddenly oppressive, suffocating. It was hard for him to breathe.

"No one else is going to play Hedda." Sebastian was whispering now, the words hissing from his lips, and now the violence was in his eyes. "I heard her. I remember."

Andrew felt unable to speak. Instinctively, he moved closer, reached out his hand, but Sebastian looked through him as if he were invisible, and then his eyes closed, and he breathed deeply, as if inhaling some exquisite aroma.

"Don't you feel her?" There was pity in the question.

Andrew's arm dropped back to his side, his fingers trembling. He remained very still, afraid to move again, afraid to speak. There was such an unearthly, delicate balance between them—it was like standing close to a sleepwalker on the edge of a precipice—

Sebastian opened his eyes. They focused on a point somewhere beyond Andrew, and his pupils were very black, fully dilated.

"Don't you smell her perfume?"

Andrew's stomach lurched. Involuntarily, he stepped back, staring aghast at his son. The grandfather clock against the far wall of the room ticked insistently. The rain rattled more loudly against the glass. Andrew licked his lips to moisten them. In his entire life, he had never felt such fear.

"Sebastian," he said faintly. Then more strongly, his voice piercing the air with urgency. *"Sebastian."*

The eyes blinked. The lashes flickered violently, convulsively, as if in the throes of an unconscious nightmare. Andrew was aware of being drawn almost hypnotically to Sebastian's eyes, as if the rest of the face he knew and loved so well had suddenly become no more than a covering, an outer casing.

Another blink, steadying now. And Andrew saw that the vision was returning to them, and a brief, searing relief washed away a fragment of the terror from his heart. For several moments they stared at each other, Andrew searching Sebastian's face, still unable to read his expression, unsure whether it was confusion he saw there now, or fear.

And then, just as Andrew felt certain he could endure it no longer, Sebastian came back. Had he been asked to describe the new change in his son's face, Andrew could scarcely have found the words, for the difference was almost imperceptible. Just that. A coming back, as if from a trance. And as abruptly as it had begun, it was over. Simply over.

Sebastian raised his left arm, and looked at his watch.

"It's getting late," he said. "I think I'd better get going. Jeremy and I have a breakfast meeting." There was a note of weariness in his voice, and he touched his temple gingerly with two fingers, as if his head ached.

Andrew forced himself to speak. "Are you—?" The words caught in his dry throat.

"What, Dad?"

Andrew swallowed. "Are you feeling all right?"

"Perfectly." Sebastian shrugged. "Just a little tired. And you know how I hate breakfast meetings." A small crease etched itself across his brow, but not even the tiniest trace of self-consciousness betrayed the normality of his words.

Still Andrew could hardly speak. He felt too shaken, as if his very foundations had been ripped away from beneath him. It was inconceivable, but Sebastian was behaving as if the last few minutes had not happened at all.

"You look a bit tired, too, Dad." Sebastian reached out and touched his father's shoulder, gently. "Better call it a night," he smiled, "or Virginia will be blaming me for wearing you out before the wedding."

The same old Sebastian, loving, straightforward. Normal.

Andrew was aware of the need to speak out, knew that what had just taken place needed to be confronted, but he also knew that he was too shocked to deal with it now.

"All right to drive?" he managed to say.

"Absolutely."

"Sure?"

Sebastian looked a little surprised. "Dad, I'm fine."

Mechanically, Andrew went through the motions of walking to the front door, of embracing his son, of watching him walk across the gravel driveway to his Jaguar, his shoes crunching sharply in the silence. The rain had stopped again, and a rich scent of damp grass and soil wafted off the Heath. It was a beautiful night.

"Good night, Dad," Sebastian called again, opening the car door. "Sweet dreams."

Andrew waited until the Jaguar had rolled quietly out of the drive into the road. Then he shut and bolted the heavy front door, switched off the lights in the hall and then in the drawing room, and returned to his armchair.

The dark seemed easier to bear, somehow, than the sham normality of electric light. He sat for a long time, in the same chair in which, just a short while before, he had leaned contentedly, sorting past into future. Just a few minutes, and now suddenly, inexplicably, that future seemed to hang in the balance, no longer seeming safe and assured; and even the past, for reasons he did not yet understand, felt like an illusion, almost a deceit.

Andrew tried to get his bearings again, to bring himself under control. Just a few minutes, that was all, so why did he feel as if he had been thrashed by some invisible force?

I'm overreacting, he told himself. Perhaps Sebastian did have too much to drink, maybe the cognac on top of the claret at dinner—he ought not to have let him drive home.

He pounded the arm of the chair with his fist, then tried again to relax, taking deep breaths, filling his lungs and letting the air out as evenly as he could. He *was* overreacting absurdly, of course. He was a lawyer, after all, a man with a logical mind. Something had happened tonight that, in the space of five minutes or so, had ripped a wound in his calm. There had to be a rational explanation; logic must play its part. What, exactly, had happened, and why? And what was it, in his own mind, that made him so certain and so terrified that the episode had nothing to do with drink or with anything else so normal as that?

What had set off those awful, confusing moments? What had they been speaking about? He couldn't remember, it seemed to have happened a long time ago. Anguished, Andrew tore at his gray hair with both hands, and the small pain at his scalp pushed away a little of the fog in his brain, and then the cold memory was there.

Diana. Of course. They had been talking about Diana. The actress, not the mother or wife. Sebastian's recollections. Intensely nostalgic, of course, perhaps a little idealized, but lucid. And then he had veered away so obliquely, as if the normal, familiar Sebastian had abruptly shut down.

The part that killed her, Sebastian had said. Hedda Gabler. And then, what? *No one else is going to play her*.

A half-formed, fuzzy memory—the root, he was suddenly certain, of the intense, exaggerated quality of his fear—flitted past Andrew's closed eyes, and he kept them deliberately tightly shut, reaching for the memory urgently in case it disappeared again. And then it developed with almost photographic clarity.

A letter. Folded white notepaper, covered with neat, clear, rounded handwriting. A small blue ink smudge in the top right-hand corner. A letter from Sebastian, written at Marchmont. *Why, for God's sake, think of that now?* How old had Sebastian been then? Fifteen, no, sixteen. In a flash, Andrew found that he remembered the teenaged gravity of that particular letter. And he remembered, too, that it had concerned a bizarre attack on a boy playing the lead in their school play, and that Sebastian's shock and disgust at the attack had come through clearly in every line.

That killed her. The present came back, jolting Andrew again. His son's odd, savage tone.

Hedda.

He stood up and began, in the dark, to pace the floor, his feet silent on the carpet, longing to shut off the thoughts, but unable to, cursing the photographic memory that had aided him all his professional life, easing his path first through examinations and helping him, so often, in courts of law. That damnably retentive inner eye now dredged up the trivial scene, more than ten years earlier, when he had opened that letter . . . the breakfast table . . . the sunshine streaming in from the garden . . . a little marmalade clinging stickily to his fingers, so that Andrew had wiped them carefully before starting to read . . .

Killed.

Andrew sat down again, the trembling returning. From Sebastian's earliest childhood, his most dominant characteristics had been his common sense and his innate sensitivity to the feelings of others. Andrew could not recall a single occasion when his son had shown the slightest tendency to violence of any kind. And yet tonight there had been such undeniable fury seething beneath those strange words. And then, mere moments later, that uncanny retreat into himself, before those truly bizarre words which Andrew had found the most frightening of all:

Don't you feel her?

Andrew tore himself from the chair. He was being ludicrous, allowing his imagination to race crazily ahead of reality. That letter had been an entirely natural account of an unpleasant event that had taken place at school, nothing to do with Sebastian at all. The fact that the play had been *Hedda Gabler* was coincidence—

Then what about that ecstasy? *Don't you smell her perfume?* And that wide, vacant stare.

A sudden giddiness overwhelmed Andrew, buckling his knees, and he fell to the floor, crouching on the carpet on all fours, like an animal. His head was spinning, he felt nauseous and faint. It occurred to him that he was on the verge of a heart attack—he anticipated the pain, like a blow from an ax, waiting for it to strike his chest. But the long, shuddering moment passed, and no agony came to finish him off, just a terrible weakness. Tentatively, he moved, so that he could lean against the edge of the sofa, waited until the nausea had receded and his head felt clearer, and then he got up slowly, holding on for support.

The grandfather clock struck midnight. Unsteadily, he walked out into the cool hall. Perhaps he was ill, he thought. His hands were icy, his cheeks hot. He had to get to bed, to rest. He began to climb the staircase, shaking his head.

Imagination, he told himself. *Sleep is what I need.* In sleep he would shed this madness . . .

But escape was not so simple. Lying still sleepless in bed, with dawn only an hour away, Andrew knew by now that those fears would not be shaken off. He had not misheard those words, had not mistaken the tone behind them, nor misread the expression in his son's eyes. Sebastian had been a beautiful child, and now he was a man, handsome, strong, brilliant, triumph spreading before him. A son to be proud of. Yet a dam had burst in Andrew Locke's mind, and now there seemed no stopping the flood of awful terror.

Dear God, he prayed silently, *let me be wrong.*

But a small, malicious voice in his head said:

You are not.

In the morning, once Andrew had showered and shaved and dressed, once he had spoken on the telephone to Virginia, heard her sweet, low voice, he felt a little better. He stood at his bedroom window, looking out over the vista of heathland. It was a perfectly clear morning, and he could see right into the heart of the City of London, could see the dome of St. Paul's, made tiny by distance but gleaming in the morning sunshine. Perhaps, he thought, at a distance of a few more hours, the events of the previous night might also shrink to a saner perspective.

He went downstairs, to Ellie and the breakfast she laid out before him every morning, tried to chat normally, tried to eat something and to read his newspaper, but he knew that there was no point to the charade. It was impossible to pretend to himself that nothing had happened. There was only one way to reassure himself, and that was by seeing Sebastian again, right away, face to face.

Sebastian had only just returned from his breakfast meeting when Elspeth told him that Andrew had arrived.

"Dad." Sebastian stood at the open door of his office. "What a surprise. Not at the office?" He looked fit and vigorous, and entirely normal.

"I have an appointment in St. James's," Andrew lied, "and I'm early, so I thought I'd just look in."

"Come in."

"Can we get you some coffee?" Elspeth asked.

"Dad?"

"Not for me, thank you."

Andrew steeled himself as soon as the door was closed.

"Bumped into an old acquaintance just now," he began. "In Bond Street. Father of a chap who was at Marchmont with you, I think. Anthony Jacobs."

Sebastian, shuffling papers on his desk, glanced up. "Dan's father?"

"That's right. You remember him?"

"Certainly. Didn't know him well—he was a year or so older."

"Odd thing," Andrew said lightly. "We were chatting for a moment, talking about Marchmont, and Jacobs mentioned that dreadful incident you once told me about, the school play that was canceled."

"That's right. Dan was the director. *Hedda Gabler*." Sebastian gave a small shudder of memory. "Horrid business. Dan Jacobs was calm, I remember, very much in charge."

It was an entirely spontaneous response. Casual. A brief pause in the midst of work to recall an old, half-forgotten event. Distressing once, but over long ago. A natural reaction. Andrew felt as if his blood had ceased to flow for many hours, and had now begun to flow again. The relief warmed him. Just one more question, he thought.

"Did they ever find out who was responsible?" he asked.

Sebastian, looking down at papers again, shook his head. "Not to my knowledge."

His voice was innocent. Yet when he raised his face again to look at his father, Andrew realized that his eyes were rather more empty than innocent. Devoid of feeling. Like a swift short circuit. Unnatural.

And then the telephone rang, and the moment was past. The son he knew so well, the man he knew, spoke briefly, smiled at his father as he went toward the door, blew him a kiss. And Andrew passed Elspeth with hardly a word and the wannest of smiles, and outside, in Albemarle Street, where the world passed to and fro in its steady weekday pattern, he began to walk automatically, turning left into Piccadilly, and just past the Royal Academy he saw an empty taxi and hailed it, and asked the driver to take him back to Hampstead.

"Is anything wrong, Mr. Locke?" Ellie was vacuuming the stair carpet when Andrew came through the front door.

"Not at all, Ellie," he said, with forced brightness.

She unplugged the cleaner and came down into the hall. "Did you forget something?" She peered at him more closely, her eyes bright and concerned behind her spectacles. "You're looking tired, if you don't mind my saying so. Not feeling ill, I hope, not so close to the wedding."

"No, Ellie, I'm fine, really." Andrew went directly to his study and opened the door. "I've a few papers I need to deal with here, that's all."

"That's good," she said, and smiled. "A sensible idea spending more time at home just at the moment. Would you like a cup of tea?"

"Maybe later."

He closed the study door, took a bunch of keys from his pocket, and unlocked the deep bottom drawer on the left side of his desk. It was full to the brim with papers and sundry items; a fair cross section of more than twenty-five years of sentiment was crammed into this drawer. He withdrew an armful and heaped it onto the desk top.

It took over an hour to find the letter. There were so many things to distract him: photographs that had been left out of albums or frames, certificates, the pair of white baby's booties, now grimy and frayed, the only time Diana had ever knitted anything, school reports—all promising, almost to the point of brilliance, illuminating Sebastian's future.

But the letter was there, as Andrew had known it would be from the instant he had remembered it.

The damage looked much worse than it really was, thank heaven, Sebastian had written, *and the Doc doesn't seem to think there'll be any scar or anything. But the whole school's in an uproar . . .*

There was a ragged newspaper clipping, too, from the local Buckinghamshire paper, that Sebastian had brought home in the school holidays and that Andrew had forgotten about, which told of acid taken from a school laboratory and mixed with lipstick.

. . . it's almost impossible to conceive, Sebastian's letter had gone on, *of anyone being capable of such wickedness . . .*

Andrew read both items three times, then folded them carefully and placed them in his wallet. Then, as an afterthought, he removed them again and locked them back, with the other papers, in the drawer. Safer there, from other eyes. One never knew.

He took the Bentley to Gower Street, and parked right outside the big university bookshop. Three quarters of an hour later, he emerged with a parcel under one arm and drove on to Foyles in Charing Cross Road, and this time, when he returned to the car, there was a parking ticket under a windscreen wiper, but Andrew left it there, uncaring, and drove directly back to the Vale of Health.

"Ellie?" he called out as he entered the house. There was no answer and he called once more. *"Ellie!"*

Satisfied that she must have gone out shopping, Andrew went into the study again and locked the door behind him. Sitting in his leather chair behind the desk, he used his paper knife to slit open the paper wrappings of both packages, and lifted the books out, one at a time. They felt heavy, and he handled them carefully, gingerly, as if they were volatile enough to explode in his hands. He placed them one upon the other beside the pigskin blotter that Virginia had bought him at Smythson's for his last birthday, and leaned back in the chair.

His study window looked out onto the driveway, a beautiful weeping willow bowing low to scrape the glass occasionally when the wind rustled its branches. A young woman, tall in jeans and red wellington boots, strode past in the road with her labrador bitch, heading for the Heath, muddy after the night's rain. A blackbird sang joyfully in an oak tree, and, if he troubled to listen, Andrew could hear the soft whirr of the mid-afternoon traffic climbing East Heath Road.

Andrew missed the therapeutic hours of walking his dogs. Rufus and Jasper, his old golden retrievers, had both died years before, and Andrew had never had the heart to find another dog, until recently, when Virginia had begun to encourage him to think about it, for she loved animals and felt that a house was not a real home without at least one dog and one cat.

"I've missed having pets since Matthew died, but it never seemed quite fair living in a flat," she had said.

"We'll find a dog after we're married," he had promised her.

"Perhaps we could go to Battersea," she'd suggested.

"I think I might find that too heartbreaking," he'd said.

"But worthwhile if we could give some poor creature a home."

Thoughts of happy homes and weddings and domestic pets seemed far-off fantasies to Andrew now. He averted his eyes from the beauty outside the window and looked at the misery piled before him on his desk. Fear and self-hatred rose in his throat like bile.

"No," he said quietly. "Not today."

He stood up and unlocked one of the cabinets behind him. Then he took the books and placed them on the top shelf, and then he shut the cabinet and locked it again. They were here now, in his house, but he wasn't ready. He could not look at them. Not yet.

For the next few days, Andrew remained, for the most part, locked in his study with the books and his thoughts, emerging only for meals and a short night's rest. The telephone rang frequently, his partners and staff concerned, Virginia and Sebastian anxious about him. Andrew instructed Ellie to tell callers either that he was engaged in urgent work or that he was out of town, but after the third day he took the receiver off the hook for much of the time.

"But Mr. Locke, that means that no one will be able to ring," Ellie said in some consternation.

"Quite."

"But it might be urgent—Mrs. Hart or Sebastian might need you, or there might be a crisis at—"

"I'm sorry, Ellie," Andrew said, already on his way back into the study, "I simply don't want to be disturbed."

"But—"

"I shall be telephoning Mrs. Hart and Sebastian quite regularly, so they shan't be worried." He relented a little. "And you needn't worry either, Ellie."

"I most certainly am worried about you," Ellie said, firmly. "You look shocking, Mr. Locke, quite ill, as a matter of fact."

"I'm not ill."

"Then you'll be making yourself ill if you go on like this."

Andrew closed the door. It no longer seemed to matter what Ellie or anyone else thought. Even Virginia's feelings were suddenly of secondary importance. He telephoned her, as he had promised Ellie, each morning and evening, aware that otherwise she would insist upon coming to The Oaks.

"It's just pressure of work," he lied. "With the honeymoon so close, you'd expect it to pile up."

"At the office, perhaps, but hardly at home."

"Too many distractions at the office, I'm better off here."

Virginia was unconvinced, worried after speaking to Ellie, and, finally, angry, sure that he would, as Ellie was fretting, make himself ill if he continued to drive himself in such an uncharacteristic fashion. Her fiancé was a painstaking man, she admitted, and a stickler for detail, but Andrew had always known when to pause, how to make space for pleasure and relaxation.

"This is foolish, darling," she told him. "You're alarming everyone."

"There's no need to be alarmed," he said, more stiffly than he intended.

"Andrew, please, this just isn't like you. You must stop it at once, or at least tell me what's wrong."

He could not tell her, and he could not stop. Over and over again, Andrew forced himself back into the past, trying to remember and to analyze each stage of Sebastian's development, going over the painful period after Diana's death, trying to pinpoint any sign he might have missed at the time, of the slightest abnormality. But he always came back to Sebastian's well-adjusted attitude, to the way his son had helped him to come to terms with their loss, the fact that he might have been destroyed without him.

He went back further, too, examining Diana's relationship with Sebastian. She had clung so tightly, he had known that even then. Had she overprotected him? Yet even as a small boy, Sebastian had been gregarious and they had both encouraged him to make friends. For hours on end, Andrew delved into what he knew about his son's independent, adult life. The most extraordinary facet of it was surely his success, and despite Sebastian's undeniable ambition and dedication, like his father he knew how to relax. Andrew considered his social life; girlfriends were certainly abundant and varied. He thought that Sebastian had probably not yet known a great love or passion, but in his twenties that surely was nothing to be especially concerned about. There was plenty of time for love—he, after all, had not met Diana until he was in his forties, and it had taken him until his seventieth year to fall in love again.

Within a week, the ravages of Andrew's emotional pain showed in his appearance as well as his behavior. He hardly slept, and never without bad dreams, and he lost five pounds in weight. On the two occasions, toward the end of the week, when Virginia and Sebastian forced him to see them by appearing, together, at the house, they were horrified by his gauntness and uncharacteristic snappishness, but Andrew felt unable to confide in Virginia and could hardly bear to look his son in the eye.

On the eighth night, after three hours of sleepless misery in bed, Andrew went quietly down to the study and unlocked the cabinet behind his desk. He took out the books, as he did every day, and sat down.

He felt strangely peaceful. Isolated and remote, as if the panic had suddenly receded, leaving him with a curious, dull acceptance of what he could no longer turn away from. He sorted through the titles, selected the one that he had, until now, refused to open, and laid it on the blotter. The lettering on the cover swam fuzzily. He felt in his dressing gown pocket for his leather spectacle case and put on his glasses.

The title sprang clear under the light of the desk lamp. Just one word. Very direct.

Insanity.

chapter
11

On the fifteenth of June 1972, at half past eleven in the morning, Virginia and Andrew were married, according to plan, at Caxton Hall near St. James's Park. It was a glorious day, and the air rang with gaiety as the newlyweds stepped, laughing, from the registry office to the clicks of cameras, cries of congratulations and showers of confetti. Virginia's younger son, Jamie, was trapped by a demanding job in California, but Hugh, the older, had come down from Edinburgh for the occasion with his wife and their little daughter, and as family photographs were posed for, the child giggled with delight as Sebastian balanced her on his shoulders and Jeremy Mariner told her wicked stories.

They lunched at the Mirabelle, just a few close friends and family, and afterward, Sebastian drove his father and new stepmother to Heathrow to catch the early evening flight to Nice. The luggage was checked in, and while Virginia chose a novel for the journey, Andrew and Sebastian went to the bar and bought two glasses of Perrier water to drink a final toast.

"Long life and happiness, Dad," Sebastian said. "I love you both."

"Virginia loves you too." Andrew smiled. "I don't have to tell you how I feel, do I?"

Sebastian shook his head, put down his glass and took a close glance at his father. Andrew had emerged from the bout of reclusiveness that had worried them all so much—it had seemed an eternity, yet it had only been about a week, and Sebastian and Virginia had had no choice but to accept his reassurances that all was well. Yet Sebastian still felt a nagging doubt.

"Dad," he said now, hastily, seeing Virginia approaching. "Are things all right with you now? I know what you've said, but are you quite sure there's nothing you'd feel better sharing with me before you go?"

Andrew's answer came swiftly and readily.

"I'm absolutely fine, Sebastian," he said. "Absolutely content." He paused. "So long as you are, too."

Their eyes met, and the intensity in them matched as perfectly as the blueness of their color. There was love in them, and tenderness and care. And fear.

Each rediscovery of the Hôtel du Cap in Cap d'Antibes brought fresh pleasure to Andrew, but on this arrival his joy seemed especially profound. It was Virginia's first visit, but her expression was sublimely happy as she climbed out of the taxi, straightened her salmon pink linen suit, and surveyed the cool, graceful lines of the cream-colored hotel with its pale blue awnings and shutters.

"Oh, Andrew, you were right—this is *the* most beautiful place," she said with delight, sniffing at the air. "And the scent!" She inhaled, closing her eyes. "Pine and jasmine—and mimosa, and what else?"

"Bougainvillea," Andrew said, "and roses, of course, and you'll have to ask a gardener if you want to know the rest." He tucked his arm into hers. "Come on. There's much, much more, believe me."

The first week of the honeymoon passed blissfully. Every morning they awoke refreshed and at peace to the glorious sight of the hotel's quiet park bordering, on both sides, the broad gravel path that led right down to the Eden Roc Pavilion, the swimming pool and the Mediterranean. Sometimes they breakfasted in bed, sometimes on their balcony, sometimes on the terrace overlooking the gardens, listening to the clear, gentle sound of morning tennis being played on the nearby courts.

They sunbathed for a while each day, and often it was warm enough to don bathing suits and swim in the pool, and usually they lunched at Eden Roc, too lazy and contented to venture out; but once, they drove up to Saint-Paul-de-Vence, and another time they admired the Legers in the museum at Biot, and one evening, they rented a little scarlet Peugeot and braved the Grande Corniche for the sunset views. Virginia observed the sparkle returning to Andrew's eyes and was satisfied that whatever had troubled him before the wedding seemed to have melted away. They both found this almost constant companionship idyllic, delighted in one another. Andrew felt a million miles removed from his anxieties, and indeed, as the days passed, they seemed more and more ludicrous. He abandoned his fears by day and slept in tranquillity by night.

As much as they loved being together, they made it a routine to take a brief time apart each day. Having lived as a single man for so many years, Andrew had inevitably become accustomed to privacy, and Virginia, too, enjoyed moments of solitude. Most afternoons, she would go up to their room before Andrew, to shower and change, and then she might go into Antibes to visit the hairdresser or browse in the boutiques. Andrew would wait until she had finished in the bathroom and then take his turn, before going into Juan-les-Pins, where he would buy the English newspapers at the bustling *papeterie* and sit down at one of the pavement cafés to read, while sipping a Dubonnet or a *café noir*.

On the tenth day of the honeymoon, he sat down at a table outside the Pam-Pam, ordered his drink, lit a Havana and, entirely at peace, began to read. He went through *The Times* first, then the *Telegraph*, then idly turned the pages of the *Daily Express*.

It was such a short piece that he might just as easily have missed it altogether, yet his eyes fell on it as if it were the only item on the page of theater news and gossip.

Peter March announced plans yesterday for a new West End production of *Hedda Gabler*, following hot on the heels of his successful *Wild Duck*. March was enigmatic when asked about casting, though—

Andrew read no further. Panic engulfed him, seizing him by the throat. He stood up, fumbled in his pocket and threw a note onto the table without even glancing at it. He left the newspapers, the breeze catching the edges of the pages, turning them over and whisking them onto the ground as Andrew began to walk, slowly, numbly at first, then more quickly—too quickly—back along the main street, past the casino, past the beaches, quiet this afternoon in the cooling wind, past the Juana and the Provençal and the Belle Rives hotels, toward Cap d'Antibes.

It was a long walk, much too long, but Andrew had not thought to flag down a taxi, had not thought to pause even for an instant, but as the incline grew steeper and the Hôtel du Cap was not yet in sight, he was forced to stop. He could hardly breathe, and there was a searing pain in his side.

A stitch, he thought, *that's all it is*. But just the same, he rested at the side of the road, leaning against the rock wall, perspiration trickling down his face, his heart pounding as if it would burst, his lungs battling for air.

Dear Christ, he prayed, *not now, please God not now*. And after a while, as he slumped on the wall, some of his strength returned to him, and he pulled out a linen handkerchief and mopped his forehead and eyes. The hotel was still so far away, but the only taxis passing him were all occupied—he couldn't make it. He closed his eyes. The newsprint swam before them . . . *new production* . . . There must have been other *Hedda*s, he tried to rationalize; if he checked back when they got home to London, he was bound to find any number of productions over the last decade—

But Sebastian had been a student then. He hadn't been an agent, whose whole raison d'être was to be aware of who was going to be casting what play. Andrew straightened up. However much he prayed that he was wrong, that this damnable terror was all in his own overwrought, perhaps even senile imagination, he *had* to get back, he had to go home, had to watch Sebastian, to stay close to him.

And the fear rose again inside him, powerful and strengthening, and he made his way up the rest of the hill.

Virginia was horrified when she saw Andrew's state, incredulous when he insisted on returning to London immediately, and infuriated when he refused to explain what had happened since she'd last seen him just a few hours before.

"If you're trying to shield me from worry," she said, "I can assure you I'm half out of my mind already!" She had been dozing on their bed when he'd arrived, wearing a bathrobe and longing for his return, but now all relaxation had disintegrated and she was pacing the room.

"I'm sorrier than I can say, darling." Andrew had grown calmer since he'd had an opportunity to sit down in the cool of their room. "If I could share this with you, I would, you must believe me."

"But you don't trust me." Virginia was pale.

"I trust you with my life." Andrew tried to take her hands, but she snatched them away. "There's no one on this earth I trust more."

"Just not enough to explain to me why you want to cut short our honeymoon."

Andrew flushed darkly. "I realize how extraordinary this must seem to you—"

"I've married a master of understatement," Virginia said cuttingly, close to tears.

"—and I know that by not sharing this with you, I'll probably leave you imagining things far more terrible than reality."

"Then *tell* me."

"I can't." Andrew shook his head, his eyes bleak. "I wish to God I could, but I can't."

"Very well then." Virginia opened one of the wardrobes and began taking her dresses off their hangers and throwing them onto the bed.

"What are you doing?" Andrew asked.

"What does it look like?"

"Darling, you mustn't—I want you to stay here, relax, enjoy it till I can get back." He picked up two dresses, but Virginia pulled them out of his hands. "It's madness for you to ruin your holiday, too."

"This isn't a holiday," she said, chokingly. "I thought that it was supposed to be a honeymoon, and I'll be damned if I'm going to take it on my own."

There was nothing Andrew could say or do to comfort her. They were married now, and he loved her unreservedly, but his fears were his own. He would not lie to her, and if he confided in her now, he would always feel that he had betrayed Sebastian.

There was no flight till morning, but once Virginia's anger was spent and her hot tears of frustration shed, they agreed to make an effort and changed for dinner down at Eden Roc.

Outside, below the big picture windows, waves crashed onto rocks and sea spray lifted high into the air, white and frothy. There were no stars tonight, and the moon dodged heavy, gathering clouds, emerging now and then in a watery crescent.

The silence between them was heavy with unhappiness. For more than a year, Andrew had done everything in his power to surround Virginia with adoration and comfort; in every way imaginable, he had protected and cherished her, had made a great and sincere effort to share every facet of his life with her. Yet now, without warning, she found herself feeling abandoned by him, though it was clear to her, even through her anger, that he was even more wretched than she was. She had hoped that once they were seated in one of their favorite settings, Andrew might open his heart to her, but he seemed hopelessly preoccupied. He hardly touched the steak he had ordered, just sipped at his Bordeaux and stared out into the night. Virginia wished that they had stayed in their room, for this beautiful restaurant was designed for pleasure and intense conversations, for wit and romance. Misery had no place here; despair belonged upstairs in privacy, or perhaps out there, on the black sea, whipped up to a frenzy with the waves.

"I know this is connected to whatever happened before the wedding," Virginia said, unable to keep away from the subject any longer. "I knew then, however well you tried to fob me off, that it was something awful."

Andrew said nothing, just fingered his napkin.

"I've tried and tried to imagine what it might be." Virginia was near tears again, her jaw quite stiff with the effort of holding them back. "The obvious thing, of course, was that you were afraid, in London, that you might be terribly ill—and that you must have learned this afternoon that—"

"No," Andrew said.

She sat very still. "You're not dying."

"No," he said, softly, full of anguish for her. "There's nothing wrong with me, my darling."

"Swear it."

"I swear it."

"And Sebastian? He's not ill either, nor in trouble?"

"No." The pause before his answer was imperceptible.

Virginia watched her husband. His elegance seemed somehow diminished tonight; the distinguished, silvery hair and thick eyebrows looked simply white, the attractive lines were deep, painful wrinkles of age and worry. Each mouthful he attempted to swallow seemed to threaten to choke him, and when he spoke, each word was husky with unhappiness. He looked old. And she loved him more than ever.

"I love you," she said.

He looked up into her eyes. "Even through this?"

She waited before answering. "I think I shall love you forever," she said. "Even if you try to make me hate you."

"Is that what you think I'm doing?" he said sadly.

"I have no idea what you're doing."

*   *   *

Tactfully silent about their scarcely touched plates, their waiter offered them first cheese and then the dessert trolley. They declined both.

"Just coffee, please," Virginia said.

"For me, too." Andrew waited until the waiter had gone, and then he got to his feet. "Will you excuse me, darling, for just a moment?"

"You're all right?" she asked.

"Of course."

Virginia seldom smoked, but she had bought a packet of cigarettes earlier in the week, and now she took one from her handbag and allowed a passing waiter to light it for her. She inhaled the smoke and looked out at the dark Mediterranean. The rocks below looked forbidding and lethal; it was hard to believe that just that morning, sunbathers had perched on them, relaxed and happy.

Gradually, vaguely, she became aware of a little commotion outside the restaurant. Voices were raised, and out of the corner of her eye, she thought she saw a man running past the entrance. An argument of some sort, she thought, or perhaps a romantic tiff. She looked back at the window, at her own shadowy reflection. Straight-backed, very still, lonely. The waiter brought their coffee, poured a tiny cup for her and moved quietly away. Virginia raised one hand to her cheek and found it damp with tears she had been unaware of shedding. Acutely embarrassed, she wiped them quickly away and stirred her coffee.

A small group of people out in the hall seemed, she realized at that moment, to be looking in her direction. And then the maître d'hôtel came hurrying toward her table. His face, she saw, was very pale.

Virginia's heart lurched with sudden, crushing terror, and she jumped up, overturning her cup so that coffee ran over the white cloth and down onto the carpet.

"What is it?" Her voice was tight with fear.

The maître d'hôtel leaned close, his mouth almost against her ear so that other guests would not hear and be upset. "Will you please come, Madame Locke. Your husband—"

But Virginia was ahead of him already, running, oblivious of heads craning at every table. The maître d'hôtel paused to pick up her handbag and to stub out her cigarette and to direct a waiter to clear the spilled coffee and change the cloth; and then he followed her, wishing, for once in his life, that he were not in charge, that he were still a young waiter without responsibilities.

At the door of the gentlemen's cloakroom, two men, one the attendant, barred Virginia's way.

"Let me pass," she said quietly, and something in the timbre of her voice cut through the silence, and they moved aside.

Andrew lay near the door, facedown on the stone floor. One of his arms was outstretched, fingers spread, as if reaching for something, the other arm folded unnaturally beneath him. A man with dark skin, curly black hair and wearing a snowy white shirt was kneeling beside Andrew, about to place his own folded jacket beneath his cheek. He stopped when he saw Virginia.

For one more brief moment, she clung to hope. She opened her mouth to scream at the men standing around like a small, silent Greek chorus. *Do something*, she wanted to scream at them. *Fetch help!*

But she did not scream, or even speak. She stood frozen, and the stranger beside her husband began to move again, placed the jacket beneath Andrew's poor, dead face, as if it might protect him from the cold, hard stone. And then he stood and, unable to look Virginia in the eye, withdrew.

The maître d'hôtel, uncertain how best to aid her, took her arm, gently, for a moment, and then, feeling how rigid she was, released her again. Later on, he would tell others how greatly her courage had impressed him. But it had nothing to do with courage. Virginia stood alone. She felt brittle, like an aged, hollowed-out tree. True feeling, she knew, would come later, for she knew all about desolation and grief and loss and agony. For now, she felt nothing. Dead.

A voice somewhere behind her muttered, "*Voyage de noces*," and Virginia became conscious that a little crowd had gathered in the hall. Sympathetic words rippled toward her, tiny, icy stabbings of pity. And she stirred, then, and turned to the maître d'hôtel, to the poor, white-faced man.

"Would you please clear the room, Monsieur?" Her voice was low and almost steady.

"Of course, Madame."

They melted swiftly away, respectfully, their murmurs receding.

"Shall I leave you, Madame?" the maître d'hôtel asked.

"Please."

He closed the door. They were alone together.

*   *   *

In the *Daily Express* the morning after Andrew's death, a few indifferent lines were printed:

Following the news that his "angels" have flown, producer Peter March has announced that he is abandoning plans for a new production of *Hedda Gabler*.

Sebastian, sitting in the first row of the aircraft carrying him to Nice, read the follow-up lines almost mechanically, hardly noticing the tiny, involuntary jolt of reaction produced by the words. The same response that yesterday's column had provoked. He had wondered at it for an instant then, and then the faint headache he had woken with had taken a fiercer grip, and he had forgotten.

This morning, Sebastian was buried in sorrow, wrapped in his blanket of grief. The words meant nothing to him.

c h a p t e r
12

The funeral took place on a wet and windy afternoon just sixteen days after the wedding. Andrew was buried beside Diana in Hampstead Cemetery, and many of those who came to give their support and comfort to Virginia and Sebastian were the same people who had shared in their joy a fortnight earlier. Both Virginia's sons were present this time, as well as Andrew's own colleagues and clients, and there were more than enough of the rich and famous to attract the press. Most came for the grieving widow and son, but some still came because of Diana Lancaster, who had introduced many of them so lovingly to the unassuming, attractive barrister three decades earlier.

Sebastian stood beside his stepmother, his right hand lightly placed beneath her arm, reassuring rather than supporting. Virginia, petite beside him, was pale and resolute, her characteristic dignity perfectly maintained, and Sebastian knew that only he could feel the unbearable tension that charged her whole body; and even when the heavy clods of wet earth were shoveled onto the lid of the coffin, he doubted if anyone else observed the tremors of grief that shook her.

The matter of his father's place of burial had troubled Sebastian deeply, for it had always been understood that Andrew would lie beside Diana. Now, of course, that no longer seemed right to Sebastian, yet Virginia had no such qualms.

"Andrew belonged to your mother for almost thirty years," she had said to Sebastian. "He never belonged to me. I just borrowed him for a little while."

"He loved you completely."

"I know that," Virginia said, and squeezed his hand, grateful to him for his thoughtfulness. "But still, it seems only right that your parents should lie together, and you mustn't feel that it diminishes what Andrew and I shared."

Sebastian found it hard to speak about their loss without weeping. The shocking suddenness, and the desperate sadness of the timing of his father's death, had devastated him, but he found that he was a man able to mourn, naturally and intuitively, without the shame and embarrassment that seemed to stifle some people at such times.

"He was the best father I could ever have imagined," he told Jeremy in the crowded drawing room at The Oaks after the funeral. "He was everything to me, father, friend, even partner. He was the most sensible man, and yet"—he poured himself a second whisky and lit a cigarette—"and yet the emotional side always mattered most; he never made a decision for the sake of common sense if it was going to cause anyone grief."

"He was my hero," Jeremy said, quietly.

"Was he?" Sebastian didn't hide his surprise. "I didn't know."

"No reason why you should have known." Jeremy shrugged. "Don't suppose Andrew knew either. He knew I respected him, must have known I liked him." He paused. "I haven't found that many people to admire—intensely admire, that is."

"I've always thought you admired your father."

"Yes." Jeremy smiled wryly. "Mostly for putting up with my mother, and me, come to that. I admired Louis Schwartz, not only for giving me a chance in New York. But your dad—I think he was a hero from the beginning, when we were in kindergarten. He was my idea of a Viking lord, and he was always there for you."

"He was very fond of you," Sebastian said, softly. "I remember the day I sprang the idea of our partnership on him, and he hardly hesitated for an instant."

"He knew I'd never let you down," Jeremy said.

* * *

The funeral over, there were other decisions to be made. Virginia's possessions had all been transferred to The Oaks before the wedding, and Sebastian was determined that she should remain in the house.

"But it's your home," Virginia protested.

"Neither technically nor morally," Sebastian said.

"If I'd been living here with Andrew, I'd probably agree with you, but we never spent a single night here together."

Sebastian was adamant. "I have a home of my own," he said. "It suits me, I like it. Dad intended that you should live in his house, and if you choose not to—and I can't stop you, of course—then I suppose it'll have to be sold." He paused. "Which I would hate more than I can begin to tell you."

"That sounds like emotional blackmail," Virginia said, gently.

"I'm sorry." He thought for a moment. "How about a compromise? You settle in, for a while—Ellie's already told me she'd like to stay on. And if you'll have me, I'll stay with you both until you feel at ease."

"And if I don't feel at ease?"

"Then we'll think again."

Sebastian stayed for four weeks. For the first two, visitors came and went in a steady stream. He and Virginia were alternately relieved and irritated by the callers; they wanted to be alone, yet they recognized their need to be occupied and surrounded, for it postponed the time when their loneliness would be inescapable.

Two weeks after the visitors stopped coming, Sebastian moved back to Mayfair. It was selfish of him, he was aware, yet sensible. The house that he had loved all his life, and which he had looked forward to having filled again with happiness and warmth, now seemed cold and gray. And he knew that he had to leave Virginia to make her own way, before she grew too dependent on his companionship. He hoped that she would elect to remain permanently at The Oaks, but he promised that if she decided she could not face it alone, he would help her to search for a new home.

It was time, too, to return fully to work. Through the early weeks, Jeremy had shouldered the burden, but the agency's success did not seem, fortunately, to yield to bereavement, and it was apparent that operations had to return to normal if they did not want to put that hard-won success at risk. Back at Locke Mariner, Sebastian became even more aware of how intensely he was going to miss his father. He seemed to see Andrew in everything he did; he had been so instrumental in almost every weighty decision Sebastian had ever made.

It was early in August when Virginia invited Sebastian to the house to start the inevitable sifting through of Andrew's belongings.

"There are some things," she said, "that you might prefer to handle personally. I know we both dread it, but I suppose it has to be done."

"Are you sure you're ready?" Sebastian asked, knowing that he was not, might never be.

"Of course I'm not," Virginia said. "But better get it over with, don't you think?"

"Tomorrow morning?"

"I'll expect you."

Virginia had made a start by the time Sebastian arrived, and neat stacks of Andrew's suits, shirts, ties and pullovers lay on the four-poster in the master bedroom.

"One pile, I thought, for one of the charities," she said, quite briskly, though the redness of her eyes made it apparent she had been weeping over her work. "Those few items, on that side, I'd like to keep—foolish, I know, but I particularly loved him in that blue pullover, and the tie was his favorite."

"I gave it to him, several birthdays ago."

"He told me." Virginia made an effort, and went on. "I wasn't sure if you wanted this kind of keepsake or not—maybe you can pop up later and have a rummage."

"I will." Sebastian hesitated. "I thought, perhaps, if you didn't mind, I might try tackling Dad's study."

"No," Virginia said. "I don't mind a bit. All that paperwork." She paused, guessing that Sebastian was trying to protect her from personal mementoes relating to Andrew's first marriage. "He was quite a hoarder, wasn't he?"

There was a light tap at the door and Ellie looked in.

"Would you be ready for a cup of tea yet?"

Sebastian smiled. "I haven't even begun yet, so I don't think I deserve one."

Ellie's lower lip quivered, but she bit on it firmly. "Just thinking about this kind of work takes tea," she insisted. "I'll make it good and strong."

*　*　*

Sebastian had not entered the study since his father's death, and now he realized that it was because, of all the rooms in the house, this one was Andrew's most personal place, and with the door closed behind him, Sebastian felt his presence most acutely.

Sitting down behind the desk and inserting one of his father's keys into the locked center drawer, Sebastian wavered, abhorring the intrusion into what had been private. But there was no alternative.

He found few surprises. A few files for which Andrew's partners had been searching; copies of legal documents and some important letters; a collection of his own schoolboy letters from Marchmont; and most of his correspondence from Edinburgh. This proof of the loving, nostalgic aspect of his father's character moved Sebastian deeply, and he set them to one side to look at more closely later, before turning to the first of the three steel cabinets against the wall, in which he found the store of memories from which he had wished to protect Virginia: four thick leather albums containing clippings of articles and reviews of Diana's performances, scores of photographs and, tied with red ribbon, her love letters . . .

It was in the last cabinet that he found the books. He picked the first from the top of the pile, idly glancing at its title, and then he took the others, one by one, and placed them slowly on the desk.

He went, after a little while, to fetch Virginia.

"Have you seen them before?" he asked her.

She shook her head, as baffled as he was. "Never. Andrew never expressed the remotest interest in psychology or psychiatry. And since my first husband was a psychiatrist, it would have been bound to come up in conversation, wouldn't you think?"

"Perhaps," Sebastian suggested, "they're something to do with a case he was working on."

"Should I send them to his office?"

Sebastian thought. "If they're needed, they're bound to be asked for. I should just forget about them if I were you." He felt a strong desire to put the books back where he had found them. He didn't want to look at them anymore; he felt as if they had touched on something a little morbid and somehow distasteful.

But later that night, after Sebastian had gone home, and Ellie had retired to bed, Virginia returned to the study and unlocked the cabinet again. The discovery had unsettled her, and she found herself wondering whether there might perhaps be some connection between those ugly books and the mystery that had so acutely distressed Andrew in the weeks before his death.

The books all had one topic in common: mental illness. Individually, their subject matter ranged from neuroses, obsessions and compulsions to depressions, psychoses and schizophrenia. Might it, Virginia wondered, have been some awful, irrational fear about his own state of health that had caused Andrew's haunted, pinched look before the wedding?

"No," she said aloud. "It's too absurd."

And yet his bizarre switch of behavior on the last day of his life forced her to consider it, making her shiver with misery. The books, she noticed, were all marked in numerous places, some with bookmarks, but in some places the corners of pages had been turned over, a habit of which Andrew had strongly disapproved.

Virginia opened the first book, then shut it again. She felt utterly drained, emotionally and physically. She had done too much, too soon, and besides, what was there to be gained now by burrowing into what might have been one of the few dark patches in Andrew's life? He had known sadness, of course, even tragedy, but overall, his seventy years had been filled with success and light. Better, by far, to dwell on that.

She sighed and stood up, replaced the books again on the top shelf and turned away. And then, as an afterthought, she locked the cabinet carefully, and went slowly and wearily upstairs to bed.

c h a p t e r
13

K atharine Andersen, with her lovely, active life, her wonderful, caring David and their perfect Manhattan apartment, was restless. It was hard to understand why that should be so. She grew angry with herself, wondering if she was destined to become one of those perpetually dissatisfied women who invariably wanted whatever it was that they did not have.

"Do you think I'm too much like my mother?" she asked Sam Raphael, in one of her attempts at self-analysis.

Sam frowned. "There wasn't much wrong with Louise, you know, except that she never stopped loving Jake, but wouldn't admit it."

"Yet she withdrew from their marriage." Katharine knew she was being tactless, knew that it was hardly an appropriate conversation to have with her stepfather, but they'd been this route before, numerous times, and she knew that Sam, remarkably perhaps, didn't seem to mind.

"She only withdrew because her grief over Annie was too intense for her to handle."

"So how come I feel this urge to withdraw from David?" she asked, helplessly.

Sam smiled. "No one can answer that question except you. And maybe David. Talk to him."

* * *

With no work on the immediate horizon, and with Laszlo Eles out of reach in Europe, Katharine's sense of being trapped, and her guilt about feeling that way, grew stronger. She knew Sam was right, knew that the one person she ought to trust with her emotions was David, but it was late November, one night just after Thanksgiving when they were getting ready for bed, before she found the courage to tackle him.

"It isn't you," she said, desperately anxious to minimize the hurt she knew she was bound to cause him. "It isn't one single thing to do with you—it's all me, inside me."

"I know that," David said. He sat on the edge of the bed, his face suddenly pale. "In a way, I wish I didn't. At least if it was something I was doing wrong, maybe I could try to fix it."

"No," Katharine said quickly, sitting down beside him. "You mustn't even think about fixing anything about yourself. I love you just the way you are. It isn't you."

There was a moment of silence, and then David got up and walked over to the window.

"What scares me most, I guess," he said, slowly, "is that the problem may not be either with you or with me. That it may be 'us,' that maybe we're not meant to be a couple."

"But we're a wonderful couple," Katharine said.

David sighed, and in that moment, Katharine saw the fear in his eyes, and she knew that he was frightened of losing her, and she had a great urge to go to him and put her arms around him, to hold him and try to make him feel as safe as he always made her feel. But this was not the time. It had taken her too long to come to this point, and there was no sense in going back until it was all out in the open.

"Okay," David said, suddenly. "I have a suggestion."

"You do?" Katharine, too, was frightened now.

"It's strictly a short-term idea, it doesn't really resolve anything, but it may just give you the breathing space you need. Your uncle —your great-uncle—"

"Henrik?"

"He writes often, doesn't he? And isn't he always inviting you to visit him in Denmark?"

"Sure, but—"

"Why not go?" David's brown eyes were keen again now, the fear gone for the moment and optimism taking its place. "A trip abroad, on your own, to your father's homeland, might be just what you need."

"You could come with me," Katharine said.

"That would sort of defeat the object, don't you think?" He came back to the bed and, drawing her gently closer, kissed her hair. "Stop thinking about me, for just a little while, okay? This trip is for you, all for you. I'll still be here when you get back."

"Are you sure?"

"Of what? That I'll be here?"

"That you don't mind."

"I mind," David said. "But I need you to be happy."

Katharine arrived in Copenhagen in the middle of December. She had not been in Europe since she was five years old, and although in some ways she might have wished to satisfy her longing to see London or Paris as an adult, before any other city, this felt like a safer, more appropriate entry into another world. In England and France she had no family, knew no one. Here, at least, she had her great-uncle.

"This is wonderful, wonderful," Henrik exulted when he met her at the airport. "You are beautiful, beautiful, just as I thought you would be!" He put his left arm around her and hugged her warmly. "Did you know," he asked, easily, "that I have only one arm?"

"Daddy told me, and my grandmother," Katharine said, but she was glad, nonetheless, that Henrik had mentioned it in such a relaxed manner, for the first glimpse of his empty right coat sleeve had, in spite of her preparedness, shaken her a little.

"How is Karen?" Henrik asked as he took her luggage trolley from her and walked beside her toward the exit. "She hasn't written in quite a while."

"She's quite poorly these days, I think, though she's so well defended by Mrs. Nielsen, her nurse-companion, that it's sometimes hard to discover anything about her, let alone get through to see her."

"What is she like, this Gudrun Nielsen? Does she care properly for Karen?"

"No doubt about it. She's very starchy—"

"Starchy?" Henrik queried.

"Stiff, formal. But I've watched them together, and she's quite different with my grandmother, very gentle and rather humorous. I think they're good friends."

They emerged into the sunlight. It was bright and invigoratingly cold, and Katharine was grateful for her fur-lined coat.

"You will need a hat," Henrik told her. "It isn't windy today, but you'll find it has quite a bite to it when it blows."

"Are we taking a taxi?"

Her great-uncle shook his head. "I brought the car. If you wait here with the bags, I'll bring it to you." He looked at her and laughed. "You're wondering how I can drive without my right arm."

"No, I'm sure you—"

"I have a specially converted little car, and I drive like a demon. Are you afraid?"

"Terrified."

Henrik Andersen was sixty, just four years older than his nephew, Jake, would have been had he lived, the closeness of their ages the result of Henrik's father's late second marriage. He was tall and broad, with snowy-white hair and blue, piercing eyes, and as Katharine had already experienced, capable of bestowing an almost bearlike hug in spite of having only one arm.

He had lost his right arm in the early days of the war, in a training accident while serving with the Danish army. Burning with frustration and fury as the Germans had invaded his country, Henrik had been forced to sit on the sidelines with his fellow Danes with the knowledge that, even if he had been able-bodied, since this invasion had been labeled a "peaceful occupation" supposedly carried out to protect the country's neutrality, there was no official state of war between Denmark and Germany.

Until August of 1943, the country's internal affairs, though closely influenced by the Nazis, had still fallen legally under Danish rule. When the government resigned that August, however, Germany had stepped up its powers, but by that time, the resistance movement in Denmark had been running like a magnificently oiled, human machine.

Even without his right arm, Henrik had vowed to play his part to the full. In the early days, when the seeds of resistance were still being sown in London, Henrik trained his left arm and hand, forcing himself on and on until he felt confident and capable. It was not enough for Henrik to be able to write legibly, or to make love to Anne-Marie, his wife, or change his baby son's diapers; Henrik wanted to be capable of riding his bicycle, of learning to use a secret transmitter, of loading and firing a pistol and of breaking a Nazi's neck.

To this end, he had used his tireless self-training and sheer willpower to anesthetize the pain he still suffered, doing anything and everything that might help his left hand to become more dexterous, even taking on his wife's sewing, holding a stick in his mouth as a primitive substitute for his right hand. Although Henrik had never fought a single German directly, he had assisted with the printing of one of the various Resistance newspapers, and had taken part in numerous strikes and demonstrations. And, most notably, in the first days of October of 1943, days nominated by the Nazis for the roundup and deportation of the Jewish population, Henrik had, in a small way, helped in coordinating the successful rescue and transportation to safety in Sweden of 90 percent of Hitler's intended victims.

Anne-Marie, his wife, had died two years after the end of the war, and, unable to tolerate their family home in Jutland without her, Henrik had brought Erik, their son, and Agnes, their daughter, to Copenhagen, taking a lovely, spacious apartment on Esplanaden, an elegant street facing Winston Churchill Park. The apartment was just a short walk from the harbor, from Kastellet, the seventeenth-century citadel, and from the museum of the Danish resistance movement. It seemed, to Henrik, a perfectly suitable location for him, with its poignant reminders of terrible and glorious years, and yet he realized that at least he would not remain as rooted in the past as if he had stayed in Jutland.

"My brother," he explained to Katharine during their first afternoon together, "died before the war, and his widow, Karen—"

"My grandmother."

"That's right. She took their only son, Jacob—your papa—to America in 1934."

"You must have been very lonely," Katharine said, "after you lost your wife."

"Of course, but I still had the children, thank God, and I still had many wonderful friends from my resistance days. And to occupy myself I had kept one out of the three antique shops that my brother and I had owned before his death. It's still here, still open, in Bredgade—you must visit it."

"I'd love to." Katharine paused. "But neither Erik nor Agnes lives in Copenhagen now, do they?"

Henrik shook his head, filled his pipe with tobacco and lit it. "You don't mind the smoke?"

"I like it."

He puffed for a moment. "Erik lives in Stockholm with his family, and Agnes in Aalborg, in the north."

He had five grandchildren, he told Katharine, but alas, he saw too little of them, and few of his old friends were still alive, and so his life had quieted, his horizons had narrowed. He still went, most days, to the business, but it was perfectly managed, and he sometimes felt that he was more in the way than of real use, and with the rest of his time he walked his two miniature schnauzers—now sitting beside him on the settee—and listened to music, and smoked one of the many pipes from his collection.

The dogs, a bitch named Fanny and her brother, Asger, were the chief reason behind Henrik's reluctance to travel far afield. They were his constant companions, going almost everywhere with him, and while Asger had nearly pined to death on the one occasion Henrik had left them in a kennel, it had taken Fanny a month to recover from her panic after the only flight she had ever endured.

"Since then," Henrik said, "I have only left Copenhagen if I could travel either by car or by train—the dogs love trains." He paused. "That was part of the reason that I didn't come to America for your parents' funeral, but only part."

"I understood," Katharine said.

"No, I don't think so. The real truth was that Jacob's death brought back my own losses, long ago as they were, and I'm afraid that I became very depressed for a time afterward."

"I didn't know. Your letters were so wonderful, and the fact that they kept on coming. They comforted me far more than one short visit might have done, especially as I don't think I was taking in too much at the time."

"I hoped you would come here, to me," Henrik said. "Jacob used to write to me about you, while you were small, then while you were growing up. He was so proud of you, your papa—he always sent me copies of the programs of the plays you were acting in at school, and then later, when you were designing at university."

"I was very proud of him," Katharine said, softly.

"You miss him very much, of course, and your mother." Henrik's pipe had gone out, and he lit it again. "I met Louise only twice, when they came to visit me. She was a beautiful woman, and very intelligent, and gentle, I thought."

"Yes, she was, all those things."

"You look much more like Jacob than her. Your coloring, your height, though your eyes"—Henrik peered closer—"I never saw eyes such a color before—your photographs did not do them justice."

They got along wonderfully well. Henrik was young for his age, a warm, vigorous man with a fine sense of humor and a great capacity for enjoyment. Katharine was fascinated, at last, to be able to see the city in which her father had grown up, and her great-uncle was delighted to show it to her. Copenhagen, he told Katharine, was not at its best, for Tivoli, as popular with the Danes as with tourists, was closed for the winter months, and besides, it was very cold; but on the other hand, Christmas was just two weeks away, and there was an air of festivity in the streets, and in the restaurants, bars, cafés and stores. Henrik drove Katharine right around the city, walked her through all the museums, took her to Christiansborg Castle to see Parliament in action, and drove her across to Jutland to see where her grandparents had lived.

"It's all so unlike anything I imagined before I came," Katharine told Henrik. "When I thought about Copenhagen, I had an image of a compact little town, rather colorful and quaint, I suppose. Whereas in fact it's much more spacious and stately—all those impressive, dignified old buildings and those wonderful, elegant squares."

One of the city's greatest charms was that one moment one could be strolling along a narrow, cobbled side street and the next one might emerge into space and splendor. Having grown up in Washington, D.C., Katharine was, of course, accustomed to handsome, venerable architecture, but this was all so *old*.

"I sound like a real American tourist, don't I?" she laughed.

"That's what you are," Henrik said comfortably. "Nothing wrong in that."

"I'll tell you what else is wonderful," Katharine went on enthusiastically. "Your air. It smells cleaner and clearer than any I've ever breathed. And you don't have traffic jams—and I don't know if it's just because it's too cold for sensible people to be out on the streets, but compared to what I've grown used to in New York City, this is almost deserted."

As she relaxed and unwound, Katharine began to see Copenhagen as a huge, sprawling stage set, felt her creative juices starting to flow as she wandered around. She bought a sketchpad, pencils, charcoal and pastels, and once Henrik had left her to herself, she worked as she went, gathering ideas for future, as-yet-unknown projects.

The statues, she thought, were marvelous, for Copenhagen was full of highly original, often impressive sculptures: the Bull and Dragon fountain in Rådhuspladsen, the Water Mother in the Glyptotek, the extraordinary Gefion fountain in the park near Langelinie, close to Henrik's apartment. Sitting alone, after a long morning's chilly sketching, in a comfortable, snug brasserie at a window table overlooking Kongens Nytorv, the city's largest square, Katharine saw the Danish Royal Theatre over to the right, and the baroque structure of Charlottenborg opposite; and she had a sense of gazing out over a grayish but magnificent stage scene into which an invisible master hand was adding a cast, for added conviction, of motor cars and pedestrians, and bicycles and dogs.

But it was in the home that Copenhagen's true charms and its approachability were most evident. Her great-uncle's five rooms were filled with antiques, yet they were still snug, cozy rooms. It was possible to sprawl on a settee eating a sandwich, without feeling a trace of guilt, and the fact that Fanny and Asger were allowed to bury their bones beneath silk cushions and to sleep on the beds at night made Katharine feel even more comfortable and at home.

"I'm ready now," she told Henrik, after ten days. It was almost eleven o'clock in the evening, and they were listening to a Chopin piano concerto in the sitting room.

"For what?"

"You told me I should tell you when I was ready to talk over the problems that brought me here." She paused. "It's taken me until now, when I'm almost due to go back home, but I think I'm about as ready as I'll ever be."

"Then let me light my pipe, and get really comfortable, and then we can begin."

Katharine waited until Henrik was settled.

"The fact is," she said, "I guess I don't really have any problems." She paused. "Or rather, I feel so damned guilty about feeling that I do—have problems, that is. Are you following me?"

"Not yet."

"My life, since I moved in with David, has been wonderful. Happy, comfortable, well ordered. Fun, even. And David is about as good and fine and loving as any man could be."

"Go on."

Henrik let Katharine talk, encouraged her to let it all out, a little at a time or, sometimes, in rapid, if brief, bursts. His great-niece, he felt, had been brought up perhaps a touch too correctly; her education and environment had taught her too much restraint, a little too much reserve. It was as if because Katharine was aware that she led a privileged life from the point of wealth and luxury, she felt ashamed of feeling, or at least admitting to feeling, fear or unhappiness. And life, Henrik thought, had not been so overly kind to her. First, the loss of her little sister, an untimely introduction to sickness and death, then her parents' divorce and then their own tragic deaths. And because she had been twenty-one when that had happened, Henrik surmised, and an adult, Katharine had not let herself admit to her true feelings: that deep down, she was just a child, an orphan, alone and afraid.

"Your David," he said, when she had, at last, finished, "sounds like a very decent man."

"He is."

"But if you are not sure about him, then perhaps he isn't the right man for you." Henrik tapped ashes out of his pipe. "Life is long, and full, and worth living to its best, my dear Katharine. The man you choose to spend it with must be that right man. Elusive, sometimes, but you have to keep on looking until you're certain."

"How can I be certain?"

"You will know when you are, take my word for it. You're too special—everyone is too special—for second-best."

"But David Rothman *is* the best."

"For someone else, maybe. Not necessarily for Katharine Andersen." He struck a match, puffed at his pipe for a few moments, then blew out the match and went on. "A surgeon, like Jacob, is fine, of course. And a good man is even better. But where is it written that a bus driver or an actor, or a writer or a lawyer might not be better for you, just for *you*?"

Katharine said nothing.

"I think you wanted me to tell you to stay safely with your David. Is that right, do you think? I think that you are afraid to hurt this kind, good man, and afraid of the emptiness if you leave him."

"Maybe," she said quietly. "I'm often afraid."

"We are all afraid, much more often than we like to admit." Henrik paused again. "I cannot, will not advise you to choose either way in such an important matter. But I do advise you to listen to your inner voices, to your heart, and to take heed. Take your time, Katharine, take all the time you need. And be a little kinder to yourself."

*   *   *

David did not fight her over her decision to move back into her own apartment. Katharine had waited until after Christmas to break it to him, partly because she had wanted to feel quite certain in her own mind that she was doing the right thing, and partly because she couldn't bear to make David miserable in the middle of the festive season. But in the event, her anxiety had made her so jumpy and strained that she had known she was spoiling it all for him anyway, and she felt ashamed of herself for that. Guilt, guilt, guilt—she was weary of feeling guilty. Henrik was right; this was no basis for any long-term commitment, let alone for marriage.

She left on New Year's morning, 1974, after the most sublime night they had ever spent together. They had made love with a combination of desperation and tenderness, and Katharine had felt closer to David than ever before. First thing in the morning, when she woke, she felt suffused by warmth and joy—but then it came back to her; her resolution to leave and the months of confusion and heart-searching that had gone before, and it seemed both foolish and wrong to go back on her painfully made decision now.

"This isn't the end of anything," she said to him, wanting to cling to him, wanting to hold on to their last moments in the warm, secure bed. "At least not so far as I'm concerned. Though I'd understand if you wanted to finish it."

"You know I don't," he answered. "You know that I don't want you to leave, either, though I think I understand."

"Do you?"

"I'm trying to."

He was a rock all through the rest of that morning, putting a brave face on the misery of it all, taking her over to her place himself, insisting on carrying her bags. Katharine had stressed repeatedly that she was just stepping back a pace so that she could examine her feelings more rationally, but she knew that it was far too large a pace for David, who had no doubts about her, no fears, no qualms, only love and care and respect.

"Shall I put on some coffee?" she asked, awkwardly, once they were inside her apartment and the front door was closed.

"Not for me, thank you."

"Okay." Katharine felt so inadequate and so cruel that her voice trembled, and David was white-faced, and she felt that he was close to breaking, and knew that she should let him go.

"Well," he said, "I guess you need some time to unpack, get used to the place again."

She nodded. "It's going to be strange."

"Yes." His eyes were dark and sad. "For me, too."

"Will I see you later? I mean—"

David's smile was small and wan. "Back to dating. I've always hated dating."

"We're not back to that," Katharine said, desperately. "I'm not throwing it all away, David, I swear it, it means too much to me."

"I know that." He shifted a little. "But if you don't mind, I think I'll take a rain check—let's leave it for today, okay? Give us both a chance to settle down."

"Okay," she said, miserably.

"Call me, if you need me." He took her left hand in his; it was the first time he'd touched her since they'd entered the apartment. "I mean that. Anything you want, any problems."

"The same goes for me," Katharine said, and her voice was husky with tears ripe and ready to fall. "I love you, David."

"I love you, too, Katharine."

She began to weep the instant the door closed behind him, only just held back the sobs until she was sure he was out of earshot, and then she sat down on the creamy, still almost pristine sofa—her own, lonely, cold sofa—and she sobbed for a long, long time. And then she found a bottle of wine, and got herself drunk, and entered the first afternoon of the new year more confused and wretched than ever.

Karen Andersen died in February, and the funeral brought back dark memories for Katharine, but she was aware that her gloom was even more deeply rooted than that. Living alone again, seeing David two or three times a week but always coming back to her own bed, Katharine's sense of her life being an ill-fitting jigsaw did not lift.

She acknowledged how intensely she missed living with David, but she remembered too vividly how she had felt before, and although she realized that she was likely to lose him altogether if this unsatisfactory period of limbo continued for much longer, she felt powerless to change the course of events.

It was in April, thirteen months after the mugging and their meeting, that David told Katharine that the situation had become intolerable for him, that he could no longer bear it. That he was thirty-three years old, not twenty, and that he would sooner not see her at all than have this maddening, tiny share of her.

"I still love you, you know that, don't you?" he said, when he'd finished telling her that it was over. "I would marry you in an instant, if I thought it was what you wanted."

"I know." Katharine's voice was only a whisper.

"But it isn't, is it?"

"I can't," she said.

And this time when he went, out of her apartment and out of her life, there were no more tears for Katharine, and hardly any pain. It was much worse than that, for she felt nothing at all.

Only dull acceptance.

c h a p t e r

14

The bar of the Carlton Hotel on the penultimate night of the 1974 Cannes Film Festival was mobbed, smoky and reeking of whisky, pernod and a stifling mix of perfumes. Sebastian, reluctant to go farther into the crowd, stood at the entrance, looking for Jeremy. Many of the drinkers were red-eyed and heavy-lidded from the battle fatigue of the days and nights that had gone before; some of them looked crumpled and seedy, their faces, if not their clothes, looking slept in.

Sebastian spotted Jeremy seated at the bar, glass in hand.

"Sorry to be late. What are you drinking?" He checked Jeremy's glass, then signaled to the barman. *"Comme d'habitude, s'il vous plaît, monsieur."*

"How did it go?" Jeremy asked.

"Well." Sebastian looked around. "We'll talk details upstairs, but they want Barbara so badly we can practically write our own contract."

"They know she won't travel without the boy?"

Sebastian nodded. "And that she has to be in London two weeks before Christmas. All agreed."

Since Barbara Stone had come to Locke Mariner as their first big name, she had never regretted the move. She had filmed a comedy thriller with Michael Caine in 1972 that had become a huge box-office success, and her last London play had transferred to Broadway to rave reviews. With her old television series being repeated in the United States at peak viewing times, and with several successful talk show appearances under her belt, including two with Johnny Carson in the space of six months, Barbara was being hailed as almost an American. Only last month, her photograph had appeared on the cover of *Today* after her Tony nomination, and now, in Cannes, Sebastian had, for the first time, consolidated the kind of financial deal that her new star status merited.

"Have you called her?" Jeremy asked.

"Not yet." Sebastian tasted his Armagnac, enjoying its slight roughness, and a slow smile spread over his face. The business today had been executed in the agreeable atmosphere of the Negresco in Nice, but the festival was exhausting. He knew that it would be a long time tonight before his over-stimulated brain slowed down enough to allow his body rest, which was probably just as well, since he had a long drive ahead of him.

"Still leaving town tonight?" Jeremy asked, reading his mind.

"Definitely."

Sebastian disliked Cannes at the best of times, and this was certainly not the best, but while this town might be suffering indignities, there was still a wealth of charm and beauty in easy reach, and he had long since promised himself that he would leave this evening and drive up into the hills to Saint-Paul-de-Vence, where he had made a reservation at the Colombe d'Or.

"Why don't you come up with me, Jerry?" he asked, aware that it was a pointless question, since Jeremy thrived on the festival atmosphere, and his company for the evening and night was almost certainly lined up and waiting. Jeremy, Sebastian knew, seldom slept alone.

The Locke Mariner business partnership was looked upon these days as one of the most forceful in the business, but as their success had grown, so had their own acceptance that they were, as individuals, still immensely dissimilar. Sebastian and Jeremy had different tastes in almost everything, and contrasting life-styles, and yet there was one parallel in their lives, never discussed between them, that had nothing to do with the agency. Sex without love. But there, too, were vast differences, for Jeremy was bisexual and, increasingly, promiscuous. It had been rumored, jokingly but maliciously, that Jeremy Mariner would sleep with anything that moved—even a rabbit, if it was good-looking enough, and though Jeremy had heard the gossip, he did not trouble to try to squash it. He was highly sexed, perhaps oversexed, and, like Sebastian, he had never been involved in a loving sexual relationship. But unlike his partner, it was not because he was incapable of mixing the two. Jeremy knew precisely why it was. He loved Sebastian. Was in love with Sebastian. Had always been in love with him, he sometimes thought. And would never, if they both lived to be a hundred, tell him how he felt.

Jeremy suffered for it, had always known that while Sebastian was more than fond of him, cared for him deeply and had a respect for him uninfluenced by any amount of rumor or malice, Sebastian could never return his love. Sebastian Locke was the best, the brightest, the most decent man Jeremy knew. There was nothing shabby or cheap or mean about him; as an adult he was the same golden boy he had been at school, a man incapable of betrayal or of deliberate unkindness. But Sebastian was entirely heterosexual.

Jeremy had a good life. He had a luxurious home in Chelsea, he drove a Morgan, he had plenty of money and the great good fortune to thrive on his work, yet Sebastian was still the best part of his life. He had learned how to cope with his feelings, knew that it was wiser, on a night such as this one, to remain in Cannes while Sebastian went alone up to Saint-Paul. Jeremy knew how to live every day to the full, was aware of the pain that he suppressed, but he knew, too, that he would never walk out on his partner, whatever the cost to him, emotionally, of staying.

It took Sebastian twenty minutes to maneuver his rented Mercedes out of the town. The Croisette this evening was a menace, with too many drivers and pedestrians apparently incapacitated by drink or drugs, and Sebastian was glad he had restricted himself to just the one Armagnac. Outside the Martinez, the road was blocked by a Volkswagen and a Citroën involved in an accident; the damage looked minimal, but the drivers were out of their cars and one of them, a heavyset man in T-shirt and shorts, was cursing and gesticulating. Sebastian sat in the car, resigned and amused, while drivers behind him leaned on their horns, and a pretty young prostitute wandered up to the Mercedes, gave him a good view of her behind and about thirty seconds to make up his mind, before sauntering on to the Fiat behind him.

The quarrel settled and the embattled drivers gunning their engines and driving away, Sebastian put his car into gear, glanced into his rear-view mirror to see the young prostitute moving back to the pavement outside the hotel, and put his foot down on the accelerator. The week had been interesting, and today had been successful and pleasant enough, but now his urge to leave the coast behind him and get up into the hills was intense.

The Côte d'Azur had lost much of its appeal for Sebastian since Andrew's death in Cap d'Antibes. It was not particularly rational, he accepted, to associate a heart attack that might just as well have occurred anywhere else with a place or a part of the world. But whereas in the past touching down at Nice Airport—where the aircraft coasted so low over the blue Mediterranean that one felt almost close enough to touch the tiny white yachts and sailing boats—had always given Sebastian a special pang of delight, these days it only brought back his arrival on the June day in 1972 when he had come to collect his father's body.

It was just before two in the morning when the Mercedes twisted around the last uphill bend and arrived in Saint-Paul-de-Vence. Even the low growl of his engine seemed to disturb the hush of the place, to offend the dark, old walls. The night porter at the Colombe d'Or was dozing, and Sebastian felt almost sinful when, after checking into his room, he left the house again, wanting to stretch his legs.

The view from the garden was not as perfect as he knew, from past experience, it would have been a few hours earlier. Then, the lights all down the hillside, where the tiny villages punctuated the vineyards and flower gardens, would have twinkled profusely. It was very dark now, the moon high and small in the sky, but the incomparable perfume of the region still hung in the air, the soft fragrance of jasmine and mimosa. Sebastian inhaled deeply and realized how completely exhausted he was. His flesh was beginning to throb with that last-ditch weariness it was impossible to deny, and leaving the garden, and passing the night porter, asleep again, he went back to his room.

He undressed, leaving his clothes over a chair, and poured himself a drink from the duty-free bottle of cognac he'd packed in his case. And then he turned out the light and lay naked on the cool sheets, the soft air from the open window caressing his skin while he finished his drink.

After a while, feeling a little chilled, he slipped beneath the covers. He couldn't sleep. His muscles still ached, tiny nerve ends twitched in his legs and arms, and he realized that the cognac had acted as a stimulant, instead of as a relaxant. He lay on his back, his eyes open.

He thought of taking out a book and reading himself to sleep, but it seemed too much of an effort. He thought about Jeremy, wondered, idly, who he was spending the night with in Cannes, and then he thought about Barbara Stone and the contract he'd negotiated on her behalf earlier in the day. He often lay in bed thinking about agency business. Too often.

In the two years since Andrew had died, Locke Mariner had, more than ever, become Sebastian's whole life. As a rich and ongoing pattern of success had unfolded, they had been forced to move to larger offices at the beginning of the year, a few hundred yards further along Albemarle Street. In spite of their continuing desire to keep the expansion of the agency under firm control, Sebastian and Jeremy had realized their obligation to minimize errors that might arise out of understaffing. Elspeth Lehmann still managed the office, of course, but they had brought in two new secretaries, a full-time bookkeeper and a part-time legal adviser. These days, when Sebastian was not at his desk, working out new campaigns or strategies with Jeremy, or trying, with Elspeth, to improve administrative methods, he was in theaters, screening rooms or in the offices and conference rooms of television and film companies. Jeremy was wholly committed to Locke Mariner, but he liked to play as hard as he worked; when offices in Britain closed for the day, Sebastian was on the telephone to clients or companies operating in different time zones, or he was entertaining, or being entertained.

Physically, Sebastian looked and felt fitter than ever. Professionally, he was agile, discerning and as tough as he needed to be. In what private life he allowed himself time for, he was good-natured, discriminating, easygoing and generous. Women continued to move eagerly in and out of his life with exhausting swiftness, but love remained, for him, an undiscovered myth. Sebastian recognized all too clearly the shortcomings of his existence, knew there was too little warmth in it, however satisfying it was in other ways. He continued, regularly, to see Virginia, who had remained, as he had hoped, at The Oaks, involving her wherever possible in agency socializing, but beyond his genuine fondness for his stepmother, he knew no ways to fill the emptiness that Andrew's death had left.

Three months after returning from France, Sebastian and Jeremy, in Los Angeles to help smooth the way for Simon Kean, now on the brink of international success, found themselves unexpectedly faced with a chance to sign Locke Mariner's first big American name. Michael Jaffe was a dark, tousle-haired actor with Slavic features, whose dramatic ability and sex appeal had drawn hundreds of thousands of fans into cinemas in several countries. For more than three years, he had won leading roles in some of the finest and most fortunate films of the period. Michael Jaffe was a star.

Jeremy, in this instance, was the right man in the right place at the perfect moment. Jaffe had just reached agreement with his own agent—a small outfit in Manhattan to whom he had remained loyal since his early days in theater workshops—to the effect that he intended to look for additional representation to cope with the European work he wanted to do. The agent in New York was Louis R. Schwartz, the man who had given Jeremy Mariner his first job in the business. When Jeremy called him from Los Angeles, as he usually did when he was anywhere in the United States, Schwartz put him in touch with Jaffe without hesitation.

"If he likes you," Schwartz told Jeremy, "you and your partner'll have to come to New York so's we can get this straightened out."

"Tomorrow suit you?"

"Tomorrow's the Sabbath, Jeremy."

"Since when are you religious, Lou?"

"I'm getting old," Schwartz said. "I'm hedging my bets."

"Do you think Jaffe will like us?" Jeremy asked.

"I wouldn't have suggested it if I didn't think so."

"How come he isn't going straight to one of the big agencies, Lou? I mean, don't misunderstand me, we're happy he isn't, but most stars of Jaffe's caliber like sheltering under one big umbrella."

"Michael's a Brooklyn kid," Schwartz explained. "Big business brings him out in a rash. He likes intimacy. You and Locke should suit him well."

Jaffe liked Jeremy and Sebastian. He liked Locke Mariner, adored Elspeth Lehmann, loved the way the British offices were run, thought that London was paradise next to New York.

"Don't get me wrong, guys—New York's the greatest city in the world. New York is home. But London's something else." Jaffe sought a word that might make him sound less like every other tourist, but failed. "I guess they're right. London is *class*—you guys are class, all of you."

"What can we say?" Jeremy laughed.

"Thank you about covers it," Sebastian said. "We feel the same way about you."

"One thing," Jaffe said. "How come you don't have an office in New York? I don't mean for me—I'm with Lou Schwartz for keeps, may he go on forever. But Locke Mariner is class, like I said. You'd do great over there too."

"Perhaps," Sebastian said. "One day."

"But not yet," Jeremy confirmed. "We're considering it, but we're not quite ready for that kind of move."

"That's a pity," Jaffe said. "I have a friend—a great actor. He's had the lead in a prime-time show on NBC for nearly four years, and he's getting itchy feet."

"Who is it?" Sebastian asked.

"His name's Sam Raphael."

"Jack Granville in *Star Rider*," Jeremy said.

"That's the one."

"Didn't he play Larry Cotton in *Going Forth*? I'm pretty sure I saw him, in '68, at the Lyceum." Jeremy half closed his eyes. "And is he the Raphael who played Richard the Third with the Folger Theatre in Washington in 1970?"

"I'm impressed," Jaffe said.

Sebastian smiled. "My partner is a walking casting directory."

"Raphael's good," Jeremy said.

"I know it, Sam knows it, but his agent—not unreasonably—thinks that a prime-time Western's the best thing that could happen to an actor past his first flush—Sam's over fifty, but he still has the stuff, and he has a yen to play a theater again."

"And if something big and right comes along," Sebastian said, "unless he's free to grab it with both hands, it may be too late."

"He's talked to me about switching agents," Jaffe said.

"He ought to have someone who respects his needs," Sebastian agreed.

"He needs you guys."

15

"Paris?"

"That's what I said, Katharine."

"You want me to go to Paris, now?"

"Is there something the matter with your ears, *kedves*?"

"It's just that I can't believe it. The timing—"

"You can't go?"

"On the contrary—the timing is just so perfect! If you only knew how much I want to get away, to get out of this city—Laszlo, you're an angel and a genius."

"The second I already knew—the first is news to me."

No sooner had Laszlo Eles returned to New York from his extended trip to Europe than he had contacted Katharine, his favorite assistant, to discuss his next project, a musical to open at the Winter Garden Theatre in October. To be set in and to be titled simply *Paris*, lavishness was to be the key word and the budget was to be sumptuous.

"Book by Gerard Legreque, music by Howard Blaustein, lyrics by Sydney Kane—"

"Designer, Laszlo Eles," Katharine finished for him.

"Of course." Eles smiled. "With Katharine Andersen." He paused.

"And Zizi Markheim has agreed to create the costumes—we are to work together, which may not always be easy—"

"Or peaceful," Katharine added. "Have you met with her yet?"

"In Milan. She knows precisely what she wants, as I do, though we have yet to learn what the composers want, and neither of us, of course, has any intention of giving way either to them or to each other." The Hungarian winked one dark eye at her. "I think the results, in any event, will be miraculous."

"Can I start reading?"

"Right away." Eles paused. "Are you with us, darling Katharine?"

"Of course I'm with you."

"Good. Then take the book, and go pack your bags."

"What for?"

"Paris."

Since Katharine was to be Eles's number one assistant on the show, and since he had come to trust her unreservedly, she found herself playing a much more vital, integral role than on the previous productions on which they'd worked together. Laszlo knew Paris inside out, but he wanted Katharine to familiarize herself with the city, too, and so he had decided to send her, for the whole month of June, to stay at the Ritz, since *Paris* was to have three sets: one in a suite at the most famous hotel in the world, one in a Saint-Germain street café and one in the Luxembourg gardens.

"I see Paris, *kedves*," he told Katharine, "through the eyes of the Impressionists, and though I want our audiences to feel, as accurately, as realistically as possible, that they are inside the Ritz and in the park, and idling away an afternoon in the café, I want them, at the same time, to be absorbed into the fabric—into the soul of the city."

"I understand."

Eles shook his head. "Impossible, until you have seen it for yourself. If you are truly to understand what I hope to achieve for this show, you must experience the great works of art side by side with Paris itself. You must taste it, *kedves*, smell it, feel it."

Katharine immersed herself in Paris, thought of it as a young girl burying her face in the sweetness and joy of her first bouquet. It was love at first sight, as she had felt sure it would be, and when she stepped out in the mornings into Place Vendôme, it was without hesitation, without the slightest trace of anxiety or even reserve. Any apprehensions she might have had, before her arrival, about coming alone to the city of romance, had melted away in the first hours. A twenty-five-year-old woman in Paris did not need a man at her side in order to take pleasure in the city; Paris alone could make her feel beautiful, make her feel alive and vibrant and unique. Besides, Katharine was not here to make love, she was here to work.

But how could one, with any justification, think of it as work? To wake in the morning in a suite at the Ritz, to sample some of the finest food on offer in the world. To wander through Saint-Germain-des-Prés, to sit with a sketchpad in Les Deux Magots or Café de Flore or, late in the evening, in the rue de Furstenberg. To see the views from the Butte of Montmartre, to try to capture the intensity of the artists' faces in the Luxembourg gardens and to stand in the Jeu de Paume or the Orangerie, drinking in the glories of Pissarro, Renoir and Monet. Katharine had never felt so fortunate as this, had never felt so completely content with her own company, or with herself.

She returned, in July, to a stiflingly hot Manhattan from which there could be no further escape, for the composers and producers were ready to make their presentation to Eles, without which they could not begin their actual work. Once that had begun, Katharine knew that Laszlo would drive himself and her on and on, through the worst conditions, oblivious of anything and everything but achieving what was, as yet, only a glimmering canvas in his own mind.

When Laszlo collapsed, in his studio, at the beginning of August, they were less than halfway through the first stage of their work.

"It is his heart," Erzsébet, his wife—known to their friends as Betty—told Katharine when she arrived a few hours later at New York Hospital.

"Is it bad?"

"He has been lucky, they say, thank God, but if he wants to make a complete recovery, they insist he take a full rest for at least six weeks."

"Will he do what they say, do you think?"

Pale but composed, Betty smiled. "What do you imagine, my dear? You know him well enough."

"I can't imagine Laszlo resting," Katharine admitted.

"No. Neither can I."

Once over the worst of his illness and his initial fright, Laszlo fought his cardiologists and nurses just as Betty and Katharine had feared he would, tooth and nail.

"Nothing," he declared from his bed, "can persuade Laszlo Eles to abandon a show before completion, nothing short of death!"

The doctors, his wife and Katharine tried everything they could to persuade him to cooperate, while the producers and composers bit their tongues, secretly willing the great designer to stand firm.

"If they make him stop," Sydney Kane said direly, "it will kill him."

"For God's sake, Sid, don't say such things." Howard Blaustein's myopic eyes were round with horror.

"How far has he got with the designs?" Gerard Legreque, flown in from Monte Carlo, wanted to know.

"No one knows, except maybe the assistant." Kane paused. "When I had my coronary," he said, warming again to his theme, "they wanted me to quit for three months—I went back to work after five weeks, and look at me, I'm still here."

"Knock on wood," said Blaustein.

On the thirteenth day after his collapse, three days after Betty had taken him home, Laszlo confounded everyone by announcing his retirement.

"I don't believe it," said Blaustein.

"He's just jerking us around," said Kane.

"I think not," said Legreque.

"I never trusted him, damn Hungarian," Kane said.

"Come on, Sid, that's not nice," reproached Blaustein.

"I don't feel very nice, Howard."

"Perhaps Eles is dying," Legreque said somberly.

"Then let him finish his work first," said Kane.

Katharine was shocked and dismayed.

"I didn't know they wanted you to retire altogether, Laszlo."

They were in the Eleses' sitting room in their apartment on Central Park South, and the designer was seated on the sofa wearing a pale gray silk dressing gown and soft calf slippers.

"They don't," he said.

"I don't understand. Isn't there some middle ground between a few weeks' rest and putting yourself out to grass for keeps?"

"Not for me, *kedves*." Laszlo, as always, was adamant. "For me, it has always been all or nothing. I cannot work with a stopwatch in one hand, Katharine, switching off my inspiration when it's time to take a pill or have a sleep."

"But can you stop?" she asked him, gently. "Can you bear it?"

"I think so. I have done great work, and I am almost satisfied." He took her hand and squeezed it. "I guess I don't want to die yet, and I find that Betty wants to keep me around a while longer, too." He smiled. "I thought for sure she would be glad to be rid of me. I'm a lucky man."

"Of course you are." Katharine was ashamed. "I'm sorry, Laszlo. I'm being selfish. It was just such a shock—it never occurred to me for an instant that you might want to retire."

Betty having insisted that Katharine stay and have lunch with them, Laszlo announced, as his wife served them grilled monkfish and leaf spinach, that he had another shock in store for Katharine.

"I told you, earlier, that I am almost satisfied with my work."

"So you should be," Betty said.

"Please, Erzsébet, don't interrupt."

"Don't you speak to me like a child."

"I apologize."

"I accept your apology."

"You were saying?" Katharine said, trying not to laugh.

"I was trying to say that I shall only be able to begin my retirement with any peace of mind if you are allowed to complete the designs for *Paris*, and to oversee the final sets."

Katharine stared at Eles. "You're not serious."

"Why not?"

She thought she might burst with gratitude and affection. "They'd never allow it."

"Why do you say that?"

"Because I'm an assistant."

"So? We were all assistants once, even I."

"But for a show like this one, they want the best, and whoever they do pass it on to will employ their own assistant." She smiled lovingly at him. "It's wonderful of you to think about me, Laszlo, especially right now, but you don't have to be concerned—I'll give them whatever help they ask for, and then I'll bow out gracefully."

"Are you crazy?"

"Laszlo," Betty said, with mild reproof.

He banged the table with his fist and his knife fell off the table. "You speak like an idiot schoolgirl, not a talented designer!"

"Laszlo, don't be so rude, and remember your heart," Betty said, more firmly this time.

"Kuss!"

"Don't tell me to shut up!"

"Please," Katharine said, anxiously, "don't fight on my account."

"We always fight," Laszlo assured her. "And you still sound like a schoolgirl. There is absolutely no question of cooperating with another designer. Everyone has been enthralled by our sketches, by all our plans. No one else in New York, or in London or Paris or Berlin, for that matter, could have the breadth of vision that I, the one and only Laszlo Eles, have brought to this production—"

"Of course not, dear," Betty said, a little caustically.

"Don't *interrupt!*" He went on. "No one else has such exquisite taste and judgment, not even you, darling Katharine, or not quite yet, at least—"

"Never," Katharine said.

"Modesty," Eles glowered at her, "is charming, I'm sure, for a well-brought-up girl in Georgetown, but completely stupid for a woman close to the top of her profession on Broadway."

"All right," Katharine said, laughing, "I'm brilliant."

"You could be. One day. Perhaps."

"Finish your fish, Laszlo," Betty said. "And stop all this talking and excitement or you'll wear yourself out."

"I'm nearly through," he said, and suddenly there was a weariness in his voice that made both women glance at him anxiously. "I have just one more thing to say, and then there's an end to it. Either they take Katharine Andersen, and they pay Katharine Andersen the going rate, and give full *credit* to Katharine Andersen, or I shall set fire to the work we have done so far."

"You wouldn't." Katharine was horrified.

"I would." Laszlo picked up his fork. "And then they would have to start from scratch and pay twice through their noses. Let's see how they like that."

The producers fought Laszlo hard for a few days, but after Katharine, coached by the great designer, gave Kane, Blaustein and Gerard Legreque an early taste of what was to come, they were sufficiently fired up to come over to her side.

"Eles knows better than any other designer I can think of," Blaustein said, "how to make our work come alive, how to suck an audience up out of their seats and make them part of the show."

"We've talked it over," Kane concurred, "and we think that at this stage, we'd rather give ourselves over to Katharine Andersen—even if she is a nobody—so long as she has Eles's blessing."

"Eles has far too much pride," Legreque added, "to vouch for someone less than terrific, don't you agree? After all, ultimately, it will be his own reputation on the line."

"Gerard's right," Blaustein said. "Whatever else Eles has done over the years, however often he's been called a genius, this is his endorsement, and if it turns into a disaster, that's what he'll be remembered for."

The job her very own, Katharine panicked. Everything that had been strong and sure in her dissolved, turned to mush. She was only a halfway decent designer, for pity's sake. She was, no matter what Laszlo said, an *assistant*. If she tried to do this, she'd be a laughingstock—she'd have to get out of New York City—hell, she'd have to get out of the country!

For a week after the producers had given her their blessing, she neither ate nor slept. A great longing to see David overwhelmed her. He would understand how she felt, he would tell her to let herself off the hook, that she was allowed to say no to them all, would agree with her that there was no shame in remaining anonymous and insignificant.

And then she realized that she was lying to herself, that David would say nothing of the kind, and that though he would always be gentle and ready to pick up the shattered pieces if she failed, he would be the first to point out to her that she just might *not* fail, and that if she didn't try, she'd never know.

Sam came to dinner at the end of that week, just as her emotions were on the turn, and added the finishing touches to her decision.

"It's time you woke up to yourself, Katharine," he told her sternly. "If you turn this down, you'll not only be letting down Laszlo when he needs you most, but you'll be letting yourself down—"

"I know, Sam."

"Besides which, not only will no one ever give you another chance, but you won't deserve one."

"I said I know, Sam."

"You do?"

"I've already decided to do it."

"That's great," he said, and hugged her. "So what are you doing sitting around here? Get to work, woman—it's showtime."

The show took over completely. There was nothing like theater for total absorption; it was easy to immerse yourself in theater, for it was a world in itself, a life that it was possible to live for twenty-four hours of every day if you wished it, and sometimes even if you did not. Katharine began by employing her own assistant, fired her after two days and then hired a seventeen-year-old named Dixie Callaghan. Dixie was tiny in build, red-haired, green-eyed, and the brightest spark Katharine had ever met. She was good at her job, she thought that Katharine was gifted, glamorous and the most incurably beautiful woman she'd ever known, and she thought that the designs were pure heaven.

And they were pretty wonderful, Katharine conceded, putting it all down to Laszlo, even her new ideas, the innovative additions that were all her own. She was still working under his influence, she told herself, even if he was recuperating with Betty at their home in Switzerland, having vowed to stay out of New York until opening night.

"The Ritz set, of course, is pretty much perfect already," she said to Dixie. "But then Laszlo and I agreed from the day I came back from Paris that just staying in a suite at the Ritz is a theatrical event of the grandest kind, so all we had to do was to be true to the hotel and the rest would just follow."

"I'd love to go there," sighed Dixie.

"Well, you can't go anywhere just at the moment," Katharine said, "except to the carpenters' shop."

Dixie grinned. "I swear to God, boss, I wouldn't even sail round the Greek islands on Jack Nicholson's yacht right now, even if he got down on his knees and begged me."

"Does Jack Nicholson have a yacht?"

"I don't know, but I wouldn't leave you even if he had."

Getting the Luxembourg set right was much less easy, since the beauty of the gardens was in the eye of the beholder and tremendously affected, Katharine had noticed even in a single month, by changes of light and temperature and, of course, by mood.

"This is where I really need you to be involved," she told Gerard Legreque on the telephone. "The book speaks for itself, of course, but we want you to feel completely happy with the way we've captured it."

And then there was the café set, seeming almost perfect in itself and yet—and then Katharine realized that this, of all the sets, would never be complete without people, for Saint-Germain without its characters was nothing.

She called Zizi Markheim at her salon in Avenue Montaigne in Paris. "It's time for us to get together, Madame," she said.

"*Bien sur*, Katharine," Markheim said, equably. "If you speak with my secretary, she can squeeze you in, I'm sure. When are you flying in?"

"You don't understand, Madame. It's important that you see the sets and that we discuss the costumes in situ."

"*C'est impossible.*"

"Surely not," Katharine said, more firmly. "Laszlo assured me that you had agreed to be in New York at this time."

"What I may have agreed with Laszlo," Markheim said, with disdain, "has no real bearing upon our relationship."

For the first time, Katharine really bristled. She had known that Zizi Markheim was a notoriously difficult woman, and it had occurred to her before telephoning to plead, but then she had remembered that Laszlo never begged, Laszlo insisted.

"I am surprised," she said, mildly.

"*Pourquoi?*"

"Laszlo led me to believe that you were passionate about your designs, Madame Markheim."

"My passions are hardly your concern, my dear Katharine."

"Naturally they're not." Katharine paused. "I don't mind sharing mine with you, though, Madame, and at this time, I am passionate about my sets for *Paris*. I'm convinced that unless we stand together at this point, so that my sets become a perfect foil for your costumes, the third act of the show may fail."

"Surely you can send me sketches and photographs, perhaps a model or two—"

"Impossible." Katharine pushed on. "I also feel that you and I should become involved with the casting of the Saint-Germain extras." She paused. "Unless you don't care who wears your clothes, Madame."

Zizi Markheim's sigh was audible.

"Not before next week."

Katharine smiled. "Next week will be perfect, Madame."

Katharine began to thrive on this new flexing of muscles, this wielding of a creative power she had not guessed she possessed. Dixie was a wonderful support, her defender and protector, seeing to it that her boss, as she insisted on calling Katharine, remembered

to eat sensibly, and to rest, and to find time for the occasional swim
and massage to keep herself strong and supple.

Rehearsals began in early September, and with the last bout of
work on the sets well in progress, and in the hands of the carpenters,
prop men and painters, Katharine was able to sit in on rehearsals,
exactly where she loved to be most, in the heart or, as Sam Raphael
described it, in the "crotch" of the theater.

"All through my childhood, right through school," Katharine told
Dixie, "that was what I assumed I was going to do."

"To act?" Dixie was surprised. "But I imagined you'd always been
an artist."

"Have you always been sure what you wanted, Dixie?"

"Only since my tenth birthday. Before that I wanted to be a train
driver, then a clown, then president."

"Of the United States?"

"Sure." Dixie's green eyes flashed. "But then, on my tenth birthday
my folks took me to see a revival of *Annie Get Your Gun*, and after
about three minutes I wasn't in any old theater, I was really there,
with the Wild West Show, and after that, I wanted to know how they'd
done that to me—"

"And got hooked."

"And how." Dixie looked curiously at Katharine. "So were you any
good, boss, at acting?"

"I wasn't bad, I guess."

"Which means, knowing you, that you were great. So what made
you switch to design? I mean," she added quickly, "I'm glad you did,
but why did you?"

"All kinds of reasons," Katharine said, cagily. "Some of them sound,
some of them not so sound."

"But you're happy you took up design, aren't you, boss?"

"Happier than you can imagine, Dixie."

The huge sets were not transferred to the Winter Garden Theatre
until two weeks before opening, and Katharine watched feverishly
as Laszlo's concepts and her own were brought to life under the
rigid auspices of the stage director, stage manager and master car-
penter.

"Boss, you're a genius," Dixie said rapturously, as expert hands
hung and folded the precious fabrics that Katharine had insisted on
importing for the Ritz set.

"Do you think Zizi will approve?" Katharine and Zizi Markheim had been on a first-name basis since the Frenchwoman had caved in and come to New York to consult with Katharine.

"She may not admit it right away, but I'll bet my boots she'll secretly think it's completely gorgeous."

Katharine and Dixie sat in on the interminable lighting rehearsal, biting their knuckles and gnawing their fingernails when their glorious color schemes were almost bleached out by bad decisions, or when the shadows of trees in the Luxembourg gardens fell incorrectly; and during one dance rehearsal, when a young man fell heavily, ripping a back cloth, Katharine leapt out of her seat, barely managing to stifle a scream of anguish.

"Quit worrying, boss," Dixie said heartily, though she, too, had found herself perspiring with alarm. "It's going to be fine."

"What good is fine?" Katharine snapped. "*Fine* is okay weather—*fine* is how you say you feel when you have a lousy head cold but you don't want to be a grouch."

"Okay, then," Dixie said, knowing that Katharine hardly ever snapped. "It's going to be sensational."

"Of course it's going to be sensational if half the chorus kick their damned feet through the Medici fountain!"

Dixie sighed. "I give in. It's going to be the pits. A disaster."

Katharine glanced at her warily. "That bad?"

The first dress rehearsal went like a breeze. Everyone loved the sets, the cast most of all, and the most delicious thing for Katharine was when, at two separate moments, actors sought her out to tell her what a glorious difference the sets had made to their own conviction; and one actress even told Dixie the next day, that when she had left the theater after rehearsal and found herself on Broadway, she had felt genuinely startled, as if she had expected to step out into the heart of Paris.

Total panic returned during the second dress rehearsal, two days before the first preview. Katharine felt as if she were about to be torn violently away from her new, precious and oh-so-generous theater family—from the men and women who wanted her sets to succeed, just as they wanted their own work to be noticed and noted with pleasure at the very least. As if she were going to be hurled over the spotlights and across the orchestra pit to the merciless wolves, to the audiences who paid real money for their tickets, to the critics who could seal the fate of a show or a would-be, jumped-up, self-seeking, so-called designer with a single blow of the pen.

And worst of all, more truly terrifying to Katharine than anything or anyone else, there would be Laszlo Eles, her mentor, her friend, who had handed it all to her on a golden platter, and who would be in his rights to kill her, to hang, draw and quarter her if she betrayed him.

"He'll kill me," she told Dixie.

"No, he won't."

"You don't know Laszlo."

"No, but I can't wait to meet him."

"Even if he's going to kill me?"

On the evening of the first preview, Katharine hid in the smallest of the dressing rooms, and when Dixie found her, she had just climbed up on a chair.

"Isn't it too soon to hang yourself, boss?"

"I'm not. Yet."

"So what are you doing?"

"Trying to disconnect this damned loudspeaker."

"Why?"

"So I don't have to hear the boos or catcalls."

"Would you like me to help you?"

"No, thank you." Katharine glared down at Dixie. "And I don't want to talk to anyone when it's over."

"Not even me?"

"Only if you promise not to talk about the show."

And then it was opening night.

"I'm not going," Katharine told Sam, when he came to pick her up.

"Of course you're going."

"No." She sat down on a straight-backed dining chair. "Look at me, Sam. My body has seized up."

"Your body is just fine," Sam said, calmly. "What you need is a stiff drink."

"I couldn't swallow it," she said hoarsely. "I feel as if I've been paralyzed, Sam—I can hardly catch my breath."

"You'll manage." He looked at her severely. "Do you want a drink or not?"

Katharine shook her head. "I told you I can't."

"Then it's time to go."

"I'm not *going*—" Her voice was shrill. "If you force me to go,

Sam, you'll have to carry me, and it'll be your fault if I die, simply die of terror!"

Katharine did not die, and *Paris* was a smash hit, and the stars of the show acted and sang and danced like stars, and Howard Blaustein and Sydney Kane and Gerard Legreque were ecstatic. And Bill Fuller, the director, embraced Katharine, and Joe Pirelli, the choreographer, kissed her and Dixie on both cheeks, and Katharine felt as though her entire body had been bathed in purest, lightweight gold, and she could float or fly or do *anything*—

And then there was Laszlo, linking arms with Betty, looking tanned and fitter than she'd ever seen him, and for one more minute Katharine froze again, ready to slide back down into the role of subordinate, of hireling, staring tentatively into his attractive face, trying to get past the warmth of his smile to detect the truth that would lie beneath.

"Kedves," was all he said. But Katharine saw that the smile was deep and true, in his dark eyes as well as on his lips, and there was real approval in it, and affirmation, and genuine, sincere pleasure, for her and for himself.

The producers threw a party at Sardi's, and Katharine was only half aware of sailing into the restaurant on Laszlo's arm, past a sea of faces and popping flashbulbs, and after that it was all sheer delight and terrific champagne and food that she scarcely tasted.

She felt a touch on her arm, after about a half hour, and she turned around, and David was standing there, handsome in a tuxedo.

"Hello, genius," he said quietly.

They embraced, and David hugged her hard, and kissed her once, on the lips, and then drew back.

"Do you know," Katharine asked, "how glad I am to see you?"

"Are you?"

"More than anyone."

"You know the show's a real smash, don't you?"

"Think so?"

"You only have to look around and listen—and I don't just mean here." David's eyes were as gentle and loving as they had ever been. "I hung around for a while in the foyer at the theater, and I tell you they loved it."

"Did you like the sets?" Katharine asked, feeling suddenly shy.

"I thought I was in Paris," he said simply. "Especially in the café.

I thought any moment I was going to see Hemingway or Gertrude Stein—it was that kind of sensation. I can't remember ever being quite that absorbed in a scene before."

"Thank you," she said, overwhelmed.

"You deserve your success," he said. "Every ounce of it."

Someone tapped Katharine on the shoulder then, and she had to turn away from David for an instant or two, and when she turned back again, wanting to tell him how truly happy she was to see him, and how much she had missed him, David had vanished. She looked around the restaurant, scanning faces and backs, and then she realized that he had gone, and a cloud of sorrow touched her for a moment, darkened her evening. But then Dixie came running over, wild in emerald satin and long pearls, red hair all frizzed out, to drag her by the hand to talk to someone who was just *dying* to meet her. And Katharine pushed David out of her mind, and went on with the party.

It was the best night of her life, she knew that, a night to be stored away forever. She missed her parents, thought especially about Louise, knowing what the evening and her success would have meant to her mother, and at one point she went to the payphone on the first floor and telephoned Henrik collect, only realizing when he answered sleepily that it was five in the morning in Copenhagen.

"Oh, God," she said, "I'm sorry. I didn't mean to wake you."

"Don't worry, don't worry," Henrik assured her. "I wanted to hear, I was so excited for you—tell me."

"It went wonderfully, though it's too soon to say how well we're going to do."

"But the people tonight, they loved it?" Henrik, more awake now, sounded eager. "And you, are you pleased with yourself?"

"I'm so pleased I'm going to be insufferable."

"About time."

"Are you well?" Katharine asked. "And Fanny and Asger?"

"We're all just fine," Henrik said. "And we all miss you and hope you will come to us again soon."

"I love you," Katharine said, and blew a kiss into the telephone, and then she went back to the party, still walking on air.

Dixie was crying drunkenly on Katharine's shoulder, telling her how much she was going to miss her, and the first strands of tension had begun to twist through the air as the company became aware that the early reviews would soon be through. And Bill Fuller, the director, was making an impromptu speech, steeped in champagne, telling everyone how much he loved them, and how magnificent the show was, whatever the critics might say, and the audience had made it pretty clear what they thought, and the lines into the box office had been jammed since long before the previews, and that's what happened when so much talent came together—

And then Katharine saw him for the first time.

The stranger was tall and golden, his hair straight and beautifully cut, the color of corn, but true, not out of a bottle, and he was slim and his tuxedo was the best tailored in the room. And he was talking to Sam Raphael, animatedly, and his eyes were blue and earnest and clear, and his nose was almost, but not quite straight, which was the absolute making of a face that might, otherwise, have been too perfect, like a model's.

He gesticulated with his hands, but only slightly, just small, eloquent sketches of movement with his fingers, and then Sam said something that made the stranger laugh, and Katharine heard him for the first time, over the heads of the crowd. And his laugh was deep and rich, and his eyes and mouth stretched with his smile in a wonderfully genuine way, and she felt as if her heart had been squeezed, and she knew that she was staring.

And then he looked her way, and his laughter stopped.

And it began.

c h a p t e r

16

S ebastian was in New York to negotiate Barbara Stone's transfer, from London to Broadway, with the successful Peter March production of *Antony and Cleopatra*. Michael Jaffe had told Sam Raphael, currently in the city during a break from filming in Colorado, to expect Sebastian's call, and when they had met, over drinks in the Blue Bar at the Algonquin, the two men had hit it off, just as Jaffe had predicted.

"The pity of it is," Sebastian had told Raphael, "we can't be of any real use to you right now."

"Because you still have no office in New York." Raphael shrugged. "Any plans on the horizon?"

Sebastian nodded. "We're looking at an existing agency in the city."

"For a takeover?"

"It's possible. It's even probable. But in the meantime—"

"In the meantime, I have a contract for one more season with *Star Rider*, so we have a little time to play with." Raphael looked at Sebastian quizzically. "You're not really all that hungry for expansion, are you?"

"Michael must have told you how we feel about staying compact."

"He did. It's unusual."

Sebastian smiled. "We want to stay hungry for our clients, and the best way to do that is to stay reasonably lean. That doesn't preclude expansion altogether, though—it just means we have to do it our way."

The day before Sebastian was due to fly back to London, Sam Raphael had invited him to attend the opening of *Paris*, the new musical at the Winter Garden Theatre.

"Having a good time?" Raphael asked him in the first intermission.

"So far."

"It gets better."

"You've seen it?"

"I saw a preview." The audience began to move back into the auditorium for the second act. "There's a party later at Sardi's. Care to come?"

"I have an early start."

"If you like the rest of the show, come. There are some people you should meet."

"Okay." Sebastian smiled. "Just for a while. Thank you."

In a fine mood after the final curtain call, Sebastian was glad he'd agreed to go to the party. The music had been good, with three songs immediately memorable; the performances had been fine, Legreque's plot strong enough to hold the audience throughout, and the sets and costumes had been stunningly beautiful. Sardi's was crowded and smoky, but the food was good and the atmosphere was dizzy with triumph. Sebastian met a half-dozen people whom he enjoyed meeting, and another half-dozen it made good business sense to meet, and he drank more champagne than he usually did or had intended to, and he thought, as he had many times in the past, that no other city was better at throwing good first-night parties than New York City.

He was deep in conversation with Sam Raphael, talking about Paris—the city, not the show—talking about their favorite restaurants and nightclubs, when Sebastian had the sense that someone was looking at him, and turned to see who it was.

His breath caught in his throat.

She looked like an exotic creature, he thought in that first instant, yet she was, at the same time, entirely woman. The most wonderful-looking woman Sebastian had ever seen. She wore Kenzo silk kimono pants and top, all pale gold with tiny white sequins stitched along every seam and around the neckline. She was tall, almost as tall as he was, in high-heeled gold sandals; her hair was long and wavy, a rare dark blond, streaked with gold, and her eyes were unique, too, amber as a cat's eyes, but utterly human, full of sparkle and life and spectacularly infectious joy and excitement.

He could not look away. He felt powerless to do anything but stand and stare. Until he saw a flush, delicate but unmistakable, on her cheeks and, suddenly embarrassed, he averted his eyes and took a fresh champagne glass from a passing waiter to try to break the spell.

It was unbreakable. She had moved away a few feet, was talking to a girl, a wild young thing with frizzy red hair and a vivid green dress, and Sebastian saw that their conversation was animated and happy, and he took advantage of the woman's preoccupation to stare at her again. She laughed at something the girl said, and the sound reached Sebastian's ears and he wanted to capture it, to seize it and remember it, wanted her to laugh again, for him. A man approached her, put an arm about her, gave her a hug, and she smiled into his face, and Sebastian hated the man, felt a surge of unprecedented jealousy—but then he saw her slip tactfully but decisively out of the embrace, and he had never known such relief.

He felt a touch on his arm and turned.

"Sam, I'm sorry."

"What happened to you?" Sam looked amused. "One minute we were in the Latin Quarter, the next you were gone."

It had been only a few moments, yet it had seemed, to Sebastian, timeless.

"I'm sorry," he said again, and made an effort to return to their conversation, but he knew that his eyes kept seeking her out again, kept moving back to her, and he saw, with the profoundest pleasure, that she, too, seemed drawn to him. She was evidently popular and in demand, more alive and vibrant than any of the people clustering around her, and her beauty was extraordinarily incandescent.

"Ah," said Sam, "now I understand."

Sebastian smiled. "You must forgive me." He paused. "Who is she?"

"My stepdaughter, as a matter of fact."

"You're kidding."

"Actually, my former stepdaughter. I was married to her mother for nearly six years."

Sebastian experienced a new thrill of happiness. Fate. They had been meant to meet tonight. This thread of destiny, starting out with Michael Jaffe and his introduction to Sam Raphael, and the fact that neither he nor Jeremy had been free to visit New York before now —and now this chance invitation to the show and this party.

"She wasn't in the show, was she, Sam?" he asked, keeping his voice low. "I'd have noticed her, even if she'd been in the back row of the chorus, and she's no chorus girl, though she could be a dancer."

"She's not a dancer, she's a designer. *The* designer."

"Of this show? Of *Paris*? That's wonderful," Sebastian rejoiced, for he had found the sets tonight quite brilliant, and so there would be no need for polite half-lies when they met, when they spoke, and she was talented as well as beautiful, and they *were* going to meet now, of that he was quite, quite certain. It was inevitable.

"Her name," he said, suddenly urgent. "Tell me her name, Sam."

"Katharine Andersen," Sam said, gently.

Something stirred, deep inside Sebastian.

"I met a girl by that name once," he told Sam. "She was five years old, and I was seven."

Sebastian shut his eyes, and she came back to him. Blond and pretty and bold, for a five-year-old, and a girl, that was what he and Jeremy had said about her. He smiled at the memory and opened his eyes.

"Impossible, of course. There must be hundreds of Katharine Andersens in the world, thousands." He paused. "I think we called her Kate."

"I don't think anyone calls this lady Kate," Sam said.

"She was in London with her parents, on a visit from Washington. She came to stay over at our house." Sebastian was still remembering. "Her mother was an actress, I think."

"Louise Grahame," Sam said, quietly. "Louise Grahame Andersen, to be exact."

Not a coincidence, after all. Fate. Sebastian believed in fate.

"Introduce me, Sam," he said. "Now."

They both knew, immediately—Sebastian for the very first time in his life—that they were in love. Close up, he found her even lovelier, now that he could see how soft and perfect her skin was, how truly rare those amber eyes, how soft and generous and sweet her lips. Close up, Katharine thought, with a rush of excitement, that he was much, much more attractive, and he wasn't smiling that wonderful smile anymore, he looked serious, almost grave, and the look in his clear blue eyes touched her heart, gripped her soul—

Sam was speaking. "And this is Sebastian Locke."

And when she heard his name, she, too, closed her eyes for a moment, remembering a boy she had met when she was five years old, remembering his father and his friend, Jeremy, and their house and the housekeeper, and their garden, and the portrait of his mother, his famous mother. Who had died on the day they had met.

"I remember," she said, and she found, with astonishment, that her eyes were moist with tears, for she remembered that that had been her first awareness of death. Before Annie, long before her parents. And here they were, more than twenty years later, and this was what they called destiny.

c h a p t e r

17

They left Sardi's together, took a cab to his hotel, the Carlyle on Madison Avenue, sat down for a few moments in Café Carlyle and ordered a bottle of champagne.

"Do you really want this?" Katharine asked Sebastian.

"More than anything."

"I think I've had enough."

His face fell. "Already?"

"They kept refilling my glass at the party, and I think I kept on letting them."

"You're talking about champagne," Sebastian said.

"Of course." Katharine paused and saw the relief on his face. "You thought I meant us—you thought I'd had enough of *us*? But we've only just begun."

He smiled into her eyes. "I know."

They left the champagne without tasting it, for neither of them wanted or needed to drink, they wanted to walk, to talk, to be together, to absorb being together. They walked south along Madison Avenue, past all the little private galleries, past the Whitney and the Westbury, went on walking until they turned right into Sixtieth Street and then headed back north again along Fifth Avenue. Katharine's feet, encased in their high-heeled gold sandals, had begun to ache badly after the first ten blocks, and after the next ten, they were almost blazing pain, but she didn't care, her feet didn't matter, nothing else mattered now except being with him.

"You're tired," Sebastian realized suddenly, feeling a pang of guilt. "You must be absolutely exhausted after the day and night you've had, and I'm making you walk when you ought to—"

"No," she said quickly. "I'm not really tired, it's only these silly shoes, they're not really meant for walking."

"Oh, God, you're limping, and I didn't notice."

"It's nothing, truly."

He wanted to pick her up in his arms and carry her, but he was afraid of frightening her, of startling her away when he'd only just found her.

"Why are there never any cabs in this city when you really need one?" he said, frustratedly.

"We don't need a cab," Katharine said, gently. "We're nearly there."

"Where?"

"My place."

She kicked off her sandals the instant they were through her front door, and the first things she saw were the pale pink and white roses filling her hallway.

"They're glorious!" Katharine fished out the cards. "From Laszlo and Betty—they're so *good* to me. And these are from Sam—" Her eyes, already sparkling, blazed with pleasure. "I don't believe it—he says the notices are *great*—oh, thank God! How could they get these here so *quickly*?"

"We left Sardi's over an hour ago," Sebastian said, enjoying the clear delight on her face. "I expect New York florists keep long hours."

The light was flashing on the answering machine in the living room, and there was a message from Dixie, confirming that the critics loved *Paris*, and why the hell had Katharine left so early?

"They all love you, don't they?" Sebastian said, softly. "All those people." He had heard the warmth in Dixie's voice, and he knew already, without needing to be told, that Katharine Andersen was a woman who elicited warmth and affection and, he guessed, loyalty.

"I love them, too," she said. "Oh, God, I'm so happy—I've never been so happy in my life."

"I feel the same," Sebastian told her. "And lucky, oh, so lucky."

"Really?"

He wanted to tell her that he felt that way because, looking at her, he saw that a part of the light in her face, a part of the joy, was there because of him, not just because of the good reviews, or because of her loving friends, but he thought she might think him too sure of himself, and that was so far from the truth.

"I'm afraid," he said, "at the same time."

"Of what?" she asked.

"I'm afraid this isn't really happening, that it's a dream."

"Want me to pinch you?"

"Yes," he said, "please."

And he saw that when Katharine smiled, tiny dimples formed in both cheeks, and he saw, when she brushed the long, dark gold hair back, away from her face, that her neck was fine and smooth, and his hands ached to touch her, but he waited, held back, knowing it was too soon.

Sebastian was due at JFK early that morning. It would not be the first time he had gone back to a hotel just to collect his bags and check out, without any time for sleep. Within a half hour of being introduced to Katharine, he had found himself planning how swiftly he could return to New York. Within two hours, he knew that he would not leave on the morning flight, knew that nothing could persuade him to leave until he could be sure that Katharine, too, understood that this was not just some temporary, passing madness, but much, much more.

He left her at four o'clock, still sheathed in her golden silk. He had longed to peel it away from her, had yearned to make love to her, had sensed that she wanted him, too, but he had not even kissed her. There would be time for that, plenty of time, it was better not to rush. And besides, he was afraid to make love to her. He was twenty-seven years old, and he had never been in love before. She was everything he had ever longed for, the way he felt was all he had ever hoped for, and it would, he hoped with all his heart and soul, be different in that way, too. But still he was afraid that it might not be.

He came back, uninvited, at ten o'clock, loath to wake her, but anxious that she might be an early riser and be gone if he left it any later. The doorman looked at him suspiciously as he buzzed the apartment, and it was several minutes before Katharine answered him, and Sebastian felt suddenly certain that he would be sent away, but the doorman told him to sit in the lobby for fifteen minutes and then to go straight up.

Katharine was at her open front door when he came out of the elevator. "Good morning," she said. "What a lovely surprise."

"Did I wake you? Your doorman seemed disapproving."

"Not at all. That's just Ike being protective."

She wore a pair of blue jeans and a T-shirt, and her feet were bare, her toenails varnished pale pink, and Sebastian knew he must have disturbed her in the shower, for her hair was tucked up in a white turkish towel tied turban-style around her head. And when he passed her, and she shut the door, he caught a whiff of baby soap and shampoo and talc, and he saw that her face, without a trace of makeup, was even lovelier than it had been the night before.

"I hope you like croissants," he said.

Katharine looked down at the paper bag in his hand with pleasure, and back up into his face with even greater pleasure. "I love croissants," she said.

And all Sebastian's emotions kicked up inside him, and he felt quite absurdly happy and confident and reckless, and he kissed her then, before she could move away, and it was an entirely different kind of kiss to any that he had ever experienced. This was not a prelude to lovemaking, it was a prelude to love. It was sensuous, so sensuous that he felt a charge all the way to his toenails, but it was far more than that, it was warm and gladdening, and excited and welcoming.

"Don't stop," she whispered, feeling him draw away a little. Her face was flushed, her eyes were startled and luminous, her heart was racing a million beats a minute, and she saw that he, too, looked dazed, as if he hardly knew where he was. She smiled at him. "On the other hand, maybe I should make us some coffee."

Sebastian nodded, slowly. "Coffee sounds good."

Katharine put out her hand, and he took it, and she led him to the kitchen. "I thought you might change your mind and catch your flight after all."

"I told you I wouldn't."

"I know."

He gripped her hand. "I'll never lie to you, Katharine Andersen."

Katharine looked up into his eyes.

"I believe you," she said.

*   *   *

They lunched, later, at The Sign of the Dove, and then they walked again, in Central Park this time, and then Sebastian dropped her off at the theater.

"Can I see you later?" he asked.

"I want to see the show again, this evening." She looked apologetic. "Could you bear it?"

"I'll see it twice a day, if you'll let me sit beside you."

"Just tonight," Katharine said. "There are some things I want to check out—I was too terrified last night."

They sat in the dress circle, and Sebastian studied Katharine's face as she gazed down at the stage, at her work, and he loved her shy smile when she caught him looking at her, and they held hands, like teenagers. And after the show, they were hungry again, and they both felt like eating rare beef, so they went to Gallagher's and ate prime rib, and then they took a cab back to the Carlyle, and sat listening to Bobby Short. And then Katharine's eyelids began to droop, and Sebastian walked her home, and they kissed again at the door, and then he left her, for she was exhausted, after all, and he was still a little afraid.

Katharine lay awake for a long time that night, unable to switch off her thoughts. It was all so like a dream that perhaps she didn't need to go to sleep; the success of the show, the kindness of people and then, at the absolute crest of the wave, Sebastian.

"Sebastian Locke," she said, softly, into the dark.

She remembered him so vividly, as a boy, remembered feeling grateful to him because he'd been kinder to her than his friend, remembered thinking him handsome, even at seven, and wanting to impress him by climbing trees even though she'd been afraid of falling.

She knew that he had canceled his flight that morning because of her. She knew that he was as attracted to her as she was to him, and it puzzled her a little that he had held back after their kisses, and yet it was all part of it. Of the mystery. Of what had made their meeting so utterly different—so different from the way it had been even with David. Darling David, whom she'd felt so happy to see, less than an hour before she had first set eyes on Sebastian. Loving David, who had been so comfortable, so safe. Too safe, she supposed.

She shut her eyes and tried to think about David's face, the beloved features she'd seen just over twenty-four hours before, and that had stayed with her for months and months after their split . . . the curling brown hair, the gentle, loving eyes . . . She could still remember them, of course, she could describe them to herself, but suddenly it was impossible to conjure them up in her mind's eye. She turned over, thought about David's fine, long-fingered surgeon's hands, but when she put her face into the pillow, she saw, instead, Sebastian's hands, narrow, too, and capable, but more expressive, more eloquent. Hands that would be wonderful lovemaking hands . . .

Her body ached to be touched by him. She wondered how long it would be before he was ready, before he felt certain that she was ready for him.

She sat up and switched on the bedside lamp. It was four o'clock. She considered calling him, waking him. What if he left the city without telling her? What if she had been too distant, if her signals had not been clear enough? She had always been too reserved, too Georgetown for New York, too hesitant for some men. What if Sebastian thought she didn't really want him? What if he left on the morning flight today?

And then the panic slipped away, and Katharine turned out the light and lay back again. And she did not call him. And she knew that he would not leave.

In his suite at the Carlyle, Sebastian, too, was awake. He knew that it was only possible for him to stay one more day in Manhattan. He had urgent matters to attend to in London, he had clients depending on him, Jeremy champing at the bit to discuss their possible American takeover, Elspeth needing a little time off.

Twenty-four more hours to court the woman he was quite certain he loved, to woo and win her. To make love to her, if she would have him. And to discover, for better or worse, if, this time, it would be different.

He felt like a teenager, yearning and uncertain, yet his fear of failing Katharine, of failing himself, was a passionate, adult fear. For losing Katharine Andersen was not to be compared with losing any of the other lovely girls he had known and lost because of his own emotional impotence. Losing Katharine would, he realized, leave a great, terrible and permanent void in his life, be an ultimate waste, a true desolation.

He thought of planning the day meticulously, then remembered the evening, a few years ago, that he had so carefully tried to shape with Sabrina Bright, and which had ended so disastrously. And yet a certain degree of planning, since he was not on home territory, was essential, and he sensed that it might be good for them both if they could leave behind the tensions and throb of this city, where pressures seemed to grow and expand, to feed on themselves and to take over.

He called Sam Raphael at first light.

"Hello?" The actor's voice was slurred with sleep.

"Sam, I'm sorry to wake you."

"Sebastian? What's up?"

"Nothing, Sam. I know it's early—"

"Early? It's the middle of the fucking night."

"I know—"

"So what do you want?"

"I need a recommendation"— Sebastian spoke quickly, his voice both apologetic and urgent—"for the prettiest, easiest day trip out of the city."

"You're kidding me."

"I've never been more serious." There was no point in prevaricating. "Sam, I'm in love with her, and this is my last day, and I need it to be perfect. You know Katharine very well, you know what she enjoys, what makes her happy—"

"Okay." Sam was awake now, and trying to take notice. "At least you're honest—I guess I must think you're honest or I wouldn't want you for my agent."

"Where should I take her, Sam?"

"Will you give a guy time to breathe?"

The morning was warm and sunny as they drove, in a rented Japanese car, up the Hudson River Valley, left the skyscrapers and the ugly industrial sprawl near the city, took Route 9 and made for Putnam County. They passed Tarrytown, detoured a little way to take a look at the Sleepy Hollow Restorations, and arrived at the Hawk House Inn in good time for lunch.

"Oh, my," Katharine said, with pleasure. "This is lovely."

"God bless Sam Raphael," Sebastian agreed.

It was an old and delightful, blue-and-white clapboard inn near the river, and the dining room was charming, with a beamed ceiling and inglenook fireplace, overlooking a pretty garden.

"This was a wonderful idea," Katharine said, once they were seated in a bay window. "It's lovely to get out of the city for a few hours."

"I know you've been stuck there for months." Sebastian picked up his menu. "I'm surprised you don't have a weekend place. Don't you feel stifled in the summer?"

"I shared a house on the Island last summer, with David. It was heaven, being able to escape, especially in August."

Katharine had told Sebastian about David on that first night, as they'd walked and talked after the party. She had wanted, immediately, to tell him everything about herself, wanted him to know it all, just as she had wanted to know all about him, and David Rothman had been—still was, if she was honest—an important part of her life.

"We're not as good at weekends in London," Sebastian said. "Maybe because the city's so spread out, so the need to get away isn't as intense as here."

"Do you still live in that same district?"

"Hampstead?" He shook his head. "I have a house in Mayfair, in the heart of London. It's a tiny, white house, couldn't be more different from The Oaks."

"I remember your old house," Katharine said. "At least I think I do, but you know the way it is with really old memories. They get blurry, a little misleading, like dreams."

"Not always," Sebastian said. "I remember you so clearly." He smiled. "Little Kate, telling us ghost stories—you even impressed Jeremy, which was no mean feat."

"I remember he didn't like me much."

"Didn't he? He probably did, but he wouldn't have wanted to admit it. Jeremy's like that."

"And now he's your partner."

"Yet we never planned it that way. That was fate, too." Sebastian paused and looked at her intently. "It seems the best things are."

They ate prime ribs and then cheese, and drank a good red wine, and they talked quietly, not as hungrily as they had the previous day, but just as comfortably and easily. They shared their pasts in light-hearted snatches and anecdotes and opened up the darker recesses more willingly and freely than either of them had with anyone before. Katharine had only a vague memory of Andrew Locke, much hazier than her recall of Sebastian and Jeremy, but she knew that Sebastian's father had been gentle with her, and she remembered that she had thought him very tall and handsome, and she felt genuine sorrow at his death, and deep sympathy for Sebastian and his stepmother, for she understood all too well the shock of sudden loss. And when Katharine told Sebastian about Jake and Louise's untimely, shattering deaths, he wanted to weep for her, and when she talked about the traumas of her decisions to uproot her life in Washington and to abandon her course at Carnegie Mellon, he admired her more than ever.

"Have you ever regretted those moves?" he asked her.

"Not at all." She shook her head slowly. "Not really. I was taking quite a chance, of course, dropping out like that, but after Sam introduced me to Laszlo, everything seemed to drop into place. Just lucky, I guess."

"Talent like yours has nothing to do with luck." Sebastian watched her color a little with pleasure. "You shouldn't sell yourself short. You must know how good you are."

"I'll admit I've surprised myself a little. But no matter what anyone, including Laszlo, says to the contrary, the whole concept for the *Paris* sets was his, not mine."

"What comes next?" Sebastian asked.

"I don't know."

He leaned forward and placed his right hand, palm upward, on the tablecloth, and with a slow, steady, deliberate movement, Katharine offered her left hand in response, letting it hover for a moment in the air before laying it over his, her palm up, too, so that her hand fitted snugly into his, like an abstract image of two lovers curled closely in slumber.

They both shivered a little, felt the same piercing, sweet rush of desire, and Sebastian squeezed her fingers gently, and Katharine took her hand away and laid it in her lap.

"Would you like coffee?" he asked, softly.

"No," she said. "Thank you." Her voice was low and clear. "No coffee, no dessert, nothing more."

"I'll get the check."

"Yes," Katharine said. "Please."

He paid the bill and they left the dining room and went, with hardly another word, to the reception desk, for he had not dared to presume to reserve a bedroom, but now he knew that it was what they both wanted, what they needed, more than anything. What was right.

It was a charming room, with a canopy bed, and there was a calm about them both, in spite of their mutual, powerful longing, and they stood in the center of the room, a few feet apart, looking into each other's faces, waiting.

It was Sebastian who closed the gap between them, gently putting one hand under Katharine's chin, tilting up her face before he kissed her with infinite tenderness.

They drew apart again, for one more, brief moment, both exquisitely aware that these were the last seconds before they would be irretrievably joined. Committed.

And then they were undressing each other, Katharine's red cotton skirt fell to the floor, Sebastian kicked away his jeans, he tugged at her white voile, buttonless blouse and pulled it over her head, and her mane of hair tumbled in disarray, and he unfastened her silk brassiere and she, laughing, tugged at his underpants. And the rush of joyous relief, the desperately longed-for sensations of skin on skin, of muscle and sinew and fragility and strength, overtook them, drew them onto the bed, with no time to pull off the counterpane. They felt each other's pulses throbbing, imagined they could almost hear the blood pounding madly through their veins.

And their lovemaking began, and continued, and they were equal participants, his hands, her hands, feeling, probing, discovering— Sebastian wanting to devour her, to adore her, to pour himself into her, but holding back, loving her—Katharine surging toward him, wanting him, every inch of him, wanting him to cover her entire body, loving his fingers, his tongue, his penis, the smoothness of his skin, the slender strength of his hips, the roundness of his buttocks. And the passion mounted and soared, giddily, wildly, lustily, ecstatically, until it seemed to them that the room around them was on fire with the heat of their bodies and the sunshine that flooded through the windows and beat upon them as they came together, arching and thrusting and loving . . .

And afterward, Katharine slept for a while, and Sebastian watched over her, kept her close to him, her head in the crook of his arm. And he covered her with the counterpane, and he kissed her hair tenderly, and he felt not the slightest, tiniest, remotest urge to move away or to be alone.

This time there was no end to love with the end of lovemaking. It was as he had always dreamed it might be, exactly as he had always known it ought to be, but far, far better. Katharine was so utterly beautiful, outside and within, and he wanted all of her, needed her with him completely, entirely. And he knew now that it was Katharine for whom he had been waiting, all his adult life.

* * *

He returned to London for just four days, throwing the agency into confusion by announcing during a staff meeting the first day that he would be flying back to New York for at least one more week, perhaps more.

"What is going on?" Jeremy asked, after the meeting.

"I told you."

"You've met a woman."

"Not just a woman. Katharine."

"Whom I met when she was five, I know, and she's Sam Raphael's stepdaughter—"

"Former stepdaughter."

"And she's designed the sets for *Paris*—"

"Which is a smash, did I tell you?"

"Twenty-five times. I still don't see why you have to fly straight back to New York."

Sebastian looked at Jeremy, trying to be patient. "You really don't see, do you?"

"No."

"I'm in love with her, Jeremy." He paused, for effect. "I've never been in love before in my whole life, and I have no intention of losing her. The thought of being apart from her for a few days is bad enough, but any more than that is intolerable."

"Why can't she come to London?" Jeremy asked, reasonably. "Her work is more or less done, isn't it? Yours is not. You have clients here who depend on you."

"Who depend on us. You'll be here, and I won't be gone forever."

"How long, exactly, will you be gone?"

"As long as it takes."

Katharine was at Kennedy to meet him. The weather had changed, and she was all wrapped up in a heavy sweater and raincoat with a long scarf around her neck.

"I was scared you wouldn't come."

"How could you doubt it?" He held her tightly.

"I thought maybe this was too good to be true."

He twisted the ends of her scarf round his wrists. "Can we get out of here, please. I want to unwrap all this and see what's underneath."

"Don't you remember?"

He kissed her mouth. "You're the one who said memories can be unreliable."

"Where are you staying?"

His hesitation was minimal. "Your place, if you'll have me. I mean, if it's a problem, I'll go to the Carlyle or anywhere, so long as—"

"Let's go."

"Are you sure?"

"Do I have to carry your bags?"

There was never any doubt for either of them. For the next four days, they were together all the time, were never apart, never had the slightest need to be apart. They were days of the sweetest discovery. Sebastian learned a whole new range of emotions, susceptibilities and capacities, became aware for the first time of the sheer joy of basic physical familiarity when set apart from pure sex; understood the warmth of constant companionship and, also for the first time, experienced the fierce, sharp sting of jealousy if Katharine so much as smiled at another man.

"I thought you were still in love with David," Sam said to Katharine on the telephone on the third morning, while Sebastian was in the shower.

"I thought I was, too," Katharine admitted. "It sounds corny as hell, I know, Sam, but I guess I never knew what love could be like."

"Until now."

"You like him, don't you, Sam?"

"Would it make any difference if I didn't?"

"Not to the way I feel about him, no. But it matters to me what you think, Sam, very much."

"I like Sebastian," Sam said. "I liked him as soon as I met him. I hope things work out so that he can become my agent, but I'm a lot more concerned that they should work out for you two."

Katharine had tried, briefly, to compare the way she felt now with the way it had been in the early days with David, but it seemed beyond comparison; whether it was simply because David was not Sebastian or whether she had simply become open and ripe for commitment, she could not tell. But either way it came to the same thing.

"We love each other," she told Laszlo.

"Obviously."

"You don't approve."

It was the fourth evening of Sebastian's stay, and Laszlo and Betty had come to dinner to meet him. Katharine was whipping the cream for dessert, when Laszlo had come into the kitchen.

"You don't need my approval." Laszlo relented. "In any case, it's not true that I don't approve. I've only just met Locke, and I think he seems like a fine man, and it's transparently clear that he loves you."

"So what's the problem?"

"No problem, except I'm afraid you're going to do something rash, and that we're going to lose you, *kedves*."

"You could never lose me, Laszlo," Katharine said, touched. "You're one of the very best friends I have in the world."

"Will you marry Sebastian?"

Katharine went on whipping cream. "He hasn't asked me."

"You're blushing, Katharine."

"I'm just hot from whipping."

"He will ask you," Laszlo persisted. "What will you answer?"

She put down the bowl.

"Dessert's ready," she said.

On the fifth night, they went to see *Paris* again, and afterward, they went to Alessandro's on Park Avenue for dinner, and after their wild duck with cherries, while they were waiting for the *soufflé Alessandro* to be prepared for them, Sebastian reached for Katharine's hand.

"Marry me."

Katharine stared into his face and said nothing.

"I know it's crazy, in a way, and much too fast, and—"

"No," she said.

"Oh, God."

"No, it isn't crazy, and no, it isn't too fast."

Sebastian's heart lurched with hope. "Are you saying yes?"

"Ask me again."

He held on to her hand as if he were holding on for dear life. "Will you please, please marry me, Katharine Andersen?"

Katharine's eyes filled with tears.

"I will."

They were married by a judge two days later, Sam Raphael and Dixie Callaghan their witnesses. Dixie was entirely swept away by the romance of the wedding dash, but Sam was bemused and anxious about the haste. Katharine had tried to explain to him that Sebastian, not ordinarily an outlandishly impulsive man, simply could not bear to wait for the complications of a more traditional wedding.

"And you?" Sam had asked.

"I believe that this means everything to him," Katharine had said, simply. "I think it would be different if his parents were still alive, but he says that I'm his family now, and he has this vast longing to bring home his bride—he says he feels in his heart that it's the right thing to do, right for us both."

"And you," Sam had said again, "what do you feel?"

"I want to marry Sebastian. There isn't a single doubt in my mind. And I don't seem to care whether I marry him in a church or in a judge's chambers, or in a field—I just want to be with him, to make him happy."

"And you're going to go to England?"

"Yes, Sam."

"But you're an American, Katharine."

She had smiled. "But I love an Englishman."

"We can have our marriage blessed," Sebastian told Katharine, as they sat, holding hands, in the back of a limousine en route to the judge's chambers, "if that's what you want—we can have it blessed in a church in England, or in New York or Washington, or even in Denmark, if you like." His expression was fiercely tender. "I mean it, Katharine, anything you want, anything at all, so long as you don't make me wait one more day to make you my wife."

"We're crazy, you know," Katharine said, but her face was filled with laughter and joy. "This whole thing is insane—I just don't *do* this kind of thing, at least I didn't until I met you."

It was true. Katharine Andersen had seldom acted on wild, mad impulse, but she recognized that falling in love had rendered her a little insane, and if that was so, then she wanted to stay that way forever, and if Sebastian had wanted her to fly to Jupiter with him, she would have agreed. And the wondrous part of it was how calm she felt, how utterly right it seemed to her.

"Are you really sure?" he asked her, softly, while they were waiting, with Sam and Dixie, for the judge. "I mean, are you quite, quite sure this is what you want?"

"One thousand percent," she whispered. "I know I said it was crazy, but marrying you feels like the clearest, most completely sane thing I've ever done in my whole life."

She wore a white Yves Saint Laurent suit she had bought the previous year, and a wide-brimmed hat with apricot trim and matching gloves and shoes, and Dixie had organized her bouquet of lilies and soft peach roses and baby's-breath, and Sam had given her a pale blue garter.

"Are you wearing something old, boss?" Dixie asked.

Katharine touched the single strand of pearls around her neck. "They were my mother's, Dixie, so I'm all set."

"You look—" Dixie shook her head. "I can't find the words. You always look beautiful, boss, but today—"

"Thank you, Dixie." Katharine squeezed her hand. "And when are you going to stop calling me 'boss'?"

"Never." Dixie leaned closer. "That's the only thing that really pisses me off about this whole thing, boss."

"What?"

"If you're going to live in London, how are we ever going to work together again? I mean, you are going to keep on designing, aren't you?"

"I don't know," Katharine said. "Probably. Maybe. Perhaps. And the really wonderful thing, Dixie, is that I don't seem to care."

They honeymooned in Venice, just six days at the Gritti Palace, days of undiluted heaven, steeping themselves in the wondrous un-realities of this city of the sea, with its magical beauties and dark corners, all so familiar from a wealth of paintings and films, floating here and there, all out of time, as their meeting had been. Waking with the dawn light, and making love, and sleeping again, and break-fasting on their balcony, man and wife, lovers and friends.

"Look at the ceiling," she murmured, later, as they lay again in their big bed. "Isn't it the most wonderful you've ever seen in the whole world, my darling?"

"It is, angel," he agreed, but he was looking at her face, and at her hair, fanning out over the pillows, and at her neck, and shoulders and down at her breasts, at their pale, perfect nipples, and down, at the gentle swell of her belly, and still further, at the dark gold tousle of her bush. "The most wonderful," he said, kissing her.

And later, in their gondola, she said, "Did you ever see a sky like this, my love? It's the most perfect sky anywhere, except maybe in heaven."

He looked up at the sky, and she was right, it was a perfect, clear blue, even though summer was well past, and then he looked down again, at the small, extra wonders of her face, for he noticed more each time he studied her, marking them in his mind, memorizing them: the delicate sprinkling of freckles on her wonderful nose that had appeared with the warmth of the sunshine, the way the dimples sprang into her cheeks when she smiled, the tiny creasing of laugh lines between her nose and the corners of her mouth, the wondrous softness of her mouth.

"You're right, angel," he said, again, for that was how he thought of her now, his angel wife, and he wished, more than anything, that his father could have met her, for he knew that Andrew would have adored her as much as he did.

And the honeymoon slipped sweetly on, and they dined at Harry's Bar, and fed the pigeons in the Piazza San Marco, and embraced in the narrow, dark alleys while skinny cats wound themselves around their ankles, and they wandered over arched bridges and wrinkled their noses at the stagnant canals; and they sat silently, holding hands, in the cool peace of small churches, and listened to the tolling of bells in the Campanile, and soaked, together, in perfumed baths, and dined from room service, and thought they might drown in love.

chapter 18

Virginia was at Heathrow to meet them, her face strained with nervousness, but as soon as she saw the newlyweds emerging from the customs hall, her doubts and anxieties vanished. Their sheer happiness communicated itself to her immediately, as well as Katharine's beauty and radiance and her understandable apprehension at arriving in a new country not to visit, but to live.

"Welcome." Virginia stepped forward, took Katharine's hands in her own and kissed her warmly on one cheek. "I can't tell you how delighted I am to see you."

"No kiss for me?" Sebastian asked.

"A big one." Virginia stood on tiptoe to embrace him. "Darling, I understand you already. One look at your beautiful Katharine, and I understand it all."

"You're very kind, Mrs. Locke," Katharine said, relief washing over her as she saw that the petite and attractive older woman was absolutely sincere. "I have to tell you that I feel I know you already. Sebastian's told me so much about you."

"In that case," Virginia said, "you'll know that I mean it when I ask you please not to be so formal. I'm just plain old Virginia, and I hope we're going to be the best of friends."

* * *

They went by taxi to Sebastian's house, and Sebastian insisted on carrying Katharine over the threshold while Virginia paid the driver, and then inside, while Katharine looked avidly around the small but elegant sitting room, eager to learn more about the husband she scarcely knew, Sebastian found a bottle of champagne in the refrigerator, opened it and filled three glasses.

"To my beautiful wife," he said, raising his glass.

"To you both," said Virginia.

"To us all," Katharine added.

"How do you like it?" Sebastian asked her. "Let me show you round, and you can tell me what you want to change."

"Before you do that—" Virginia said, and stopped.

"Go on," Sebastian said.

"All right." Virginia took a breath. "I know you've only just come off the plane, and you must both be exhausted—"

"We've only come from Italy," Sebastian said, "and I, for one, have never felt better."

"And you, Katharine?"

"I'm fine," Katharine said. "Truly."

"Then I suppose now is as good a time as any to tell you that I don't think you should be thinking about settling down here, in this house."

"Why not?" Sebastian asked.

"It's a charming little house, modern and perfect for a businessman on his own, for a bachelor." Virginia paused. "But you have a wonderful house in Hampstead."

"Oh, no," Sebastian said firmly. "Absolutely not, Virginia. The Oaks is your house, you've been living there now for over two years—"

"Unhappily," Virginia interrupted, and then, seeing the distress on Sebastian's face, she shook her head. "That's an exaggeration, of course, darling. I haven't been exactly miserable, but I'm not going to pretend any longer that I've been happy."

Katharine looked at them both. "Maybe we should sit down." She thought. "Or maybe I should go upstairs, look around?"

"Please don't think about being tactful." Virginia sat down in one of the armchairs. "I need you to hear this, Katharine. It concerns you directly, for one thing, and in any case, we're all family now."

"Come and sit here, darling." Sebastian drew Katharine down beside him onto the sofa. "Go on, Virginia, please."

Virginia went on.

"Amongst other considerations," she said, "you're a married man now, and though, of course, it's much too early—and it's not my place to discuss such things anyway—you may decide, perhaps, one day, that you want to have children." She paused. "That's what The Oaks is for, what the house needs."

Neither Sebastian nor Katharine spoke, so Virginia continued.

"There's no warmth in it for me, Sebastian, not without Andrew, but it's still such a wonderful house, and I care about it."

"I'm sorry, Virginia," he said, quietly. "I should have known how you felt."

"How could you, when I never told you? I didn't want to burden you with my feelings, and quite frankly, until you told me that you were going to be married, I didn't waste too much time considering how I really did feel. There didn't seem much point."

"But you think there is now."

"I know that The Oaks came to me, by law, because I was Andrew's wife," Virginia continued, "but I could never feel that it was mine. He and I never spent a single night under its roof, and I've never stopped considering it your family home, Sebastian."

They all sat in silence for a few moments.

"Darling?" Katharine said, gently. "What do you think?"

"I don't know what to think, except that I've been incredibly selfish, not realizing how you felt—no, don't tell me I had no way of knowing. I should have known anyway." He paused, his brow furrowed. "Where would you like to live, Virginia? By the sound of it, you must have somewhere in mind."

"I have." Virginia's tone became brisker. "I'd like, very much, to find a nice flat, perhaps with a terrace, near Hyde Park. Somewhere in walking distance of Harrods, with lots of lovely restaurants and shops and cafés to keep me busy without too much effort."

"That sounds lovely," Katharine said.

"It does, doesn't it?" Virginia smiled at her. "Of course, you must be thinking I'm dreadfully presumptuous, since we don't have any idea if you're going to like The Oaks, let alone want to live in it."

"Katharine will have to see for herself," Sebastian said.

"I have seen it," Katharine reminded him.

"You were five years old," he pointed out.

"You surely don't remember it, do you?" Virginia asked.

"I remember some things," Katharine said. "Mostly, though, I think it's the atmosphere that comes back to me, and its size—I remember I thought it was huge."

"Everything seems rather bigger than it really is when we're five, don't you think?" Virginia said.

"I know I liked it then."

"Even if you still feel that way when you see it again," Sebastian said, "there'll be dozens of things you'll want to change."

"It is an old-fashioned house," Virginia agreed, "but particularly splendid." She stood up and walked over to the French windows that overlooked the tiny town garden, and her voice grew quieter, less robust. "There's a glorious garden there, and a magnificent drawing room, with oak beams and a huge fireplace, though Ellie and I seldom bother to light a fire—" She turned around to look at Katharine. "Ellie Wilkins is the housekeeper, by the way, one of those loyal and wonderful family retainers you read about in novels—"

"She was there all those years ago, wasn't she?" Katharine asked.

"I think Ellie more or less came with the house," Sebastian said.

For the first time Virginia looked at him imploringly. "I want to go, Sebastian. I really need to start again, on my own."

He stood up. "You'll never be on your own, not if we have anything to do with it."

"I know that, darling." She came over to him. "It's just too sad, too hard for me, living in Andrew's house without him." She took his hand. "I bless you for wanting me there, I know you only intended to be kind."

"Kindness had nothing to do with it."

"If you say so." Virginia smiled up at him. "Anyway, all that's beside the point now. And there's nothing more we can discuss until Katharine's seen The Oaks."

"Why don't we go now?" Sebastian suggested.

"Right now?" Katharine, still seated, looked up at him, startled.

"I'm going to drive Virginia home, anyway—I don't really want to leave you all alone on our first afternoon in London." He paused. "Unless you're too worn out."

"I can get a taxi," Virginia said.

"Of course you can't," Katharine said swiftly, and stood up. "So let's go."

"Sure?" Sebastian looked at her. "You don't have to feel pressured by all this, darling."

"Will you stop?" Katharine laughed. "You're both forgetting I've been living in New York for over five years—pressure is what we have for breakfast."

*   *   *

They drove up to north London in Sebastian's black Aston Martin, with Katharine squeezed into the back in spite of Virginia's protests, but Katharine felt that she wouldn't have cared if they'd made her ride on the back of a motorcycle, so long as she could see where they were going. She had forgotten how big the city was, and as they drove up Heath Street in Hampstead, she gasped with delight.

"How can this still be London?"

"London's full of charming little districts," Virginia told her, "though Hampstead is one of the loveliest."

"We're almost there." Sebastian turned into East Heath Road, and then left into the Vale of Health. "This is the road—and this"—he turned into the drive—"is The Oaks."

For several moments, as Katharine stood in the driveway looking at the house, she said nothing at all, simply looked, allowing herself to react, to feel.

"I did remember," she said, softly.

It was a breezy afternoon, and the sounds of creaking branches and rustling leaves on the ground and of birdsong filled the air, giving her a sense of freedom and tranquility.

"I think it's wonderful," she said.

Virginia opened the heavy oak door and went directly upstairs to allow them to look around without her. They stepped into the wide entrance hall, and Katharine saw the lovely leaded and stained windows, the ornate ceiling, the graceful, arched entrances to the drawing and the dining rooms—and almost immediately, she felt what Sebastian's parents had responded to when they had first fallen in love with the house after the war. This was a sensitive house. The oak would respond to mood, to different people and tastes and feelings, and Katharine knew, instantly, that it would be a terrible house in which to be unhappy.

"Poor Virginia," she said, very softly.

"Yes." Sebastian felt shame, again, at his insensitivity.

"To have been coming to live here with so much optimism and joy, exactly as we've come to London—and then not even to have been able to spend one single night with your father." Katharine took Sebastian's hand and gripped it.

She understood how Virginia must feel. She believed her when she said that she wanted to leave. There could only be ghosts here for her, only lost hopes and dreams.

"What about us?" Sebastian asked, reading her thoughts.

"It's different for us," she said.

The house had a personality, she knew that already, a character of its own. And it was welcoming her, she felt it.

They would be happy here.

They wanted to be happy, oh, how they wanted it. Sebastian
needed that happiness. Sebastian, my dearest friend. Katharine's
husband. Diana's son. That last, of course, was the most important
of all, far more than even he could have realized.

I told you before, I think, that I didn't hate Kate, and that was
no lie. But it isn't true to say that I didn't resent her. I was
consumed by my resentment of her. Or rather, by my jealousy.

Kate changed everything. Spoiled it. Took Seb away from me.
So I tried my level best to spoil things for her, though, of course,
in doing that, I did more harm to him, to my friend. I behaved
rather badly, especially at the beginning, but then people were
accustomed to my bad behavior. Except Seb. He's always been
the exception in my life, the best thing, the best person—the
person for whom I wanted to be at my best.

Jealousy does terrible things to people, doesn't it? Or maybe
it's love we ought to blame. Love gets too much credit, I sometimes think. You only have to think of what it did to the three of
us.

PART
Two

19

They agreed to take their time. Virginia would look, in a leisurely fashion, for the right flat, and Katharine would visit The Oaks as often as she liked, getting to know the house and making up her mind, gradually and naturally, which parts she might want to redecorate or even redesign. In the meantime, she and Sebastian would live in Mayfair, but Katharine would not allow herself quite to settle, would not regard the little mews house as home. The Oaks was going to be home.

Sebastian returned to Locke Mariner on their third morning back in London. He was accompanied by Katharine, as he had hoped, feeling, with uncharacteristic machismo, like the proudest of men bearing a glittering prize, longing to show her off. Katharine, for the first time since her arrival in the country, felt true nervousness, but Elspeth Lehmann was at the door to greet her with a warmth and courtesy that swiftly became genuine pleasure as she perceived the younger woman's earnest desire to be liked.

"Where's Jeremy?" Sebastian asked.

"Not in yet."

Sebastian said nothing, but Katharine saw a hint of surprise in his eyes, for the two men had not seen one another since Sebastian had left London for New York, and she knew that her husband had been eagerly anticipating their meeting.

"Everyone here is dying to meet you, Katharine," Elspeth told her. "You don't mind if I call you Katharine, do you? Mrs. Locke sounds so very formal."

"And I might not even realize you were talking to me." Katharine smiled. "There's so much to get used to."

"There must be," Elspeth said sympathetically. "And you mustn't hesitate to ask me for anything, if you think I can help."

The two secretaries and Max Wolf, the bookkeeper, hardly troubled to conceal their curiosity, and Katharine was suddenly aware that she must have been the object of much speculation over the past two weeks.

"I'm going to rescue my wife now," Sebastian said, after several minutes of questions about New York and Katharine's show and, of course, their honeymoon, "and sit her down in my office with a cup of coffee."

"They're all so nice," Katharine said, when the door was closed. "And this," she said, looking around Sebastian's office, "is even nicer."

She was almost more fascinated by this room than she had been by the Mayfair house, for that, she had noticed immediately, no matter what Sebastian might say, had smacked of impermanence; apart from the antiques and objets d'art that he had collected, the little house had a transient, almost throwaway feel about it.

"This," she said, with a sense of satisfaction, "is you."

"Is it?" he said, lightly, though he was obviously pleased. "It's just a work place, of course, but I'll admit I'm fond of it."

"Of course you are."

Katharine knew already, very well, how important, how fundamental the agency was to his life. The office was an elegant and tranquil room, spacious, with a washroom and tiny galley kitchen adjoining. Its style was simple and efficient, lightly sprinkled with touches of beauty. His writing desk was rich, burnished mahogany, inlaid with dark green leather, the wall behind it taken up entirely with bookshelves. Two Matisse lithographs hung on the left-hand wall, where Sebastian could clearly see them, and a romantic little Chagall original hung opposite.

"It's a beautiful office," she said.

There was a light rap on the door, and it opened.

"Jerry." Sebastian rose. "At last."

He stood in the doorway, a shorter man than Sebastian, but very slim and dark and superbly dressed.

"This," Jeremy said, "I take it, must be Mrs. Locke."

"This is Katharine." Sebastian's face was filled with pleasure. "And this is a moment I've been looking forward to." He took Katharine's hand. "Darling, I'd like you to meet Jeremy Mariner."

Katharine smiled at Jeremy. "We've already met, though you probably don't remember me."

"I remember you rather well." He looked at her, studying her. " 'My, how you've grown' is the first thing that comes to mind."

"I'm not the only one." Katharine paused. "I'm very happy to meet you again, Jeremy."

She returned his gaze, trying to take him in. His face was narrow, sharp-featured, and his dark eyes smiled at her well enough, but it was a sardonic smile, she thought, with a pang of disappointment, and insincere.

"I haven't congratulated you." Jeremy kissed her cheek.

"You've hardly congratulated me," Sebastian said.

"It wasn't easy to, since you were apparently hiding out." Jeremy looked steadily at Sebastian. "I should have liked to have been at your wedding, but then you must have known that."

Sebastian put one arm around Katharine. "I'm afraid we've upset quite a few people." He smiled, easily. "It was entirely my doing— I just couldn't bear to wait. I thought Katharine might change her mind if I gave her time to reconsider."

"I don't think she would have done," Jeremy said.

"No," Katharine agreed, "I wouldn't."

"Perhaps Seb thought he might be the one to change his mind," Jeremy suggested. "He managed to stay a bachelor for twenty-seven years, after all."

"Not once I laid eyes on Katharine," Sebastian said, quietly. "Everything changed the moment I saw her."

"I hope," Katharine said to Jeremy, "we can be friends."

Jeremy smiled.

"I'm sure," he said.

"He hates me," Katharine said to Sebastian later, when they were alone again.

"Of course he doesn't."

"He certainly resents me, you can't possibly deny that."

"He's just upset that we married in the States."

"I can understand that. He is your best friend, after all."

Sebastian sighed. "I suppose, if I'd been thinking clearly, I'd have asked him to fly to New York." He shook his head. "But I wasn't thinking about anyone except you."

"You'll have to make it up to him," Katharine said. "Do you think he may be concerned that our marriage is going to somehow affect your relationship?"

"There's no reason for him to think that."

"Still. I think it's important that you spend some time with him now, away from the office. Have dinner with him tonight—"

"I want to have dinner with you."

"We have our whole lives to have dinner, darling," she persisted. "I think maybe Jeremy just needs you to reassure him that nothing's altered."

"But it has."

"Not between you and him." Katharine paused. "I think it's quite understandable if some people are a little dubious about us—both Sam and Laszlo told me they thought we were rushing into marriage, that we ought to take time, make plans."

"You're not having any regrets, are you?" Sebastian looked anxious.

"Not a single one." Katharine smiled. "But good, true friends are hard to come by, don't you think? I think their feelings are just too important to be ignored."

Sebastian and Jeremy had dinner that night at Rules.

"Katharine thought you hated her," Sebastian said, coming directly to the point.

"Of course I didn't hate her," Jeremy said, hardly looking up from his menu.

"That's what I told her." Sebastian paused. "It wasn't exactly the warmest of greetings, though, was it?"

Jeremy put down the menu. "Perhaps I didn't find it the warmest of settings. Trotting her into the office to meet the staff—and by the way, this is Jeremy."

"It wasn't anything like that." Sebastian was dismayed. "How could you possibly think of it that way? I was longing for you both to meet, and it seemed the most natural—"

"Might have been more natural to invite me to the house, don't you think?" Jeremy suggested lightly. "Though I suppose it was the extension of the honeymoon—outsiders not welcome."

"I'm sorry, Jerry."

"For what?"

"Everything. Not getting enough of a grip on myself to be able to plan the wedding properly." Sebastian shook his head. "It wasn't fair to Katharine, either, I see that now, but I felt almost obsessed by the need to make it happen—I felt as if she might disappear in a puff of smoke if I didn't act instantly."

"Get the ring on her finger." Jeremy picked up the menu again. "I understand, I think."

"In the heat of the moment, it never occurred to me that you might be able to fly out and join us—idiotic of me."

"Don't give yourself such a hard time, I told you it's okay."

"No, it was thoughtless, and I'm sorry."

"Ready to order?"

"What do you think of Katharine? Isn't she wonderful?"

"She's very lovely." Jeremy paused. "Beef, I think."

Sebastian looked frustrated. "Jerry, we're talking about my wife. It matters to me what you think."

"Does it? It shouldn't." Jeremy smiled. "But I do think she is very lovely to look at. And she's obviously a clever girl, and she seems to love you. Beyond that, I don't know her yet."

"She's the best thing that's ever happened to me," Sebastian said, quietly.

"I'm glad," Jeremy said.

As Sebastian became embroiled again in agency business, paying the inevitable price for his unscheduled absence, Katharine and Virginia began to spend a great deal of time together. They found Virginia's new flat together, in Montpelier Square, which it was agreed, after numerous talks and meetings with solicitors, that Sebastian would buy, while Virginia wrote The Oaks over to him. And while Virginia helped the younger woman to find the best shops and stores in various parts of London for her own needs, Katharine busied herself with the decoration and furnishing of Virginia's flat.

"You need a new kitchen," she said.

"I suppose it isn't very clean," Virginia agreed.

"And a nice new bathroom."

"Surely not?"

"The bath looks as if it's been used by a football team, and I don't think the plumbing looks too reliable, do you?"

"No," Virginia admitted, "I suppose you're right."

"Should I be minding my own business?" Katharine asked, suddenly embarrassed. "I'm so sorry, Virginia, I have no right—"

"I'm absolutely delighted to have your help," Virginia assured her. "I've always been worse than useless with this kind of thing."

"It's just that you're leaving behind so much space and comfort, and we want you to have everything you could possibly want."

"And I shall, my dear," Virginia said gratefully. "With your help."

Having both the house and flat to work on was a boon to Katharine. It was almost like designing a theater set, better in some ways, for even if it was only for a handful of people instead of for weeks or months of audiences, it would make all the difference to those few people's everyday existence.

Katharine found that she had a gift for transforming even the most disinterested workmen into eager craftsmen. She flattered, coerced and charmed electricians and painters and plumbers, and on the rare occasions when Sebastian had time to spare, he marveled at her talents and realized all over again what a brilliant soulmate he had found. When he was called out of town for several days that December, Katharine and Virginia spent even more time together, sharing their loneliness over lunches and dinners and endless cups of coffee and tea. The difference in their ages seemed immaterial to the warm friendship that was growing between them, though it was true that there was a certain fragility about Katharine that brought out the maternal instincts in Virginia; and their relationship was a source of great comfort to Katharine, who, despite her undeniable joy with Sebastian, was finding the strains of putting down new roots in another country formidable.

She had not driven since leaving Pittsburgh, but now Katharine bought herself a little blue Renault 5, and most mornings, she would grit her teeth and battle through the erratic London traffic to Hampstead, where she would inspect the progress made on the house and collect Virginia. Then they would either shop and lunch, or visit an exhibition, or go to a matinee, or sometimes, if it seemed practical, they would treat themselves to excursions into the countryside. They shivered in the chilly, early December winds that blew in the charming streets of Windsor, Eton and Oxford, wishing it were spring— but then they would discover tiny English tearooms with low, beamed ceilings and blazing fireplaces, serving real cream teas with scones and homemade strawberry preserves, and they would be happy, after all, that it was still winter.

*   *   *

In the second week of March, Virginia moved into the completed flat in Montpelier Square, and one week later Sebastian and Katharine were due to move into The Oaks. At five o'clock that morning, the telephone on Sebastian's bedside table rang shrilly, waking them both.

"Hello?" He fumbled for the light switch and looked at the clock. "Who's this?"

"Darling?" Katharine turned over to look at him.

"Christ," he said. "Is she all right?"

"Virginia?" Katharine sat up, alarmed. "Is it Virginia?"

Sebastian shook his head, still listening. "Yes, of course I can come. Where? I'll be there as soon as I can." He hung up the receiver. "It's one of our clients, Elaine Christie—"

"What's happened to her?"

Sebastian was already out of bed. "She's taken an overdose—some kind of sleeping pills." His face was grim. "She's twenty-three, for Christ's sake, why would she do a thing like that?"

"She's alive?"

"They're still working on her at the Middlesex. They found my name in her diary—they can't find any relatives, so I have to go."

"Of course." Katharine pushed back the duvet. "I'll make you some coffee—"

"No time, sweetheart."

"Would you like me to come with you?"

He shook his head. "No point us both sitting around waiting. In any case—" He stopped. "I forgot."

"What?"

"Today. We're moving today."

Katharine put her arms around him. "Don't worry about that."

"But I can't just leave you today, of all days. I'll call Jeremy. Elaine's his client, too, he can go to the hospital."

"Are you sure?"

Sebastian was already dialing Jeremy's number. "Damned answering machine—where the hell is he?"

"You'll have to go," Katharine said. "There's nothing for you to worry about here, honestly. Virginia's due at eight, to help with the packing, and Harrods will be here at nine—and Ellie's waiting at the other end."

"You really don't mind?" Sebastian pulled on his jeans, looking doubtful.

"Of course I mind, but this is more important. Anyway, we're pretty well organized, so you just get to the hospital, and see what you can do for her."

Sebastian called Katharine several times until the telephone in the Mayfair house was disconnected, but it was after ten in the evening before he arrived at The Oaks.

"She's asleep," Ellie whispered to him at the front door. "Poor thing, she's had quite a day. And so have you, by the look of you. Is the girl all right?"

"She will be, I think." Sebastian gave her a hug. "You must be out on your feet, too, Ellie. Why don't you get on up to bed?"

"I'll be doing that, unless you need something."

He shook his head. "Just some sleep."

"It's wonderful having you back here, you know," Ellie said. "Like old times."

Katharine, in grubby blue jeans and one of Sebastian's large white cotton shirts, was in the drawing room, dozing in one of the big armchairs that she had had reupholstered and covered in a flame-colored velvet as close in shade and texture to the original fabric as she had been able to find. A fire flickered weakly in the grate, and beside Katharine, on the coffee table, a bottle of Cristal champagne stood in a bucket of half-melted ice, two glasses next to it on a silver tray.

Sebastian bent down and kissed her gently awake.

"Hello, angel."

"Hi." She sat up, sleepily. "What time is it?"

"Quarter past ten. You poor thing, having to cope with the whole move on your own."

"Hardly on my own."

"I hate myself for leaving you." He sank down on the sofa.

"How's Elaine?"

"They pulled her through, and she seems, thank God, to be glad to have survived, poor, crazy girl. But she didn't want to be left alone, and since one of the doctors said that her emotional state needed more looking after now than the physical side of things, I had to stay."

"Sure you did."

Even through her own exhaustion, Katharine could see the extent of his weariness. There were shadows under his eyes, his hair was tousled—she knew by now that Sebastian was always immaculate, unless he was in bed—and his shirt was open at the neck with the tie he'd grabbed early that morning, stuffed into a jacket pocket.

Looking around properly for the first time since he'd come into the drawing room, Sebastian could hardly believe what Katharine had achieved.

"This is amazing."

"What is?"

"This room." Suddenly finding his second wind, he stood up. It was the same room he had always known, and yet it was not.

"Do you like it?"

His possessions, the items he had collected since moving to Mayfair, were in the room, blending with the old, and other new, small additions, nothing too much, nothing too extreme—an ornament or two, the antique silver tea caddy Katharine had found at an auction at Phillips, the pair of cut-glass claret jugs from another auction at Sotheby's, a delicate grouping of plants.

"I love it," he said.

Already, a slightly different, younger, but very discreet touch was at work, like soft, fresh spring air, not intrusive but nonetheless permeating the atmosphere. Yet nothing that had been integral or important to this room had been adulterated.

"I tried to keep everything that was beautiful and old," Katharine said, softly. "I didn't want to spoil anything."

"And you haven't."

Sebastian looked at the fire glowing feebly—perhaps for the first time in years, he thought, remembering what Virginia had said about not being bothered to light fires. A fleeting sadness swept over him as he thought about Andrew again, and how much he would have loved Katharine, how she would have adored him. But as he looked at his wife's wonderful eyes, intently waiting for him to be ready, so utterly sensitive to his needs and feelings, every trace of sorrow passed away like forgotten mist.

"Let's have some of this champagne."

He opened the bottle with a small pop, and poured, and Katharine rose, and they sipped for a moment, then put down the glasses and held each other, gently, quietly. And Sebastian stared into her face, silently acknowledging a brand-new awareness. He felt suddenly as if some vital part of himself had been absent for a long, long time, a lack that he had never, consciously at least, noticed.

"What are you thinking, darling?" Still in his arms, Katharine sensed the change in him.

"That this isn't just coming back," he murmured. "It's coming into a whole, complete home. I feel as if a long-lost fragment of myself, that I'd forgotten, has been returned to me, as if it's just slotted into place." He held her tightly, knowing it was her doing. Since his earliest childhood he could not remember experiencing such a sense of absolute love. Such a full measure.

"Shall we go upstairs?" Katharine asked him, gently.

"Why don't we?"

He let her go, damped the fire and turned out the lights, and she held out her hand to him and drew him out of the drawing room and up the broad staircase to their bedroom. And Sebastian hesitated only for an instant before entering the room that had been his parents'. And then he opened the door, and halted in sheer astonishment.

Katharine had hardly allowed him entry to this room since work on the house had begun, and for the past two weeks he had seen nothing of it at all, only too glad that she had taken its redecoration upon herself.

"Now I understand," he said.

"What do you understand?"

"Your desire for secrecy."

For this, of all rooms, had undergone a complete transformation, yet somehow Katharine had, while creating an entirely fresh, new bedroom for their new life, managed to intermingle precious memories. The light-hearted blue-and-white color scheme from their honeymoon suite in Venice, so easy to wake up to; the style of canopy above the four-poster bed that Sebastian recalled from the room they had first made love in, back in the Hawk House Inn; and the bedposts themselves were, he realized, from his parents' own bed, though Katharine had had them polished to a lighter, warmer hue.

It was the most beautiful of bedrooms. The walls and carpets, overall, were creamy, with added warmth thrown up from the soft Persian rugs touched with tender rose and a blue that was softer than powder; the curtain pelmets were swagged, while the drapes themselves hung generously, but unfussily, to the floor. A chaise longue stood below the foot of the bed; Katharine's dressing table, spacious with bowls of flowers and a pair of small, shaded lamps, stood at the big window farthest from the bed—she had given over the dressing room to Sebastian, liking the intimacy of preparing for night and brushing her hair in the morning in view of her husband. And though the bed was romantically canopied, she had dispensed with curtains, so that it stood openly and invitingly, the focal point of the room in spite of the lovely armchairs and the graceful cheval glass that Katharine had perfectly matched to the bedposts and the legs of the chaise longue.

"Do you like it?" Katharine asked, made suddenly nervous by his long silence. "I need you to like this room."

In response, Sebastian picked her up and swung her lightly round, as if she were no heavier than a feather, and then he hugged her tightly, kissed her once, on the lips, and pushed the door shut with one foot.

"You do like it," Katharine said, in his arms.

"More than words can ever express," he said, huskily, and then he put her down and began removing her clothes, an item at a time, meticulously and tenderly kissing every single part of her body as it was laid bare.

"Dear God, I love you," she whispered, and she waited until she was completely naked, her skin flushed, her nipples erect and aching, before she did as he had done, caressing him with her lips, very lightly, as she stripped him of his shirt and unbuckled his belt.

"Angel"—was all he said, for he could hardly speak, could only fall, with her, onto the bed, their new bed for their new life.

Beginning to kiss her again, more demandingly now, Sebastian felt all the unpleasantness and sadness of the day melting away, felt himself growing erect and strong and filled with life and desire. Katharine was playful tonight, kittenish in her movements, deliberately tantalizing him, teasing him, flicking the tip of her tongue over him, voluptuously wriggling, taking his hand and rubbing it over her soft, warm skin and then kissing each of his fingertips in turn, so that he was inflamed with the need to have her—

—And then, without warning, another force, demanding equal acknowledgment, startled him, took him by surprise. It came over his shoulder, out of nowhere, creeping insidiously around him like a stealthy will-o'-the-wisp. The old, familiar, strangely beautiful but disembodied scent of Mitsouko, and Roger et Gallet soap, and Leichner makeup. Diana's scent, the inexplicable nocturnal comforter of Sebastian's childhood, his adolescence and even, occasionally, of his adulthood, that had never disturbed, never required explanation—

Yet suddenly, now, as Katharine writhed languidly in his arms, fully aroused, her skin silken and hot, her thighs open, her body awaiting him, eager and ready, the fragrance seemed to assail Sebastian, to wrap itself around him, over him, the perfume no longer delicate, but heavy, cloying, sickening—

"No—"

With a violent jerk, he pulled away from her. He heard her startled gasp, was aware of her dismay, but he could only lie rigid, on his back, his body icy and impotent, cold perspiration on his forehead and in his palms.

"Darling, what is it?"

He was hideously aware of Katharine beside him, anxious, waiting for him to say something, but he felt unable to move or to speak.

"Sebastian, darling, what's the matter?"

Her voice was puzzled and concerned and gentle, and at last, with a difficulty bordering on physical pain, Sebastian forced himself to respond.

"I don't know," he said, clenching his fists so hard beneath the duvet that the nails tore into his skin. "I think I must be more exhausted than I realized."

"Of course you are." She kissed him, tenderly, on the forehead, her hair brushing his lips. "All that horror, in the hospital."

"I'm sorry."

"Nothing to be sorry about, sweetheart." She moved away from him, toward the other side of the bed. "You just get some sleep now."

He lay motionless for a long time, until the only sound in the room was his wife's soft, even breathing as she slept peacefully beside him, and he thanked God that she had accepted his explanation, and that she was asleep and blissfully unaware. He was numb now, filled only with silent horror at the grotesqueness of what had just happened to him, and he knew that he could never share it with Katharine.

For it had seemed to Sebastian as if the scent, the hallucination he had always been sure he had summoned from his subconscious out of some kind of need, believing he could master it, banish it at will if he wished to—as if, without warning, it had grown from a small, delicate sweetness into a swollen, ugly mutation. Threatening. Smothering him.

And the worst part of all was the sense of revelation it had brought with it. The feeling, at the very height of their passion—the sickening, shocking feeling—that he and Katharine had not been entwined in an act of love. But of incest.

It was after ten when he awoke. The bedroom was light, though the curtains were still drawn, and Katharine was beside him, propped up on one elbow and watching him, a small smile on her lips.

"Good morning, sleepyhead."

"Hello, angel." He smiled back at her. "Been awake long?"

"A while. I've had a bath and I've made coffee."

"So how come you're back in bed?"

"I felt like looking at you. I love watching you in the morning."

Sebastian half closed his eyes again and stroked the soft, downy skin of Katharine's forearm. He had slept so deeply and dreamlessly, he thought, after that bizarre, waking nightmare. He remembered it now, but realizing how happy he felt just waking and seeing Katharine beside him, he knew that it must have been nothing more than a prelude to jagged, overtired sleep, brought about by the traumas of the previous day. A night terror, nothing more.

"Are you okay?" she asked, gently.

"I'm fine, darling."

She snuggled down next to him, and he ran a finger from her chin to the base of her neck and down into the warm valley between her breasts. He felt her small shiver of pleasure and opened his eyes. Her nipples were erect beneath the pale silk of her nightgown, and with a surge of intense desire, he drew her up so that she was lying on top of him.

With one swift, graceful movement, Katharine slipped the night-dress up over her head, and her hair flew into a halo of dark gold, and she put her hands on his shoulders, and pressed the full length of her body against his, her breasts, her belly, her bush, her thighs—

And the horrors of the night spun quietly away from Sebastian's mind, and were forgotten.

c h a p t e r
20

The spring and early summer of 1975 passed pleasurably. Sebastian and Katharine were happy together, had no regrets, and Locke Mariner continued to thrive. Virginia, in her new home, felt as if a great weight had been taken from her shoulders, and Jeremy, it seemed, had resigned himself to Katharine's permanence in their world. Indeed, now that the Lockes were quite settled in The Oaks, and Sebastian's attention was once again fully focused on business, Jeremy began to appreciate the new air of ease that accompanied his partner into the office most mornings.

His own social life was far removed from theirs. When Jeremy was not involved in agency entertaining, he spent his leisure hours in a quite studiously debauched manner. A steady procession of lovers of both sexes continued to pass through his Chelsea flat, some staying for two or three weeks, but never longer; and while these days he drank in moderation and found that smoking pot tended to bring on his asthma, he took so much cocaine that the membranes of his nose had begun to be affected. But nothing was allowed to interfere with his efficiency at Locke Mariner. It was his own company, after all, and still the only thing he wanted to do with his life—but primarily, he would never let Sebastian down, would never betray him.

Of Katharine, of course, he was jealous. He had never known such jealousy before, but then Sebastian had never been in love before. Jeremy found that he could not hate her, she was simply too nice to hate, and besides, he had to recognize that she adored Sebastian, would do anything for him—and how could Jeremy hate anyone who loved Sebastian? He preferred, on the whole, simply to avoid Katharine's company, and on the occasions when it was impossible not to join them for dinner or at a party, Jeremy tended toward chilly politeness.

"Does he ever explain to you why he dislikes me?" Katharine asked Sebastian, after Barbara Stone had seated her beside Jeremy at one of her Sunday lunch parties.

"Of course not, because he doesn't dislike you," Sebastian dismissed the idea. "No one could."

"Plenty of people could, sweetheart. There are all kinds of reasons for not liking someone." She gave a small shrug. "It's all right, I guess—Jeremy isn't ever actually nasty, or even rude."

"But it troubles you, all the same."

"It's just a pity, that's all. I want, so much, to like him. And in a way, I do, because he's your best friend as well as your partner, and I can see how fond he is of you."

"I'll talk to him," Sebastian said.

"No, darling, don't."

"I'd like to sort this out."

"You'll make it worse." Katharine smiled. "Time's the only thing that's going to change the way Jeremy feels about me. I'll just have to be a little more patient."

But as Sebastian repeatedly observed Katharine's reserved, but painstaking efforts to break down the barriers that Jeremy continued to put up, he became increasingly angry.

He challenged him one day, at a quiet moment in the office.

"What exactly is your problem with Katharine?"

Jeremy looked up from his desk, surprised. "I didn't think I had a problem with her."

"But evidently you do, since you make it so abundantly plain that you don't like her."

"On the contrary." Jeremy's face was impassive, his voice calm and careful. "I like Kate very much, naturally. She's a likable person."

"She's also highly intelligent," Sebastian said sharply, "and far too sensitive not to be upset by your lack of warmth." He paused. "Jerry,

I care too much about you to let our relationship go to pieces because you, for reasons I can't begin to understand, refuse to be honest about this."

"You want honesty?"

"Of course."

Jeremy's smile was tight. "You and I have known each other most of our lives, yet for a long time, all we've really had in common is Locke Mariner."

"Our friendship goes far deeper than that, surely." Sebastian was distressed. "I trust you, for Christ's sake, more than anyone."

"Except Kate."

"Well, of course I trust my wife, but this is about you and me."

"I thought it was Katharine you wanted to talk about," Jeremy said. "Seb, I trust you too, with my life, you know that. But Kate and I have absolutely nothing in common except for our relationships with you. You are our only common ground."

"Isn't that enough reason for you to make an effort?"

Jeremy's face hardened. "Listen to me, Sebastian. I leave here at night, and I go home, and I screw whoever's available, and I use cocaine, and I live in another world."

"And I wish you didn't—I wish you'd spend more time with us. We both want you—Katharine, too, that's why she's always trying to get you to come to visit, or go out to dinner—"

"Katharine is a lady," Jeremy said, more gently. "She's sensitive, and she's clever, just as you said. And she may have worked in the theater, and she may have met us both when we were all kids, but the fate that you believe brought the two of you together again has nothing to do with me."

"Does that mean you won't even try to get closer to her?"

"If Kate got close to me," Jeremy said quietly, "my way of life would sicken her."

"Your way of life isn't nearly as bad as you make out."

"Leave it," Jeremy said.

"I can't."

"Then I'm sorry."

The only element that had remained constant all through Sebastian's life was the house that was now once again his home. Yet in some ways even The Oaks seemed to be changing. After more than twenty years of restraint, when even in festive moments its beauty had seemed muted, now, like a long-neglected woman given the opportunity to flaunt herself, the house was coming into its own again. It had always been a splendid backcloth for entertaining, and at last, just as Andrew and Diana had done, Sebastian was in a position to make full use of that potential.

His pleasure in their home was a little marred, however, had been ever since that first traumatic night. Every evening, when he and Katharine climbed the staircase to go to their bedroom, a small frisson of something akin to fear caressed Sebastian's spine. It wasn't that he was visited by the hallucinatory scent each time they made love —on the whole, their lovemaking was as lusty and satisfying as it had consistently been while they were still living in Mayfair. But on three separate occasions since the first, that previously benign fragrance had become so oppressive that Sebastian had felt compelled to turn away from Katharine. She had clearly come to accept his occasional impotence as nothing more serious than a symptom of overwork and fatigue, and it was true enough that the incidents had coincided with nights when he had been more drained than usual, but nevertheless, they unnerved Sebastian.

Sometimes, he lay in bed beside Katharine wanting with all his heart to make love to her, and yet he felt afraid to reach out. It was as if some malicious sprite was lurking close by, waiting to pounce, to spoil their love, to twist and distort and taunt. Then his heart would beat wildly in his chest, and his hands would grow clammy with sweat, and he would be overwhelmed by self-disgust, until he felt able, once again, to regain his control. Katharine was right, he re-assured himself, forced himself to believe. It was fatigue, stress— nothing more.

But although she was genuinely unconcerned by the occasional bouts of impotence that troubled her husband, Katharine was not quite as contented as she let him believe. Certain that she had made the right decision in marrying Sebastian and moving to Britain, she still missed her friends and her work, missed America if truth were told.

"London's wonderful," she told Virginia, one June afternoon, as they sat in the garden at The Oaks, sipping fresh lemonade. "But it's so very different."

"I'm sure it must be quite hard for you, at times," Virginia said. "I haven't ever been to New York, or anywhere in the east, though I've visited Jamie, of course, in California."

"They say the West Coast is almost like visiting another country,

too," Katharine said. "I traveled very little, before I came here—
perhaps that's why I find it tough, sometimes."

"New customs to learn, to adapt to," Virginia sympathized. "Trying
to fit in all the time. I think you manage admirably, my dear, and in
any case, I'm sure that Sebastian wouldn't want you to change anything about yourself."

"I suppose not." Katharine paused, watching a pair of magpies on
the lawn. "Though being married to him isn't always easy, either.
Oh, I guess he's happy—he tells me he's never been so happy,
but—"

"But?"

"There's this underlying tension in him that troubles me sometimes." Katharine smiled. "Sebastian's the most enigmatic man I've
ever known, he's hard to keep up with. In business, he's so volatile
and he has such energy, he's so poised and confident."

"But—?" Virginia prompted her again.

"But at home, sometimes, I sense a lack of confidence. A kind of
uncertainty."

"About what?"

"Himself, I think." Katharine hesitated, then went on. "You know
how demonstrative and warm Sebastian is most of the time—but he
can be remote, too, sometimes, almost untouchable." She paused
again. "And when he's like that, it's as if he's all wound up, but there's
a great big untapped reserve of softness inside him, and it's up to
me to touch on just the right chink in his armor, so that it spills out
again."

"But it's worth waiting for?"

"Of course it is."

Virginia thought for a few moments. "Perhaps Sebastian simply
isn't accustomed to the intimacy that comes with marriage. I'm not
talking about sex, of course—Sebastian must have had dozens of
girlfriends before meeting you, darling, but he's never lived with a
woman before." She smiled. "I think he's very like Andrew in many
ways. He was such a conservative man, and yet once I agreed to marry
him, he became such a romantic that he made me feel almost a girl
again."

"Sebastian's certainly a romantic," Katharine said.

"But though I think I knew Andrew very, very well," Virginia went
on, "there were times when I couldn't begin to decipher his inner-
most thoughts." She smiled. "Perhaps it's a Locke characteristic."

"I guess no one can ever know what's really going on inside

someone else's mind," Katharine said, leaning back contentedly so that the sun bathed her face. "And some things ought to be private."

Virginia watched her for a moment.

"Do you think you might be just a little bored?"

Katharine sat up. "Bored? The last thing I am is bored."

"But you're accustomed to working, surely?" Virginia persisted. "And not just at some ordinary, dull job that you might be glad to escape from. Too much time on your hands to think, to analyze things that don't really need analysis."

Katharine picked up the glass jug of lemonade on the garden table and refilled both their glasses. "I haven't thought about working—at least, not for a while now. First, there was the house—"

"And my flat."

"And then there was just coming to grips with all the changes."

"But now?"

"I guess I thought it might be too tough, breaking in all over again."

"I imagine it might be," Virginia admitted. "But you're a talented professional, my dear, with a fine record." She smiled. "And I suspect that Sebastian would be the first to want to help you—once he knows that's what you want." She paused. "If you do want it."

Katharine felt the breeze ruffle her hair.

"I'll give it some thought," she said.

She spoke to Sebastian a few days later.

"I'm not asking for help—or not too much, at least. I just want to be pointed in the right direction."

"I understand that, darling."

"Do you think I stand a chance over here?"

"With your talent? No doubt about it."

"So who should I talk to?"

"Leave it with me for a day or two. I'll have a word with Jerry, see what he suggests."

"Jeremy?" Katharine looked doubtful. "Do you have to?"

"He handles more clients on the production side than I do, and he's better at keeping his ear to the ground than I am." Sebastian looked at her. "Jeremy's a professional. When it comes to work, you couldn't deal with a better man."

Katharine was silent for a moment.

"Okay," she said. "That's fine—talk to him."

"You're sure?"

She nodded. "It might be good for us all." She smiled. "At least then Jeremy and I might have something we can really talk about at dinner parties, besides the damned weather."

Jeremy telephoned her two days later.

"Seb tells me you're thinking about getting back to work."

"That's right." Katharine paused. "What do you think?"

"Why don't we have lunch?"

"Really?" She was startled. "Do you have time?"

"I'm free tomorrow—how's that with you?"

"It's great. Thank you, Jeremy."

"Don't thank me yet."

"Where and when?" she asked.

"Do you know The Gay Hussar in Greek Street?"

"Not yet."

"I'll see you there at one tomorrow."

Katharine arrived first, and ordered a glass of white wine at the table to help calm her nerves. It was hard to visualize Jeremy Mariner becoming her ally, but that didn't stop her hoping that this might prove a turning point, in more ways than one.

He arrived at just two minutes past one.

"Am I late?" He stooped to kiss her cheek, lightly.

"I was early."

"Thanks for coming." Jeremy signaled to a waiter.

"Thanks for suggesting it."

"You're a potential client." He looked at her drink. "Another glass of wine?"

"No, thank you, I'm fine."

He ordered a glass of champagne and turned his attention back to Katharine. "So tell me, what do you want?"

"To get back to work."

"I know that already—I need to know what exactly you're hoping to do next. Another musical? Straight play? Are you hoping to break into opera or ballet? First thing we need to work out is direction."

Katharine smiled. "I guess I was looking at it a little more humbly than that. I'm a newcomer over here, after all."

"But hardly a newcomer to the business."

"That's true. But I know very little about the theater in Britain."

"Theater is theater," Jeremy said. His champagne arrived, and he picked up the glass. "Cheers."

"Cheers." Katharine drank some wine. "I was hoping that you might help me get started again—point me the right way."

"I'm sure I can do more than that, Kate."

She smiled again. "No one except you has called me that in years."

"That's how I think of you," Jeremy said. "That's what you told us to call you when you were five, wasn't it?"

"I'm surprised you remember."

"I told you I remembered you well." He paused. "Do you mind my calling you Kate?"

"Not at all."

Jeremy ate his *gulyas* with a hearty appetite, while Katharine found herself unable to contemplate anything heavier than a dish of lightly marinated salmon.

"What you can put out of your mind," Jeremy told her, "is your idea of carrying around a portfolio or résumé of your career."

"But isn't that the correct approach?"

"You designed the sets for *Paris*," he pointed out.

"On Broadway—I can't expect people here to have seen it."

"It doesn't matter if they've seen it or not. What matters is they've heard of it—more to the point, they've heard of you. You're a fabulous designer, Kate. I haven't seen your sets either, but I have ears."

Katharine was dubious. "But surely you're not suggesting that I just sweep in, wherever you send me, and say here I am, don't expect me to prove myself, just take it or leave it?" She shook her head. "That kind of attitude in the States from someone trying to break in would get you kicked all the way from Broadway to Iowa, and then some."

Jeremy smiled. "But you're not just any American trying to break in. They'll expect a fairly gung-ho approach from the designer of a big smash musical."

"Even though you have such wonderful designers of your own?"

"All out of a handful of schools," Jeremy said, dismissively.

"Great schools, with fine reputations."

"True, but all schools stamp their mark on students, their style. You dropped out of Carnegie Mellon, didn't you? You completed your training at the hands of a master."

"I certainly did. Do you know Laszlo Eles?"

"We haven't met, but naturally I know of him." Jeremy paused and leaned toward her, his manner confidential. "You're an individual,

Kate, that's all I'm saying. Don't make the mistake of being too modest. If the right production comes along, you won't need them, they'll need you. Just remember that."

Two weeks later, while Sebastian was working late in his office, Jeremy looked round the door.

"Do you have a moment?"

"Sure."

Jeremy sat down facing him.

"Scotch?"

"Please."

"What's up?" Sebastian asked. "Problems?"

"An awkward one."

"Tell me." He set two whisky glasses on the desk.

"It's Kate."

Sebastian looked up, surprised. "What about her?" He paused. "Does this have something to do with the meeting you set up for her this afternoon?"

"That's right." Jeremy waited a beat. "Have you heard from her?"

"Not yet—I think she was going to meet Virginia when she was through. What's this problem?"

"It's a little awkward."

"So you said. What exactly is awkward?"

Jeremy picked up his glass. "I had a call about an hour ago, from Aileen Fisher at CWP. She was at the meeting with Katharine and the Fitzwalters, and she seemed a little concerned."

"About what?"

"Katharine's attitude."

Sebastian's eyes narrowed. "What about her attitude? Jerry, will you stop tiptoeing around and come to the point?"

"Aileen felt that Kate was arrogant."

"Arrogant?" Sebastian laughed. "Are we talking about the same Katharine? My wife doesn't have the first idea how to be arrogant."

"I agree with you." Jeremy shrugged. "Kate's always seemed very modest to me, very reserved."

"Of course she is." Sebastian was angry. "What the hell is Aileen Fisher talking about?"

"Apparently, Kate arrived without her portfolio—"

"She told me that was your idea."

Jeremy shook his head. "Not exactly. I told her that there wasn't any need to go in like a novice, which was the way she seemed to be thinking. I only used the portfolio as an illustration, as a metaphor."

"Which she took literally, and I don't blame her."

"But I certainly never would have suggested that she tell Ken and Barry Fitzwalter to fly to New York if they wanted to see her work."

"Katharine said that?" Sebastian was stunned. "I don't believe it."

"Aileen had no reason to lie."

"Are you sure you didn't tell her to say something like that?" Sebastian asked ironically. "A small metaphorical joke, perhaps?"

"Am I in the habit of insulting producers?" Jeremy asked, mildly, then paused. "Sebastian, don't take this the wrong way, but you've never worked with Kate, have you?"

"You know I haven't."

"Do you think perhaps she has a more forceful attitude to her work than to her private life?"

"Not according to Sam Raphael, or Dixie Callaghan, her assistant, who told me that Katharine was the most wonderful, gentle person she could imagine working with—not that I needed telling."

"Then I have no explanation." Jeremy shrugged again. "Maybe it was just one of those clashes of personality—maybe the Fitzwalters had already decided who the job was going to before Kate went in."

Sebastian's anger had not abated. "In that case, Katharine should never have been sent to meet them. There's no reason for her to have been exposed to that kind of nastiness."

"She's a big girl," Jeremy said. "She made it on Broadway—I'm sure she can handle a little London bitchiness."

"I don't doubt that she can," Sebastian said coolly. "That doesn't mean that I want it to happen."

Katharine was outwardly calm when Sebastian spoke to her that evening during dinner at home, but he could see that the encounter had upset her.

"I'm a professional—or at least I hope I am," she said, "but I sure as hell didn't come off looking like one."

"The Fitzwalters know you're a professional," Sebastian said, "and a damned fine one. Jeremy thinks—and I agree—that they'd probably made up their minds before you even got there."

"I doubt that." Katharine paused. "I hated going in there without something to show them, but Jeremy insisted that would be down-grading myself."

"He says he intended that as a metaphorical piece of advice, not to be taken absolutely literally."

"Does he?" Katharine said dryly.

"Don't you believe him?" Sebastian asked.

"Do you?" She shook her head. "Don't take any notice of me—
I'm really angry, but with myself, not with Jeremy or anyone else.
I've been around long enough to know better than to listen to advice
that I don't agree with."

Sebastian looked at her. "What are you saying? That Jeremy deliberately misled you?"

"No, of course I'm not saying that." Katharine shrugged. "If I think
back now, I guess he was just trying to boost my confidence. And he
wasn't wrong to do that—I was feeling very jittery about trying to
break into a new marketplace." She smiled, ruefully. "And I was
certainly right about that, wasn't I?"

"One bad meeting means nothing, angel."

"One lousy meeting," she amended, "and with two of the biggest
producers in town."

"It was bad planning on our part," Sebastian insisted. "We'll do
better next time, I promise."

"Let's not rush things, okay?"

"Whatever you say."

It was another three weeks before Katharine felt ready to broach
the subject again. It was a Sunday evening at the end of July, one of
their all too rare quiet times together, and they were sitting in the
room on the first floor which Sebastian had converted into a tiny
private cinema where he could watch videotapes of artists' performances, or old movies, just for entertainment.

The final frame of *Un Homme et Une Femme* had just faded away,
and the almost aggressively romantic quality of the film had left
Katharine restless and invigorated. Looking at Sebastian, still sitting
comfortably back in his soft leather armchair, mellow and relaxed,
she decided that now was the perfect moment to talk.

"My career," she said.

"What about it, angel?"

"I've been thinking about things."

"I knew you were. I didn't say anything, because I didn't want to
push you again, until you were ready."

"That's just it," Katharine said. "I'm not sure if I am ready."

He smiled, still very relaxed. "There's no urgency. You just take
all the time you need—there's so much for you to get used to. And
when you say the word, I'll start making inquiries." He paused. "I

think I'll look after you myself from here on, rather than Jeremy, don't you think?"

"I'd certainly prefer it, though—"

"Though what?" Sebastian looked at her. "Would you be happier with an independent agent, darling? I hadn't thought about it, but if that's what you want, I'd understand."

"Why on earth would I want another agent," Katharine said swiftly, "when I'm married to the best?" She stopped again.

"What is it, darling?" Sudden alarm flickered in his eyes. "Are you missing New York? Are you considering working over there?"

Katharine laughed. "Of course not—the last thing in the world I want is to be separated from you."

"Thank God for that." The relief in his face was conspicuous. "It's just that I'm aware that if you'd stayed over there, the offers would have been stacking up by now, whereas over here, it may take a little time and effort to get the ball rolling."

"I don't really mind about that," Katharine said.

"But you do want to get back to work, don't you? I felt, when we met, that you loved it so much."

"I did. I do, I guess." She tried to explain. "But for a whole bunch of reasons—I don't understand them all myself—the prospect of starting over again, of selling myself in this new marketplace, fills me with dismay instead of excitement."

"You're underestimating yourself, Katharine. After *Paris*, you're an established name."

"That was what Jeremy tried to tell me."

"And he was right."

"I'm not so sure. Not in London, where there must be dozens of gifted British designers who would fight tooth and nail before they let an American steal jobs from them."

"I'd say 'earn' was a more appropriate word than 'steal.' If you win a show, they'll respect you for it."

"Maybe." Katharine paused. "This may be just a passing phase, sweetheart, but I'm not so sure I feel like fighting all that hard."

Sebastian stood up and walked slowly over to the built-in cocktail cabinet. He took out a bottle of cognac.

"What exactly do you have in mind then, if not design?" He poured cognac into two snifters. "I may be wrong, but I don't envisage you sitting here at home for too much longer."

"You're not wrong."

"So what is it you want?"

He looked at her from that end of the room and saw, with a pang, how intense her confusion was. She was so extraordinarily lovely, and he hoped more than anything that he was making her happy, but he knew that she would not, and should not, settle for a life of leisure.

And then, suddenly, Sebastian knew what it was that Katharine was made for. And in that same moment, he realized precisely what the magic ingredient had been that had drawn him so inexorably to her side at Sardi's that night last October. It had been more than beauty, for there had, after all, been many other beautiful women there that night, as there were in many places, most nights.

It had been her talent. A certain, rare kind of talent.

There was a portion in Sebastian's mind that had become increasingly adept, over the years, at focusing with magnetic sureness upon what it, usually instantaneously, recognized as exciting and exceptional potential. That, he realized now, was what had happened in Sardi's that night: a professional attraction of great strength. But once they had met, stood close to one another, that initial recognition had been confused by the other intoxicating new emotions that had made him temporarily forgetful of everything except the phenomenon of falling in love. The realization, now, did not lessen that love. Rather, it strengthened it.

"Sebastian?"

Katharine's voice stirred him.

"I'm sorry."

He walked back to her, gave her one of the glasses. He felt as if a cymbal had crashed in his brain, and instantly, secretly, he had begun to calculate, to think like an agent instead of a husband.

"What is it you want, Katharine?" he asked her again.

It was vital, he decided, to be cautious with her. She was, he knew, fluctuating between contentment and insecurity, her emotions peppered with homesickness and the anxieties of settling into a new environment. If he was heavy-handed with her now, she was bound to shy away, perhaps irrevocably.

Katharine took a sip of cognac. "I wish I really knew."

He decided to sow one gentle seed. "What about acting?"

Her eyes widened. "I'm not an actress, I'm a designer."

"But you told me," Sebastian said, lightly, "when we first met, that your first, instinctive love was acting—your inheritance from your mother, you said. You told me you won every lead in every school play—you even admitted that you were good."

"But I chose design. I rejected acting for art."

"Only because you blamed your mother's career for your parents' divorce. You said that Sam pointed that out to you, and you realized he was right."

"That wasn't the only reason, it couldn't have been," Katharine said. "I knew how tough the life was—a life of constant rejection, a life of selling myself was never my style."

Sebastian smiled at her. "You've just been telling me that about stage design, and you managed to get to the top in that field in New York City, the toughest marketplace, as you put it, in the theater." He paused. "If you'd stayed with acting, with your first love, there's no telling what you might have achieved by now."

"Too late to think about that."

"Is it?"

"Of course it is." She looked at him. "Anyway, surely if I had been suited to the profession, if it had been right for me, I wouldn't have given it up for anything."

Sebastian said nothing, only smiled, allowed the new thoughts to percolate for a few minutes in her confused mind. He sat down beside her, drank a little cognac and took her hand.

"How good were you?" he asked, at last. "Did you really believe you were good, before you decided to go with art?"

A tiny glint of defiance shone briefly in Katharine's eyes. "Yes," she admitted. "I think I was quite good. But I didn't want the life, or maybe I knew I couldn't be dedicated enough." She shook her head. "In any case, why are we discussing this now? I'm twenty-six years old, and I'm married, and that means more to me than anything."

"You mean you're scared of repeating your mother's mistakes."

"I just mean I'm not an actress."

"All right." Sebastian tilted back his chair and raised his hands as if surrendering. "I understand, it's okay. But there's no need for you to be defensive, with me of all people."

"I didn't know I was being defensive," Katharine said.

"It was just that I suddenly had an impression that you wanted to talk about old times—and I always want to know more about you and all the strange ways our interests seem to overlap."

For a few moments, Katharine was silent.

"You're right, of course. There's no harm in remembering." She smiled. "And even if I have buried all those old instincts, it is good to think back to the parts I played, and to the rehearsals."

"Tell me," Sebastian said quietly.

Katharine shrugged. "Not that much to tell. Except that I loved it all—the comradeship, the fabulous surge of adrenaline during performance, even, in a gruesome kind of way, the stage fright." She paused. "Of course, most of those things factor into why I love scene design—"

"Not performance, though."

"No, but I still feel I'm part of the company, of the family—I know it's not the same, I'm only on the periphery. My finished work, my sets, are drawn right in, they become part of the heart and soul, while I can only sit back and watch."

They sat talking well into the night, more absorbed than ever in each other. From time to time, Sebastian gave Katharine a gently encouraging nudge back into those youthful days when she had still dreamed of theater on the other side of the footlights, then sat back again to watch and listen to her responses.

"Hypothetically," he said, "purely hypothetically, if you could have your pick today, what roles would you give your soul to play?"

"I don't know," she said. "It's been so long since I gave it any thought."

"Think now."

"I can't, just like that."

"Yes, you can. Let yourself go—what's the first role that comes into your head that you think you could play?"

"Rosalind," Katharine said instantly, and blushed.

"As You Like It." Sebastian smiled. "Romantic."

"I designed the sets in high school."

"I would love to see you play Rosalind."

"Not my soul, though," Katharine said. "You asked if there was a part I'd give my soul to play. There isn't. That's what I meant about not being right for acting."

"What about television?" Sebastian asked, changing tack. "What about film?"

"No."

"Why not?"

She shrugged. "I always felt I belonged in theater."

And again, Sebastian smiled.

*   *   *

It was after two in the morning when Katharine, lightheaded enough on the mixture of cognac, the power of Sebastian's careful but persistent proddings, and her own stirred-up imagination, felt ready to shed some of her inhibitions.

"I think I remember Rosalind's epilogue," she said, shyly. "Do you feel like hearing me?"

"You bet I do." He squeezed her hand. "Only if you're comfortable with it, angel."

"It's just been such a long time since—oh, what the hell, here goes nothing." She got to her feet, a little unsteadily, and laughed. "I think I must be drunk."

"Go on, sweetheart," he coaxed her, gently. "I'd love it."

Katharine began, and for the first few words her voice trembled, and her hands, and she wished she had not begun, had not imagined that she could feel so awkward before her husband, and her eyes sought an impersonal spot on the far wall beyond him—

And then it fell back into place. She knew that she was totally lacking in experience and ignorant of technique—but the magic of it was still there for her, the pleasure of using her voice, of disappearing into another human being, even for just a few minutes.

Sebastian forgot that she was his wife. He was an agent, a purveyor of talent. And as such, he was seeing Katharine Andersen Locke for the very first time.

She was a novice, of course, and the piece she had chosen came out of schoolgirl memory, was not a speech that any professional would select to audition with, yet Sebastian realized immediately that Katharine had three essential qualities—the innate intelligence that was no surprise to him; a clear, warm voice, startlingly more English than he had imagined possible; and almost faultless, natural timing. But far more, infinitely more compelling than all those things was the fact that it was quite impossible to look away from her.

If, as was to be expected, Sebastian had begun to become familiar with Katharine's beauty as the months of living together had passed, that familiarity vanished there and then. As in New York, that first time, he was staring at her again, raptly, at her wonderfully constructed face, at the perfect combination of fine bones, soft skin and rare eyes; he was seeing how at one moment she had a look of untouchable dignity, and the next, a soft, sparkling humor that was just a breath away from a wistful vulnerability.

But the eyes through which Sebastian saw Katharine now were

not romantic eyes, nor loving eyes. They were cool and assessing, observing each transition and checking once, twice, to be sure he was not mistaken, that love had not twisted his judgment.

". . . and, I am sure, as many as have good beards, or good faces, or sweet breaths, will, for my kind offer, when I make curtsy, bid me farewell."

She finished, stood very still, waited for him to speak.

"Wait," he said. He rose abruptly from his chair and strode quickly to the door and opened it.

"Where are—?"

"Please," Sebastian said. "Just wait."

He was back within minutes.

"Here," he said, and thrust a script into her hands.

"What is it?"

"It doesn't matter—it was the first script that came to hand, what it is is of no consequence." He looked at her intently. "Sarah Bernhardt could read a telephone directory and make audiences weep, Katharine."

"I'm not Sarah Bernhardt."

"Humor me." He took the script back out of her hands and opened it at random. "Here—read both parts, just as it comes."

Katharine stared at him, then down at the open pages. "Don't I get time to read it first?"

"No." Sebastian sat down again and folded his arms.

"Darling—"

"Please, angel," he said, quietly, urgently. "Do it for me."

Something inside her toughened, almost visibly. She lifted the script higher and raised her chin. Her dark gold hair brushed one cheek, and she tossed it back. And began to read.

Sebastian felt professional detachment dropping away from him, like the shriveled skin falling away from a snake, revealing brand-new, living and sensitive flesh. There was no possibility of remaining cool now. The incomparable thrill of new discovery and the burning anticipation that invariably accompanied the greatest of those discoveries surged through him as he listened and watched, giving nothing away.

She had it, he was certain. What some people called "star quality," and others called "charisma." She had *it*.

Until this minute, his relationship with Katharine had been the most candid and open he had ever known. Yet now, suddenly, for the first time, Sebastian felt himself drawing back, away from her, felt a kind of uncharacteristic stealth creeping over him as he began, privately, silently, to plan a strategy—spinning the first strands of an unpredictable and intricate web that even he did not yet quite understand.

c h a p t e r
21

"It's all destiny," Sebastian said to Jeremy the next evening, as they sat in Jeremy's office waiting for a call from Los Angeles.

"Crap," Jeremy responded. "Kate's a designer, not an actress."

Sebastian shook his head. "Other way around. Katharine's been working as a designer, but what she is is an actress."

"But she's a good designer."

"Yes, she is. Katharine's a multitalented woman." Sebastian's eyes were determined and clear. "But her destiny is in acting."

"Sebastian, listen to yourself." Jeremy was exasperated. "Any minute now, you'll be talking star signs and full moons. You're an agent, not a fucking fortune-teller."

"I know how it sounds." Sebastian smiled. "But if you'd heard her, seen her, you'd feel exactly the same way." He paused. "Katharine derailed herself at a vulnerable time of her life, chose the wrong route, it's as simple as that."

"But even if that's true, it's much too late to turn back now. She's twenty-six years old—a little old for drama school."

"Not necessarily, but there are other ways, as you know, more than most." Sebastian was very calm. "And it's hardly unheard of for people in our business to change direction. Any number of actors become directors or writers."

"And bimbo wives of rich executive producers find their ways into fourth-rate movies, but I hardly think Kate fits that description."

Sebastian's eyes grew harder. "I don't have time to waste in fatuous arguments, Jerry. I'd hoped for a little cooperation."

"Regardless of my opinion?"

"In this case, yes."

"Just one more little question."

"Yes?"

"Does Kate agree with you about this?" Jeremy paused. "Is she ready to give up everything she's worked for, to start all over again on something she decided to ditch years ago?"

"She's ready to give it a try."

"Because it's what she wants, or what you want?"

Sebastian raised a brow. "I didn't know you were so interested in Katharine's feelings about anything."

"It's your feelings that interest me," Jeremy said. "I don't think I've seen you as fired up over an idea as this for a long time."

"Katharine's my wife. Is it really so surprising?"

Jeremy smiled. "More fascinating than surprising."

Before two months had passed, Katharine found herself plunged deep into a world unlike any she had known. No sooner had she admitted to a pang of excitement at the notion that it might not be too late to think again about an acting career than Sebastian had snapped into action.

"Take it easy," she had said, panicked by his energy. "I'm not as certain as you are that this is right."

"It's right, angel," he had told her. "Trust me."

"You know I do."

"I won't commit you to anything that you don't agree with one hundred percent, okay?"

And she had smiled and nodded, for she did trust him implicitly, and loved him more than ever for the new, dynamic spark in his eyes that she knew was for her, all part of his desire and will to make her happy.

Sebastian worked strenuously, but diplomatically, pulling all the strings that it made sound sense to pull in order to win Katharine her first professional acting engagement and, with it, her provisional Equity card. He might, as easily, have drawn her in through a small film role, but that was not the direction he had decided to map out for her, and besides, all Katharine's roots were in theater, and theater was where he saw her so vividly, in his mind's eye.

Sebastian understood the workings and standards of British repertory theater as well as, or perhaps even better than some other London agents. He persisted in his belief that those companies still cradled some of the finest talents of tomorrow, and there were by now few theaters in the entire country that either he or Jeremy had not visited over the past few years.

"What do you think about the Bromsgrove Playhouse?" he asked Jeremy, one morning in mid-August.

"I try never to think about it," Jeremy replied.

"Well, think about it now, for Katharine's debut."

"You're kidding."

"Never been more serious."

"It's a dump." Jeremy laughed. "You are kidding, aren't you?"

"It's perfect for our needs at this time," Sebastian said. "They're doing *Arsenic and Old Lace* and *All My Sons*, with a Pinter double bill sandwiched between. There are three reasonable parts for Katharine—"

"An American designer playing Pinter in Bromsgrove?"

"Katharine has excellent standard English, you'd be surprised."

"I would."

"Wait and see," Sebastian said, easily.

"Let me get this absolutely straight," Jeremy said. "You want to send your beautiful, sophisticated, successful American bride to an industrial town in the Midlands for a couple of months—"

"Three and a half months."

"—to cut her teeth in a mediocre company—"

"I want Katharine to serve her early apprenticeship without too much pressure," Sebastian explained, patiently. "The Playhouse is ideal. Alan Bridehouse was down last week, and he's seen her and wants her. He knows Katharine's a beginner, and you and I know it's not a great company, but they'll correct her mistakes, smooth over her rawness, and they'll be kinder to her than some."

"And if she's as good as you claim," Jeremy added, "they won't be sharp enough to recognize her potential prematurely."

"You see?" Sebastian smiled. "I knew you'd understand."

*   *   *

Katharine arrived in Bromsgrove for her second meeting with the director of the season, awash with doubts and confusion. The older parts of the town were attractive enough, with some half-timbered houses and a sixteenth-century grammar school, but she found the drabness of the flat she was to live in for the duration of her engagement depressing.

"Couldn't I stay in a hotel?" she asked Sebastian on the drive back to London. "Birmingham's close enough, isn't it?"

"Not if you want to fit in. You'll find it hard enough, as it is."

"I usually fit in pretty well," Katharine said.

"I know you do, angel, but this is going to be different."

She sighed. "I guess I know what you mean. I went through some of that in New York when I first got there. I had my apartment on the Upper East Side, and there I was, a humble college dropout, trying to break in, and there were plenty of people who didn't like it."

He took her hand and squeezed it tenderly. "I just want to do all I can to see that people don't give you a rough time."

"Do you think they'll resent an American getting work?"

"It may not help," he admitted. "You're also very beautiful, you've been a big success on Broadway, and you're rich."

"I'm hardly going to brag about that," Katharine said.

"You won't need to. Actors are the sharpest people in the world, my love. They'll smell the money, and the success, and however decent they are, chances are they'll resent it."

She tried to smile. "I'll work it out. I'm going to Bromsgrove to learn from them, after all. I'll just have to make sure they know it."

Sebastian glanced at her quickly, his eyes searching. "You're sure that you want to do this, aren't you? I mean, you're not just doing it for my sake?"

"I most certainly am not," she said, indignantly. "I may love you a hell of a lot, and this may not exactly be my idea of paradise—and I sure as hell *hate* the idea of being separated from you—"

"I'll come up as often as I can."

"We'll still be apart."

"Maybe you shouldn't do it—"

Katharine's voice was firm. "I have a contract now, and I'm going to fulfill it if it kills me. And let's look on the bright side—if I get through the next three months still loving the theater, then we'll know for sure you're right."

* * *

Virginia, outraged when Katharine told her the news, confronted Sebastian the very next morning at Locke Mariner.

"How can you even *consider* depositing Katharine in a place like that?" she demanded. "Heaven alone knows London's been enough of a culture shock for her, but now you don't just intend throwing her to the wolves—you want to abandon her."

Sebastian tried to explain. "We chose—"

"I can't believe you could be so heartless," Virginia swept on. "And I certainly refuse to believe that poor darling Katharine had anything to do with the decision—I doubt if she'd even heard of Birmingham, let alone Bromsgrove."

"May I speak now?" Sebastian asked mildly.

"If you can say anything that can possibly make me think this is anything other than cruelty."

"Of course it was my idea. Naturally, Katharine knew very little about British repertory theater—"

"Then how on earth—?"

"Virginia, please give me a chance."

She kept silent, her lips tightly compressed.

"I chose that particular theater, in that particular place, for reasons I consider perfectly sound. Katharine wants to act, and since she is quite old by beginner's standards, and since the profession is not exactly holding its breath waiting for a London agent to push his wife out on stage like some Mr. Worthington, there was hardly a surplus of companies willing to try her out."

"But surely that's precisely why you ought to be discouraging her," Virginia said, impatiently.

"Katharine is a mature, successful and independently wealthy woman, wouldn't you agree?" Sebastian asked.

"You're stating the obvious."

"So do you think she'd be likely to submit to the quirks of her husband, unless she agreed with him?"

"Perhaps not," Virginia said, unconvinced. "But I still think that it's tantamount to planting an orchid in a bed of weeds."

Sebastian had never seen Virginia so angry. "Darling, please try to see that this isn't as simple as it looks. Katharine understands that it's important for her to stay in a less-than-luxurious rented flat, so that she doesn't arouse envy. She went through those kinds of problems in her early designing days in New York, she knows how important it is to try to fit in."

"Do you think she will fit in?"

"I think so." Sebastian paused. "She's as green as they come, and she's going to make mistakes, but if she makes friends, too, Katharine can use this engagement as a perfect training ground."

"What if it's all a disaster?"

"If she fails, then she can come home to The Oaks knowing that she tried. On the other hand, if she succeeds, she'll come back hungry for more. Either way, I know she'll survive."

"And what about your marriage?" Virginia asked, quietly. "Will that survive?"

"Of course it will," he said with perfect confidence.

"It's a long separation, darling."

"But I'll be going up at weekends." He shook his head. "I hate the idea of being apart from Katharine just as much as she does, but we're in love, Virginia, and we're very happy."

"You truly believe this is a wise decision?"

Sebastian took Virginia's hand. "I do, I swear it. It's the right decision, for Katharine's future happiness. For us both."

The Playhouse worked its spell on Katharine from the start. In the graceless street in which it stood, it was an incongruous structure, warmly decorated and ornately carved, with a small, gilded foyer, an icy barnlike auditorium, a splintery stage and damp-smelling, uncomfortable dressing rooms. It was worlds apart from the Winter Garden Theatre in New York City, but once the artists were backstage, slapping the Max Factor onto their faces, it was earthy, archetypal theater nevertheless, and its scent could burrow its way into the bloodstream just as forcefully as it would in Shaftesbury Avenue or on Broadway.

As she settled down, Katharine realized how much confidence all the years behind the scenes had given her, and how much she owed to Laszlo and, before him, to her time at Carnegie Mellon. She had an ability to mix with and to adapt to all types of people, and she was no longer as fearful as she had been in the past.

"I guess I enjoy a challenge these days," she told Virginia, on the telephone one evening in the second week of rehearsals for *Arsenic and Old Lace*. "Oh, I'm still terrified—I had the biggest anxiety attack just yesterday. But I know how to face up to it now, knock on wood."

"Are they treating you well, darling?"

"They couldn't be kinder." Katharine's voice was bubbling with excitement. "It's all a little strange, of course, but in a way, this whole thing, just being up here, feels as much like acting as the onstage work—sometimes I don't really feel like myself at all."

It was another life, another world entirely. Katharine had told no one in the States either about the switch of direction to acting or about Bromsgrove. She did wonder what Laszlo or Sam or Dixie would say if they could see her here. Or David. She thought that he would probably hate the idea, would have tried to dissuade her from going through with it and then, being David, would have given her all the support she needed. But David didn't know, and Katharine was happier not thinking too much about him. And as for the others, as much as she loved them, it didn't really matter what they thought. It was Sebastian who mattered most. Her husband, her lover, her best friend and now, she recognized, her motivating force. For she knew, deep down, that whatever she might say to the contrary to Virginia or to anyone else, she was only really here, in this alien little Midlands town, because Sebastian wanted her to be.

The people she was working with were being kind and generous to her—she had not lied to Virginia about that. And Katharine could see that Sebastian had chosen wisely, if at first glance strangely, for her sake, for the third-rate quality of the productions, brought about by paltry budgets rather than lack of talent, shielded her, allowed her to step gently into this new role. The sets were modest, the dimensions and perspective all wrong, and Katharine's fingers itched to get to work on them, but that was not her job. She had a new line of work now—or at least she had for the moment—and Sebastian had not twisted her arm, had not forced her to take it.

They said that the people who loved you often knew you better than you knew yourself. If Sebastian, who had already come up four times in two weeks, said that the light in her face was most brilliant when she was acting, who was she to disagree with him?

Arsenic and Old Lace went down well with the audiences; Alan Bridehouse seemed more than satisfied with Katharine's work; and although she knew that she was almost as alien to some members of the company as a visitor from Mars might have been, she was, at least, making no enemies. When the Pinter double bill opened, however, in the middle of October, it played to half-empty houses, and although they had high hopes that the Arthur Miller play would improve things considerably, Katharine could not imagine anything even approaching euphoria ever raising the roof of the Bromsgrove Playhouse.

By the end of November, Katharine was heartily depressed. It was damp, dismal and cold. The work was stimulating and enjoyable, and she felt that, in time, she would look back on these three months as a truly worthwhile experience, but late at night, when she went back to her lonely flat, anxieties about her continuing separation from Sebastian niggled at her until the early hours.

"Are you all right, my love?" he asked her, when he came up for the first night of *All My Sons*.

"I'm great," she lied.

"If you wanted to come home, I'd understand."

"I want to come home more than anything," she said, "because I miss you like hell, but I'm not leaving till the final curtain on the last night."

"You're a trouper." Sebastian held her tightly, inhaled the fragrance of her hair. "I miss you, too, angel, more than I can ever tell you."

"Only another twenty-six nights to go," she said, nuzzling against his shoulder, then drew back, looking at the overnight bag behind him. "What did you bring me?"

Each time he drove up to see her, Sebastian brought Katharine a few delicacies and comforts from London, and their reunions were always so romantic—with candlelit picnics out of Fortnum & Mason hampers enjoyed on the living room floor on a rug bought from Harrods, followed by nights of lovemaking and tenderness—that Katharine always forgot, for a while, about the damp and the inadequate central heating and her isolation.

"Tonight," Sebastian said, "we have Beluga and Dom Pérignon."

"Lovely," Katharine said, leaning against him again.

"And"—he turned around and opened his bag—"we also have aromatic oils of sandalwood and"—he took out three glass phials and read their tiny labels—"and patchouli and geranium, which I am assured are known for their relaxing and sensuous qualities when used in body massage."

"Oh," Katharine said, softly, and sat down on the edge of the bed.

"Don't just sit there," Sebastian said. "We need glasses."

"We don't need glasses."

"We don't?"

"What we need is for you to bring those little bottles over here and for you to take my clothes off."

"And then?"

"And then you're going to teach me the art of massage."

"We can't do it on the bed, the oil will ruin the mattress." He pulled her sweater up over her head.

"The floor's too cold, sweetheart," Katharine murmured, unbuckling his belt.

"How long's the kitchen table?"

Her amber eyes opened wide. "You're joking, aren't you?"

"Massage is traditionally given on a table," Sebastian said, taking her by the hand and leading her into the kitchen. "It's long enough." He leaned his weight against it. "And strong, too. We need a bath towel—"

"Yes," she whispered, and unzipped his trousers. "And we'd better draw the curtains."

"Christ," Sebastian said, his hand inside her panties. "You're wet already, angel." He pulled her against himself, feeling his own erection hard and urgent.

"No way," Katharine said.

"No way what?"

She tilted her pelvis, rubbed herself against him. "No way you're getting out of giving me that massage."

He let go of her, and his blue eyes glittered.

"Get two towels," he said, huskily, "and then get up on that table."

"I don't want to stain the pine."

"Fuck the pine," Sebastian said.

When Sebastian was gone again, back to London, the lonely days until December 10, the end of Katharine's engagement, stretched dauntingly ahead. Her fellow actors and the stage crew were friendly, and she went with them to pubs and drinking clubs, but when she was alone, Katharine began eating for comfort. The food was alien, too, yet she found it oddly consoling: steak and kidney pies, sausage and mash with Bisto gravy, Spam and baked beans, all so down to earth, so solid and secure. When she felt in need of something more exotic, there were the items that Sebastian had left her, and there was a Chinese takeaway, and an Indian restaurant run by a courteous and hospitable married couple.

And then there was chocolate, the beginnings of a new love affair with slabs of Cadbury's and mugs of strong tea with Kit Kats—and on the evening, after the show, when Katharine telephoned Dixie in New York to wish her a happy Thanksgiving, she was forced to smile at herself, at what she considered her ultimate transformation into an Englishwoman. For instead of turkey and cranberries and pumpkin pie, Katharine had, in front of her, cod and chips wrapped in newspaper, and the only American thing on her table—her pine table blessed with fragrant patches of patchouli oil—was a bottle of Heinz tomato ketchup.

On the eleventh of December, having said her farewells to the company the previous night, Katharine took a taxi to Birmingham and caught an early train to London. Sebastian had intended to come up to fetch her, but knowing that his visits had already disrupted his schedule, Katharine had insisted on traveling back alone.

"You've taken most of my stuff home already—I think I can just about manage two suitcases," she had told him. "How about you meet me at the station on Sunday afternoon, sweetheart? That way you can do all your boring paperwork in the morning, and I can have you all to myself when I get back."

Now that the day had come, however, Katharine found that she was itching to get out of the flat. She thought of calling Sebastian to let him know, then decided she'd wait and telephone him from Euston.

It was a cold morning, with a fierce wind blowing onto the crowded platforms. Katharine found a porter, loaded him up with her possessions and went directly to make her call.

Ellie Wilkins answered on the third ring.

"It's Katharine, Ellie—how are you?"

"All the better for hearing your voice, my dear, but I know you haven't telephoned to speak to me."

"Where is he? In the bath?"

"He went to the office very early, my dear."

"Did he?" Katharine said, "Okay, Ellie, I'll call him there."

Sebastian's private line rang several times before Jeremy Mariner picked it up.

"Don't either of you ever stop working?" Katharine asked lightheartedly.

"Kate? Where are you? Seb was trying to reach you."

"I'm at Euston Station."

"But he wasn't expecting you until this afternoon."

"I couldn't stand it a moment longer." Katharine glanced down into her purse. "Jeremy, could you put Sebastian on, please—I don't have any more change."

"He isn't here."

"Has he gone home?"

"I'm afraid not."

"Is he coming back? I could jump in a cab and come to the office to surprise him."

"Sebastian isn't coming back, Kate. He's on his way to Heathrow."

"What for?"

"He's trying to make the next flight to New York."

"You're kidding, Jeremy. Tell me you're kidding."

"Afraid not. We had an important telex last night—problems with Michael Jaffe. We both came in early to see if we could sort something out from this end, but it was no go."

"Couldn't you have gone?" Katharine's voice was tight.

"Too much on."

"More than Sebastian?"

"I thought so." Jeremy paused. "I'm sorry, Kate. I know you must be disappointed, but I'm sure he'll call you later."

"I'm sure he will."

"Though I doubt there'll be time at the airport."

"Of course not," Katharine said. "Good-bye, Jeremy."

It was the first time that Katharine had ever been really angry with Sebastian, but now she was mad as hell. A part of her brain registered that she might be overreacting, but right that minute, sitting in the back of a taxi on the way back to Hampstead, the larger part didn't give a damn. There could be nothing going on in New York that could possibly warrant his flying out today, of all days, and if there was, then Jeremy could surely have gone. She expected nothing more of Jeremy Mariner, of course—she suspected it had probably amused him to give her bad news. But Sebastian knew how much she was longing to see him, and he'd said that he felt the same way. They'd been apart, give or take the odd day and night, for three and a half months, and Katharine had been *aching* to be with him again. Maybe she was being unreasonable, but what it came down to, so far as she could see, was that Sebastian did not feel the same way, whatever he might say.

By the time she reached the Vale of Health, she knew exactly what she was going to do. Ellie, having seen the taxi, was waiting for her at the open door.

"You've just missed him, my dear—he called from the airport, ever so upset about having to go without seeing you."

The taxi driver heaved her cases into the hall, Katharine tipped him with a five-pound note and shut the door.

"Upset, was he?" Her voice was light.

"You do know, then, my dear? About New York?"

"Yes, I know. Jeremy told me."

"He didn't say anything to me before, you know, or I would have told you when you rang."

"I know that," Katharine said, more gently. "Don't worry, Ellie."

"The kettle's just on the boil—come and have a cup of tea."

Katharine stooped and kissed her on the cheek. "Sorry, Ellie, no time for tea. Things to do. I'll explain later."

"I could bring a pot up to you."

Already on her way up the staircase, Katharine turned. "Do you think you could make that coffee? I ran out of decent stuff days ago and I'm dying for a cup."

All the pleasure that Katharine had been anticipating at seeing The Oaks again, at smelling all Ellie's wonderful polishing, at coming into their bedroom again for the first time, was absent, yet she was so busy, so bent on her task, that she scarcely noticed. She made two telephone calls, ran a bath, took off her clothes and dumped them into the wash basket. Ellie brought her a tray with a pot of freshly brewed coffee and home-baked shortbread, and Katharine, with her eyes on the clock on the mantelpiece, drank two cups and ate all the shortbread. And then she took a swift, efficient bath—there would be ample time for laziness later—before she tipped all the contents of her suitcases out onto the bed, set aside all those modest, deliberately shabby working clothes, took out silk underwear, pure wool, cashmere and leather, and began to pack again.

"I've called a cab," she told Ellie, downstairs in the hall with her cases by the front door. It was less than an hour since she had arrived home. "And now I'm going to Heathrow."

Watching Katharine take her ranch mink coat from the hall closet, Ellie's eyes brightened. "You're joining Sebastian."

"No, Ellie, I'm not." Katharine checked in her bag to see that she had her passport and credit cards. "I'm going to Copenhagen to visit my great-uncle." She shut the bag. "And no, Sebastian does not know, and no, I don't care if he does get upset."

"Are you all right, my dear?" Ellie looked anxious.

"I'm fine." Katharine fought her sudden desire to cry and managed to smile at her. "It's just that I think I want to have my first real fight with Sebastian, and the bitch of it is, he's not here for me to punch his damnably gorgeous nose."

Henrik was overjoyed to see her again, as were Fanny and Asger, who yelped like puppies and bounced around Katharine for over an hour before they settled down on the bed in her room to watch her unpack.

"Come in, Uncle Henrik, please," she called to him. "I'd love your company while I get straight." He came in, as big and broad and fine-looking as she'd remembered, wearing a blue cable knitted pullover, the right sleeve pinned, as usual, to prevent it from dangling uselessly. "I can hardly believe how good it feels to be back."

Henrik sat on the bed, and the schnauzer bitch draped herself across his knees while the dog leaned against him. "I confess I'm just a little disappointed, Katharine."

"Why?"

"Obviously, I wanted very much to meet your husband."

"And he wants to meet you, but right now I'm afraid all you have is me and some honeymoon photographs."

Henrik put out his hand, and she took it, felt him squeeze it, gently.

"First quarrel?" he asked.

"How did you know?"

He shrugged. "Easy, easy. You said you were away from home for three months, and now you came back and he went away. So you're angry with him, no?"

"Furious."

"That's fine, that's normal." He smiled, and his craggy face was alight with pleasure. "And I'm the lucky one, for I have you for a few days—and you look beautiful, of course, but a little tired."

"I am pretty tired," Katharine confessed.

Henrik stood up and shooed the dogs off the bed and out of the room. "So what you do first is you have a long bath, and then you take a rest, and you don't worry about anything at all."

She soaked for almost an hour in a foam bath, massaged fragrant body lotion into her skin and lay down on the big, soft bed, wrapped in an even softer bathrobe, with Fanny, who had sneaked back into the room, lying by her side. Henrik cooked dinner that evening, and Katharine marveled again at his one-armed adeptness, for almost no task seemed impossible for him, and the dinner was superb.

After they had eaten, while they were drinking their coffee, the telephone rang, and it was Sebastian, calling from New York.

"Are you all right?" His voice was guarded and apprehensive, trying to gauge the level of anger that had driven her to Copenhagen. "I was worried sick when Ellie told me you'd gone."

"Were you?" Her uncle had tactfully left the room, but Katharine was still conscious of his being close by, and so she forced a light-hearted, casual note into her voice. "I suppose you think I was ecstatic when I heard you'd gone to New York?"

"Do you imagine I'd have gone if it hadn't been vital?"

"I must be dumber than I realized. I thought that having me back home might be more important to you than business."

"I was desperate, darling. I tried everything to get out of going—"

"Your partner could have gone."

"Jeremy had commitments—"

"And you didn't."

"It wasn't as simple as that, Katharine. We had about half an hour to make the arrangements, and Jeremy dug his heels in. I owe Michael Jaffe some loyalty, too—"

"The agency owes him."

"You're right. And if there'd been just a bit more time, I'm sure Jeremy could have sorted out his problems, but—"

"But as it was, yours were easier to sort out," she said frostily.

"Katharine, I feel so miserable without you."

"You've had three months to get used to it."

"That's not true—I got up there every chance I had."

"I didn't realize it was such a sacrifice." Katharine knew perfectly well that she was being a bitch, and she could hear how unhappy and frustrated Sebastian was feeling, but though she had every intention of forgiving him eventually, she was not ready to just yet.

"I love you, Katharine, you must know that."

"I thought I did."

"I'm going to get finished here in record time."

"Don't rush on my account."

Sebastian was silent, and Katharine guessed he was biting back an angry response.

"Will you call me tomorrow?" she asked, still coolly, then added, "If you have time."

"I'll have time." He paused. "Are you ever going to forgive me?"

"Maybe."

"I love you."

"Good night, Sebastian."

"I wish to God I were there with you."

"So do I," Katharine said, stiffly, and put down the receiver.

For the next two days, Katharine continued to luxuriate and to try to repair the minimal but still, to her, noticeable damage that the weeks of careless diet, theatrical makeup and stress had inflicted on her. She went for long walks with the dogs in Churchill Park and ran, on her own, to the tip of Langelinie and around the park, her breath misting in the frosty air. She went to a beauty salon on Strøget, the long pedestrian shopping street, and had the works, hair treatments, manicure, pedicure and massage; and she went shopping, bought two beautiful sweaters in a boutique on Østergade and a blouse in Chanel, bought a lovely figurine from Royal Copenhagen Porcelain and found a handsome new pipe for Henrik at W. Ø. Larsen.

Sebastian was calling her three times a day, and Katharine knew that he must be setting his alarm so that he could speak to her first thing in the morning, Danish time. She had, by now, almost entirely forgiven him, but she had made up her mind not to let Sebastian know that for certain until they were face to face.

On the third day, Katharine spent the morning with Henrik at his antique shop in Bredgade before lunching with him in the brasserie at the Hôtel d'Angleterre. And that evening Henrik let Katharine loose in his kitchen so that she could try her hand at some Scandinavian recipes she'd found in an old, leatherbound cookery book, and it was wonderful to feel so much at home, to be so easy and relaxed.

And then Sebastian telephoned again, this time from London.

"I thought you were going to be another few days," Katharine said, not troubling to hide her pleasure.

"I promised I'd finish as quickly as possible, angel."

"You did." She felt warm and bubbling at the prospect of seeing him. "So will you come over and join us?"

"In Copenhagen?"

"Sure. My uncle's itching to meet you—it's wonderful here."

Sebastian's sigh was weary. "There's nothing I'd love more than spending a few days with you there, sweetheart, but leaving London so unexpectedly has fouled up a few things at the agency." He paused. "If you want to stay on with your uncle for a few more days, I'll understand. I know how fond you are of him."

"That's what I'll do, then."

The new chill in Katharine's voice made Sebastian wince.

"Darling, you're misunderstanding again."

"Am I?" she said. "I doubt it." There was a hard lump in her throat. "Anyway, I will stay here, as you suggest—I know I'm welcome. And if you find a moment to spare over the next week or so, maybe you can call again."

And she put her finger on the hook and cut off the call.

It was Virginia, again, who told Sebastian what she thought of him, put him straight.

"You can't be surprised, surely, by Katharine's reaction," she said to him when he telephoned her next morning from the office. "You're still almost newlyweds, and you've already spent far too much time apart."

"And I've hated every moment," Sebastian said.

"But it was your idea to send her to Bromsgrove."

"Not because I wanted to be separated from her."

"I should hope not."

"I had no choice but to go to New York, Virginia. Katharine's not naive, she knows about business."

"Being a loving woman has nothing to with naïveté," Virginia told him crisply. "I thought you were aware of how fortunate you've been in finding Katharine."

"I'm very well aware—I thank my lucky stars every single day." Elspeth opened his door, and Sebastian waved her away. "But she's not making things exactly easy for me, Virginia. I drove myself nuts to get in and out of New York faster than I thought possible."

Virginia was not letting him off the hook. "And you thought that she would leap onto the first plane to fly back into your arms. As for not making things easy for you, what about Katharine? What about what you've made her endure over the past three months?"

"For God's sake, if I've told you once I've told you a hundred times, Katharine wanted to go, she wants to be an actress."

"And now she's clever enough to realize that a holiday, however brief, is just what you both need before you try to settle straight back down into normal home life again."

"I'd love a holiday with Katharine," Sebastian said frustratedly, "but there just isn't the time right now."

Virginia was exasperated with him, and a little sad. It was curious, she thought, that a man with such a brilliant mind, blessed with so much sensitivity to others, should be so obtuse with the person he loved most in all the world.

"Sebastian, my darling, do try and listen." She struggled to be gentler. "If you really couldn't go to Denmark at this moment, then you ought to have asked Katharine to come home right away. She might have thought you selfish, but at least she would have known that you wanted her."

"Of course I want her."

"Then she must think you have a strange way of showing it."

Sebastian waited only five minutes before calling Henrik Andersen's apartment again, his whole body tensed up as he prayed that Katharine was home.

"Darling," he said as soon as he heard her voice, "I'm coming, after all. I can't stand the thought of another day without you, I'll go crazy if I don't see you soon."

The connection was so crystal clear that he could hear her soft sigh of pleasure before she answered him.

"Are you certain you want to come?"

"One hundred percent."

"Are you sure you can find the time?" There was no irony in her voice, it was just a straight, candid question.

"I'll be coming on the first flight tomorrow," Sebastian said.

"No," Katharine said.

"Yes."

"I mean there's no need," she explained, and her voice was filled with relief and happiness. "Because I'm going to fly home instead."

"Are you sure you're ready?"

"I'm ready."

He met her at Heathrow, and his breath caught in his throat when he had his first glimpse of her, just as it had that first time in Sardi's, as if he had forgotten the effect that her beauty had on him, and their drive back to Hampstead was filled with holding of hands and loving looks and golden silences.

And Sebastian had arranged everything ahead of time with Ellie, and he knew that dinner was taken care of. And they went upstairs together, and Katharine unpacked and ran a bath. And Sebastian leaned against the bathroom wall watching as she washed herself and as the puffs of foam laced her shoulders and her neck, and he drank in the sight of her and felt himself harden with desire.

"Come here," Katharine said huskily.

"No, angel."

"Why not?" Her nipples, too, were tipped with foam, and her lips were parted, longing to be kissed.

"Dinner first."

"You're very organized," she said.

"It's about time, don't you think?"

The dining room was exquisite. The lights were dimmed, and Ellie had put Georgian silver candlesticks on the table, and she had made an asparagus cream soup from a recipe that Katharine had given her, and a grilled Dover sole with lobster sauce that Virginia had explained to her over the telephone. And Sebastian and Katharine drank a perfect Pouilly-Fuissé and sat opposite one another in tall, carved chairs, and gazed into each other's eyes. And there was a velvety hush in the house, mellowing every sound, the brushing of solid silver cutlery against Dresden porcelain, crystal glasses chinking, their own voices, soft and gentle, their laughter filled with happiness.

It was a rapturous reunion. Not for many months had their minds been so finely in tune. For the first time since July, Sebastian forgot completely to think of Katharine as an aspiring actress. She was his wife. His best and dearest friend. His lover.

"Do you think we could go upstairs now?" Katharine asked, softly, when they had finished their coffee.

"Are you sure you wouldn't like a cognac first?"

"Quite sure."

"In that case."

There was no haste as they climbed the staircase, hand in hand—an eager anticipation more forceful than any they had known since their first time, at the inn, but no clumsy impatience, no awkwardness. The heat was there, the urgency was mutual, but they both keenly felt the sense of liberty and time and space that marriage had given them. There was no need to rush. They were free to wallow in sensuality as unhurriedly as they wished.

"Undress me, please," Katharine whispered, when they were in the bedroom with the door closed.

Sebastian shook his head. "I want to watch you."

"I'd like that, too."

Her eyes pored over him, over the beauty of his body, the strength and sweetness of him, the long limbs and the flat stomach and the hands that would soon be touching her skin, and the raptness of the face, the blue eyes, watching her at the same time.

Sebastian switched off all the lights then and opened the curtains, so that Katharine's pale skin glowed luminously in the moonlight, and only then did he go to her, kissing her mouth first, needing her to feel all his love, all his tenderness, all his passion through that first kiss, and then he bent his head and brushed her breasts with his lips with slow, savoring hunger. And Katharine moaned with delight, and she began to caress him, to move against him, and she twisted her head to kiss him back, and they lay down, at last, on their bed, and her hair, shining almost silver in the moonlight, spread itself over the pillows.

And then, just when it mattered most, at the moment of supreme joy, at the absolute peak of their rediscovery of each other, the very thing that Sebastian had dreaded for so long, but of which he had believed himself rid, came back to torment him. It was all around him—in his nostrils and in his mouth and his throat—he felt immured by it, unable to breathe—

Katharine tightened her arms and legs about him. He was already deep inside her, but Sebastian only half heard her groan of pleasure, only half felt her beginning to rock and roll her hips, hardly recognized his own moaning. Outside, a large black cloud blotted out the moon, and darkness fell over the room, covered them on the bed like a gigantic black bat shading them with its wings. The scent was overpowering, unbearable, choking. The bedroom began to spin around Sebastian, he felt sick and faint—

He stared down at Katharine through a mist of pain, saw her face contorted with passion. And the fragrance swept over him with a final, defeating onslaught, and that repellent, disgusting feeling of incestuousness invaded him again, and he had no choice—he had to tear himself out of her body, to wrench himself free.

"Oh, God, *no!*"

His cry was of such strength, of such revulsion that Katharine lay, for several moments, too dazed, too shocked to move, and when she did manage to reach out and turn on the bedside lamp, she saw that he was sitting on the edge of the bed, his face buried in his hands.

"Sebastian," she whispered, "what's wrong with you?"

He was shaking violently, she could feel it through the mattress.

"For pity's sake, darling, tell me."

He could not speak, was beyond words, was trying to summon up the strength to stand up, to leave the room, to escape.

"How on earth can I help if you won't talk to me?"

She put out her hand, and touched his back, and Sebastian leapt as if she had burnt him.

"I'm sorry," he said, chokingly.

Katharine watched him walk into the bathroom and close the door, heard the key turning in the lock. She heard the sound of him vomiting, and then of water running, first in one of the handbasins, and then in the shower. She wanted to go to him, but the locked door meant that she was not wanted, and that wounded her more than anything, more than the time apart, more than his going to New York, more than anything else.

And when he did return, after a little time, his trembling quieted by the shower, his body cooled, Katharine was lying on her back in their bed, the covers drawn up to her chin, rigid and awake, her eyes open and watching him, waiting.

Sebastian tried to speak, had no idea what to say, knew that if he did not find the words now, the damage would grow and grow.

"I can't explain," he said. "I'd give anything to share this with you, but I can't."

Katharine closed her eyes, rolled away and lay stiffly on the far side of the bed. And Sebastian looked at her naked, condemning back, and he knew that he could not touch her now, could do nothing to redeem himself or the moment.

And if he had thrust a knife into her, he doubted if he could have felt a greater self-hatred.

c h a p t e r
22

In the eight days that remained between then and Christmas, life in The Oaks settled back into a tolerable replica of how it had been before Katharine had gone away. But although undeniable love and caring continued to flow between them, the carefree spark of spontaneity had, for the time being, at least, disappeared.

Neither of them had mentioned that night. Sebastian could not bring himself to try to explain, could see no way to explain something that even he could not begin to understand and which he sought only to forget. And Katharine, too, longed to bury it together with the other symptoms of what she could only see as rejection. She was busy now, with preparations for the party they planned to give on New Year's Eve, and so at least she was able to concentrate her energies upon that, and on making their first Christmas in The Oaks as happy and peaceful as possible.

At night, however, the memory hung heavily between them. They went upstairs quietly, cautiously and, almost always, with enough time separating them to allow the first to feign sleep when the second came to bed. They lay, still and silent and apart, and they were both filled with pain.

* * *

Four days before Christmas, on Sunday afternoon, Sebastian came home early from the office and found Katharine standing in the back garden staring at one of the barren flowerbeds.

"Hello, angel." He kissed her lightly on the cheek and put a long, almost paper-thin, gift-wrapped package into her hand. "To be opened now."

"Now?"

"Right away."

She tore off the paper. "Airline tickets?"

"Look at them."

Katharine looked. "London-Geneva-London."

"For you, me and Virginia," he said. "And from Geneva, we pick up a car and drive to Gstaad."

"Skiing?" Her eyes had widened. "I haven't skied for years."

"It'll come back in no time."

Her face fell. "The arrangements—the party, Christmas."

Sebastian took both her hands in his. "This is more important than any arrangements." His eyes pleaded with her. "I've rented a chalet outside Gstaad, and I've sent a rail ticket to your uncle."

Katharine could hardly believe it. "Is he coming?"

"I spoke to him this morning. He's coming, with the dogs." He went on, urgently. "And we can be back in good time for the party, and please, please, Katharine, let me do this for us."

Virginia protested a little.

"You two should be going alone," she said, predictably. "It's foolish for you to encumber yourself with an old woman—and I haven't been on a ski slope for more than twenty years—and besides, I have absolutely no suitable clothes."

Neither Katharine nor Sebastian paid any attention.

"We aren't going without you," Katharine told her. "And we have a full half day to go shopping, and Elspeth has already told me that so long as we go to Simpson's and Lillywhite's, that's enough time to get all we need."

"And the rest you can buy in Gstaad," Sebastian added.

"You're going to love Uncle Henrik," Katharine said, more excited than she had been in months. "And I know he's going to think you're wonderful."

"Poor man, being saddled with me for company."

"Virginia, darling," Sebastian said. "Stop talking and go shopping."

*   *   *

The chalet was exquisite, perched on the lower slopes of the Rellerligrat, sun-drenched and with an unhindered view of Gstaad. They were in easy reach of everything, the spectacular shopping, the charming cafés and *Stüblis*, the Palace Hotel—and yet they were as away from it all as they wished to be. The ground floor was open plan, with a magnificent fireplace so tall that it continued up through the mezzanine, part of which was a gallery overlooking the sitting area of the ground floor. The rooms on the first floor, however, though all spacious, were nevertheless intimate and romantic, all but two with fireplaces and bathrooms *en suite*, and timber abounded, on ceilings and walls, and as logs in the copper stands by the side of every hearth.

Henrik arrived one day after them, with Asger and Fanny.

"Twice in one month," he said to Katharine with great pleasure when they all came to the station to welcome him. "And you, my dear friend, I am more happy than you can imagine to meet you at last."

Sebastian gave him his hand, and Henrik shook it vigorously.

"It's good of you to have come, sir," Sebastian said. "After all, we didn't exactly give you much notice."

"Who needs notice for family and winter sports? And please call me Henrik." Henrik turned his attention to Virginia. "Is no one going to introduce me to this beautiful lady?" He took her hand and kissed it. "Though I know quite well that you must be Mrs. Locke."

"Virginia, please," she said, disarmed. "I see that Katharine was right about you. She told us that you are the most charming man she's ever met."

They dined in on Christmas Eve. A maid, named Lilianne, came into the chalet three times each day, to prepare breakfast, make beds and clean, and to cook and clear away lunch and dinner, if required; but on this evening, Virginia and Katharine had insisted on helping Lilianne to create something special, and it was a memorable and joyful feast of coquilles Saint-Jacques, Chateaubriand with foie gras, and soufflé Grand Marnier.

They went down into the town for midnight mass, and it was as perfect a service as they could have dreamed of, and when they emerged, it was snowing lightly, and the faces of the congregation were wreathed in smiles of contentment. Henrik and Virginia went

directly back to the chalet after the service, and Sebastian and Katharine went for a cognac to the Palace Hotel, but they did not stay
long, for they felt, almost as soon as they had sat down, a mutual
desire to go back, too, to be alone.

Lilianne had turned down the covers in their room and had placed
two long-stemmed red roses on white lace cloths on their pillows,
with a festive red candle on each bedside table. Sebastian went to
light them both, then came back to Katharine's side, his eyes resting
on the long mirror on the wall at the far end of the room.

They were standing close together, yet there was a ghostly, oddly
detached quality about their reflection. Their faces and bodies were
in shadow, and only their fair heads shimmered in the light. Sebastian
felt a sharp pang of loneliness, suddenly intensely afraid of the sensation of separation that had come over him, and Katharine, sensing
his fear, looked anxiously up at his face.

"What is it?" she asked, gently.

He looked away from the mirror, down at her lovely face, saw
how full of love it was for him, and a new sense of urgency replaced
the fear. Quickly, he went to the bombé cabinet in which he had
stacked his pullovers and came back to her side holding a small,
slender, gift-wrapped box.

"Give me your coat," he said, softly, and placed the box into her
hands.

Katharine tore away the paper and saw that it was a leather Cartier
case, and within it lay an exquisite necklace of diamonds and South
Sea pearls.

"Merry Christmas, my love."

She lifted it out of the case, her fingers trembling, and the light
from the candles caught some of the stones and sent a kaleidoscope
of sparkling fire over the walls and ceiling.

"It's the most beautiful thing I've ever seen," she whispered, and
tears glimmered in her eyes. "I thought this trip was my present—
God knows it was more than enough."

"Nowhere near enough."

Sebastian took the necklace from her, fastened it about her throat,
and then he rested his hands on her shoulders, not moving, just
feeling her close to him, blessedly close. He wanted to tell her how
he felt, yearned to describe the exact, remarkable intensity of his
love for her, the utter preciousness of that love to him, but he could
not find the words.

Katharine reached up and took his left hand from her shoulder, and silently, intuitively, she led him to the long mirror and stood beside him.

"Look," she said.

And Sebastian saw that the disturbing quality of detachment, and the irrational fear that it had produced in him, had gone. Perhaps, he acknowledged silently, it had never really existed. He looked at their reflection now, and it was clear and strong. They stood close together, as one, hands clasped, their faces contented and calm. Perfectly real. Perfectly substantial.

"Make love to me," Katharine said, softly.

And as she turned to face him, and he saw the intensity of the love in her eyes, strength and joy flowed through Sebastian, and he knew that, tonight at least, all would be well.

There were more gifts the next morning before they went to the Palace for their festive luncheon. A Chagall lithograph from Katharine to Sebastian, this one for their bedroom, not for his office; a pair of heavy silver photograph frames from Virginia to them both; a Meissen harlequin which they gave to her; and from Henrik two Victorian silver scent bottles for Katharine and Virginia, and a Georgian seal, its stem modeled as a tiny stage with open curtains, for Sebastian.

"When I saw that the intaglio was engraved with your initials," Henrik told him, "I could not resist it."

"It's superb," Sebastian said. "Much too generous."

"No more so than your generosity, my friend."

The only shadow of the day was cast by a package that Jeremy had asked Virginia to give to Sebastian; a magnificent gold cigarette case engraved in the bottom right-hand corner with the Locke Mariner logo, and inside, in tiny letters, TO SL FROM JM.

"It's very handsome." Katharine admired it.

"Isn't it," Sebastian said, but his eyes were angry because Jeremy had so blatantly excluded Katharine, and he shut the case with a click and dropped it dismissively into his jacket pocket, and the tiny shadow passed.

The holiday was superb. As a skier, after a slightly nervous start, Katharine presented a trimmer, more expert figure than her husband, but what he lacked in finesse, Sebastian more than made up for in courage bordering on uncharacteristic recklessness. Every morning and afternoon they skimmed the slopes in almost perfect unison, and if they were not skiing, they tobogganed or skated or threw snow at each other. They felt as if the short break was, indeed, as they had both hoped, the cure for all the tensions that the past few months had brought. Even if it could only be a brief interruption in the normal scheme of things, the diamond-sharp air and, above all, their abiding, overwhelming passion for each other, made it as wonderful a holiday as their honeymoon in Venice had been.

"We're not the only ones, either," Katharine said to Sebastian on the penultimate day. It was dusk, the time the French called *l'heure bleue*, a time for lovemaking, and they were snuggled close under their duvet, both savoring each moment.

"You're just a hopeless romantic," Sebastian teased, knowing that she was thinking about Virginia and Henrik.

"You can't deny they're enjoying each other."

"I certainly can't."

Katharine stroked the inside of his left elbow. "Wouldn't it be absolutely wonderful if they fell in love, darling? Don't you think it would be wonderful?"

"I'm not sure Virginia's ready for that, angel." Sebastian kissed her right earlobe. "Though yes, I agree it would be pretty marvelous."

"Wonderful," she murmured again.

"Well?" Katharine asked Virginia on the flight back to London while Sebastian dozed after their light lunch.

"Well what, darling?"

"Uncle Henrik, of course."

"What about him?"

"I've been dying to know, but Sebastian said it would be tactless to ask you."

"Ask me what exactly?" Virginia's eyes were merry.

"Do you like him?"

"Certainly I like him—how could I not?"

"But do you *more* than like him?" Katharine persisted. "I only ask because I'm sure he was crazy about you."

"Of course he wasn't." Virginia paused. "What makes you say that?"

"He told me that you were the most wonderful woman he'd met in at least ten years."

"You're inventing that, Katharine."

"And you're blushing." Katharine glanced sideways at Sebastian and then back again at Virginia. "Go on, while he's still asleep."

"You're impossible, darling." Virginia smiled at her. "All right, I will admit to just one thing, but you must promise not to blow it all out of proportion."

"Cross my heart and hope to die."

Virginia's expression grew somber. "It's simply that after losing Andrew, I never thought it possible that I would find joy in Christmas again." She took Katharine's hand and squeezed it. "But thanks to you all—including Henrik, of course—I have."

The weather that New Year's Eve was nothing short of hostile, a night, Sebastian said when they were getting dressed, straight from the pages of *Macbeth*, with gales and rain blowing across the Heath in violent, drenching gusts, sending sodden bracken and loose branches whistling eerily into the night air. But The Oaks, tucked securely as it was into the Vale of Health, its handsome frontage illuminated by floodlights, provided a vision of welcome sanctuary for its guests as they hurried across the gravel drive from their cars, heads tucked well down under umbrellas that were almost useless in the wind.

"Lord, what a night," Barbara Stone cried, almost swept through the front door by a strong gust. "I need a mirror and a drink, darlings."

Sebastian, sleek in a black velvet jacket with a snowy white shirt and burgundy cravat, stood at the door greeting visitors, while Ellie took coats and gifts and Katharine directed the women to where they might repair their ruined hair.

"The house looks like absolute heaven," Barbara told her. "It was always lovely, of course, but you've worked miracles, darling."

"I haven't done that much," Katharine said, candidly. "I think the house has done most of it itself, with a lot of help from Ellie."

Barbara was right, for if The Oaks was beautiful under normal conditions, tonight it was nothing less than magnificent, and not for the first time, Katharine had a sense that it was far more than an inanimate shell, that it had moods of its own, reflecting feelings. And tonight, with fires burning hospitably in the drawing and dining rooms and in the broad paneled hall, the wood itself, gleaming richly from Ellie's lashings of linseed oil, seemed to unbend a little more in welcome.

Katharine realized now how right her instincts had been to avoid gimmicky party decorations. The house needed nothing in order to shine. Her only concession to flamboyance had been in the small sitting room, where she had re-created a New York–style piano bar, intimately lit and staged around the hunched-over figure of Billy

Jacques, the celebrated jazz pianist she'd borrowed for the night from Giselle's. Already that room was full to bursting, and as authentically smoky as any bar, and Billy was singing throatily and sharing bourbon with some of his admirers.

Their guest list had been their most meticulous creation. While the party was, inevitably, a predominantly theatrical event, Sebastian knew how necessarily the boundaries of his business overlapped those of many others in order to survive; and by half past ten, the guests included two fashion designers, three lawyers, two international bankers, a photographer, a hairdresser, a plastic surgeon and a psychiatrist, as well as producers, directors, writers, impresarios, casting directors, fellow agents and, of course, actors. Most of Locke Mariner's clients were present, with the exception of those working too far afield to make the journey, and even Michael Jaffe, flying in to London for a charity premiere, had promised to be with them before midnight.

Katharine had never felt better. Whichever way she turned, she was aware of eyes focusing on her with admiration, sometimes with envy. She wore a beige-and-gold chiffon, Directoire-style, full-length dress, high-waisted and so sheer that it was almost transparent, cut low to emphasize her figure and to complement perfectly the diamond-and-pearl necklace Sebastian had given her for Christmas.

"Stunning, Kate," even Jeremy had said as he'd arrived, an adoring brunette on his arm. "At least two million dollars."

As the night unfolded, Katharine, with the detachment afforded a hostess, observed their guests settling into pockets of diverse amusements, watched and listened to the merriment, the warmheartedness and, at times, the bitchiness disguised by smiles and kisses. There was a curious exultation for Katharine this evening.

"It's strange," she said to Virginia in a quiet corner, a little after eleven o'clock, "since I've lived in this house for nine months, and we've given so many dinner parties a thousand times more intimate than this—but I really feel in harmony this evening."

"With Sebastian?"

Katharine nodded. "And with The Oaks. With my life. I haven't felt quite this way before."

"It takes time," Virginia said, "to feel at home."

"It's feeling that I belong here now," Katharine said, softly. "To some of the people here tonight, I'm Sebastian Locke's wife. To others, I'm Andrew's daughter-in-law. To some, perhaps, who knew Sebastian's mother, I'm simply a part of the next generation."

"And that troubles you?"

"Until now, I think perhaps it did, a little. All those links with a past that isn't mine—"

"When you have a wonderful background of your own," Virginia said, completing the thought.

"Exactly." Katharine smiled at the older woman's perceptiveness. "It took me a long time to grow up, you know, and I think that when I finally did learn how to be independent, I liked it, got used to thinking of myself as an individual."

"A free spirit."

"You were right, a few months ago, when you said you thought I ought to go back to work—but it was Sebastian who saw what I really needed. I don't think many husbands would do what he did for me—push me out so that I could find my feet."

"I was very angry with him for doing that," Virginia said. "I thought he was running a terrible risk."

"Of what?" Katharine asked. "Of losing me?" She shook her head vehemently. "He could never do that." She smiled again. "In any case, being away from home seems to have made it all even more precious to me. I may be just Sebastian's wife to some people—all those things I said—but I'm also Katharine Andersen Locke, and I'm entitled to my place in this house. I belong here."

There was only one person who still did not, and never would, she felt sure, accept her. Jeremy might have complimented her earlier, and he might speak affably to her as he generally did these days, but there was no warmth in him for her. Katharine watched him now as he worked the room, slipping from one person to the next, charming, calculating, his clever, sardonic tongue laced with honey, his narrow eyes flirting and undressing and flattering. She disliked him so much at times, wished she could simply disregard him. Just because Jeremy was her husband's partner did not mean that she had to like him—and yet she knew how absolute Jeremy's loyalty was to Sebastian, and she realized that most of what she felt about Jeremy was sadness, because she felt unable to break through the iron layers of his mistrust and dislike.

At twenty minutes to twelve, Katharine opened the front door to find Michael Jaffe standing on the threshold.

He kissed her. "I come bearing gifts. Or one, to be precise."

Katharine looked at him. He was windswept, and a little out of place in brown cords and a turtleneck, but she saw no packages.

"Close your eyes," he said, and she obeyed. "Okay, now open them."

She gave a yelp of joy.

"*Laszlo!*" She flung herself into his arms. "You said you couldn't come—I can't believe it!" She drew back. "Where's Betty?"

"In California, getting ready to be a grandmother."

Katharine closed the door and looked at Michael. "You are the cleverest man in the world. If you hadn't introduced Sebastian to Sam Raphael, we'd never have married, and now, as if that weren't enough, you bring me the most wonderful surprise I could wish for."

"It was Sam who found out we were both flying into London the same day," Michael told her. "So Laszlo and I thought we'd surprise you."

"Come in and have a drink, and something to eat—you must both be famished." She linked arms with the Hungarian. "Laszlo, you're more handsome than ever—how do you do it? And why aren't you in California with Betty? Not that I'm complaining."

"I'm here to talk a little business that couldn't wait," Eles said.

"Business? Really?"

"And why not business?" His dark eyes twinkled. "You think I'm past it?"

"Never, but you did tell us you'd retired." Katharine gripped his arm in sudden excitement. "You're not going to work here, are you?"

"Anything is possible, *kedves.*"

"Where's Sebastian?" Michael asked.

"I wish I knew." Katharine scanned the crowded hall, then checked her watch. "If you find him, either of you, please pin him down for me—I need him for midnight."

"I spent New Year's in Britain about ten years ago," Michael said. "I remember chimes at midnight—are we having chimes tonight?"

"The chimes of Big Ben and Scottish bagpipes, too," Katharine said, "but if I don't go and check on a few things, we may not have anything at all."

At five minutes to midnight, Katharine still had not found Sebastian. Not a single guest in the house had an empty champagne glass; the net of balloons suspended over the front hall was ready to be released; but as Katharine stood just outside the dining room surrounded by merriment and anticipation, she was suddenly swamped by a sense of panic.

"Looking for someone?" His voice came from behind her.

"Darling—" She spun around, buried her face against his shoulder. "I thought I wasn't going to find you in time."

"I was looking for you everywhere." His eyes, too, were relieved.

"Have you seen Michael Jaffe? And Laszlo's here—did you see him?"

"I saw them." Sebastian took her right hand. "Come on."

He drew her through the crowds of people, all wishing them well, to their favorite spot before the fireplace in the drawing room.

"Listen," Katharine said.

In the last two minutes of 1975, a hush fell over the house, broken only by the eerie, persistent wailing of the wind in the trees outside, and the haunting, melancholy sound of the bagpipes as the piper walked the house bidding farewell to the old year.

"It's been the best year of my life," Sebastian said, softly, looking down at Katharine, leaning against him, her eyes half closed. "I never knew it was possible to love anyone so completely."

"Do you know how much I love you?" Katharine asked, urgently. It surged through her, stronger and more powerful than any feeling she had ever experienced. "Do you know that I would do anything for you?"

"And I for you."

Everywhere around them, party guests stood close together, some already embracing, others hovering expectantly. There seemed a sudden need in the air for love, for sharing, for touching. And then the chimes began. They echoed through the paneled hall and glowing rooms, resonant and inexorable, each second being left behind forever, and Sebastian and Katharine were oblivious to the crowd, oblivious to everything except each other.

"I want this year to bring us even closer," he said against her ear, then kissed her mouth.

"No more separations," she said, fervently.

"Not if I can help it, angel."

After a moment, Virginia came forward, her eyes brimming, and the three of them embraced—and then Jeremy, too, joined them, and then there were the telephone calls, from Henrik with his son's family in Stockholm, and from Sam, still in the old year, in New York, and for just those few minutes at least, all their thoughts were joyful and loving and hopeful.

*　　*　　*

In less than an hour, the old rules were back in play, the novelty of the new year already wearing off, 1976 no different from 1975, after all. The party still had hours of life in it, the champagne was still flowing, voices were growing noisier. Sebastian stood in a corner and watched Katharine dancing with Michael Jaffe, her gold-streaked hair gleaming beneath the lights as she moved with grace and rhythm, laughter dimpling her cheeks.

He felt a touch on his arm and turned around.

"Jerry, all right?"

"Peter March wants to talk, Seb." There was a glint of excitement in Jeremy's eyes.

"Now?"

"Good a time as any. I said we'd join him in the library, okay?"

"I'll bring a bottle."

Sebastian's pulse had quickened. This, they both knew, was likely to be a turning point for Locke Mariner, since they had learned that March, the head of one of London's most innovative production companies, was seeking investors in an exciting and, as yet, unnamed new project. Jeremy and Sebastian had, for some time, been in agreement that this should be their way forward: financial involvement in substantial productions and, eventually perhaps, their own production company.

"Come and dance." Katharine, a little breathless, was beside him.

"Sorry, my darling, I'm just off to a meeting in the library."

"Now? Who with, for heaven's sake?"

"Peter March and Jeremy—"

"In the middle of our own party?"

"It's important, angel, believe me."

"It had better be."

Peter March was sitting on an upright chair. He was a dapper, small man, with sparse but beautifully combed white hair and a neat, white beard.

"It's good of you to spare the time," he said to Sebastian, then nodded to Jeremy. "Both of you."

"We're very interested to know what you have to tell us," Sebastian said. "And it's a pleasant moment to talk, though Katharine tells me I'd better not be away for too long."

"She's absolutely right." March smiled. "I'll come directly to the point, or rather three points. The first being Sam Raphael, with whom

I've already spoken, and who I understand is your wife's stepfather."

"And a good friend," Sebastian said.

"The second point is Barbara Stone." He paused. "This is really, I suppose, partly in the way of being a rather early, perhaps even premature, availability check."

"What's the third point?" Jeremy asked.

"Your money," March replied.

In the small sitting room, now the quietest of the party rooms, Billy Jacques was playing soft, romantic, late-night music while Laszlo Eles and Katharine sat at a corner table.

"It's so good to see you," she told him.

"I wanted to look at you, *kedves*, talk to you, see what the British have done to you."

"What's the verdict?"

"You look much the same," Laszlo said, studying her. "Even lovelier, perhaps, which must, I imagine, be due to being in love—but still the same Katharine Andersen, thank God."

"I feel the same," Katharine said, "though it took a little while to get used to things over here. It's a different world, Laszlo, in many ways—and I miss my friends."

"We miss you, too, Katharine." He peered at her intently. "The most important question is whether you are happy, *kedves*? Completely happy?"

"With Sebastian?" She smiled. "We've had our ups and downs, of course, but I haven't regretted marrying him for a single moment."

Billy Jacques began singing "Night and Day," and for a few minutes everyone in the room stopped talking.

"Is it true," Laszlo asked, after a while, "about the acting?"

"Who told you?"

"If you wanted it to be a secret, you shouldn't have told Dixie."

Katharine laughed. "No secret." She smiled again. "Can you imagine me in a Harold Pinter play?"

"I imagine you can do anything you set your mind to, *kedves*."

"And you, Laszlo? What are you planning? Why are you really here?"

"In London, to discuss a new show. Here, tonight, to be with you, of course—and to put a proposition to you."

She sat forward, fascinated. "Tell me."

"Larry Sherman has written a musical based on Galsworthy's *For-syte Saga*. I thought at first that it might be a most dreadful idea, but in fact it's quite wonderful. Sherman hopes that I may emerge from retirement to design the show."

"And will you?"

"Perhaps." Laszlo paused. "My decision will be affected a little by your reaction, Katharine. Does the idea attract you?"

"You want me as your assistant?" Katharine's pulses raced with excitement.

"No," Laszlo said, and shook his head exasperatedly. "Are you still thinking of yourself as an assistant, even after *Paris*? Katharine, I want to work with you, as equal partners, collaborators—" He shrugged. "Though perhaps it would not be entirely equal, since my doctors and Betty still insist I must not overtax myself."

"What does Betty think, about your working again?"

"She knows I'm bored and even more impossible to live with than I used to be. She thinks it would be pleasant to spend a few months in London." Laszlo looked at Katharine. "So, what do you think?"

"I don't know," she said, honestly. "I'm honored, of course, and I'm very touched—but I'm also a little confused."

"Because of the acting?"

"Yes." Katharine paused. "I loved it, Laszlo. I'd forgotten how much I loved it. I'd buried my memories of acting, of wanting to act, so completely—if Sebastian hadn't woken me up to it, I guess I'd never have realized."

"Yet you're such a talented designer." Laszlo shrugged. "Is there a law that forbids you from designing and acting?"

"I suppose not," Katharine said slowly, and smiled. "It's certainly worth thinking about." The little crowd in the sitting room applauded Billy Jacques, and she stirred. "But not right now. I'd almost forgotten that I'm supposed to be the hostess of this party." She stood up. "Will you forgive me, Laszlo?"

He rose, too. "Go back to your guests, *kedves*." He took her hand, and kissed it. "But promise to think it over. If you wish, I can get the score and book for you to look over."

"How long are you in London for?"

"One week."

"How long do I have to make a decision?"

"Seven days."

"This new project of mine," Peter March was saying to Sebastian and Jeremy, "is, of course, in its earliest stages of development, but

Sam Raphael is very keen for you to be involved, and Noël Harvey and I are hoping to alert a few more choice names well ahead of time."

"What exactly is the project?" Sebastian asked.

"Three Ibsen plays." March stroked his beard. "After we produced *The Wild Duck* in 1971, I planned to continue a year later, but I wasn't entirely satisfied with the early plans and so we abandoned the project."

"And now?"

"Now we plan three brand-new translations by a young man named Gunnar Nyquist"—March, conscious of the half-open library door, kept his voice low and confidential—"which have been adapted by Susannah Rand into three striking plays, innovative but, one hopes, not too inoffensive to the traditionalists."

"Noël Harvey directing, I take it?" Jeremy asked.

"Quite."

"Which plays?" Sebastian asked.

"A Doll's House, An Enemy of the People," March said. "And *Hedda Gabler*."

Sitting facing the door, Sebastian noticed Katharine coming out of the sitting room with Laszlo Eles. He saw her kiss the older man, then saw Michael Jaffe approach Katharine, putting one arm around her waist. Sebastian's eyes were drawn first to Jaffe's face, checking with an instant flash of jealousy for signs of flirtation, and then to his wife's.

And then, suddenly, an entirely different image struck him.

Jaffe and Eles both seemed to fade away, and Jeremy's and March's voices and the sounds of the party all receded into a blurry mist. March was continuing to speak, to sell and to tempt, but Sebastian scarcely heard him.

In a single flicker of his mind's eye, he saw Katharine, center stage in a new role. The sudden sensation of irony was staggering in its intensity. Sebastian felt his life turn full circle. This, he knew abruptly, was what he had begun, unwittingly, to prepare her for. It was for this that he had been drawn to her side in New York.

He stared at Katharine. She was perfect.

"We're speaking to as few people as we need to at this stage," March was saying. "But Raphael is passionate to play Ibsen in London, to the extent of investing in the productions, and Noël and I both feel that Barbara and Nora are meant for each other, and I hope that

you may at least consult with me before committing her to a conflicting contract."

"But what we're really here to talk about," Jeremy said, "is the
possibility of Locke Mariner's investment, isn't it?"

With a supreme effort, Sebastian forced himself to pay attention
to the conversation, dragged his eyes away from Katharine and back
onto the producer's face.

"I know, of course," March went on, "that you can't possibly commit yourselves until you've seen the scripts and heard some detailed
plans, and we're going to be speaking to several other potential
backers, but—"

"But you'd like to know if we're interested, in principle," Jeremy
said. "Sebastian?"

Sebastian nodded, slowly, consciously calming his senses, com-
posing himself. He looked into Jeremy's eyes, recognized that his
answer was positive, but that he was waiting, as he still so often did,
for him to take the lead.

"Yes," he said, addressing March. "In principle, the answer is yes."

The conversation ended, Jeremy left the library with the producer,
hungry again and going in search of the breakfast that was being set
out in heated dishes in the dining room. But Sebastian remained
seated, the noises of the party ebbing again under the force of his
own thoughts.

Katharine as Hedda.

Since boyhood, he had had dozens of dreams and aspirations, and
he had achieved many of them. Now he felt gripped by a sense of
ambition and excitement more powerful than any he had previously
experienced. This was fate again, of course, but fate alone could only
direct them; if this ambition for his wife was to be fulfilled, Sebastian
knew that he was going to have to use every last ounce of his professional guile. There were plans to be laid, and his mind was already
beginning to buzz with them.

While far beneath the surface, a fragment of his subconscious
stirred. A long-buried enemy, half-sleeping for many years.

Katharine as Hedda?

c h a p t e r
23

"We'll have to start thinking soon," Sebastian said after dinner on the first Wednesday of the year.

"What about?" Katharine, feet up on the sofa, stretched luxuriously.

"About getting you some more work."

"It's too soon to think about that."

"Resting already. That's no way to build a career."

"I'm only just starting to relax into being home again, sweetheart," Katharine said lazily. "Gstaad was heaven, and having the party was wonderful, but I could use a little peace."

Sebastian lit a cigarette. "I'm only suggesting we give it a little thought," he said casually. "There's no guarantee you'll find another engagement for months yet, but we need to talk about your needs, training, that sort of thing."

"Actually," Katharine said, sitting up, "there's another possibility that I've been thinking over." She hesitated. "I didn't want to talk about it until I'd had a chance to weigh up my feelings."

"Something to do with Laszlo, I take it?"

"You know about it?" She was startled.

"I know that Eles is in town to talk about the *Forsyte* musical." He smiled at her expression. "You forget that's my job, knowing what's going on. I'm right then?"

"He wants me to design the show with him."

Sebastian felt a small, throbbing ache in his left temple. "And how do you feel about that?"

"I'm not sure."

"Try explaining it." He paused. "If you want to talk it over with me, that is."

"Of course I do," Katharine said.

"I'm surprised you didn't before now, that's all."

"I guess I didn't want to think about it myself, so soon after the party. We've been so happy, so relaxed, I didn't want to spoil it."

Sebastian drew on his cigarette. "How did you feel when Laszlo first mentioned the show to you?"

"Excited." She paused. "But uncertain."

"Was your first instinct to do it, to go back to design?"

Katharine stood up, suddenly restless. "I had two reactions, one on top of the other. In one way, I felt overjoyed at the thought of having a chance to repeat *Paris*—but at the same time, I had a sense that it was going backward, not forward."

"Not necessarily," Sebastian said, easily. "It could be another major opportunity for you, and having Eles in London is something that won't happen again in a hurry."

"If ever."

He watched her as she wandered over to the window, then back again to the fireplace. "You do have to understand one thing, though, Katharine. If you go back now, I think you're turning your back on an acting career forever."

"That's what I was afraid you'd say."

"I did think," Sebastian said, a little more forcefully, "that when you made your decision last year, you realized you were undertaking a real commitment."

"I did," Katharine said. "But there are other considerations, too."

"Such as?"

"If I choose acting, chances are I'll have to work out of London again, at least for a while. If I choose the musical, if I choose working with Laszlo, I get to stay at home."

"Now you're making it sound as if our marriage is holding you back from doing what you really want."

"I happen to think our marriage is important."

"Do you think I don't?"

Katharine sank down again onto the sofa. "This is silly. This is why I didn't want to talk about it yet."

"We have to."

"Not until I'm ready."

"I thought you were a professional, Katharine," Sebastian said, quite sharply. "And, frankly, I thought you were more courageous than this."

"I don't see that courage has much to do with anything," Katharine said, stung.

"Hasn't it?" he said, brusquely. "Learning a new craft's damned hard work, and living in discomfort might have been tolerable for a limited time, but I'm sure you'd sooner not go back to it."

"I see." Katharine was bristling now. "And you think I'd consider taking on the musical because it's the soft option, do you? Let me tell you, Sebastian, there's nothing soft about stage design, and I don't imagine for one second that Laszlo and I would find adapting to British theater in the least bit easy."

"Perhaps not," he said, "but at least you'd still be riding the crest of the wave rather than wading about in the mud at the bottom."

"So now you think it's my ego that's going to decide?" she said, angrily. "Do you really think me so shallow, so cowardly that a little discomfort and even a little humiliation would stop me fighting for what I really wanted more than anything?"

"I've never thought you either shallow or a coward," Sebastian said.

"All the time I was studying at Carnegie Mellon," Katharine went on, "there was always a part of me that felt guilty because I was there under false pretenses—because I didn't have the same hunger for design that the other students had."

"You never told me that before," Sebastian said, quietly.

"Because I hardly admitted it to myself. My mother knew I'd taken a wrong turn, but I thought her judgment was way off, and when Sam tried to make me stop and think, I was sure I'd worked it all out. And then, in New York, once it all started coming together for me, once I'd met Laszlo, I was convinced I'd made the right decision."

"Are you saying now that you're not sure?"

"I don't know what I'm saying."

"If Laszlo hadn't turned up on New Year's Eve, would you have wanted to go on acting?"

"I think so."

"Yes or no? Come on, Katharine, you must know that, at least."

"All right—yes—"

"Yes, you would have wanted to go on acting?"

"I said yes, goddamnit, yes." She jumped up again, and glowered down at him. "I never knew you could be such a bully, Sebastian."

"Only because I care so much."

"So much that you can't wait to get rid of me again."

"That's the last thing I want to do, and you know it."

"But if I turn down Laszlo and turn myself over to you, you'll have me buried back in some little theater that no one important ever visits, so that I can go on learning, training, getting experience—"

"Don't you think you need experience?" he asked.

"Of course I do—that's not the point."

"What is the point?"

"The point is that I love you," Katharine said exasperatedly, "and I hated being separated from you."

Sebastian stubbed out his cigarette and stood up, facing her. "If I swore to you that I'd do my best to make sure we weren't separated again—at least never for more than a couple of days at a time. If I told you that I'd never leave you in a place like that again, that it would all be better next time, *all* of it—would you go on with it?"

She stared at him. "You really believe I can do it, don't you?"

"You know I do."

"You think I have enough talent."

"I'm a professional," he said quietly. "You may be my wife, but I have better things to do with my time than take on a client I don't think talented."

Katharine was silent for several seconds.

"All right then," she said, at last.

"What do you mean?"

"I mean all right—okay—you win. You believe in me, I believe in you. I'll do whatever you think best."

Sebastian looked at her intently for an instant, as if measuring the truth of her words, and then suddenly he threw his head back and began to laugh. Full-blooded, loud laughter, his whole body shaking with it.

"For God's sake, Sebastian, what's so funny?"

"Nothing," he said, and the laughter distorted his voice. "Nothing's funny at all, angel. You're just the most wonderful creature in the world, that's all—"

With one sure, strong movement, he stooped and picked Katharine up in his arms, as if she were almost weightless.

"Sebastian!" Katharine pounded his chest. "Put me down!"

He carried her out of the room and up the staircase and into their bedroom, and Katharine, staring up into his face, seeing the intensity of the desire in his eyes, on his taut mouth, stopped struggling and relaxed against him.

He kicked the door shut with one foot, put her down and, without the slightest preliminary, began to undress himself rapidly, feverishly, leaving his clothes where they fell on the floor.

"Sebastian?" Katharine stood very still.

He grasped her by the shoulders and kissed her, a deep, almost savage kiss, and she felt a shiver of excitement, for he had never kissed her that way before, and her body, her whole being responded avidly, with equal passion. He drew back and tugged her sweater up over her head, unzipped her jeans, plunged his hand greedily between her thighs and pulled her hard against himself. A tiny flicker of something akin to fear shot through Katharine. Sebastian was always the most deliberate of lovers, almost always careful to maximize her pleasure, but tonight was entirely different. He seemed near to frenzy.

"Darling—"

He didn't answer, seemed beyond answering, and Katharine saw such a febrile gleam in his eyes that abruptly she felt overwhelmed by the isolating, irrational sense that he had forgotten who she was, that she no longer mattered.

Grasping her wrists, he pinned her arms to her sides and pushed her back onto the bed.

"Sebastian, don't—not like this—"

His hands were everywhere, not stroking or caressing as they usually were, but possessing, invading, sliding down her back, squeezing her breasts and her buttocks so hard that she cried out.

"For God's sake, stop it!"

He entered her, roughly, thrust hard into her, drew back, thrust again and again. A part of her registered fear, another part anger, and yet she offered little resistance now, was not even certain that she wanted to resist, for the memories of those nights of rejection were still raw wounds in her mind, and besides, she *wanted* him. But as he thrust, kept on thrusting, as she felt him filling her, hammering into her, as she went with him, moaning, bucking, wildly, frantically, Katharine opened her eyes and stared into his face, and she saw that he was more oblivious to her than before, and that his eyes were filled now with a pain that went deeper than the blunted, bittersweet male agony that often accompanied the last seconds before climax—

"Darling," she cried out, but he seemed not to hear her, and a few moments later, he gave one great groan and ejaculated, convulsively, into her. And then, almost instantly, while she still felt the tremors of that final lunge, he withdrew, and that act, too, was detached and destructive, as the rest had been, and she was left empty and sore and alone, while he rolled away to the far side of the bed.

Katharine lay very still. The only sounds in the room were the ticking clock on the mantelpiece and their breaths, in and out, unsteadily. She was utterly confused, unsure if she felt more angry with him or with herself. She did not know whether to leave the bed, leave the room, or to challenge him. And then she remembered the awful pain in his eyes, and the anger dissolved, and pity took its place.

She moved closer to him, tentatively, cautiously, and put out her hand to stroke his hair, half expecting him to jerk his head away. But at the touch of her fingers, he turned and she saw that his eyes were wet with tears, and she put out her arms, and as he came into them, she trembled with relief.

They lay that way for a long time, outwardly at peace, but she knew that it was not a natural sequel to love, as the lovemaking itself had been so far from natural. Generally, Katharine relished those tranquil, mindless moments after sex, their limbs still linked in exhausted, heavy warmth, but now, though their bodies were limp, there was no relaxation in them, and she fancied she could almost hear their minds ticking in time with the clock.

At last, the tension too uncomfortable for her to bear, she spoke.

"Will you tell me now?" she asked, softly.

"Tell you what?"

"What's wrong with you—or perhaps it's me."

"There's nothing wrong with you."

"Then why?" Still she spoke gently, carefully. "You've never been that way with me before."

"No," he said. "I'm sorry."

"It's okay."

"No," he said again. "It isn't."

She waited another moment.

"Is it something to do with what we were talking about before?" She paused. "Are you sure—I mean, are you really sure you won't mind if I have to go away somewhere again? We talked about what I felt, but we didn't—"

"For Christ's *sake!*" Sebastian jerked right out of her arms. "Can't you stop playing games?" He was on his knees, straddling her.

"I'm not." Breathless with shock, she stared up at him. "Sebastian, what on earth is wrong with you?"

"You still don't understand this, do you?" He grasped her shoulders painfully hard. "You're not taking it *seriously*. If you don't want to act—if you can't fulfill this one thing—"

"Sebastian, are you crazy? Let me go!"

"Don't you *understand?*" His eyes were dark with rage, the skin around his lips white with fury. "I can't relate to you anymore unless you're acting—I can't even *fuck* you, for God's sake! It just doesn't work for me anymore."

"I don't know what you're talking about!" Katharine tried to push him away, but he kept his grip on her shoulders. "You're frightening me, Sebastian!"

"I don't want an ordinary, pliable, stay-at-home woman, Katharine," he said, and his voice was clipped and harsh and desperate at the same time. "I fell in love with you because you were so different— it wasn't just your beauty or your sweetness—it was your *talent*. Don't you see yet? I can't love just any woman—I never could. You were the first, you're the only one I've ever loved!"

He released her suddenly, then, and she escaped, clambered off the bed, grabbing at the bedspread, needing to cover her nakedness. Sebastian lay back against the pillows, exhausted, one hand covering his eyes, and Katharine saw that his mouth was trembling.

"Oh, God," he said, quietly. "Oh, dear God, what have I done?"

"I don't know," she whispered, staring down at him.

He took his hand away from his eyes, and she saw the anguish in them, and the most terrible fear. "Are you going to leave me?" he asked, so softly she could hardly hear the words.

She shook her head slowly, unable to speak.

"I wouldn't blame you if you did," he said.

"Do you want me to?" she whispered.

He looked up into her face. "I would die if you left me."

"No, you wouldn't."

"I would want to die."

For several moments, neither of them spoke again. Sebastian lay still, on the bed, and Katharine stood, the bedspread held tightly against her breasts, a few feet away. She wanted to stay there, a safe distance from him, from this new capacity of his to frighten her, to wound her—but she looked into his eyes, saw the annihilation in them and, stronger than anything, the love, and she felt it drawing her, magnetlike, back to him. They were married, after all, he was her husband, and however ugly, however shocking and destructive those words had been, she had not a grain of doubt that he loved her more desperately than ever.

She sat down, on the edge of the bed, and put out her hand, and he took it, held on to it like a lifeline. They remained that way for a long time, as if the fragility of their relationship, of their marriage, was all there, held in the warmth of those two clasped hands.

"I have to ask you," Sebastian said, at last.

"Don't."

"I have to."

She said nothing.

"Have you decided"—his voice was low and tense—"what you're going to do?"

Katharine sighed, very softly.

"Yes," she said.

She knew that she was telling him what he needed to hear, and she told herself that it was, after all, what she wanted, too, and it seemed, anyway, a small price to pay to calm him, to soothe him. To end it.

"Yes," she said again. "I have decided."

"What?"

His tension transmitted itself to her, passed through his hand.

"I'll go on."

"You'll tell Laszlo no?"

"I'll tell him," she said.

And she felt him relax, felt the fingers unclench, saw the muscles go limp, saw the relief in his eyes, and the gratitude. And, dully, she knew that this battle, at least, this strange, incomprehensible battle, was at an end.

Katharine lay awake for a long time that night, deeply troubled and perplexed. It was the apparent key to soothing Sebastian that she could not begin to comprehend. Why should he be so obsessed by her becoming an actress, when he had so loved her work as a designer when they had first met? She let her mind travel back over the months. It was true to say that their lovemaking had been much more spontaneous and relaxed when Sebastian had visited her in the flat in Bromsgrove, and when he had been so intently absorbed in creating her new career. But why? Why should he need her to have that kind of success? Especially since he was surrounded by that sort of headiness every day of his working life. Would it not be more probable for him to want, and to need, an unambitious, home-loving woman?

Yet even if she were able to find an answer to those questions, they would not explain the sudden explosion of sexual violence that her initial agreement to continue had sparked—

I can't even fuck you unless you're acting.

Katharine shuddered, for that was exactly what their sex tonight had been. There had been no love in it, only wildness and, at the very start of it, a kind of triumph.

She thought about those other times, when he had so abruptly left her side in the midst of lovemaking, when she had felt so abandoned, so rejected, and she realized that they, too, were symptoms of the same problem. Yet they had taken place before they had ever discussed the possibility of her switching careers, so where, in God's name, was the link with what had happened tonight?

I need help, she thought, a little while before dawn. *He needs help.* Yet who could she speak to about such intimate problems? Virginia would be too distressed, had been through too much sadness already to burden her with more. The only other person close enough to Sebastian, who cared enough about him to be trusted, was Jeremy, and Katharine would sooner die than confide in him. *And if I tell Laszlo, or call Sam, they'll tell me leave him, to come home where I belong.*

Where she belonged. They wouldn't understand, for they hadn't seen how Sebastian could love, how tender he could be, how gentle. They would not understand that she did belong here now, with him, in this house, that this was her life now, this was her marriage. She remembered how wary she had been of marriage to David, remembered telling herself then that total commitment was only for when one knew, without a shadow of doubt, that it was impossible to be without the other person. The shadows were certainly here now, she thought. But not the doubts.

She fell asleep as the sun rose, and when she woke again, Sebastian was next door in the dressing room shaving with his electric razor. She got out of bed very slowly, already tense and uncertain what to expect of him. But when he walked into the bedroom, it was as if nothing at all unusual had happened between them.

"Good morning, angel."

"Good morning," Katharine said, and when she moved toward him to kiss him lightly in greeting, he pulled her to him for the kind of prolonged kiss that would, on any other morning, have filled her with gladness. Only today, on this particular morning, the pieces just did not seem to fit.

"I'll admit I'm very sad, *kedves*," Laszlo said to her two days later, when they met in his room at Claridge's.

"But you do understand, don't you?"

"Not at all." He smiled. "I know what you told me, and all the reasons are sound and fine, and I wouldn't argue with any of them, if your eyes convinced me that you believed in them."

"I do believe in them, Laszlo," Katharine said. "I'm just unhappy at having to say no to you. I would have loved, so much, to have worked with you again."

"I know that, *kedves*."

"You told me, on New Year's Eve, that you believed I could do anything I set my mind to." She forced herself to brighten. "I guess I've set my mind to acting."

"And taking several months off to design a musical would disturb that mind-set," Laszlo said.

"I think so. Sebastian says that there's a real momentum in his plans for me. I did some basic training in the Bromsgrove Playhouse—and it was pretty basic, believe me—and if I stop now, he thinks it'll be tougher than ever for me if I try to start again later, if not impossible."

"But are you sure you want this, Katharine? You have such a gift for design, for seeing a show as a whole entity—will it really satisfy you to be one single element, to be just one actor?"

"I told you at the party, I loved it."

"Even those small, insignificant roles, in that miserable place?"

"But the magic was still there." Katharine took a breath. "Even when we had almost finished the work on *Paris*, Laszlo, even at the very best time of my life on that side, I still used to look at the actors on stage and know that they were the ones making it happen—they were the ones on the inside, they were the heart and soul of it."

"And Sebastian truly believes he can make you a star."

Katharine laughed. "I doubt that. I don't think 'star' is in his vocabulary, he's too down to earth for that, too British. But he seems to believe that I have the talent and the potential to make it."

"And what, exactly, is 'it'?"

"Who the hell knows? And in a way, who the hell cares, so long as I'm doing what I want to be doing, and we're happy together."

"And are you?"

"Happy?" Katharine smiled again. "I told you, on New Year's."

"I know, I know," Laszlo said, a little wryly. "You told me."

Having secured Katharine's promise to continue her apprenticeship, Sebastian threw himself wholeheartedly into business, working for all his clients, as well as his wife, with every ounce, and more, of his former, unquenchable zeal. Unaware of the target at which, ever since the talk with Peter March, Sebastian had begun to direct her, Katharine followed his guidance unswervingly, presenting herself at every audition to which he sent her and attending all the various classes he suggested might be good for her.

"Your standard English is pretty good," he told her, "and you're a fine mimic, but if you're going to build yourself a real career in this country, you need to be able to eradicate every trace of your own accent on demand."

Two afternoons each week, Katharine went to a voice and speech coach in Kensington; on Monday mornings, a movement teacher came to the house to work with her; and twice a week, Katharine took classes at the Dance Centre. Every Sunday morning, a drama coach named Freddie Buchanan-Smith came to Hampstead to train her until lunchtime, when they broke off to eat with Sebastian, and then Freddie and Katharine would drive to Chalk Farm, where Freddie had the keys to an empty warehouse in which they could concentrate on projection.

Her next real opportunity came along at the end of February, when Katharine auditioned for and won the part of Laura in Tennessee Williams's *The Glass Menagerie* at the Briars, a theater center with a burgeoning reputation in Barnstaple in Devon.

"I can't believe it," she told Virginia, ecstatically, when they met for lunch at Richoux near Virginia's flat. "It's one of my absolute favorite plays and Laura's such a wonderful part. Poor, crippled Laura always reminds me of my 'Yellow Period.' " Seeing Virginia's puzzled expression, she explained. "That's how I labeled my life when I first moved to Manhattan—I was so scared of everything."

"I think of you as a very courageous young woman," Virginia said.

"Not at all." Katharine shrugged. "I've gotten better, of course, I'm stronger, not nearly so afraid of taking risks. And I never was anything like Laura Wingfield—I had a solid, sane family background, to begin with, and no physical disabilities."

"But you feel you can empathize with her well enough to play her?"

Katharine nodded. "Sebastian thinks I need to lose a little weight."

"You?" Virginia exclaimed. "That's the most ridiculous idea I've ever heard. You have a wonderful figure."

Katharine smiled at her. "Don't worry, he loves my shape as it is, but he says Laura has to be more than slender, she needs to be so fragile that the audience thinks a puff of wind could blow her over."

"But isn't that part of the skill of acting, darling? Giving an illusion of fragility—even fat people can seem frail, surely?"

"You're right, of course," Katharine agreed. "But I think Sebastian's right, too. At this point, I need all the help I can get, and losing a few pounds may just make it that bit easier to get right inside Laura."

"Well, you just be careful," Virginia said, anxiously. "You're going to need your strength, especially when you start rehearsing."

"You don't have to worry about me." Katharine looked down at her salad Niçoise. "I'm incapable of eating this kind of thing for long—I'll be back on real food in no time."

Katharine liked Barnstaple immediately. It was a charming market town on the Taw Estuary just ten miles from the Bristol Channel and not far from the wildness of Exmoor. The West Country people were warm and friendly, and in contrast to the miserable flat in which she'd lived in Bromsgrove, Sebastian had, this time, found her a delightfully furnished cottage on the outskirts of town. It had a small, well-maintained garden, a thatched roof and a working fireplace, and when Sebastian joined her, as he did, faithfully, every weekend, Katharine noticed with pleasure how swiftly and easily he seemed able to shake off the strains and burdens of the week. She loved his being there; it reminded her of their early weeks together in his little mews house, those easygoing days before they'd moved into The Oaks and the pressures had begun to mount.

There had been no more bad moments between them since that awful night at the beginning of January, and although Katharine realized that she ought to have confronted Sebastian afterward, have insisted that they talk about what had happened in the light of day, she had veered away from every opportunity, afraid that she might do more harm than good. He behaved as if nothing untoward had ever happened, was his old, controlled, vigorous and loving self, and so she had found herself wondering if she had, perhaps, blown the incident out of proportion.

Rehearsals for *The Glass Menagerie* would last for three weeks, and they would play for a further five. From the first day, Katharine found it the most stimulating work she had ever done. The other three members of the cast were gifted, highly intelligent and experienced professionals, and their working sessions, though far from gentle, were filled with fascinating debate, mental struggle and hard physical work. Helen Hardy, playing Amanda, Laura's mother, was a fine actress and a kind soul who, from the beginning, took Katharine under her wing, helping her in the tiny dressing room that they shared, with her makeup techniques, in return for which Katharine helped her with her St. Louis accent.

"You were absolutely wonderful tonight, angel," Sebastian told her after the first night. His eyes were warm and alive with pleasure and pride. "You were living in Laura's own world, and you got it just right—romantic and terribly sad, but not sentimental."

"You mean it?" Katharine asked urgently, still quivering with the excitement of performance.

"I would never say it if I didn't mean it, you know that." Sebastian paused. "And the audience loved you, too."

"You were right," Katharine said, softly.

"About what?"

"Everything. Coming here, pushing me to prepare." She smiled. "Mostly for making me see how right this would be for me."

"You look happy."

Katharine touched one of the roses he had brought her, felt the velvety softness between her fingers. "I am, darling. Very happy."

"Not sorry now that you turned Laszlo down?"

She looked into his eyes. He looked intent, but quite calm.

"I'm grateful I turned him down."

Even while she was in Devon, Sebastian continued to push Katharine, to drive her to improve her skills and build her confidence. On at least one day a week, when there was no matinee, she drove the little Renault, which she'd brought from London, up to Bristol for dance, speech and dialogue classes, and a short, concentrated series of lessons in camera techniques.

"Sometimes," she joked to Sebastian on the telephone, "I think you're trying to change me completely, that you must have hated me the way I was."

"Don't ever say things like that." He took her seriously, was appalled by the suggestion. "I just want to prepare you, to make a little use of my own knowledge to help you, so that you won't feel afraid or inadequate when the right chances come along."

"Sweetheart, I was only joking," Katharine assured him.

"Are you sure?"

"Absolutely," she said, touched by his intensity. "And I have to admit, it does seem to be helping. I feel even more stretched than I did at Carnegie Mellon, and I can actually feel my confidence growing."

"It's quality, my love," Sebastian said, gently, "and talent. You tried to bury them, I'm just helping you bring them back to life."

In the second week of April, Sebastian telephoned Peter March.

"Are you free, by any chance, this Saturday?"

"I may be," March said, carefully. "I'd need to check my diary to be sure."

"We're ready to discuss your Ibsen project." Sebastian paused. "I thought it might be pleasant to make a day of it."

"I could certainly make lunch, but—"

"Could you spare the afternoon, too?" Sebastian pressed. "There's something I'd like you to see—something that might interest you."

"How can I refuse?"

Sebastian collected March from his Surrey home and drove him down to Devon, pausing in Bath at a restaurant not far from Royal Crescent, where Sebastian suggested cold lobster and a fine Montrachet, and managed to avoid disclosing the real purpose of the excursion, before driving on to Barnstaple and to the Briars.

Seated in the small, oval-shaped theater shortly before four o'clock, March found himself, despite the excellence of his lunch, irritated.

"I see," he said, having glanced at the program. "Katharine Andersen. That is your Katharine, is it not?"

"I thought you might know," Sebastian said, lightly.

"I did not." March crossed his legs with exaggerated difficulty, emphasizing the discomfort of his small seat. "Forgive me, but I had believed your wife to be a successful stage designer."

"Also an actress."

As the lights dimmed, March's lips tightened. He loathed Tennessee Williams, always had. Having met Katharine on two occasions prior to the New Year's Eve party, his admiration for the young American woman—at least for her beauty, her intelligence and charm—had not been in question, and he had, until now, had a healthy respect for Locke, had not imagined him the type of agent to indulge a wife's whims. But then again, one could never tell.

He found himself agreeably surprised. The production was especially good, and the strength of Helen Hardy's mother and the young man playing her son was in no respect betrayed by Katharine's performance. By no means was she a great actress, March mused, but neither was there any trace of the confident, composed Washington-raised girl he had seen at her party. Her loveliness alone was touching, of course, constantly drawing the eyes from the other actors, but even that beauty had seemed quite altered by her fragility, and at the moment of Laura's first and only kiss, March had to admit to feeling almost dazed.

"I apologize," Sebastian said, as the lights came up.

"So you should."

"I was aware that you might not know Katharine was playing here."

"It was very naughty of you." March looked at Sebastian. "She's rather good, isn't she?" He got up stiffly. "I'm afraid I dislike the play, but it's not a bad production, and your wife made it more than tolerable."

Sebastian rose, too. "Shall we go backstage?"

"How could you do that to a friend?" Katharine chided Sebastian, once Helen Hardy had left the dressing room. "Poor Peter must have a hundred more important things to do than coming all the way to Devon to watch me."

"It was a very great pleasure, believe me," March said, charmingly.

"We have a little business to discuss," Sebastian said, "and I thought, under the circumstances, it might be pleasant to get out of London." He bent and kissed the top of Katharine's head. "I'm going to take Peter back to the cottage, darling, for some tea and serious conversation—how long will you be?"

"A little while, I'm afraid," she said, apologetically. "I have some errands I have to run—if you'd only told me, I'd—"

"Don't worry about us." Sebastian was brisk and cheerful. "We'll manage."

"There are scones in the larder, and fresh cream in the fridge—and there's a packet of Earl Grey, so don't use tea bags."

Sebastian smiled. "My English wife."

The two men ate their scones in the comfortable, chintzy sitting room, and March confirmed that the first of the plays was now scheduled to open at the Albery Theatre in October.

"With a run of five weeks apiece, that would take us into early February."

Sebastian poured more tea for them both. "Barbara is available, in principle, but naturally everything depends on the deal."

"Naturally." March paused. "Barbara's popularity together with Sam Raphael's charisma should prove wonderful box office, don't you think?"

Sebastian said nothing.

"But before any of these matters can even begin to be dealt with," March went on, "there's the little matter of Locke Mariner's financial involvement to be finalized."

Sebastian set down his tea cup.

"One hundred thousand pounds." He took a small bite of scone and swallowed it. "Not exactly an offer at this stage, of course, merely a suggestion."

"And a very generous one," March said, calmly, though the slight pinkness of his pale cheeks betrayed his excitement. What Sebastian was proposing was more than a mere investment. It was a major gamble, the sort of underpinning that producers dreamed about when they'd drunk a little too much champagne.

"I should like to make another suggestion," Sebastian said, "of another kind."

"By all means."

"Katharine," Sebastian said. "I feel there's something in this project for her."

"As a designer, or as an actress?" March asked.

"Katharine is an actress now, not a designer."

March was impassive. "There might, I suppose, be a small part—obviously, she isn't sufficiently experienced to tackle a major role in the West End."

"I disagree," Sebastian said, coolly. "Katharine's perfect for Hedda Gabler."

"For Mrs. Elvsted, perhaps?" March mustered a smile. "It's worth considering."

"No." Sebastian was cool. "I was thinking of Hedda."

"Surely not."

The producer reacted as Sebastian had known he would. March was a diplomat, when he needed to be, and if that superb investment was not to be tossed down the drain with the Earl Grey tea leaves, he needed to be very diplomatic at this moment.

"It's an interesting notion," he conceded, his tone amused but not in the least derisive. "But I'm afraid we could never take a chance with a novice in such a major enterprise."

"Katharine is not exactly a novice," Sebastian said. "Though I agree that it would take a certain courage to cast her."

"I'm not sure if *courage* is the right word," March said. "I don't have to remind you that I came to Locke Mariner so early in order to try to lay claim to an artist of great distinction and experience."

"And your major star will be an American TV actor—exactly what made me think about Katharine. Sam Raphael's hardly a natural choice for Ibsen, but that doesn't stop it from being a brilliant idea."

"Raphael's a distinguished Broadway actor, too." For the first time, March allowed a hint of reproof into his voice. "We shall be opening cold in London. Rehearsals will be cut to the barest minimum and every single minute will cost a small fortune." He tried to remain jovial. "You know better than this, Sebastian, especially since your own money's to be so heavily committed."

"Perhaps," Sebastian said, softly.

"I see."

"I'm going to leave it with you, Peter. I'm asking no more of you than that you take your time to think it over. Just as Jeremy and I will be thinking over our backing." He picked up his cup again. "Let the idea percolate for a while, in the privacy of your own imagination."

March said nothing.

"Katharine's talented," Sebastian went on. "You've more or less said as much. And she's a fast learner. A little more time, a little more appropriate experience and training, and she'll be perfect."

"For *Hedda Gabler*?" March looked at Sebastian. "Do you really see her as Hedda?"

"More clearly than I've ever seen anything."

At their regular Monday morning meeting in the office, Sebastian told Jeremy about the offer he'd made to March.

"A hundred grand? You're crazy," Jeremy said flatly.

"I don't think so."

"This is our first investment, and you're proposing we foot about half the bill for the entire project. More to the point, you've proposed it to the producer without discussing it with me first."

"It was the right moment to speak," Sebastian said, calmly. "March knew that it was a suggested figure, not a definite offer. But you're right, of course. I should have come to you first."

"A hundred thousand is way over the top."

"I believe in this project."

"I thought we were partners."

Sebastian took a cigarette from the gold case Jeremy had given him last Christmas. "A long time ago, Jerry, you told me there was no one in the world you'd rather invest in than me."

"That's still true. But this isn't you we're talking about."

"But it's something I have faith in."

"Fifty thousand, and I'll try and have faith, too."

"A hundred." Sebastian lit the cigarette. "I want us to have influence over these productions, Jerry."

Jeremy stood up and walked over to the window. "Barbara as Nora—Sam as Stockmann and Judge Brack, presumably. Who's going to play Hedda?"

"Undecided."

"I'd say that makes all the difference in the world, wouldn't you?"

Sebastian nodded. "I certainly would."

After the run in Barnstaple, Katharine returned to London. During the next four weeks, she attended numerous auditions and, in the fifth week, with surprising ease, she was cast in a television drama for the BBC. It was a splendid chance, and she used it well. She was to play a marriage wrecker, the "other woman" in an eternal triangle situation, and it gave her an opportunity to bring a number of angles into her acting: the sweet, sensual side that the character showed to her lover, the callous, uncompromising aspect that the wife saw, and the alternating, conflicting self-vilification and self-justification that she felt privately. The director, producers and writer of the play were pleased, and well in advance of its television showing, Sebastian secured a videotape and sent it to Peter March.

It was at the end of July that Elspeth Lehmann had a call from March's assistant, inviting Katharine to an audition. Sebastian telephoned home right away.

"This is big league," he told Katharine. "It's very important."

"You always tell me they're all important."

"This one's more so. Get yourself in the best possible shape before you go—fit in a dance class and a massage before you go to
Michaeljohn, and ask Koula to pin your hair up—"

"For goodness sake," Katharine laughed. "I've never heard you so
excited."

"I am, angel," Sebastian said. "Call it instinct."

He was lying in the bath, waiting for her, when he heard the
bedroom door.

"In here," he called. "How did it go?"

Katharine came into the bathroom, her cheeks flushed. "I'm not
sure. Pretty well, I think." She took off her jacket and bent down to
plant a kiss on his forehead. "It's such a gorgeous afternoon. I came
home by tube—the walk from the station's so pretty."

"What did you read?"

"Aren't I even allowed to sit down?" Katharine asked.

"Of course. I'm sorry." Sebastian smiled up at her. "Why don't you
get undressed and join me?"

She laughed. "I think I'll wait for you to get out."

"What did you read?" he asked again, trying to keep the tension
out of his voice.

"One scene as Petra in *Enemy of the People*, with her parents,
from the fifth act—"

"What else?"

"They asked me to read the first scene from *Hedda Gabler* between
Hedda and Mrs. Elvsted, once as Hedda and then changing around
—you know, the scene where they sit together on the sofa."

Sebastian stirred in the water. "What did Noël Harvey say?"

"Nothing much. You know how it is." Katharine looked down at
him and smiled. "You have a handsome erection."

"Yes." Sebastian picked up the soap and rubbed it over his chest.
"Harvey must have reacted in some way."

"He thanked me. He was very nice. Peter was there, too, but we
didn't speak, he just waved."

"So you came away knowing nothing?"

"But isn't it always like that?"

"I suppose so."

She glanced at him curiously. "Why are you so much more wound
up about this than any of the other auditions I've been to?"

"I'm not." Sebastian shrugged. "Maybe a little more, because we're putting money into these plays—I'd just love it if you could make your West End debut in this project."

"I did my best," Katharine said softly.

"I'm sure you did." He put down the soap. "Come here."

"Don't pull me in, this dress won't take it."

"Come sit on the side." She balanced on the edge, and he reached out his hand and drew a hairpin out of her golden chignon.

"Do you like the way Koula did it?" Katharine asked.

"It's beautiful." He drew out another pin, and the hair began to tumble. "How did you feel, while you were reading Hedda?"

"Shouldn't I be thinking about dinner? Ellie's out today."

"We'll go out to dinner." He paused. "How did you feel?"

"Where are we going?"

"Somewhere nice."

"What time?"

He wound a piece of golden hair around his fingers.

"Angel," he said.

"Yes?"

"Take off the dress and stop asking questions."

Elspeth took the call two days later, at eleven o'clock, and came directly into Sebastian's office.

"I just heard from March's office about Katharine. I thought you'd want to know right away. It's very good."

"Tell me." Nothing in the casual way he sat back in his chair altered; only the tiny pulse throbbing in his right temple betrayed his tension.

"They want her to play Petra, and to understudy Hedda."

Understudy.

Sebastian sat perfectly still.

"Who's going to play Hedda?"

"We still don't know." Elspeth looked at him. "You're not pleased, are you?" She paused. "Were you hoping for Mrs. Elvsted?"

He had to swallow before he could answer. "It was unrealistic, I know. Petra's a good beginning."

Just after six, while Sebastian was on the telephone to Sam Raphael in Los Angeles, Jeremy came in and sat down to wait until the call was ended.

"March called from New York, but your line was busy."

"What did he want?" Sebastian lit a cigarette.

"To tell us they want Barbara to play Hedda."

"You're kidding." Sebastian set his lighter down on the desk. His fingers, holding the cigarette, scarcely quivered. "As well as Nora?"

"It's Rebecca Sykes for Nora, fresh from the National." Jeremy's eyes glinted. "It's brilliant casting, Seb, don't you think? Barbara will be dynamite, pure dynamite—a sexy, electrifying Hedda. For the first time, I see a chance that our gamble might just pay off."

"Barbara's too old."

"The hell she is."

"Ibsen specifies Hedda's age as twenty-nine. Barbara's in her late forties."

"She's perfect, Seb, you know she is—and Nora's no older. Anyway, since when are you so concerned with age?" Jeremy raised an eyebrow. "You really thought they might give it to Kate, didn't you?"

"Not entirely." Sebastian took one drag of his cigarette, then stubbed it out. "They've given her the understudy, did you know?"

"March told me." Jeremy paused. "He said you might be upset."

"Do you think I'm so unprofessional?"

"I think you're human. And Kate's husband."

"In this case, I'm her agent."

"And Barbara's."

Sebastian nodded. "I'll call her."

Jeremy stood up. "Are you okay, Seb?"

"Sure." Sebastian's smile was tight. "Why shouldn't I be?"

When the door closed, he picked up a pencil and began to write, on a notepad. *Hedda—Barbara Stone. Dr. Stockmann and Judge Brack—Sam Raphael. Petra—Katharine Andersen.* He pressed so hard that the tip tore pinpoint holes through the paper, and then he took the pencil in both hands, snapped it in two, and threw it across the room.

He had been so certain that March and Noël Harvey had intended Barbara for Nora, not Hedda. He had envisaged Barbara as Nora with perfect clarity, just as he'd seen Katharine as Hedda, with her shining beauty and naturally elegant bearing. Barbara *was* too old for Hedda—God damn Harvey, God damn March for his cowardice! Barbara Stone was safe, of course, guaranteed box office, and Sebastian was as fond of her as he'd always been, but this ought to have been Katharine's part—March had known it was what he wanted, knew quite well that Sebastian had been all but buying it for her with their investment.

He lit another cigarette and stood up, his chair slamming against the bookshelves behind him. He considered withdrawing the backing, but he knew, even in the heat of the moment, that it was impossible. He could handle Jeremy, of course, but it would damage their credibility, not to mention Barbara Stone.

Damn them.

He took a deep drag of the cigarette and felt a sudden dizziness, so strong that he had to lean against the wall for support. His head throbbed—he had so many headaches these days. Too much tension. His own fault, his inability to relax.

He sat down again, shook his head. Nothing to do but have the contracts drawn up and go home to Katharine with a bouquet and with congratulations. She'd be happy enough with Petra—she'd had no idea what he'd wanted for her. She'd feel safer this way, less pressured, and that was something he ought to take into account. Katharine's happiness.

He wondered, for the first time, if she'd given her best at the audition. Had it been, perhaps, her own fault she'd lost the part? She was always so modest, so unassuming—perhaps she hadn't seemed hungry enough for Hedda? Men like March and Harvey could smell that touch of diffidence a mile off, and to them it translated into lack of drive, even lack of ambition . . .

Damn them all.

c h a p t e r
24

"I wish I didn't have to go."

"You have no choice, I know that."

Sebastian stared down at the pigskin suitcase lying, half-packed with his clothes and papers, on their bed.

"I should be here to support you. It's a crucial time."

"I'll be just fine." Katharine managed a smile. "Besides, if you were around, I'd probably be too busy for us to spend any time together." The smile became rueful. "Still, nothing new about that."

"I know." Sebastian shook his head. "It's been a bit rough lately, hasn't it? All work, for both of us."

"Sure has," she said quietly.

"I'm sorry."

"Can't be helped." Katharine's voice was light, but a slight quiver betrayed her. "We're both professionals, after all."

Sebastian looked into her face. "Maybe I should postpone this trip. If you really need me here—"

"You can't," Katharine said quickly.

His eyes grew bleaker.

"No," he said. "I suppose not."

* * *

After receiving the news, almost one month earlier, about her casting, Katharine had been delighted. She had set to work briskly, had read all of Ibsen's plays, had read the translations by Michael Meyer and Christopher Hampton of the two plays she was to work on, and had then pored meticulously over Gunnar Nyquist's translation notes, before focusing her fullest concentration on the character of Petra Stockmann. So far as Katharine was concerned, it would be the perfect London debut for her; substantial enough but manageable, a way to cut her West End teeth, to absorb excellence, and, if she was lucky, perhaps even to get noticed.

However well Sebastian had tried to disguise his disappointment, Katharine had realized that he had wanted more for her, that he had, perhaps, seen her as Mrs. Elvsted, and she could well imagine Laszlo Eles agreeing with Sebastian, perhaps giving her one of his famous tongue-lashings for selling herself short. But this was the way she was. As an actress, Katharine knew she was still a beginner. She was lucky to have Petra, and while she would, of course, study Hedda to the best of her ability, she would pray, every night, for Barbara Stone's good health.

Encouraged by Sebastian, Katharine had continued with all her classes, and he had continued, since rehearsals for *An Enemy of the People* were not to begin until early September, to send her to potentially worthwhile casting calls.

"It's important," he had told her, "for you to keep as busy as possible. Too much preparation prior to rehearsals could do more harm than good. What you need most of all is experience."

She had recorded an episode of Simon Kean's television series, filming initially for three days, with a break before further filming, and in the hiatus she had taken over a role vacated by illness for the Warehouse Theatre Company in Croydon. Katharine loved the work. Everything she touched seemed to be pointing her, she felt, in the direction that Sebastian had prophesied for her. Professionally, her self-confidence began to grow. But her happiness diminished.

Her life had altered so radically since leaving America, that she sometimes felt afraid of losing control over her own destiny, almost of her own identity. The ambitious zeal in which Sebastian had lately begun to envelop her was so powerful that she sensed a danger that it might sweep them both away from reality. Time had become a blur of activity for them both. Sebastian's own commitments kept him so frantic that he seldom emerged from Locke Mariner until ten or eleven at night, by which time he was usually drained and more than ready for sleep. For what seemed an age, he had not attempted to make love to Katharine. Only once since she had won Petra had Sebastian initiated sex, and then he had seemed more mechanical and obliging than loving, and Katharine had found herself as troublingly unmoved by him as she might have been by a stranger.

Their minds had grown progressively further apart, their bodies less and less physically attuned, their lives more frenetic. On the few occasions when work alone failed to exhaust him, Sebastian insisted they go out late at night to drink and dance at Annabel's or Tramp until the small hours. It was as if any opportunity for intimacy with Katharine had begun to frighten him.

Now, just three days before rehearsals were due to begin, he was flying to Los Angeles, and to Katharine's dismay, she felt relief more than anything. Their increasing failure to communicate on any level other than professional, had begun to distress her to the extent where she was at risk of losing her concentration on the only aspect of her life that was going well. With rehearsals almost upon her, a period when she would need all her energies, emotional and physical, perhaps it was better for them to be apart for a week or two.

A few minutes after noon the following day, a Friday, just as Katharine was about to step into the shower after her two-hour session with her movement teacher, the telephone rang.

"Hello?"

"Katharine, it's David."

The sound of his voice, tentative but warm, was so overwhelmingly welcome to Katharine's ears that she had to sit down on the edge of the bed before she could speak.

"Where are you?"

"Here, in London. I flew in on the same flight as Sam."

"How is he?"

"Great. Excited about working with you."

Katharine's right hand was trembling, and she had to support the receiver with her left.

"Where are you staying?" she asked.

"At the Inn on the Park—I'm here on a flying visit." David paused. "Can I see you?"

"How long are you here for?"

"Just one day."

Katharine hesitated. "I could do dinner this evening, if that's—"

"That's great." He paused again. "Will you both be coming?"

"No. Sebastian's away. It'll just be me."

"I think I can stand that."

When she put down the receiver, Katharine stood up and went back into the bathroom. She looked at her reflection in the mirror. Her cheeks were flushed and her eyes were sparkling.

"Oh, David," she said.

It was more than two years since they had parted, and she had not laid eyes on David since the night of the *Paris* party, when he had appeared, so briefly and touchingly, to congratulate her, but she knew now—had not considered it until now, and would probably not have allowed herself to dwell on it if she had; she knew now that she had missed David, missed her life with him. Missed him.

They met in the Four Seasons restaurant at his hotel. He was seated at a corner table when she arrived, and as he rose, Katharine saw that he was suntanned and fit, and that the touch of gray in his hair had made him even more attractive than she had remembered.

"You look," he said, "like heaven."

"You don't look so bad yourself," she answered, softly.

They kissed, just a brush of lips, without lingering, and sat down.

"White wine?" he asked her.

"Please."

Katharine sat very still as he ordered their drinks. For a moment or two, she felt certain that David was going to tell her that he'd found someone else, and was going to be married or was already married. In a minute, perhaps after she'd had a sip of wine, he'd take out his wallet and show her a photograph of some pretty woman, and maybe even baby pictures, and she would smile and clasp his hand, and tell him how very happy she was for him, and it would be a lie.

"So tell me," she said, and steeled herself.

"Tell you what?"

"How things are for you?"

David smiled. "About the same."

And his wallet stayed in his jacket, and Katharine knew that she was wrong, that he was not married or even intending to be. He was the same as he had always been. He hadn't needed to change anything much about himself or about his life, because he was fine just the way he was.

"Are you happy, David?"

"Sure." He took a sip of his Scotch on the rocks. "Though I was happier when you were in my life, Katharine." He winced a little, wryly. "I didn't intend to say that, or not right away."

"I miss you, too," she said.

"We all miss you. All your friends, the people who cared about you when you were in New York—they haven't stopped caring. All kinds of people ask about you, because it seems as if you dropped off the edge of the earth."

"I didn't," Katharine said. "I just came to England."

"Dixie Callaghan says you called her once, last Thanksgiving, and she says that she's written to you, but you haven't written back."

"Of course I have."

"Not for a long time." David drank some more Scotch. "Life isn't meant to be that way, Katharine. If you meet people, and make them love you, you're not supposed to walk away, or run away, to England or to anywhere, and even if you're happy as a lark, you aren't supposed to forget about those people."

"I haven't forgotten anyone," Katharine said, defensively.

"And are you happy as a lark?" David put down his glass. "Laszlo doesn't think you are, and neither does Sam."

All Katharine's barriers sprang up.

"Of course I'm happy," she said. "Why shouldn't I be? I have a wonderful marriage, a lovely home, a new career that I love. You may be right to scold me for not keeping in touch as regularly as I ought, but I'd be glad if you didn't listen to idle gossip."

"No one's gossiping about you—"

"Really?" All the pleasure and contentment she had felt at seeing David again had vanished. "I know Laszlo was upset with me for turning down his offer, but what gives Sam the right to spread lies about my marriage—"

"Take it easy, Katharine." David smiled a little at her anger. "Sam hasn't said anything much—"

"Nor could he, since he hasn't seen us together since the wedding."

"But he's talked to you. I know Sam respects Sebastian, and he really likes him—he just mentioned to me once that he doubted if your life was a bed of roses."

"And Laszlo?" Katharine was growing angrier. "What does he say?"

"Nothing."

"I don't believe you."

David shook his head. "I shouldn't have started this."

"No, you shouldn't, but you have, so we may as well get it out of the way."

"You know Laszlo decided not to do the show?"

"I suppose that's my fault?" Katharine asked, hotly. "And don't try changing the subject—I want to know what he's been saying about my husband."

"Simply that he has the impression that Sebastian's a natural leader, and—"

"And?"

"And that he's a little manipulative."

Katharine stared at David. "This is beneath you—I never imagined jealousy could make you malicious. Anyway, how come you've been talking to Sam and Laszlo so much?"

"Because we all love you."

"You have a strange way of showing it."

"Perhaps." David shrugged. "We're your friends, Katharine. You made your mark on us all, like it or not, and we're not about to forget you."

Katharine's anger disappeared, and in its place was a suddenly fierce sorrow and a desire to weep. She bit down on it, tried to keep going, told herself it was nostalgia, nothing more, but it was no good.

"Are you okay?" David asked, gently, seeing the change in her, aware of the tears even though they were still locked in, somewhere behind her eyes. "Do you want to get out of here?"

She nodded. "Please."

They went up to his suite, and in the lift, David put his arm around her and Katharine leaned against him, and even then, with strangers on either side, she knew what was going to happen, felt it as one might in a slow-motion, premonitory dream.

He sat her down on the sofa, and poured a cognac for her.

"That's too much," she said, her mouth still trembling.

"Just sip it," he told her, and she heard his doctor's voice, and it was so soothing, so safe.

"Oh, David." It was all she could say. She put the glass to her lips and drank a little, and it warmed her, and he sat down beside her, and she felt as if the many months of separation had never been.

"I have to say this," David said, his voice husky, "right away."

"Say what?"

"That I still love you."

Katharine said nothing.

"Not just as a friend," David said.

"No." She sat very still.

"You're still trembling," David said. "Take another sip."

"I shouldn't be here." She swallowed some more cognac, gripped the glass with both hands, as if it were a support. "I think I should leave."

"I think you should stay." Gently, David took the glass out of her hand and sat down beside her. "Tell me."

"What should I tell you?"

"Why you're so unhappy." He paused. "You can still trust me, you know."

"I always did."

"So trust me now. What's wrong, Katharine?" He took her left hand and held it. "Please, sweetheart, tell me what's hurting you."

"I don't know."

"You must know."

She shook her head. "It doesn't make any sense, David. I love him, and I know he loves me—that hasn't changed."

"But something has."

"Everything has, in a way." Katharine struggled to find the words. "It's all as it was—all in place. We're together, we love our home, we love our work, we love each other. But we're floating adrift—we can't seem to reach each other anymore. We touch, but we're not really touching, you know?"

David said nothing.

"I'm lonely." She stared down at her hand in his, and the old familiarity made her ache with sudden longing. "I guess that's what it comes down to."

"Look at me," David said. "Look at me, Katharine."

She looked up, away from their hands, into his face. Into his kind, intelligent, handsome face, and she knew it so well, knew the loving look in his brown, warm eyes, knew how the skin on his cheeks would feel if she touched him—

"David," she whispered.

"I know," he said. "I swore I wouldn't let this happen, but I guess I'm not to be trusted after all."

There were tears in her amber eyes, and a part of her mind was telling her to stand up, to walk away, to go home, but she knew that she wouldn't, that she was incapable of going at this moment and that, more than anything, she didn't want to go. And their faces grew closer and closer, and their cheeks brushed first, and then their lips, and it was such a rush of sweetness, of that familiarity again, and the sensation was so comforting, so tangible, so vivid, that Katharine knew that she could not, would not stop now, and their mouths were together, and then David's arms were around her, and the warmth and strength of him began to overwhelm her, and as he picked her up and carried her through into the bedroom, she moaned a little, but she could no longer tell whether it was a moan of protest, or of guilt, or of desire, or of love.

It felt so right. The cool, soft sheets on the bed, and the wondrous heat of their bodies. David's arms, enfolding her. David's long, fine, surgeon's fingers, stroking her. David's mouth, warm and sweet, hungry but oh, so tender. His body, compact and alive and giving and taking what she yearned to give, his legs, wrapping around her own, his hands, growing stronger, pushing apart her thighs, and all the while, the voice inside her head, urging her on, suppressing her guilt, drowning out her doubts: *It's all right, because it's David, it's all right . . .*

They lay very still, afterward, their bodies still entwined.

"What's that?" Katharine murmured, touching a scar on his right side that she didn't remember.

"Appendicitis, last summer." He stared into her eyes. "Peritonitis, actually."

Katharine burst into tears.

"Don't cry, darling."

"But you could have died," she wept.

"But I didn't, and I'm fine now, it's only a scar."

"But I wasn't there with you!" She kissed the scar, and her tears spilled onto his stomach. "You needed me, and I was thousands of miles away and I didn't even *know*!"

David laughed, gentle, chuckling laughter, and he held her tightly, and kissed her mouth and her wet eyes, and her breasts, and then Katharine, too, began to laugh, and she realized at that instant that she had not done that for weeks and weeks, and it felt so good . . .

Later, once they were out of bed and getting dressed, and Katharine was getting ready to go home, the laughter seemed far, far away again, as if it had never happened, and the heaviest sorrow weighed them both down.

"Please don't go," he said again, as he had when she'd gotten out of the bed.

"I must."

"I know." He paused. "And I have to leave London, anyway."

"Do you have to?" Katharine asked, quietly. "Couldn't you stay a little longer?"

"I have a meeting in the morning, and my flight leaves at lunchtime. I have patients waiting in New York, and operations scheduled." He paused. "And you still have a husband. Whom you still love."

Katharine could not speak.

David nodded slowly. "I guess it's time to go." He looked at her, and his eyes were full of pain. "I wanted to make you happier, darling. Don't start blaming yourself. This was my fault."

Katharine forced a smile through her tears.

"It took two."

For a little while, on her way home, Katharine almost hated David. For coming in the first place. For letting her know that he still loved her, for warming the cold, empty space inside her. For making her feel, at least for a little while, cherished, warm and safe. Most of all, for going away again. But then she realized that she could not hate David, that she never would.

She tried to tell herself, as she drove through the dark, still busy streets, that tonight had done no harm, that she must not destroy it for herself with guilt. More important, that she must not allow it to destroy her marriage. Tonight was a secret she had to keep safely locked away deep inside herself, a brief, bright, warming memory that she could think of for comfort if the nights grew too cold again for her to bear.

By the time she reached The Oaks, parked the Renault in the big drive, heard the thud of the car door and the soft crunching of her shoes on the gravel, the time she'd spent with David already seemed more like a dream than reality, and it was so strange to feel that way, because she had sometimes felt that way about her life with Sebastian.

Maybe these last few hours, with David, have been the reality, she thought, as she got undressed again, as she climbed into the four-poster. After all, David had been her reality back in the days before Sebastian had plucked her out of her own life, her own world. She felt the cool sheets stroking her body, reached out to touch the plumped, unused pillow beside her. David was the very last person she should have seen at a time when she felt so vulnerable, when she was going to need all her energy, emotional and physical.

She felt another surge of irrational resentment against him, against his gentle strength, against the old, familiar comfort of his arms, of his body—and then the emotion veered away from David toward Sebastian, for it was he who had created the loneliness and confusion inside her.

He who made her feel all alone, even when he was here.

When, just after ten o'clock that morning, a bouquet of two dozen long-stemmed red roses arrived from Sebastian in Los Angeles, Katharine's guilt was dreadful, her immediate desire to obliterate the night with David intense. The flowers, achingly beautiful, were followed unnervingly swiftly by a transatlantic telephone call.

"Angel, are you all right?"

"I am now," Katharine lied. "The flowers are lovely, darling."

"I miss you so much." Sebastian's voice was painfully unhappy and filled with undisguised longing for her. "Being away from you—" He hesitated. "I know how badly I've behaved lately, and I know I'm to blame for all our problems—"

"Sebastian, don't." Her cheeks were scaldingly hot.

"I need to say this now, Katharine. When I'm there, with you, there don't seem to be enough hours in the day, I don't have the time—or maybe I don't take the time—to look at things clearly."

"What things?" she asked, tentatively.

"Everything. I'm going to make it up to you, darling."

"There's nothing to make up for, Sebastian. If only you'd just open up to me a little more, share your feelings with me, the bad ones, not only the happy ones—"

"I know I'm to blame," he said again.

"No," she said. "It isn't like that. It's just the wall you put up sometimes, and the fact—" She stopped. She had been about to say that he didn't seem to want her anymore, but the knowledge of her own treachery had silenced her just in time.

"I know," Sebastian said, gently. "Things will be better when I get back. I swear it."

Katharine put down the telephone and wept tears of bitter anguish. She had never felt such self-loathing. She had always prided herself on her honesty, and now she had betrayed them both, Sebastian and David, and it was hard, at that moment, to be certain which was the greater betrayal.

I used to blame my mother for allowing her marriage to fall apart, and here I am, tumbling into bed with the first man who comes along, just because things have gotten a little rough.

But it hadn't been just any man. It had been David. And she had caused him more pain, as she always had.

There was only one thing Katharine was certain of now, and that was that Sebastian must never discover what had happened. No matter how wretchedly her deceit weighed on her, there was no alternative but to live with what she had done. To put it behind her.

David knew, when he called from the airport.

"You don't have to say anything," he told her, gentle as always.

"I wish we had time to talk, at least."

"I wish many things, Katharine, but it's probably better this way." He forced himself to speak lightly. "It was comfort, more than anything, for both of us. We're friends, you and I, and that's never going to change."

"I love you, David," Katharine said, helplessly. "But—"

"But you're Sebastian's wife, and I accept that."

"Will you be okay?"

"I'll be fine. And I know you will."

She remembered how he had scolded her the previous evening. "Give the others my love. Tell Dixie I'll write, when I can, and tell Sam—"

"You'll be seeing Sam on Monday," David reminded her. "Don't give him a hard time. He cares about you. We all do."

"I know."

Behind David's voice, Katharine heard the airport hum of voices and announcements, and she knew that he was being drawn away from her, felt suddenly afraid that she might never see him again.

"David," she said, urgently.

"What, my love?"

"I'm sorry."

"Nothing to be sorry about," David said. "So long as you remember I'll always be there for you, if you need me."

And I'll be there for you, she wanted to promise. But she knew it would be a lie, knew that some things were not possible.

"Be safe," she said.

"You, too—and Katharine?"

"Yes?"

"Break a leg."

The roses continued to arrive every day until Sebastian came home, and the house became a vivid, perfumed garden. The gesture was unusually theatrical and, perhaps, contrived for Sebastian, but the message of the flowers was undeniably clear to Katharine. He still loved her. He needed to prove it to her. He was desperately afraid of losing her.

Katharine was waiting for him in the drawing room the evening he got back. She felt as nervous and apprehensive as if they were two near strangers about to embark on marriage without any chance of getting to know each other first. But as soon as she saw the mixture of joy and fear in Sebastian's own eyes, her immediate anxieties dissolved, for it was so clear that he loved her, and that, surely, was all that mattered.

"You look so tired," she said, gently.

"I am pretty beat," he agreed. The hours in the plane and, more significantly, the two weeks of grueling work and battling he had endured in the crazy temperature contrasts of Los Angeles' ice-cold offices and sun-soaked poolsides had physically and mentally drained him.

"Come and relax—I'll get you a drink."

Sebastian looked closely at her. There were faint, bluish shadows under her eyes that he'd never seen before, but they just accentuated her fragility and her soft, pale skin.

"You look lovelier than ever," he said, softly, "though that hardly seems possible." He watched her, as she poured his whisky. "How are rehearsals going?"

"All right, I think." She gave him a glass and sat down beside him. "It's such a wonderful company. I told you I felt a little daunted at first, but we're beginning to settle down." She smiled. "I can't tell you how strange it is to be working with Sam."

"Your one-time stepfather suddenly playing your father," Sebastian said. "Could be worse, you could be playing lovers."

"Oh, it's great, and he's such a good actor." Katharine tried to explain. "It's just a little weird having this one solid fragment of my old life planted right in the middle of my brand-new, still strange one." She felt a warm flush on her cheeks as David's image sprang, unbidden, into her mind, and stood up abruptly.

"Don't get up." Sebastian patted the cushion beside him.

"I have some things to do in the kitchen."

"I'm sure Ellie's managing. Sit down, please, angel."

Katharine sat down. She turned her face and looked into her husband's blue eyes, saw the face she loved so much, the not quite straight nose and the fine mouth, and David disappeared again.

"I've missed you so much," Sebastian said.

"I wish you hadn't gone. I hate our separations."

"There won't be any more for a long time, I promise."

"You can't promise me that."

"Next crisis that comes up in the States or anywhere else except London, Jeremy can deal with on his own."

"What if he doesn't agree?"

"He won't have a choice."

The evening slipped sweetly by. They sat for a long while, side by side, hardly touching. Their conversation was fragmented, but contented, as they began to luxuriate in the sheer pleasure of seeing each other close to—of being in touch again. They were both painfully aware of having been given another chance. If they were to use it to reach out and touch, really touch, then they had to make sure that it would work. Resolving their problems could only come about through love and trust. They had to be ready to accept whatever came, and to be willing to work at their problems, however they developed.

It was when they were, finally, ready to go upstairs, that Katharine realized, suddenly, that Sebastian was afraid. And it occurred to her, for the very first time, that perhaps their enemy—her enemy—was The Oaks. Most of all, their bedroom.

Although it was only September, the house, without central heating, sometimes grew a little chilly, and so they had lit a fire, and now Sebastian was damping it down. Katharine sat very still, trying to come to terms with her new, disturbing thoughts.

I can't believe how insensitive I've been, she thought, appalled. She had believed herself so careful when she had arranged that room, and he, of course, had let her believe that he was delighted with it. And perhaps he had been, perhaps he hardly realized himself how much his parents' old bedroom affected him. *Or am I clutching at straws?* And yet, if she thought about it, their lovemaking had almost always been more perfect away from the house—

"All right?" Sebastian said, reaching for her hand and drawing her to her feet.

Katharine wanted to stop him, wanted to try to talk about her thoughts, but it was the wrong moment, entirely wrong, and they were already in the hall, and Sebastian was leading her up the staircase.

At least, she thought, *if he turns away from me now, I can try to understand him, maybe even help him—help us.*

Sebastian opened the bedroom door.

"Are you sure?" Katharine asked him, as he took her in his arms.

"Quite sure," he said.

Sebastian thought he had never known such fear, but he, too, had come to realize, in the long days and nights apart from Katharine, that although his problems lay within himself, they seemed accentuated by this house, his beloved house. And the understanding that his confusions might have solid roots and, therefore, be conquerable gave him new courage, and he knew that he loved Katharine far too much to let their marriage be destroyed, and so now, this evening, he took the utmost care with her, was gentle, lingering, infinitely careful.

Her body was so beautiful, so warm and soft and firm, with its familiar mounds and valleys, the small, erect nipples of her lovely breasts, the dip of her navel, the rumpled, tousled silk of her pubic hair, the heat and moistness that first his fingers, and then his mouth, discovered again, all over again

And he had known that the scent would come tonight, felt almost as if he had dared it to come. But this time, when he felt its sickening, cloying threat hovering over him, Sebastian knew that he had made himself invulnerable, and he opened his eyes wide, deliberately, and gazed down at his lovely wife, and defied the scent, turned it away and with it, the unwelcome, forbidden image of Diana, of his beloved, long-dead mother.

And it surrendered to Katharine's sweeter, softer fragrance. The past disappeared, floated away, back into the darkness, receding like a child's bad dream.

And Sebastian knew that he had, at last, won.

chapter
25

The rehearsals for *An Enemy of the People* flew by. The cut and thrust and sense of challenge that Katharine had experienced in preparation for the Tennessee Williams play seemed magnified several times over. She had felt uncomfortable, at first, about working with Sam, aware that if it had not been for David's visit to London, she would have loved nothing more. But she could not rid herself of the fear that Sam might know that she and David had slept together again, could not forget what David had told her about Sam's reservations over Sebastian. Yet after the first week of rehearsals, it had become clear that Sam only cared about her; if she was happy with her husband, that was fine with Sam. He was not her enemy; he would not, she realized, betray her.

For the first four weeks, they rehearsed at Wyndham's Theatre in Charing Cross Road, blinkering themselves to the inappropriate set on stage for the show currently playing there. Katharine was happier than she had been for a long time. In the theater, she was wholly embroiled, utterly focused, yet there was always a part of her mind able to remain on the outside, fascinated by the dedication and professionalism of the whole company. There could be few things more exciting, Katharine felt, than this blend of fantasy and intellectualism, physical hard work and trickery, those tricks that they would play day after day, after the first preview, not only on the audiences, but on themselves.

Sebastian seemed proud of her, too, lavishing unusually unequivocal praise on her whenever he sat in on rehearsals—a right, not often granted, that he had negotiated with Peter March despite Noël Harvey's disapproval. Sebastian always remained silently at the back of the stalls, keeping his own counsel.

"He's being so good to me," Katharine told Virginia. "The perfect agent, and the perfect husband."

"He does seem happier than I've seen him for a long time," Virginia agreed. "I thought he seemed a little strained before he went to Los Angeles."

"We both were," Katharine confided. "And I was concerned that when rehearsals got under way, it might be difficult at home. But it's so great, because I'm in London—I hated being away from him."

"That's all in the past now," Virginia said.

"I think it is."

The play opened to the critics at the Albery, after three dress rehearsals and four previews, on the second Tuesday in October. It was a perfect day. Katharine's body was a caldron of terror, but Sebastian was wonderful, attentive and proud, seeming to know exactly when she needed comfort and when she needed to be alone. He sent her roses, and a beautifully worded telegram, and when she reached the dressing room she shared with the three actresses playing citizens in the crowd in the fourth act, Katharine found more telegrams from Laszlo and Betty, from Dixie, Virginia, Henrik and, discreetly worded, from David.

"Okay, sweetheart?" Sam asked, peering round the door.

"No."

"Me neither."

"How can you stand this?" Katharine asked him plaintively. "How can you bear to go through this over and over again?"

"I'm crazy, sweetheart. All actors are crazy."

Thirty minutes before her first entrance, Katharine hated Sebastian, detested him for making her do this, for forcing her to endure this agony—and then, when Petra had exited for the first time, and was preparing to go on again, she loved him, blessed him for his instincts and his faith in her, for he'd been right, oh, so right.

And then later, when it was all over, after they'd celebrated in the upstairs room at the Ivy, Sebastian took her by the hand.

"We have to take a walk," he said.

"I'm a little tired," Katharine said.

"We have to, angel—just a little way."

They walked away from Covent Garden, strolled down St. Martin's Lane and into Trafalgar Square, and Sebastian reminded Katharine —though she did not need to be reminded, for she would never forget—of that other special opening night on Broadway, when they had walked through the New York City streets, she in her ridiculous, gorgeous, high-heeled gold sandals.

"You're very romantic tonight," she said.

"Do you mind?"

"What a crazy question."

Sebastian hailed a taxi.

"What about your car?" He'd left the Aston Martin in a car park near Leicester Square.

"Too much champagne. I'll fetch it in the morning."

"Will it be all right?"

He smiled down at her. "Who the hell cares? I just want to get you home."

And all Katharine's fatigue had disappeared, and when they got back to the house, Sebastian threw fresh logs onto the fire in the drawing room, and he took off her clothes and then his own, and made love to her on the seventeenth-century Savonnerie rug they had bought the previous year in Gstaad. And Katharine felt a pang of gratitude that her husband was such an intensely glamorous, fascinating man, and when one had peaks such as this, one was bound to have troughs as well, and she vowed, gazing into the flames, that she would overcome those too, when they came again, if they came.

The happiness continued all through the play's run of almost five weeks. Katharine's schedule was manageable, easy compared to Sam's, with a fortnight's break, while *A Doll's House* opened, before rehearsals for *Hedda Gabler* were due to begin. Sam went home to New York for two weeks, with gifts and messages from Katharine for Laszlo, Betty and Dixie; and Virginia brought her news, with a hint of pink in her cheeks, that Henrik, who had been corresponding with her for almost a year, had invited her to come to Copenhagen for a visit, and that she had agreed to go.

"I'll be staying at a hotel, of course."

"Of course."

"Henrik says that the d'Angleterre is very nice."

"I haven't stayed there, but I've eaten in their restaurants and it looked marvelous."

Virginia hesitated. "Are you sure you don't mind?"

"Mind? Why on earth should I mind?"

"I just thought"—the pinkness became a true blush—"Henrik is your great-uncle—I want to be sure—"

"That I approve?" Katharine was wide-eyed.

"Don't laugh at me, darling."

"I'm not laughing. I just can't imagine anything more wonderful than you and Henrik being together."

"We're not going to be together," Virginia said. "We're simply going to spend a little time together, in the same city."

"Certainly you are," Katharine said, grinning.

"You are laughing," Virginia accused.

"I'm not. I'm just happy."

On November 29, rehearsals for *Hedda Gabler* began. In spite of Sebastian's counseling that she must not, for an instant, underestimate the importance of understudying, Katharine enjoyed being able to relax and observe the action in a more detached way than if she had been a nervous participant. The understudies would have their own rehearsals, and Noël Harvey had instructed Katharine to listen intently to everything that was said, and to every stage direction that was given, keeping her own script meticulously up-to-date.

On the second Monday of rehearsals, Sebastian and Jeremy attended a full-cast rehearsal. It was the first time they had seen Barbara working her way into the role, and it was apparent that, even at this stage, she was in great shape. She looked superb, her russet hair shoulder-length and permed quite wildly about her head, her movements vigorous and her voice strong.

"God, she's good," Jeremy murmured.

Sebastian said nothing.

"What do you think, Seb?" Jeremy whispered.

He gave a small, curt nod, nothing more.

They were working their way, on stage, through the first act, and Lalla Bates as Mrs. Elvsted was letting her nervousness rise and fall as Barbara's Hedda toyed with her, and Noël Harvey was allowing them their heads, hardly interrupting them, enjoying himself. Jeremy, too, was having a good time, satisfied all over again with the casting, until he sensed that all was not well with Sebastian and, glancing at him, he saw that his face had become extremely pale and that his jaw was clenched tightly.

"Seb?" Getting no response, Jeremy touched Sebastian's left arm, and he jumped. "What's wrong, Seb?"

Sebastian shook his head, but still did not speak. His right hand went to his forehead as if it ached, and Jeremy saw that the hand was trembling slightly.

"Headache?"

Sebastian nodded. "Hell of a one."

"Do you want to leave?" Jeremy whispered. Again, Sebastian was silent. "Seb, let's get out of here—come on."

Outside, in Charing Cross Road, Sebastian leaned for a moment against a wall, breathing deeply, and then he straightened up.

"That's better."

"What was it?"

"A headache, I told you." Sebastian began walking toward his car, parked on a meter around the corner.

"Are you okay to drive?" Jeremy asked.

"Sure."

They reached the car, and Sebastian unlocked the driver's door. "I don't think I'll come back to the office."

"Good idea, go straight home." Jeremy watched his friend's face. "You're still very white, Seb. Why not let me drive?"

"What for?"

"All right, but I think I'll come back to Hampstead."

Sebastian looked at him vaguely. "Why?"

"Just a little business—I thought we could chat over a drink, relax for once."

Sebastian shrugged and climbed into the driver's seat. "Come on then."

They were less than a mile from The Oaks when it happened.

They were driving up East Heath Road, too fast. Sebastian often drove too fast, loved fast cars, loved his black Aston even more than he had his E type, but as a rule he drove well and intelligently, gauging road conditions and his own moods, and assessing potential trouble spots accurately. This afternoon he was driving fast, Jeremy thought, for speed's own sake, he was making mistakes, was not the safest of drivers on the road, but they were nearly home, and Jeremy kept silent and left Sebastian to his own thoughts. Until he lost control on one of the bends in the hill and braked badly. The Aston went into a skid, mounted the pavement on the opposite side of the narrow road, and struck a concrete lamppost.

"Shit," Jeremy said.

The lamppost had come off worst, one wing was badly dented, one headlight smashed, but neither of them was hurt, for the car was solid and tough and both men had been wearing seat belts.

"Seb?"

Jeremy waited for Sebastian to speak, to curse—to get out of the car and to take a look at the damage. But Sebastian only sat still in his seat, and when Jeremy looked at him again, he saw that if he had been pale before, now he was ashen, his eyes were closed and he was breathing in, deeply, through his nose, almost as if he were inhaling something. But what really alerted Jeremy to the certainty that something was badly wrong—what really frightened him—was the fact that Sebastian was smiling.

"Sebastian?"

Sebastian opened his eyes, but they seemed unfocused—no, that wasn't it, Jeremy thought. They were focused, but on a distant point somewhere far away, beyond the wounded Aston Martin, beyond the Heath.

"Sebastian," Jeremy said again, more sharply.

Sebastian blinked. He sat, rigidly, in his seat, and the blinking continued, became rapid and then convulsive, and Jeremy realized with horror that his friend was having a fit of some sort, a convulsion, and he had no idea on God's earth what to do.

"Seb, stop it."

Jeremy unbuckled his own seat belt, and then Sebastian's, but the other man still sat stiff and unyielding, his eyelids flickering wildly, and panic seized Jeremy, and he wanted to grab him by the shoulders and shake him back to normality, but he knew enough to be certain that he must not do anything of the sort. His mind searched frantically for information, for the right thing to do, but all his limited, useless knowledge came from films about epileptics, in which they always fell on the floor and writhed, and all you were supposed to do was to stop them biting their tongues or injuring themselves—but Sebastian did not suffer from epilepsy, and he was just sitting, blinking, while the rest of his body was perfectly still—so still that he might have been dead—and Jeremy didn't know what to *do*—

And then it stopped. The eyelashes grew still, the eyes regained their normal focus, and Sebastian turned, slowly, to face Jeremy, and for just a moment he looked vague, and then puzzled. And then he looked at the front of the car, at the wing, and at the crippled lamp-post, and he spoke for the first time since the accident.

"Fuck."

It was so natural, so wonderfully normal a reaction and so blissfully comforting, that Jeremy began to laugh.

"What the hell are you laughing at?" Sebastian stared at him oddly, as if Jeremy were mad to be laughing. "Jerry, for God's sake—"

And then he, too, started to laugh, and once he had begun, he could not stop, and his ribs ached and he could hardly catch his breath, but the laughter felt so good, and he had not had one of those uncontrollable laughing jags since he and Jeremy had been at Marchmont, and it was several minutes before he was able to open the door and have a proper look at the damage.

The laughter stopped when the police arrived, summoned by a call from a passerby. The two officers wanted to know exactly what had happened, and Sebastian told them that he had been driving too fast and had skidded, and that that, regrettably, had been that. They produced a Breathalyzer kit and asked him, politely, to blow into it, but Sebastian had not taken a drink since the previous evening, and that had only been a single Scotch, and the officers took down his details, and he was able to produce his license and insurance cer-tificate, so they made sure that the car was safe to drive, and let them go.

By the time they got through the front door of The Oaks, Sebastian was shivering, and Jeremy realized that it was not an appropriate moment to talk to him about the fit, was afraid that talking about it might even spark another.

"Has something happened?" Ellie came out of the kitchen, wiping her hands on a cloth.

"A small accident," Jeremy said, quickly. "Nothing to worry about."

"You're not hurt?" she asked, anxiously.

"Not a scratch, Ellie," Sebastian said. "Just a bump to the car."

"I'll put the kettle on," she said, promptly.

"No," Sebastian said. "No tea, thanks, Ellie."

"I think you're sickening for something," Jeremy said. "Maybe you're coming down with the flu."

Sebastian shrugged. "Maybe."

"Let's get you upstairs." Jeremy put a hand on his arm.

"I can manage, Jerry." Sebastian moved ahead, toward the staircase.

"Sure you can," Jeremy said, following him nonetheless.

"Will you call if you want anything?" Ellie asked.

"We will, Ellie," Sebastian said. "Don't worry, I'm fine."

He felt cold, chilled through, and though his head ached, he wanted a hot shower, and Jeremy stayed close to him, chatting gently, trying to be normal but afraid to leave him, still anxious about him, for even the laughter, before the arrival of the police, had not been normal or right.

"Don't you have a home to go to, Jerry?"

"I'm in no hurry."

And Sebastian didn't question his staying around after that, was easy with him now, and anyway he was too tired. And Jeremy watched as he took off his clothes, and he had not seen Sebastian naked since school, and his throat tightened as he saw how beautiful he still was, such fine, strong lines, spare and lean and all of it natural, God-given, since he seldom exercised, never ran, just played a little tennis in summer and an occasional game of squash in winter.

"Do you want a drink?" Sebastian asked, lightly.

"No," Jeremy said. "Thanks."

Looking at the other man, Jeremy knew that he needed a stiff drink, urgently, but it still seemed more important to stay in the room and watch over Sebastian, for the memory of the fit, or whatever it had been, was still fresh and frightening in his mind.

"I'll take my shower then—come in, we can talk."

Jeremy followed him into the bathroom. "Where's Kate this afternoon?"

"At one of her classes."

Sebastian turned on the shower, felt the temperature of the water for a moment with one hand, and then stepped under the hard, steaming spray—and then his left foot slipped on the wet tiles, and he lurched for an instant, and Jeremy sprang forward, was right beside him beneath the shower, supporting him, his right arm around his waist.

"I'm okay," Sebastian said.

"No, you're not."

"Just a bit unsteady, a bit groggy." Sebastian smiled, slightly, weakly. "Your clothes are going to be ruined."

"Doesn't matter."

For those few more seconds before the water was turned off, while Jeremy was still holding Sebastian—his own hair and shirt and trousers drenched, even his Rossetti shoes, his arms around the other man, feeling his solidness, his leanness, the softness of his skin—the longing and the hungering, the yearning and thirsting, the years and years of waiting and imagining and staying back, always, of gritting his teeth and keeping himself under control almost burned Jeremy alive, and he was afraid that Sebastian would notice his erection, but he could hardly bear to let him go.

And then Sebastian reached up and turned the tap, and the jet of water, mercifully, stopped.

"All right," Jeremy said, huskily, finding it difficult to speak. He led Sebastian out of the shower.

"I'm okay now," Sebastian said.

"No, you're not." Jeremy put a towel around his waist, knotted it, and put a second one about his shoulders. "Come on." He helped him out of the bathroom and into the bedroom.

"I'm fine, Jerry." Sebastian's voice was firmer, clearer. "And you're dripping all over the carpet."

Jeremy stepped away and looked at him. And he saw that Sebastian was all right again, right enough to dry himself, and to let the towels drop onto the floor, and to pull the bedspread off the four-poster, and to climb, naked, between the sheets.

"Better help yourself to some clothes," Sebastian said.

"Yes," Jeremy said. "Thanks, Seb." He walked back toward the bathroom and turned. "Seb?"

"Mm?"

"If you don't feel right by morning, stay home and get Kate to call the doc, won't you?"

"Mm."

And Sebastian lifted one hand, heavily, in thanks, and his eyes were already closing, but in sleep this time, normal, healthy sleep, and Jeremy went swiftly to take off his wet things, and to change, in the dressing room and then, just as swiftly, to leave. He was grateful to leave. He could not bear to be in the room, in the house, with Sebastian a moment longer.

When Jeremy arrived at Locke Mariner next morning, Sebastian had already been at his desk for an hour and a half.

"How are you?" Jeremy asked, sitting down.

"Fine. You okay?"

"Sure." Jeremy looked at him more closely. Sebastian appeared the picture of health, blue eyes sharp and clear as usual, the color of his skin normal, with no hint of pallor. "Headache gone?"

"I slept it off." Sebastian smiled. "I slept right through the evening—didn't even wake up when Katharine got home."

"So you had a good night?"

"I just told you." Sebastian glanced up, his expression curious. "Something wrong, Jerry?"

"Of course not." Jeremy hesitated. "It was only that the prang with the car seemed to upset you—"

"Not really." Sebastian shrugged. "All that upset me was that I ought to have let you drive."

"You've never trusted my driving," Jeremy said lightly. He stood up and began to walk to the door, then stopped. "You remember what happened afterward?"

"Afterward?"

"After the crash."

"What, in particular?" Sebastian frowned. "Jerry, what are you trying to ask me? About the police?" He paused. "You mean that touch of hysterics?"

"Yes," Jeremy said, carefully.

"You triggered me off." Sebastian shook his head, smiling at the memory. "I haven't laughed so much in years—must have been the shock, I suppose."

"Yes," Jeremy said again. "I suppose."

After three successive nights of insomnia, Jeremy paid a visit to his doctor, Douglas Lerner.

"I'm concerned, Doug," he said, "about a friend."

"What is your concern?"

"I think he had a fit, a few days ago. I saw it happen, but he seems to remember nothing about it."

"Has it happened before?" Dr. Lerner asked.

"I don't know. We haven't discussed it. I wanted to have a chat, first of all, to find out whether I need to be worried, or to worry him. He seems fine now."

"It's not really me you should be chatting to, Jeremy."

"A specialist?"

"A neurologist, I'd say."

"Can you recommend someone?"

"Of course." Lerner hesitated. "Though it'll be largely a waste of time and expense, unless the patient presents himself."

"If I'm still concerned," Jeremy said, "after I've consulted the neurologist, then I'll talk to my friend."

"I'll set up an appointment."

"Could he see me today?"

"She," Dr. Lerner corrected him. "I doubt it, but I'll try."

"Please," Jeremy said. "I don't want to wait."

"You realize that there's very little point to this consultation, don't you?" Joyce Osborne, the neurologist, an elegant, softly-spoken Scottish woman of about fifty, with pepper-and-salt hair, smiled at him.

"I realize it's obviously very limited," Jeremy agreed, "but perhaps if I describe the symptoms that I saw, you could tell me what springs to mind."

"Strictly speaking, it's unethical."

"It would be, of course, if my friend were your patient, but he's not." Jeremy looked at her. "Please."

There was not much to describe: the fit itself, if that was what it had been, the headache that had preceded it, the headaches that Jeremy knew were a fairly regular occurrence in themselves, the wild laughter afterward and then, later, the extreme exhaustion.

"He's a very controlled man, but he was out of control while this was happening. I can't be sure if that was what caused him to crash the car, or if it came about because of the accident."

"Is he a very tense man?"

"Sometimes, lately. He's very successful, there are pressures—I'd say he's been up and down for a year or so."

"But this is the first incident of its kind, so far as you know."

"Quite."

Joyce Osborne sat back in her chair. "I can understand your concern," she said.

"Are you concerned?" Jeremy asked.

"Not especially." The neurologist smiled at him, kindly. "What you have described to me sounds as if it may have been some kind of partial seizure, in itself a sudden bout of uncontrolled electrical activity in the brain."

"Is that serious?"

"Not necessarily. It's unusual, but possible, during a partial seizure, for outward symptoms to be as minimal as a little facial twitching, hardly perceptible at all, or, as you described, abnormal blinking." Osborne paused. "It's possible, also, that the affected person might experience some intense feelings during or before the seizure, fear, perhaps, or a hallucination of some kind. Do you think there was anything like that?"

"It's hard to say," Jeremy said. "The only thing he admitted to was the headache, and feeling tired." He looked at the specialist. "I know that you can't possibly make a diagnosis, but could you at least tell me the sort of things that might cause such a seizure?"

"Any number of things," Osborne replied. "Medical or neurological problems, from head injury to alcoholism, epilepsy to a brain tumor. It's impossible, and unwise, to take this any further, Mr. Mariner. This brief incident, if it was isolated, may have been caused by nothing more sinister than the shock of the car accident."

"Really?"

"Absolutely." She smiled at him again. "I recommend that you try to observe your friend for a week or two. Try not to overreact or to draw too many false conclusions."

"I think I can manage that," Jeremy said.

"If you notice anything you consider important, your next step must be to persuade your friend to see his own G.P. If there is nothing, I strongly recommend that you put the episode out of your mind."

While Jeremy tried, as discreetly as possible, to keep an eye on Sebastian, Katharine, now absorbed in rehearsals for *Hedda Gabler*, felt her marriage beginning to slide away again. All the pride and pleasure that Sebastian had taken in her preparation for and performance in the first Ibsen play seemed to have disappeared. He attended no more rehearsals; he seemed quieter in her company, almost depressed, was often brusque and sometimes uncharacteristically unkind.

"Could you work through a scene with me, sweetheart?" Katharine asked him one evening after dinner.

"I don't have time," Sebastian answered, not looking up from the papers he was working on.

"It would only take a few minutes," she persisted. "It's Hedda's short scene alone with the judge in the last act—I don't think I've got it right yet."

"I told you, I don't have time." His voice was tight, his tone curt.

"How much time does it take to read one little scene?"

"Dear *God!*" Sebastian sprang to his feet, startling Katharine and spilling the papers onto the carpet. "Where do I have to go to get some peace in this house?" His eyes were fierce with anger, his hands clenched into fists.

"I'm sorry." Katharine was shocked, but her voice was cold. "You used to show an interest in my work. Lord knows you pushed me into it hard enough."

"We all make mistakes."

"Sebastian, what is *wrong* with you?"

"Nothing." He shook his head. "I'm sorry. Just leave me alone."

Katharine was hurt and perplexed and, increasingly, angry. If Sebastian had been a confusing partner in the past, now he was a tightly closed book, sealed with a large, red, warning label. For no reason that she could even begin to comprehend, he had abandoned her, and she had no idea what to do about it.

Sebastian hardly understood himself. He knew that he had wanted Hedda for Katharine more than he had ever wanted anything, but he had believed that he had come to terms with that disappointment. The curious factor in his present gloom was that as Katharine became, as was right and proper, absorbed by and into the production, Sebastian felt a resistance in himself akin to anger. When she worked at home, when she asked him to help her with cues, he felt, oddly, like a parent faced with an offspring who seemed, suddenly, instead of innocent and beautiful, inexplicably repulsive.

Ten days after the car accident, on a Thursday evening, while Katharine was out, having dinner with Barbara Stone, Sebastian, at home, came across her script of *Hedda Gabler* on the coffee table in the drawing room.

Picking it up, he opened it. The first, unprinted page was filled with copious notes in Katharine's clear handwriting. Sebastian thumbed through the opening pages of the play, until he came to the first lines marked in red:

Good morning, Miss Tesman. How lovely of you to call, and so very early, too.

Innocuous, trifling words, yet a shivering memory assailed Sebastian briefly, and then was gone. He flipped more pages over, swiftly, moved on into the play, felt a knot growing in his stomach, then in his head, felt his scalp tightening, his pulses quickening—

I'm setting fire to your child, he read. *You, Thea, with your lovely, curling hair—*

Another flash of recall pierced Sebastian, sharper this time, and agonizingly vivid. Violently, he hurled the script away from him into the fireplace. The low, dying flames flattened out for a second or two, then rose greedily upward, licking eager blackness around the edges of the paper, and as the cover melted and the paper began to curl into ashes, he felt a balm of relief soothing his pain.

When it was done, he damped the fire, turned out the lights and went upstairs, intending to go to bed, but he felt quite light-headed, his arms and legs tingling curiously, and he knew that he was too restless to sleep. Turning away from the bedroom door, he walked on down the corridor. To a room he seldom visited.

Its coldness struck him the instant he opened the door, for it had been empty for many years. The curtains had long ago been removed, but the bars were still at the windows. The enchanting, ornately carved teddy bears designed with love, so many years ago, to protect a small boy.

Sebastian closed the door, softly, and walked over to the windows. The moon darted briefly from behind the dark, scudding clouds, casting its beams like pointing, reminding fingers, at the quilted rocking chair near the center of the room, where the boy's small bed had been. He sat down in the chair and began to rock, slowly. Back and forth, back . . . the motion was soporific, hypnotic . . . his eyelids drooped . . .

The sound of the wind, cracking eerily through the branches of the old oak trees just outside the nursery, woke him abruptly. Hard, driving rain rattled on the glass, and as the tree nearest to the windows swayed and groaned, black, darting shadows twisted strange shapes over the walls and onto the floor, creeping close to touch his feet and then flitting away again, like long, pulsating tentacles. Sebastian knew that he was afraid, and did not know why. There was cold sweat on his brow, and his heart beat alarmingly in his chest. He remembered, suddenly, clearly, his earliest taste of fear and loneliness, felt keenly the awful isolation of his life now.

I can't bear it, he thought.

He sprang up from the chair, and the creaking of the abandoned rocker joined with the groaning of the trees and the moaning of the wind. He opened the door, half walked, half ran down the corridor to the staircase and down to the hall, to the front door. He paused there for a moment, as if trying to exert some degree of self-control, before he opened that door, too, and let himself out of the house.

The air was cold, but with a wonderful purity, smelling of rain and grass and clay. Beyond the shadowy drive and the empty road lay the Heath, inky black and menacing, yet offering to him, at that instant, a measure of escape.

Slowly, steadily, he walked across the road and up onto the first high bank of wet grass and nettles. In the distance, on East Heath Road, the headlights of one of the cars driving up the hill swung briefly in his direction, picking him out like a target, and then they were gone, and he ploughed on into the dark. He stared up into the sky as he walked, and as his eyes grew accustomed to the night, the quality of the clouds and the vague, watery outline of the moon took on a beauty and stability that, it seemed to him, the muddy earth beneath his feet could not offer.

He sank onto his knees. The wind whipped his face fiercely, and the rain sank needles into his flesh and his eyes, blinding him. He put up his fingers to his face, as a sightless man might, feeling the skin of a stranger. There was a warm wetness beneath his eyes, and he realized that he was crying. Tears coursed down his cheeks, and for a while he gave himself up to the weeping like a child, covering his face with both hands, tasting his salt on them and moaning with the wind.

Until suddenly he stopped, and sat back on his heels, and thought: *This is insanity. I am insane.*

The thought had formed like a firm, perfect, round bubble in his mind. It seemed to hover with him for a few minutes, quite tranquil, and then it burst into a fresh spindrift of aching. It occurred to Sebastian, fleetingly, that he might lie down in the sodden grass, and maybe he would go to sleep, and maybe he would die. But then he knew that it was an absurd thought, and impractical and, in any case, he did not want to die.

With a sigh, he climbed to his feet, turned slowly around, checked his bearings. The bubble had gone, would not return, he felt certain, and though the pain was still there, the intolerable agony and fear had, for the moment at least, gone with it. It was time to get back to the warmth of The Oaks. He was very cold, his clothes were sticking to his skin, and he smelled mud on himself. He began walking again, back toward the lights in the distance, more briskly as he went on. He walked like someone out for a stroll, as if there had been nothing especially odd about a man dressed in pullover and jeans kneeling down in the middle of a storm-swept heath in the dead of night. As he walked, he breathed deeply, filling his lungs with the chill, wet air, striding more and more strongly, more purposefully, up through the long grass and, finally, back over the last bank onto the still silent road.

Approaching the house, he stopped suddenly. The front door was open, and a pool of bright light spilled out onto the drive. A figure stood, silhouetted in the door frame. Sebastian's breath caught in his throat. The figure was spectrally white, and its ethereal, gossamer quality jabbed him painfully in the heart with terror.

"Sebastian?"

It moved as he heard his name. And relief and awareness of his own preposterousness flooded through him, and he stepped onto the drive and heard the gravel's reassuring crunch beneath his soft-soled shoes.

"Sebastian, where have you *been*?"

Katharine stood at the open door in a cream silk negligee, her arms wrapped about herself in a futile attempt to protect herself from the cold. She was shivering, and her face was pale, and Sebastian saw, with a pang of remorse, how huge her amber eyes were with fright, how rimmed with tears.

"I went for a walk," he said. He put his arm around her, but took it quickly away again as the mud on his sleeve stained the pale silk. "I'm sorry," he said. "I took a tumble."

"Did you hurt yourself?" They stepped inside, and she closed the door. "Sebastian, what were you doing walking outside in this weather?"

"I didn't know you were home."

"I came back a while ago, and I assumed you were out, so I got undressed. But then I saw your briefcase and your keys, and I knew you must be home after all." Her eyes were still wide. "I looked all over, in the house, in the garden, and then suddenly I had this awful feeling—"

"What kind of a feeling?" he asked.

"I was frightened, for you, and I went to the front door and opened it, and then I saw you."

He smiled. "I thought you were a ghost, for a moment."

"I guess it's that kind of a night," she said.

Sebastian, too, had begun to shiver, and seeing that he was wet through, Katharine ordered him, with sudden firmness, upstairs, and he followed her quite submissively, and while he peeled off his clothes, she turned the bathtaps on full and fetched two large bath towels from the linen cupboard, and brought Sebastian in from the bedroom, where he was sitting in a dressing gown, on the edge of the bed.

She had thought, over the last several days, that she might never feel tenderness toward him again, that his recent behavior was un-forgivable, but now, as Sebastian sank down into the steaming water, she took a large bar of soap and began to wash him gently, massaging his shoulders and the back of his neck, kneading away the small, hard knots in his muscles, saying nothing, only touching.

For a time, Sebastian sat in the bath like a silent, withdrawn statue, lost in the steamy, comforting cocoon that Katharine had wrapped him in, and then, with an effort, he stood up and climbed out, and she waited and watched as he dried himself with the big, warm towels, silent and calm now, only once pausing to touch her arm in a mute gesture of gratitude and apology.

"How about a hot drink?" Katharine suggested, at last.

"Okay."

They went downstairs, very quietly, anxious not to disturb Ellie who had, until now, slept undisturbed. In the kitchen, Katharine heated some milk and searched the larder and cabinets for cocoa.

"We'll have to have chocolate," she said.

"I'll add some cognac."

They sat at the table, sipping slowly. Sebastian knew that he could not explain, and Katharine did not ask him to.

"Why are you smiling?" he asked.

"Just thinking we must look like a placid, contented, normal hus-band and wife, sitting with their nightcap in the kitchen."

"Aren't we?"

Calmly, she looked at him. "Is it normal to swing from joy to misery from one day—one minute—to the next? Or from kindness to anger?"

"No."

"Won't you talk to me, Sebastian?"

"About what?"

"Anything. Whatever you want."

Sebastian stirred his chocolate.

"Do you remember," he said, after a few moments, "what part my mother was to have played on the evening after her death?"

Katharine concealed her surprise. "No. I know my parents came to London for a premiere, but I was only five. If I knew it, I've forgotten."

"It was Hedda Gabler."

Katharine experienced a small jolt. She watched his face. He seemed composed, his expression inscrutable. "I didn't know," she said.

"I remember," Sebastian said, his voice steady, "my father telling me that she had died after the dress rehearsal. I remember that my own first visit to the theater was to watch that final rehearsal."

"I suppose you don't remember too much about it," Katharine said, very moved. "You were only seven, weren't you?"

His reply was so soft that she had to strain to hear him.

"I remember," he said.

"Tell me about it," she said, gently. "Do you want to tell me?"

"Perhaps. One day."

For a minute or two, he seemed very remote again, the remoteness that Katharine had come to hate and to fear. And then, to her great relief, he sat up straighter, and she had a sense that he was deliberately shaking off ghosts.

"Let's talk about you," he said, "about your Hedda."

"She isn't really mine, sweetheart, she's Barbara's."

"Of course she is, but you have to look at her as your own, you know that." He paused. "It's important that you don't feel constricted by great performances of the past, angel. A mature, older actress's characterization is bound to be vastly different than a younger, less experienced woman's."

For a few minutes, at least, he seemed interested again, caring, wanting to help her, and it could almost, Katharine thought, have been the old Sebastian speaking. He did not mention his mother again, but she felt that he was reassuring her, in some obscure way, that there was no risk of his comparing her with Diana Lancaster. Katharine knew Diana only from her portrait, and from the one film she had made, the film in which her own mother had also acted, but she guessed that the legendary Diana's performance, had it come to pass, would probably have been incomparable, and she did not mind that at all, felt no envy, only sadness for Sebastian.

"I thought," Katharine said, uncertain if it was a wise thing to say, but needing to say it, "that you hoped, when I auditioned, that they might give me Thea Elvsted."

"I know you thought that," Sebastian said.

"But it was Hedda you wanted for me, wasn't it?"

"It was," he said.

"Why didn't you tell me?"

"I didn't want to put too much pressure on you."

Katharine hesitated before going on. "And was it because of your mother that you wanted me to play Hedda? Because she never actually got to play her?"

His eyes were kinder than they had been for a long time, and yet they were so sad that Katharine wanted to weep.

"Yes," he said, softly. "I suppose it was."

At last, she thought she understood.

On December 21, Virginia returned to London from Copenhagen, and the following day, she and Katharine met for lunch at La Causerie in Claridge's.

Looking at Virginia, Katharine saw a sixty-six-year-old woman, more fine-looking than ever, elegant, composed and reassuring as always, but softened further by an added glow of happiness. Looking at Katharine, Virginia saw a young woman more beautiful than she had ever been, but disturbingly frailer and more nervous than before.

"I don't have to ask if you and Uncle Henrik had a wonderful time," Katharine said, smiling. "It's written all over you."

"You, however," Virginia said, "look much too tired."

"It isn't tiredness."

"What is it then?"

Katharine did not hesitate for long. She was aware that she needed, badly, to talk to someone. She had considered Sam, but it had seemed almost unprofessional to confide in him while they were working on the same show, and she knew from what David had told her that Sam had already formed negative ideas about her marriage. There was no one more trustworthy or wise or nonjudgmental in her life than Virginia.

She began at the end.

"Did you know that Hedda Gabler was to have been Diana's last role?" She paused. "That she died the night before opening?"

Virginia shook her head. "No, I didn't know that. Andrew told me once that she died shortly after coming off stage, but we didn't talk about Diana often. Even when we were just friends, long before we thought of marrying. He talked about the good times, sometimes, but not about the sadness."

"I only found out about it a few days ago."

"Is it especially significant, darling?"

"I think so," Katharine said. "It was a dress rehearsal, and it was the only time Sebastian ever saw her on stage, just hours before her death." She looked at Virginia. "I've thought about it a good deal since he told me—God knows I've little enough spare time, between Ibsen and all my classes, and trying to give Ellie an occasional hand in the house, but in the moments I do have to myself, I can't seem to think about anything except how strangely Sebastian's behaving."

"Strangely?" Virginia queried.

Katharine flushed. "I've been seeking explanations for so many things for such a long time now. Things I didn't feel I could share with anyone, not even you."

"And now?"

"Now I feel I have to share it. We need help, Virginia."

Having heard the ups and downs of the past year and more, Virginia was dismayed and shocked. She had realized that the marriage was a turbulent one, and on more than one occasion she had even feared that it might not endure, yet she had always felt certain that, fundamentally, Sebastian and Katharine were as much in love as they had been when they had first met in New York.

"I understand now why I've sometimes felt as if you were trying to avoid me."

Katharine was distressed. "I've never wanted to avoid you, Virginia."

Seeing how fragile the young woman's nerves were, Virginia hastened to reassure her. "I don't mean that I felt left out in any way, darling. I only meant to say that, knowing you both as I do, I'm sure you've wanted to keep your troubles from me." She paused. "But isn't it always better to talk to someone?"

"I feel relieved already," Katharine said. "But I feel disloyal at the same time."

"Talking about Sebastian behind his back?" Virginia smiled, gently. "If it were anyone else you'd spoken to, I might agree with you. But you must know that you can trust me absolutely, darling."

"Of course I know that." Katharine shook her head. "When he told me about his mother and *Hedda Gabler*, I thought, for just a little while, that now I could understand him. I hadn't realized, before then, that he'd wanted so desperately for me to get the part—if I'd known, I might have been able to make him see that it was impossible."

"It's rather touching, really, isn't it?" Virginia said. "The two women he's loved most in his life, both actresses."

"He made me an actress," Katharine pointed out. "Or at least, he pushed me into remembering that it was what I wanted."

"Do you regret that now?"

"Not at all. Sebastian was right, and I'm grateful. And I so hoped that after he told me about Diana, it might be a turning point for us, that we might pull together again once he'd shared it with me."

"But you think you were wrong?" Virginia asked.

"Half the time, he's more distant than ever. Not to be unkind," Katharine said quickly. "It's a strange remoteness, as if he isn't aware that I'm there at all—almost as if he isn't quite there either. Then sometimes, he seems to understand that he's hurting me, and he makes an effort—but then I'll say the wrong thing, quite unwittingly, and he'll fly into one of these odd rages."

Virginia was quiet for a moment, thinking.

"Do you think he may be unwell?"

Katharine shrugged. "I don't think so. He has too many headaches, but I'm sure that's because he drives himself so hard and because he hardly ever seems to be relaxed these days."

"Do you think it would help if I spoke to him?"

"No, I don't think it would."

"What do you think might help? Do you think Sebastian needs to see someone professionally? A psychiatrist, perhaps?"

Katharine waited several moments before answering.

"I think we should move out of the house."

"Leave The Oaks, you mean?" Virginia was startled.

Katharine nodded. "I don't think we should ever have moved into his parents' house. Sebastian's quite different when we're away— lighter, somehow, less burdened. I think many of our problems are connected with The Oaks."

"And with this play?"

"Perhaps. I'm not sure." Katharine paused again. "But at least the play will be over and done with by the beginning of February, whereas the house—" She stopped. "It's all so sad. I love The Oaks—I've put a lot into it."

"You may be wrong, darling," Virginia said.

Katharine smiled, wanly. "You mean it may be just wishful thinking. It may be our marriage that's all wrong, not the house, not the play."

"I don't mean that at all," Virginia said. "It's also possible that you're under more stress than you realize, that things aren't quite as bad as you fear they are."

"I hope you're right, Virginia."

"But you think I'm not."

Katharine's face was somber. "No."

* * *

Later, when she was alone, Virginia's mind could not rest. All that Katharine had told her had troubled her greatly. Their sexual problems, Sebastian's uncharacteristic rages, his depression and, perhaps most worrying of all, his detachment from Katharine. He sounded almost callous and cold, and Virginia knew, without a shadow of doubt, that Sebastian was a genuinely warm and kind man. She would stake her life on that. That he was capable of ruthlessness, to a degree, must also be true, since it was doubtful if he would have succeeded in his mannerly, but nonetheless razor-sharp business otherwise. But Sebastian's integrity, and his care for the individual, had remained the outstanding feature of Locke Mariner's style, and Virginia knew that his staff adored him, his clients respected him and that Jeremy, not the easiest of men, still seemed to get along with Sebastian as well as he had ever done.

At home, in Montpelier Square, Virginia looked at the silver-framed photograph of Andrew that she kept on her mantelpiece. She remembered how intensely proud he had been of his son, the way he had glowed with modest, yet unshakable pleasure whenever he had spoken of Sebastian's achievements from boyhood into maturity. These revelations of Katharine's would have done more than disappoint or disillusion Andrew. They would have caused him unimaginable distress.

Trying to relax with a glass of sherry, Virginia suddenly sat bolt upright. There were certain memories of Andrew that she had never shared with anyone, memories that belonged to her alone, and to which she normally refused thinking space because they were too painful. She had taught herself soon after his death to block them off, for they were also utterly pointless.

"He must have known."

Her thought, spoken out loud, sounded harsh in the evening hush. It was a terrible thought, yet suddenly there was no doubt in her mind. Nothing else would have affected Andrew so deeply as a major concern over Sebastian.

Virginia looked up at the photograph again. She remembered, all too vividly, the inexplicable changes that had come over Andrew in the days before their wedding, and then again in the hours before his death, and her heart ached for him all over again.

And then she remembered the books.

Her chance to be alone in The Oaks came early the next afternoon. Sebastian was at the office, Katharine at rehearsals, and Ellie was doing her carefully planned and, inevitably, lengthy Christmas shopping.

Virginia was so nervous when she paid her taxi driver that she dropped her purse onto the gravel drive, and then fumbled with the key in the lock of the front door. She had not once used it since Sebastian had insisted she keep a set of house keys after she moved out.

"You're as entitled to the run of The Oaks as we are," he had told her. "More so, if anything."

She remembered that his blue eyes had been bright with emotion as he had spoken, and that her own heart had spilled over with gratitude for his consideration. But she had never intended to use them, had taken the bunch of keys silently, and had then placed them in a drawer in her flat, and forgotten them, until today.

It was cool in the hall, and already quite dark. It smelled of furniture polish and log fires. Virginia closed the heavy front door behind her and, for a moment, leaned against it for support. Then she walked smartly down the corridor to Andrew's old study, let herself in and switched on the overhead light.

The room had not altered. She and Sebastian had both found this one of the most affecting rooms in the house, the one room that had been Andrew's entirely, and though she knew that Sebastian sometimes came in here and sat down to do a little quiet thinking, he had turned another room into his own study.

Virginia looked again at the bunch of keys in her hand and selected the one for the filing cabinet nearest the window. It opened easily.

The books were there, just as she had left them. She switched on the angled desk lamp and directed its bright beam onto the leather bindings. She felt suddenly weak and irresolute. Couldn't she leave right away, forget that she had ever seen the books? Why did she have to involve herself in this way?

But I am involved, she thought, unhappily, and steeled herself.

Two at a time, she removed the books from the shelf and placed them on the desk, blowing a little dust off their covers.

Somewhere in the house, a floorboard creaked. Virginia held her breath and tiptoed to the door. Had Ellie come in? Had she perhaps not gone out, after all? Tentatively, she opened the door.

"Ellie?" She waited a moment. "Ellie!" There was no reply, and, a little impatient with herself, she returned to the desk and drew the curtains before sitting down resolutely.

She looked down at the title of the first book.

Schizophrenia.

The print swam before her eyes, and she reached into her handbag to take out her reading glasses. And began.

For more than an hour, she followed Andrew's strange trail of bookmarks, folded over page corners and underlinings, her bewilderment growing with every discovery. Under one heading, she read an underlined passage:

Hallucinations of smell or taste may be pleasant or otherwise . . . When the patient's mood is "good," pleasurable tastes or smells may be hallucinated.

Virginia's head ached, and the brightness of the lamp irritated her eyes, but she continued doggedly from book to book.

"It makes no sense," she said aloud.

She read about personality pattern disturbances, about individuals, ordinarily outgoing, friendly and warm, who were subject to fluctuations of mood in which cheerfulness was often replaced by sadness brought about by internal factors rather than by external events.

That could apply to anyone with the blues, she thought, stoutly, and went on reading.

She read marked passages about psychotic persons showing signs of amnesia, inability to understand what others were saying, failures of attention, disorganization of thinking—and she could not begin to imagine why Andrew had ever bought such awful, unhappy books. Certainly none of these things could possibly have anything to do with Sebastian—it was frightful of her to have thought that they might.

She began to feel quite ill. Sick, old and guilty. She did not understand. Not a word of it. Her shoulders ached from bending over the books, yet still she ploughed on.

And then, in the last book but one, hidden between two pages, she found a tightly folded piece of writing paper. Unfolding it, she saw that it was an old letter to Andrew from Sebastian, written in the summer of 1963, when Sebastian must have been sixteen. A letter of term-time news from a schoolboy.

Virginia's tired eyes wandered down the page, read what Andrew had read, about an ugly practical joke, about acid, about lipstick and about a school play. Something within her jarred, tautened. Her fingers, moving automatically, pushed her glasses higher over the bridge of her nose, and she turned over the page and came to the end of the letter. And knew, with awful certainty, what conclusion Andrew must have drawn.

But it did not explain what had happened to make him buy these books. And if they were related to Sebastian, as now seemed more likely from the letter tucked away inside one of them, how were they related? Had Andrew perhaps been guilty of a fearful overreaction, of a kind of hysteria?

Even with what Katharine had told her, nothing about Sebastian pointed to anything more serious than some sort of depression or emotional disturbance. Perhaps Katharine was right about the house and, of course, about the play. Unless Sebastian had himself confided in his father things that no one else could guess at?

But hallucinations? Schizophrenia? Psychosis?

Virginia shuddered, and locked the books away again.

This was beyond her.

c h a p t e r
26

On Friday evening, Christmas Eve, the company of *A Doll's House* gave their final performance. The set would be taken down, in accordance with union rules, before midnight, and the set for *Hedda Gabler* would take its place the following Monday.

Katharine attended an understudies' rehearsal in the morning and went to a dance class in the afternoon. She dreaded going home. The spirit of The Oaks seemed, to her, to be at its lowest ebb since she and Sebastian had moved in less than two years ago, plunged deep into strange disquiet as if by an invisible, depressing hand.

Sebastian had hardly spoken to her for the last two days.

"Why are you so angry with me?" she had asked him, the previous morning.

"Angry?" He had seemed surprised. "I'm not angry."

"Then what's the matter with you?"

"Nothing."

"Something is very much the matter," Katharine had said. "And if you won't share it with me, then I don't know how to help you."

"There's nothing to share, angel." He had been calm.

"If you won't share," she had said, softly, "then there is nothing."

* * *

When she was with him, she felt immersed in her misery. When they were apart, she felt like an observer, watching from the outside the slow death of her marriage, an incurably sick creature, atrophying before her eyes. Love still penetrating, dimly, through the gloom, but its once powerful glow already dwindled away almost to nothing. Katharine doubted if she still had the fight in her to rekindle it.

It was hard to believe that just a year ago they had been in Gstaad, full of optimism. She kept that memory, alongside other cherished moments—Sardi's, the Hawk House Inn, Venice—enclosed for safe-keeping, like those miniature scenes inside the little glass globes Louise and Jake had bought for her as a child. There had been one she'd turned upside down to make the snow fall. The memory of last Christmas seemed that way to her now, trapped and lost forever. She and Sebastian were standing in separate glass globes this year. Even if they did break through and touch, once in a while, there was no real contact.

She had decorated the big tree in the drawing room anyway, with Ellie's help, and the elderly Welsh housekeeper, perfectly aware of the misery in the house, had done her best to maintain as much seasonal atmosphere as possible. Ellie's loyalty to Andrew and Diana Locke's son was unshakable. She had known Sebastian from birth, remembered him as a flaxen-haired, laughing, kind-hearted boy, but she, too, had seen the changes in him, could no longer fathom him.

Katharine came home at four o'clock, Sebastian at half-past five, and at six, they assembled in the drawing room, with Ellie, for the switching on of the fairy lights on the tree, and for a glass of sherry. And two hours later, Ellie served them dinner, formally, in the dining room, starting with Beluga caviar, Sebastian's favorite, on a silver-and-glass bed of crushed ice.

Sebastian was unreachable, veiled, for the most part, in mysterious, faroff thoughts. At least, Katharine thought, dully, there seemed to be no ugly moments in sight, no acts of actual harshness. On Christmas Eve, of all nights, she did not know if she could have borne that.

For a while, they ate and sipped wine, and Katharine made forced conversation, and Sebastian, polite but vague, smiled a distant smile. She tried, once, to close the gaping rift between them by reaching out, tentatively, to touch his hand. It was cold. He looked up, surprised, and his eyes were dull, and Katharine thought, suddenly, that she might burst with sorrow.

"Where's it gone?" she asked.

"Gone?"

"Our happiness," she said.

Sebastian shook his head, slowly, and in the candlelight, Katharine saw that his eyes were dark with pain.

"I don't know," he said, very quietly. "I wish I did."

Katharine let a moment pass.

"We need help," she said. "You must know that much."

"What kind of help?"

"I'm not sure." She paused. "A doctor, perhaps."

"Are you ill?"

"No." She tried to maintain the steadiness in her voice. "But I think you may be."

There was that smile again, distant, remote.

"I'm not ill, Katharine."

"You have too many headaches."

"I'm not ill," he said again.

"What then?"

He waited before answering. "I'm sad."

"But what's made you so sad? Is it me?"

"Not you."

"Then what?"

He shook his head. "I don't know."

Katharine spent a little while in the kitchen after dinner, helping Ellie and hurrying her along, since she was to go to her daughter's home in Aylesbury that night, in order to spend Christmas Day with her and her grandchildren.

"Will you be all right, my dear?" Ellie asked.

"I'll be fine," Katharine said, brightly.

"I'm not sure I ought to go," Ellie said.

"Of course you must go—your daughter's expecting you."

Ellie had been with the family for more than thirty years, and in all that time, she had never been anything but the soul of discretion. There were quarrels in every home, there were tensions and times of sadness, and Ellie knew that so long as there was love in the home, the bad times could be overcome.

"I've never known this house so dark," she said now.

"I know," Katharine said. "I'm sorry. It must be hard for you."

"Never mind me, my dear. It's you and Sebastian I worry about." Ellie paused. "You should take him to a doctor."

"He says he isn't ill."

"There's more than one kind of illness, don't you think?"

"Yes, Ellie," Katharine said. "I do."

After she had put Ellie into her taxi with her small suitcase and two carrier bags stuffed with gift-wrapped parcels, Katharine made a pot of coffee and took it into the drawing room. Sebastian was standing by the French windows, gazing out into the night, his breath making delicate webs of frosting on the glass.

Katharine set down the coffee tray.

"How about a cognac?"

Sebastian turned to face her, and she saw that his forehead was creased with pain.

"Another headache?" she asked.

He nodded. "If you don't mind, darling, I think I'll go to bed."

Katharine went to him and placed her right hand on his forehead. His hand had felt so cold before, and now his skin was hot.

"I think you may have a fever."

"No," he said, and moved away. "I told you, I'm not ill."

He was not especially abrupt, but it was a rejection nevertheless, another small wound.

"Go on, then," Katharine said. "I'll be up later."

A little after midnight, having checked over her plans for the morning, when she would be preparing Christmas dinner for themselves and for Virginia, Sam and Jeremy—the prospect of having even Jeremy was some comfort to Katharine now, *anyone* who might bring Sebastian out of this awful gloom—she was too restless to go to bed.

Quietly, she went into their bedroom to fetch her script. It was a fresh copy, for her original script with all her notes in it had gone astray, a loss which had caused her considerable grief and embarrassment, though she had, by now, absorbed and committed to memory all directions and alterations.

Sebastian was asleep. His breathing was even, and the peaceful expression on his face was in marked contrast with his right arm, which was flung across the bed, the fist oddly clenched, even in sleep.

Katharine took off her clothes, slipped on a silk robe, and left the room again, shutting the door silently behind her. She thought about going back down to the drawing room to work, but the room she so loved seemed to depress her these days, and she would be spending more than enough time in the kitchen later on in the day.

On an impulse, she turned and walked down the corridor and

opened the door to Sebastian's old nursery. The room was empty but for a dresser at one end, and a quilted rocking chair in the center, and there was a musty smell in the air, but the delicate animals at the windows stood out clearly in the moonlight as a memorial to the love that had once filled the room.

I'd want to keep those bars, she thought, idly, *if ever—*

For a moment, a great tremor of longing shook her, and tears pricked at her eyes. There would be no children, for there was no lovemaking anymore. Had not been for almost a month, since rehearsals for *Hedda Gabler* had begun, and with them the awful downward spiral. No lovemaking, and hardly any love.

She closed the door, and sat down in the chair.

I wonder if it was like this for my mother and father, she thought. They had been so happy, and then it had all come apart. *You think you are so intimate, and then something strange and dark worms its way between you, and suddenly you can't even seem to ask what it is. You don't dare to ask because you're not sure if you want to know. And before you know it, the sliver of dark's grown and spread, and it's turned into a chasm—*

Katharine shuddered, and looked down at the script in her lap.

In the bedroom, Sebastian was dreaming. It was an abstract dream, dotted with insubstantial images, fluctuating between tranquility and disquiet. The only constant was the scent. It was the core of the dream, the soul of it, starting as the old, familiar fragrance with its promises of serenity and comfort, but then intensifying and surging until it distorted his dream into a nightmare. The perfume, *her* perfume, cloying now, nauseating, choking, filling the dream, the room, his head, magnifying the pain there, even in sleep, to explosion point—

He tore himself out of its grasp and woke, in the four-poster, cold sweat clammy on his body.

Dazed, Sebastian got out of bed, walked, naked, to the door and opened it. He heard the soft voice, the words luring him along the dark corridor.

Katharine, still sitting in the rocker, did not hear him coming. She was wandering now, idly, through the fourth act, consolidating her lines, hearing her cues in her mind, not looking at the script, liking it close but no longer needing it. She took her role as understudy seriously, but found herself feeling glad, on the whole, not to be playing Hedda. She found the character not incomprehensible, but too unsympathetic to love, and it seemed necessary, to Katharine, to find some part of Hedda with which to empathize. She could understand what it was that Hedda sought, what she longed for, but she could not wholly be her, whereas Barbara, almost from the first day of rehearsals, had begun to establish an entity. By New Year's Eve, the night of the first preview performance, Barbara Stone would *be* Hedda Gabler.

Katharine returned to the fourth act, to the scene between Hedda and Judge Brack. The door opened and a shadow fell across the script in her lap. She looked up, her mouth curving in a small, spontaneous smile.

He stood motionless in the doorway. Naked and handsome, like an alabaster statue. Something in his face brought Katharine to her feet, the script falling to the floor, a thump of alarm jarring her.

"Sebastian?"

For a second, she thought he was still asleep. He stared right through her, and his eyes were filled with blind anger. Rage. Instinct warned Katharine not to move.

If I go to him now, she thought, with perfect clarity, *he will hit me*.

For several, interminable, frozen moments, she remained exactly where she was, the rocking chair knocking rhythmically against the backs of her legs. And then, very slowly and calmly, she began to move toward Sebastian and, as if trying to soothe a potentially savage animal, she reached up and touched his cheek.

"Sweetheart?" she murmured.

Sebastian came to life with sudden, ferocious passion. Taking her completely by surprise, he pulled her to him and tore the robe from her shoulders. His skin felt burningly hot, and his penis was rock hard with desire.

"Sebastian, please, not like this."

For another moment, he stared down at her, his pupils dilated, staring, yet still, she felt certain, not seeing—and then his hands raked down her back, and he swung her around so that she was against the wall.

"For God's *sake!*" Katharine's momentary paralysis vanished, and she began to struggle. This was a stranger, she was fighting off a violent stranger, not Sebastian at all! She tried to push back against him, but he was too strong for her. He held her back with one arm, brought his other hand down between her legs, and then his penis was thrusting against her, trying to penetrate her thighs—

"Sebastian!" she screamed at him, his name a half sob, her voice half strangled. "Please *stop* this!"

He released her.

"Oh, my God."

His arms dropped limply to his sides, and he slumped back against the wall, and there was a new expression on his face, of stupefied horror. Tears of shock ran down Katharine's cheeks, and she trembled violently, groping for her robe, pulling it haphazardly around herself to cover her nakedness.

"Oh, God," Sebastian moaned. "Oh, dear God—" His eyes were squeezed tightly shut as he moaned, and when they opened again, they were full of such a terrible self-loathing that, despite everything, Katharine's lingering fear dissolved back, as it always did, into helpless love.

"It's all right," she said, soothingly. Like a mother murmuring to her injured child, she took him by the hand. "Come on." She led him out of the old nursery and along the corridor back to their bedroom.

"Oh, Christ, I'm sorry," he said.

"You didn't know what you were doing." Katharine drew back the covers and pushed him gently into the bed and climbed in beside him. "Go to sleep, Sebastian."

He lay, for a few minutes, on his back, staring up at the ceiling, and then he turned over and hid his face from her. Katharine moved closer still, put her left arm around him.

"I'll stay with you," she murmured.

At last, he slept.

There was no real rest for her that night. It was impossible, of course, for her to shake off the nightmare she had just experienced, and when, finally, she did drift off, her sleep was haunted by bewildering, fragmented dreams.

Once, during the darkest hours, she woke—or perhaps she was dreaming—and she thought that Sebastian was standing beside the bed looking down at her, compassion in his face. Katharine did not move, feigning sleep, and after a few moments he turned away, and she felt the mattress shifting under his weight.

And the fitful, fretful sleep continued.

She woke just after nine to a lonely bed, a silent house and an overwhelming, crushing depression. There was no sign of Sebastian, but on his pillow lay a parcel, wrapped in distinctive purple Asprey paper, bound with green ribbon, and beside it a note.

Sam called, crying off. He has a bad cold, and sends much love. I'm going to collect Virginia. We'll be back before Jeremy arrives. Merry Christmas, angel.

Wearily, Katharine got out of bed and drew back the curtains, throwing a hand over her eyes for a moment against the dazzle of the morning. The world outside looked unscarred and beautiful. The lawn sparkled after a light frost, and the sun shone out of a vivid blue sky. Beyond the garden, Hampstead Heath rolled gently away, down toward the city, and Katharine saw tiny people and dogs ambling toward the horizon, and closer to the Vale of Health, a boxer dog dropped a stick at his master's boots and barked joyfully.

She turned back and picked up the Asprey parcel and sat down at her dressing table, glancing at her reflection in the mirror, fingering the shadows under her eyes. *Not as bad as it might be*, she told herself, and smiled ruefully.

She unwrapped the parcel with minimal curiosity. The gift was magnificent, kindly thought-out and generous. A miniature chess set, carved in silver and lapis lazuli. Katharine sighed, and tears sprang to her eyes. She had told Sebastian at the beginning of the month that she and Lalla Bates sometimes played chess backstage with an old, cracked and worn set, and it was kind of him to have done this, yet he had ruined it by leaving it for her to find. Surely he must have known that she would sooner have had him with her, sooner have had honesty and, perhaps, an explanation, than any number of valuable gifts.

But he knows we're past explanations. Way past.

In the kitchen, she found more surprises. Evidence that Sebastian had been working was all around. On the table stood a large bowl of freshly skinned peaches, marinating in a blend that he liked, of cognac, brown sugar, Grand Marnier and fresh peach juice, and in the refrigerator she found a bowl of chocolate mousse. He must have been up terribly early, Katharine thought, bemused.

There was more in the dining room. The table had been cleared and freshly laid, everything impeccably in place, with the Georgian silver, fine crystal and the old Flanders lace cloth that she never dared use in case it came to harm. On the sideboard, two bottles of Château

Margaux 1961 had been opened, an extravagant gesture that, for an instant, gladdened her heart, until the absurdity of their situation suffocated the fleeting pleasure and she hurried back to the kitchen to bury herself in welcome work.

She was peeling potatoes about twenty minutes later, when the thought that she had been trying to suppress ever since she had woken finally broke through the barriers of sham.

Leave him.

Katharine sat down on the chair closest to her, her hands nervous in her lap, fingers clasping and unclasping. The thought was a voice, loud in her head. She could escape from this. Sebastian was no longer the man she had fallen in love with. He was not in control of himself anymore, yet he controlled her, and she had allowed him to. Until now.

She had to leave him.

She leapt up from the chair and bolted from the kitchen, up the staircase into the bedroom, slamming the door, seeking refuge from her own thoughts. She flung herself onto the bed, her face pressed against the pillows, and she sobbed into the soft, white cotton, great racking sobs of despair, until at last she was exhausted, and she got up and went into the bathroom to splash her face with water.

She brought a moist, cool towel back into the bedroom and sat in one of the armchairs by the window, the towel pressed to her forehead. Her eyes sought out the romantic little Chagall that hung over the bed, her gift to Sebastian a year before. She remembered his pleasure, the way his eyes had shone with love. A last few tears squeezed between her eyelids, great, salty tears that dripped off her cheeks onto the chair.

I can't leave him.

The image of his vulnerability came back to her, like a snapshot clear in her mind; the way he had slumped against the wall the night before, despairing, defeated, horrified at himself.

Katharine sighed, a lonely, desolate sound that seemed to echo in the room. And then she noticed her script lying on the windowsill. She picked it up, surprised, remembering that she had dropped it in the nursery the night before, and had left it there in the confusion. Sebastian must have brought it into the bedroom this morning.

She glanced at it. There had been a small tear in the cover that had been there when she had been given it to replace her original, lost script, but now she saw that it had been repaired, neatly, with sticky tape. Another gesture, apparently, along with the work in the kitchen and in the dining room.

If only it were that simple.

It was two o'clock when they sat down to eat. Sebastian at the head of the table, Katharine on his left, Virginia on his right and Jeremy at the opposite end.

"What a beautiful table," Virginia said, as she unfolded her napkin.

"Sebastian's work," Katharine said.

"Least I could do." Sebastian lifted the first bottle of wine, ready to pour.

"I'm famished," Jeremy said.

Through turtle soup, roast turkey, plum pudding and Sebastian's desserts, they chattered and joked and were festive, until day dwindled to dusk and then to the sooty darkness of a late winter afternoon. After the meal, they exchanged their gifts and made telephone calls. Katharine and Virginia telephoned Henrik; Sebastian called Elspeth, who had the flu; and Laszlo telephoned from Switzerland.

"How are you, *kedves*?" he asked Katharine.

"Great," she said. "I miss you."

"I miss you, too."

"How's Betty?"

"She's wonderful," Laszlo said. "I saw David a few weeks ago. He asked after you."

"How is he?" Katharine's voice was steady.

"In good health." Laszlo paused. "And you? Are you happy, *kedves*?"

"As a clam," she said.

The evening progressed. Katharine knew that she had never given a finer performance. Her nerves mercifully blunted a little by fatigue, good food and wine, she sat by the log fire, demure in fine apricot wool with white collar and cuffs, her hair pinned up in a French pleat. A woman hacked into raw pieces, she thought, wryly, and glued back together for a special occasion.

Virginia, too, was wretched. Time and again, she feared that she might betray Katharine's confidences, that her own self-control might snap. This was the fifth Christmas since she had lost Andrew. Until last year, they had all been sad holidays for her, and then in Gstaad had come unanticipated happiness, and now—now there was this continuing anxiety, this unpredicted and vexing agitation. It churned her stomach, it ruined her appetite for food and for laughter. She had tried to put it away, to shelve it as she had shelved the books, but it was no use, and now she found that she was watching, listening, straining to catch some clue, a hint of something in Sebastian.

He looks less tense today, she thought. *And fitter than Katharine —she's losing weight, poor darling, and just now, when she needs all her strength.*

Virginia brought herself up short. She had to stop this blatant scrutiny, or Sebastian would notice. How long could she continue this almost obsessive search for warning signs, this mental flicking back and forth between those markings in Andrew's dreadful books and Sebastian's expressions? Observing nothing, and feeling all the more treacherous, all the more ridiculous and old, and fearful in case he should notice.

Jeremy, too, was watching.

Nineteen days had passed since their car accident, since he had witnessed the strange buildup of tension in Sebastian that had culminated in that odd, brief fit. He had seen his partner almost daily since then, had referred occasionally, lightly, to his health, and had tried hard to take Joyce Osborne's advice.

"If you notice anything important," he remembered the neurologist telling him, "then persuade your friend to see his own G.P. If there is nothing, put the episode out of your mind."

Easier said than done, Jeremy thought now, sitting in Sebastian's own drawing room after Christmas dinner, trying to behave normally. There had been nothing important, nothing tangible, at least. The odd aspirin too many, the increase in general tension, all of which could be put down, if one wished, to pressure before the holidays. Yet still Jeremy felt that there was something badly wrong.

"How's your Hedda going, Kate?" he asked her, as Sebastian poured Armagnac.

"Pretty well, thanks. I hope."

"What do you think of Barbara?"

"She's quite brilliant," Katharine said.

"And healthy as a horse," Jeremy added.

"Knock on wood." Katharine touched the coffee table.

"I'm never sure how understudies feel," Jeremy said. "One imagines some of them sticking pins in dolls, praying for the odd broken leg, or at least a touch of laryngitis."

"Not this understudy," Katharine said, brightly. "This understudy's praying that Barbara stays fit and strong."

"Though I'm sure you'd be wonderful," Virginia said, warmly, "if you were called upon. Wouldn't she be wonderful, Sebastian?"

"Certainly she would," Sebastian replied.

"Sebastian wanted Kate to have the part," Jeremy said. "He was furious when March and Harvey gave it to Barbara, weren't you, Seb?"

"Rubbish," Sebastian said, and shrugged, easily. "There's plenty of time for Katharine. The casting's been fine and strong."

"More coffee, Jeremy?" Katharine asked.

"Please."

She's unhappier than I've ever seen her, Jeremy thought. *And Virginia's not her usual self, either.* They were all acting their socks off, he realized, no one more convincingly than Sebastian himself. He was the perfect host, merry and warm and, to all intents and purposes, more relaxed than Jeremy had seen him in weeks. Jeremy could not even say, truthfully, that this outward tranquility was a masquerade. He could only sense, in his heart and soul, that it was not real.

Sebastian felt better than he had in weeks. He held up his glass of Armagnac and gazed through the amber liquid into the flames, the color so like his wife's eyes, smiling slightly into the glow. He knew that he was participating easily in the general conversation, but the words themselves no longer seemed to have much meaning. He was glad to have found the ability to converse with Katharine again, to join in, but he knew now that all that was hollow. Insignificant.

"Henrik said that perhaps next year we might all be together again," Virginia said.

"I'd love that," Katharine smiled.

Sebastian nodded, and he looked through them all back to a moment lodged, lightly now, in his memory, when this had frightened him, this curious, almost absolute, detachment. A year ago, in a bedroom in Gstaad, a room in which candles had glowed and red roses had beckoned them to their bed, he had stared into a mirror at the reflection of their marriage. For an instant, then, he had perceived himself as ghostlike and removed from Katharine, but her love had drawn him back.

She can't do that now.

Now it seemed that he had pitched away from her side again, was separated from her more completely than at that time. But there was no pain, and no fear, for he knew now that it was all a part of the pattern, of their fate.

He felt a strange ambiguousness about this new sensation. He was free from torment, yet he thought that it still lingered nearby, waiting to jostle him, to unsettle him again. He was free now, and yet he was still a prisoner, merely diverted for a while in a mellow, pleasant corridor.

And it was pleasant here, now. With his beloved Katharine, and his dear Virginia and Jeremy. In his parents' house. In Diana's fragrant, irresistible embrace.

On Monday, the set for *Hedda Gabler* was put up in the Albery Theatre. On Wednesday, at half past noon, the cast assembled, in full costume, and the slow technical rehearsal began.

"It takes an age," Katharine told Virginia, on the telephone. "They have to pull all the elements together."

"When will they have the dress rehearsal?" Virginia asked.

"They'll have three," Katharine explained. "The first one's this evening—they like to hold the first one at performance time if possible."

"And you have to be there all the time?"

"Oh, sure—I need to be."

It was a tremendous relief to be in the theater, to be away from the house. She had no sense of nervousness here, no anxiety—she thought that even if it had been her own first night for which she had been preparing, she might have felt almost calm. There was no question of complacency; it was simply that, in comparison with her personal life, even the specter of drying up on stage had lost its horror.

Sebastian, too, was working. In his office, in Albemarle Street, he sat behind his desk, receiving and making telephone calls, meeting with Jeremy and the accountant, dictating to his secretary, going over schedules with Elspeth, finding time to praise a new employee for a job well done.

He was the essence of success. A portrait of rationality. But within the framework, beneath the pleasant quilting of tranquility that had accompanied his unraveling from reality, the old scar tissue was beginning to pulse with new life, and the tiny, but indestructible enemy in his deep subconscious was starting to surge up again. Toward domination.

Katharine's period had been due on Monday, the day after Boxing Day, the day the crew had put up the set. They came like clockwork for her, always had, no matter what. Even after Jake and Louise had been killed, even after her mugging, even during the last stressful weeks before the opening of *Paris* and all through the ups and downs of her marriage. On the dot. Always.

Until now.

She had not given it a thought until late on Monday night, while she had been removing her makeup, getting ready for bed, and though she knew that she ought to have begun that morning, she had shrugged at herself in the mirror, and brushed her hair, certain that she would start to bleed during the night. But two nights later, after the first dress rehearsal, she still had not begun, and though, without doubt, there were more than enough reasons for her body to be reflecting the emotional strains she had lately been under, Katharine knew, already, that they had nothing to do with it.

Sebastian left the house early the next morning, and Katharine slept until nine o'clock. Ellie brought her breakfast on a tray, and Katharine felt hungry, ate everything, and then ran to the bathroom and threw up. And as she sat on the bathroom floor, still limp and perspiring, she felt numbed but dreadfully lonely—and suddenly there was only one person she wanted, desperately, to speak to. Not to tell him, just to talk to him, to hear his voice.

She went back into the bedroom and looked at the clock. It was not quite ten o'clock, just five, New York time, and for all Katharine knew, he might not be alone. But she had to take that chance, and even if he was with someone else, David wouldn't mind. David was her friend.

His answering service picked up. Katharine's mind flew across the ocean and pictured David dealing with some emergency, someone burned, or smashed up, and she wanted to cry out that *she* was an emergency, too, she needed him to call on her—

But instead, she spoke normally, sensibly.

"Please tell Dr. Rothman that Katharine called."

"Would you like the doctor to return your call, ma'am?"

"Yes," Katharine said. "Please."

"What message would you like to leave, ma'am?"

"Just tell him Katharine called."

"Please give me your number."

"He has it."

"Dr. Rothman likes us to take all numbers, ma'am."

"He has my number," Katharine said again, still calm, growing numb. "Please just ask him to call."

"Is it an emergency, ma'am?"

A little seed of panic poked its head up through the layer of calm, and Katharine pushed it back down again, like a gardener with a flattening spade.

"No," she said. "No emergency."

On Thursday afternoon, Noël Harvey summoned the cast for notes, and that evening, they held the second dress rehearsal. Sebastian attended the last part of the rehearsal, after which he had arranged to take Barbara Stone out for dinner. It was her birthday. She wasn't saying which birthday, was in the mood to be coy about it, though Sebastian and Jeremy both knew that she was going to be forty-eight. She had told Sebastian, whom she had always felt closer to than Jeremy, that she didn't really feel like celebrating, certainly did not want any kind of a party, so if they were thinking about a surprise, not to bother.

"Patrick's in France, in any case, with his father," Barbara had said to Sebastian a few days before, "and I'm having more than enough fun with Hedda—but dinner with you and Katharine would be just lovely, if you'd like."

That morning, however, Katharine had woken up with a sore throat.

"I think I'm getting Sam's cold," she told Sebastian.

"Better take plenty of vitamin C." He felt her forehead. It was the first time he had touched her in days. "No temperature. Do you want the doc?"

"Just for a cold?"

"You can't afford to be ill right now."

"No," she said. "Of course not."

"Are you going to be okay for dinner tonight?"

"I should think so."

But after Sebastian left, she was sick again, and the nausea stayed with her all through the morning, and at lunchtime she called him at the office and told him that she thought that it might, after all, be better if she had an early night.

"We're on our own, I'm afraid," Sebastian told Barbara, after the dress rehearsal. "Katharine has a lousy cold, and she certainly doesn't want to pass it on to you."

"Poor darling," Barbara said. "Still, I'm happy to have you all to myself. Where are we going?"

"Your birthday, your choice."

"Sheekey's, please."

Barbara ate oysters and drank a great deal of champagne, and she looked marvelous and sexy as always, full of life and turning heads, but Sebastian, close to her, saw new lines on her face and neck, and thought that she looked just a tiny bit worn, and he was filled with admiration for the way that that all just disappeared when she was on stage. Barbara was going to be one of those truly ageless, timeless women, and if she got the right parts—if they got her the right parts—she would be able to go on and on forever.

"I've never once regretted the day your father introduced me to you, darling," she told Sebastian. "Best move of my career."

"You transformed Locke Mariner," he countered. "You were our first big name, our first star."

"Six years ago next spring." Barbara picked up her glass again. "To you, darling Sebastian, the best agent any girl could have."

"To my number one, absolutely favorite client," he said.

Sebastian drank sparingly, for Barbara was drinking heavily, having a fine time but getting drunk, nonetheless, and so he would have to drive her home, and besides, he had another of his headaches. It had started almost as soon as he'd reached the theater, and it was getting worse.

Barbara and her son lived in a house at Marlow, near the river, but she kept a London flat on the eighth floor of a modern block in Pimlico.

"You will come in, won't you, darling?" she said at the door.

Sebastian glanced at his watch. "It's getting pretty late." His headache had receded a little, but it was still there, still nagging.

"Just one more drink won't hurt, surely?" Barbara headed for the kitchen. "And I know just where there's a nice bottle of champagne all ready for the drinking."

"Don't you think we've had enough?"

"I haven't, and you've hardly had any."

Clearly, Barbara was in no mood to be alone, Sebastian thought, not, at least, until she was ready to fall down drunk.

"You haven't forgotten you're previewing tomorrow night?"

"No, darling, I haven't forgotten."

Sebastian took the bottle from her to open it. "Well, if you think you can cope with it," he said, "then I'm not going to be a killjoy on your birthday."

"It's my birthday I'm having trouble coping with." Barbara got out two tulip glasses. "Anyway, I don't have to get up early, so I'm just going to relax."

Sebastian followed her into the living room. A little brown Burmese kitten lay sleeping on the cream-colored sofa.

"Hello, Nan, my sweet." The kitten woke and stretched, languidly. Barbara sat down beside it and began to stroke it. "Oh, what a beautiful purr."

"Who's this?" Sebastian asked, pouring champagne.

"This," Barbara said, picking the little cat up in her arms, "is a new friend of mine. She's called Nantucket."

"Why?"

"After the place that the man who gave her to me comes from." Barbara pulled a face. "Not especially appropriate, I suppose, for a little kitty, but it seemed right at the time. I call her Nan."

"She's very pretty."

Barbara put the kitten back down on the sofa, and went to open the doors to her small terrace. "Not too cold, is it, darling? I like having the heat up high with fresh air."

Sebastian thought about the eight floors. "Is it safe having it open, with the kitten?"

"She never goes out there," Barbara said. "First day I had her, my lovely cleaning lady was hosing the pot plants, and she caught Nan with the spray. Terrified her—just as well." She swayed a little, and held on to the wall.

Sebastian sat down in an armchair. "It went well this evening, didn't you feel?"

Barbara raised a finger to her lips. "Don't even think it, darling—much too superstitious to talk about it."

"Noël seemed quite calm."

"He'll be a wreck tomorrow."

"Am I allowed to say that I think you're quite wonderful?" Sebastian asked, lighting a cigarette.

"Of course you are, darling." She grinned at him. "Did you like my death tonight?"

"Loved it."

"I must say it's great fun shooting myself through the head every performance," Barbara said, flippantly, picking up her champagne glass. "Goodness, I despise her."

"Hedda?" Sebastian felt his headache returning, felt the band of pressure tightening around his skull.

"I respect her, too, of course. Such hypocrisy, and so aware of it."
She drank a little, and sank down on the sofa, and Nantucket, un-
willing to be disturbed again, jumped neatly off and walked into the
corner, near the radiator. "I've watched Katharine in action a few
times," Barbara went on. "She's very good, you know. I was surprised."

"Were you?"

"I thought she'd be too gentle for Hedda, but actually, she almost
frightened me." Abruptly, Barbara set her glass down on the low
coffee table and stood up. "Excuse me, darling. I'm feeling just a
little queasy."

"Do you want me to go?"

"No, no." She walked, unsteadily, toward the bathroom. "Shan't
be long. Give yourself a drop more champagne."

Sebastian leaned back in the armchair, and closed his eyes. He
felt a light, small weight on his thighs as the kitten landed on
him, and then a series of tiny pinpricks as her claws kneaded his
trousers.

"Hello, Nantucket," he said, very softly.

The room was quiet. He could hear the kitten's purring and his
own breathing, and, in the bathroom, behind the closed door, the
sound of water running into Barbara's basin, and, from further away,
down on the London streets, the sound of late-night traffic.

His head hurt. He could smell her again, had been aware of the
fragrance all evening. And yet it was not quite the same, not quite as
strong, or stifling, as it sometimes was.

He opened his eyes and stood up, the kitten in his arms. It gave
a little miaow.

"Darling?"

Sebastian looked up and saw Barbara standing over him.

"Did you drop off?"

"Must have done."

She picked up her glass and sat down.

"All right?" Sebastian asked.

"Lovely," she said.

"What perfume are you wearing?" he asked, suddenly.

"Mitsouko," Barbara said. And then: "Where's Nan?"

"Don't know. Must have wandered off."

Sebastian took another cigarette out of his case, lit it, and stood up. He stretched his legs and strolled slowly out onto the terrace.

"Barbara." His voice was quiet. "Barbara, come out here."

"What is it, darling?"

"Don't make a noise. Come out slowly." He heard her behind him. "Look."

"Oh, my God."

Nantucket was sitting, about five feet from the edge of the terrace, on the ornamental stone parapet of the building itself. Just a narrow strip of concrete.

"How on earth did she get there? She never goes out."

"Easy enough, for a cat," Sebastian said. His head pounded. "Shall I try and get her?"

"No—you might frighten her, she might go further out or even—"

"Try calling her."

"She's a kitten, not a dog." Barbara began to inch toward her.

"You can't reach her."

The kitten mewed.

"She's stuck, poor baby," Barbara whispered, distressed. "I'm going to climb up."

She picked up the small, white, wrought-iron table from the center of the terrace, her movements slow and graceful, like a dancer's, and set it down again close to the right-hand edge, as near to the kitten as she could. And then she took off her shoes.

"That's crazy, Barbara," Sebastian said sharply.

"Quiet, you'll scare her. Help me up." She climbed up onto the table. She was wearing silk trousers, and they flapped around her ankles in the breeze. "All right, Nan, darling," she crooned, softly. "I'm coming to save you."

Sebastian stood beside the table, motionless. Her perfume blew around him in a soft cloud, and he felt sick.

"Don't be frightened, darling," Barbara murmured to the cat, and her stockings slithered a little on the tabletop.

"For God's sake," Sebastian said, "you're going to fall."

"No, I'm not, I have perfect balance. Dance training," she said, boastingly.

It was the champagne boasting, and Sebastian knew now, knew that she was going to fall.

"It's all right, Nan, my sweet," Barbara wheedled, and leaned out, right over the edge of the terrace wall, reaching for the parapet. "You just keep very still for—"

She stumbled.

Sebastian sprang forward, grabbed for her as she pitched into space, caught her right ankle and the silk of her trousers.

Barbara screamed.

He held on, felt the fragile skin and bone in his hands. And then the silk ripped in his hands, and then Barbara's ankle slipped in his grasp, and she swung a little way, and he heard her head crack against the stone wall of the building—Mitsouko filled his nostrils, her screaming filled his head, together with the pounding of the blood in his ears and in his temples—

And then she was sliding out of his grasp. And he knew that he had to let go, had to. Had to.

And she fell.

When Barbara hit the pavement eight floors down, Nantucket, the little brown kitten, gave a tiny, chirruping mew, and turned herself around, and began to walk, slowly, neatly, back onto the terrace wall, and then she jumped lightly, silently, down to safety.

Sebastian stood, his eyes torn wide, staring down.

The cat looked up at him. And hissed.

And for just one moment, one long, tormented moment before the headache came back to blot the knowledge out, Sebastian knew what he had done.

Barbara had still been alive in the ambulance, they told him later, at the hospital. Alive and conscious, thinking clearly and precisely in spite of her terrible injuries. Clearly enough to tell them that it had been her own fault, they reassured him, that Sebastian had warned her not to, had tried to stop her. Had tried to save her.

It had been the champagne, Barbara had said, and her birthday had made her feel immortal.

And then she had died.

He was too shocked to drive himself home. He telephoned Jeremy, who came to the hospital to fetch him, disbelieving. And they went back to Hampstead in silence, and Katharine was sleeping soundly, having dosed herself with aspirin and hot lemon, leaving out the whisky because of the baby.

"Are you all right?" Jeremy asked Sebastian.

"No."

"Do you want me to stay?"

"No."

And Jeremy went home, and Sebastian could not bring himself to go upstairs, and so he lay down on the sofa in the drawing room. And went to sleep.

c h a p t e r
27

"I can't believe it."

"Nor can I, but it's true."

"It can't be true. It *can't* be!"

"Angel, you have to take it in. It's awful—it's ghastly, but it has happened, and all the wishing it away in the world isn't going to change that."

Katharine and Sebastian were in their bedroom, sitting on the bed. Katharine was white-faced, her eyes red and sore from weeping. Sebastian had woken her at eight o'clock with the news, wishing he might have kept it from her a little longer, but knowing that it could only be a matter of an hour at the most before the telephone started to ring. He had forced her to sip some sweet tea, thinking she might faint, but she had rallied, physically, at least, her disbelief protecting her a little.

"Tell me again how it happened," Katharine said. "It can't have been the way you made it sound—it's too horrific, too bizarre."

"Don't make me go through it again, angel."

"I know. I'm sorry. It must have been a nightmare for you." She looked at him. "You're blaming yourself, aren't you?"

"Of course I am. How can I not?"

"But you said that they told you at the hospital that they knew it wasn't your fault. That Barbara told them you tried to stop her—" She faltered. "To save her."

Sebastian was hollow-eyed. "I obviously didn't try hard enough."

Katharine ran her hands wretchedly through her long hair. "I still don't understand how she got up there—how you—" She stopped.

"How I let her?" Sebastian said, harshly. "Katharine, her kitten was out there. Barbara wouldn't let me get it, she said I might scare it and it might fall."

Katharine shuddered. "It's wicked of me, I know, but I'm glad in a way she didn't let you, or it might have been you who—"

"Stop it, darling."

Katharine began to weep again, quietly, hugging herself against the shivering that had begun as soon as Sebastian had told her.

Sebastian stood up.

"Don't leave me," Katharine whispered.

"I'm going to ask Ellie to make you some breakfast."

"I couldn't eat."

"You have to eat," Sebastian said. "You're going to need every ounce of strength today."

Katharine stared up at him, tears still wet on her cheeks. "You don't mean—"

"Of course I do."

"No." She shook her head, violently. "No, I couldn't!"

Sebastian sat down again, gently. "You're her understudy, angel."

"But surely they'll postpone the preview?" Katharine's eyes were wild with horror and dismay.

"I don't know exactly what they'll do," Sebastian said. "But whatever they do decide, you're it. You're Hedda."

"It's so—" She sought the right word. "Brutal."

"Yes, it is."

"They won't want me. Noël won't want me."

"Yes, they will."

"They want a name. A star." Panic was rising in Katharine.

"Even if they do," Sebastian said, "there's no time."

It all hit the fan less than an hour later. The police arrived just ahead of the press, and Jeremy.

"How's Kate holding up?" Jeremy asked Sebastian, in the hall, his voice low.

"She's in shock, but she's strong."

"Where is she?"

"Upstairs, getting dressed. Noël telephoned a few minutes ago."

"He was beside himself when I told him," Jeremy said.

The telephone rang. Sebastian picked it up quickly and spoke for a few moments.

"That was March," he told Jeremy. "He wants Katharine in his office at ten."

"Can she make it?"

Sebastian looked at his watch. "Just."

"Will she want to go?"

"March said that he knows she won't feel up to it—none of them do—but this is show business, ghastly as it is, and they have to talk right away."

Jeremy's mouth quirked.

"Business before mourning," he said.

When Katharine left the house, the sun was shining brightly. It had been foggy when Sebastian had woken her, but now every trace of mist had gone.

"My God," she said, softly, to Sebastian, "it's New Year's Eve."

"That's right." His voice was taut but gentle.

She looked up at him. The black taxi that had been ordered was waiting for her in the drive, engine switched off.

"Do you suppose the rest of the cast know yet?"

Sebastian shook his head. "I doubt it. Or Sam would have called."

Katharine looked wan. "I'd ask you to wish me luck, but I'm not sure what I'm wishing for," she said. "This is all wrong. More than wrong. It's monstrous."

"Yes," Sebastian said. "It is."

He opened the door for her, and she climbed into the back of the taxi.

"I wish you could come with me."

"Me too. But I have to make a statement."

"I know you do."

"Will you be all right?" he asked her.

Katharine nodded. "You're being—"

"What, angel?"

"Kind," she said.

"Shouldn't I be?"

She didn't answer.

"I'll call March's office at eleven," Sebastian said. "But if you know anything solid before that, call me here."

"Sure," Katharine said.

Katharine spent one and a half hours closeted with Peter March and Noël Harvey, before they banished her to an outer office so that they could talk alone.

"At least she knows it inside out," March said dolefully.

"She's a very professional girl," Harvey said, close to tears.

"It may be quite interesting," March ventured. "She's such an entirely different kind of Hedda. Barbara was so—"

"Stupendous."

"If only Katharine had done a little more."

"I warned you, Peter."

"We'll replace her, of course." The producer became brisker. "The office is on to it as we speak."

"It can't be soon enough."

"Hardly."

"We have to cancel tonight's preview," Harvey said. "There's simply no alternative. We'll break it to the others this afternoon and do a dress rehearsal later."

"It'll cost a fortune," March said, bleakly.

"What choice do we have? She'll go on for the matinee tomorrow, and you'll move heaven and earth to find us a name."

"And in the meantime," the producer said, slowly, "I think we'll have to engage a little public sympathy."

"Tragedy doesn't sell tickets," Harvey argued. "The moment they hear about poor darling Barbara, they'll want their money back."

"Not necessarily. Not if we tell them that Katharine Andersen is Diana Lancaster's daughter-in-law."

"Peter, darling," Harvey said, patiently, "there aren't enough people left alive who *remember* Diana Lancaster."

"We'll remind them." March paused. "You've forgotten, haven't you? I'd forgotten myself until this morning."

"Am I being dreadfully obtuse?" the director asked, wearily.

"Not at all, dear boy. It happened over twenty years ago, after all."

"What happened?"

"Diana Lancaster died," March said, with relish. "Directly after the last dress rehearsal for *Hedda Gabler*."

"Good Christ," Harvey said.

"Precisely."

Katharine went directly from March's office to the theater. She was still numb with shock, but not numb enough. In a little over twenty-four hours, she was to open on a West End stage in her first leading role, and she felt nothing but horror. Barbara was dead, horrifically dead. And she was neither qualified, nor ready to take over the part, besides which she was by now hideously aware that the management had only given her the understudy because of Sebastian's investment in the show.

Barbara's belongings had already been removed from her dressing room when Katharine arrived, and Olive, Barbara's dresser, her eyes red from weeping behind her spectacles, was waiting for her.

"I didn't believe it when they told me to come in," she said.

"I still can't," Katharine said.

"She was such a lovely lady," Olive said, and dabbed at her face with a sodden handkerchief. "And on her birthday, too."

Katharine remembered, suddenly, that she had not called Sebastian.

"I have to call my husband—he doesn't know what's happening."

"I'll leave you alone," Olive said, then hesitated, looking Katharine over with her professional eye. "Miss Stone's costumes will need taking in just a little."

Katharine's stomach churned violently.

"I don't want this, you know, Olive."

"No," the dresser said, gently. "I can see you don't. But that's what they have understudies for, isn't it? You mustn't feel bad. Miss Stone would tell you to enjoy yourself."

Katharine could not answer, and Olive left the room, closing the door quietly behind her. Katharine picked up the telephone on the dressing table and dialed. Ellie answered, told her that Sebastian had left the house a little while before and was on his way to the theater.

"Mr. Raphael telephoned for you. He heard what happened, and he said that I was to tell you to"—Ellie hesitated—"to 'hang tough.' I think that was what he said."

Katharine smiled faintly. "I'm sure it was. Thank you."

"Are you all right, my dear?"

"No, Ellie, I'm not."

"You will be," Ellie said, stoutly. "You're a brave girl."

"I don't feel very brave right now."

"God bless you."

Katharine called Virginia next, praying that she'd be at home. She answered on the second ring, bright-voiced.

"You haven't heard, have you?" Katharine asked.

"Heard what, darling?"

Katharine told her.

"Dear God," Virginia said, and her shock was clear in the words. "Are you all right? Can you cope?"

"I guess I'll have to."

"What about Sebastian?"

"He feels dreadful, of course. I think he's operating on a kind of remote control, getting through it, you know?"

"I can imagine." Virginia paused. "That's not true. I can't imagine it at all—I can't see how such a thing could possibly have happened. It's too ghastly to contemplate."

Katharine was trembling. "She was so—alive. She was so brilliant, and she was so good to me, and now I'm supposed to take over from her, and it's so *wrong*—"

The door opened, and Katharine looked up.

"Virginia, darling, I have to go. Sebastian's just arrived."

"Do you want me to come?"

"No. Thank you. There's no point—there's no time, thank God."

"Call me, if you need anything," Virginia said, anxiously. "And tell Sebastian, too—anything at all."

"I will."

Sebastian looked exhausted, and Katharine saw that the small frown lines that usually accompanied his headaches were etched between his blond eyebrows.

"What's happening?" he asked, sinking into a chair. "Peter's been unavailable, so I came straight here."

"They've canceled tonight's preview."

"But you're going on?" he asked, tensely.

She nodded. "Tomorrow. The matinee."

For a moment, Sebastian remained motionless, his hands clenched into white-knuckled fists. And then he was up on his feet, and the triumph in his eyes seemed like white-hot, blazing fire.

"I'm terrified, Sebastian."

"You'll be perfect," he said, and still the exultation in his eyes grew, until Katharine thought, for an instant, that he might crow like a jubilant cock.

"I've never seen you so excited," she said, embarrassed and

shocked, yet moved, at the same time, by the fierceness of his reaction. *The baby*, she thought. *I should tell him about the baby, right now*.

And then she realized, abruptly, that the jubilation was not for her, but in spite of her. Suddenly she knew that, though Sebastian stood just inches from her, he was far, far away from her.

"Barbara's costumes are going to need altering," she said, shakily. "Olive's waiting outside." She wanted him to go, needed to be alone for a while.

He nodded, slowly. "I'll leave you."

"Where are you going?"

"To the office. There are things to deal with. The police are coming. The coroner." Sebastian paused. "I'll be calling Barbara's boy in France. The police contacted Dupont, his father, last night."

"That poor boy," Katharine said.

"And then there's the party."

"What party?" The word made her flinch.

"It's New Year's Eve. We always have a few drinks at the office, remember?" Sebastian's voice was flat, almost vague. "I'll have to say a few words, about Barbara."

"The dress rehearsal's scheduled for five," Katharine said, quietly. "Will you be able to come?"

"I'll try."

"I'd like you to be here."

"All right," he said.

He went to Albemarle Street. Elspeth gave him a hug, Jeremy came in to talk to him for a few minutes before going out. He sat at his desk and pushed papers around.

His office did not seem solid and real as it normally did. Nothing seemed entirely real. He felt as if his head were filled with cotton wool. He touched things, tangible things, but the flesh of his fingers seemed insensate. He picked up a pen to write, but knew that he could not, set it down again and got, unsteadily, to his feet.

"I'm going home," he told Elspeth.

"But your calls."

"I'll make them from home."

"Are you all right?" she asked.

"Fine," he said. "I'll see you later."

"Should I cancel the party?"

"No," he said. "Just a drink or two. I need to tell them, myself, what happened. There may be gossip."

He heard his own voice. It sounded natural, clear, though to him it seemed as if it floated in the air, unrelated, cut off. He left the office, went to his car, turned on the ignition and began to drive.

I'm afraid, he thought, *of what is happening to me.*

He turned into Bond Street, left into Burlington Gardens and headed toward Regent Street. He drove perfectly, automatically, the hands that were not his, holding the steering wheel lightly, the eyes that were not his, checking the rearview mirror.

There's no reason to be afraid, he heard himself think. *It's just beginning. It's as it was meant to be.*

The black Aston Martin drove past the BBC into Portland Place and headed toward Regent's Park.

My destiny, his thoughts said.

A t half past three, in the theater, the atmosphere was tense. The news had been given out, the reactions had been of intense shock, of great sorrow and, ultimately, of panic. Sam was being protective, and the rest of the cast were behaving with impeccable gentleness and consideration toward Katharine, but she could sense their resentment. It was not her they resented; it was her lack of experience.

"You'll be terrific, sweetheart," Sam told her, but Katharine felt that the words were uttered out of desperation as well as kindness. She felt like a charlatan, but did not dare to confess her feelings to anyone, not even Sam. She might be a novice as an actress, but she had been exposed to theater people all her life, and she knew that she had no right to express her fears just to relieve herself of a burden. Stage fright was like an infectious virus, easily communicable and almost impossible to cure. And what Katharine felt now was way beyond stage fright.

Sebastian was in the back garden when Ellie called to him.

"I'm just popping out for a while," she called, buttoning her beige winter coat. "Would you like me to get you something?"

He stood by the rose beds, his back to her.

"Nothing, thank you, Ellie."

Ellie sighed, and turned to go.

Sebastian bent to pluck the head off a winter rose. A thorn pricked his index finger. He squeezed the stem tightly, then let the flower head fall to the ground. He raised his hand and looked at the tiny drop of blood. He felt the small sting of the prick, and it was a relief to him, for it seemed to provide proof that he was, after all, still inhabiting his body.

Still here, he thought.

He took his handkerchief out of his pocket, and wiped away the blood. And then he walked, slowly, back toward the house.

At Locke Mariner, the switchboard was flashing continuously.

"I don't understand why he left," Jeremy said to Elspeth.

"He said he was going home to make calls. It seemed sensible, under the circumstances," Elspeth said.

"But he hasn't gone home."

"Perhaps he did and went out again. Maybe he's gone for a walk." Elspeth paused. "One can understand his being upset today."

"I'll try him again."

In the drawing room at The Oaks, Sebastian heard the ringing of the telephone, but did not move to answer it.

He stood beneath the Nathan Smith portrait and looked up into Diana's face. He looked for a long time. Her sweet, enigmatic smile pierced memories into his languid, receptive brain: memories of childhood days of being loved by her. Recollections that seemed truly sharp and clear for the first time, nullifying, eradicating every anguish and every joy that he had experienced since that first, fundamental perception of love.

Everything else had been self-deception, created out of despair and longing for the purity he had believed lost forever. He knew that now. She was all that mattered. Her love had been the only love that counted. Whatever happened now, it was all for her.

By half-past four, the first signs of fog returning to the city had begun to send the cautious-minded on early homeward journeys. In St. Martin's Lane, outside the Albery Theatre, the sharp lines of the buildings had already blurred a little, the fringes of the mist drifting down to obscure the globe above the Coliseum.

"It's going to be a peasouper," the box office manager said, in the midst of handing over refunds for the evening's canceled preview. "It'll be hell getting home later."

"What's she like, this new Hedda?" her assistant asked.

"Beautiful girl. She's got something, I'd say."

"But is it enough?"

The manager shook her head. "Not nearly enough, not to fill a star like Barbara Stone's shoes."

"When's the funeral, do you know?"

"Haven't heard. There'll be an inquest, I expect."

"Really? Why's that?"

"She fell eight floors. There'd have to be a few questions."

"But it was an accident, wasn't it?"

"Of course it was, but still—"

"Poor woman."

"Quite a break for the understudy, though."

"She didn't look too happy when I saw her."

At five o'clock, prompt, the house lights dimmed, and the dress rehearsal began. Tesman's aunt and the maid delivered their first lines and, in the wings, the assistant stage manager dropped a vase onto the wooden floor with a resounding smash. In the fifth row, Noël Harvey ran a nervous hand through his sparse, curly hair and stared fixedly up at the stage, willing himself to settle down.

At the back of the theater, a carefully opened door blew a blast of cold air through the auditorium, and Sebastian slipped silently into the back row and sat down. A photographer in one of the boxes clicked his camera. And Hedda Gabler made her first entrance.

Noël Harvey grasped the arms of his seat, and then, after a moment or two, relaxed. Katharine looked wonderful. The eyes could not fail to be drawn to her, and when she spoke, her voice was clear and effortless and surprisingly calm, and the director saw that she was, truly, Hedda, and that she was also, thank God, in command.

The first act continued. The atmosphere calmed a little—not too much, just enough, so that the edge remained, sharp and fearful, not as terrifying as it would be at the first performance, but with the knowledge of it prodding at them all, driving them forward into excellence, into errors and small panics and then, back again, into excellence.

In his seat in the back row, Sebastian hunched forward, and Katharine's Hedda swam into a mist of pain. There were two voices in his head, crowding in with the ache, battling, burning tracks into his brain as they struggled for supremacy over him. One of them youthful and sweet and clear. The other vibrant, demanding and powerful.

He moaned, a soft, suppressed sound, and then he rose, groped his way past the empty seats toward the exit, and hurried out into the dark afternoon.

Jeremy, having failed repeatedly to reach Sebastian at home, tried the Albery. Noël Harvey's assistant, Giles, confirmed that Locke had been seen in the theater by one of the front-of-house staff.

"But I gather he left, rather abruptly, during the first act. They said he looked a little unwell."

Anxiety swelled to alarm. Jeremy telephoned Virginia.

"What's wrong?" she asked as soon as she heard his voice. It was the first time that Jeremy Mariner had ever called her.

"Is Sebastian with you?"

"No, should he be?"

"I was hopeful."

"You're at the office?"

"Which is where he should be."

"You've tried the house, obviously?"

"Obviously. And the theater. They say he was there, and that he left, looking ill. I'm concerned about him, Virginia."

"So am I."

"Can you tell me why?" Jeremy asked.

Virginia hesitated. "Perhaps we should meet."

"Yes," Jeremy said. "But I can't leave here for a while yet."

"No. I see." She paused. "I think perhaps I should go to the house—see if he's there. He might not be answering the phone."

A pang of fear gripped Jeremy, but he kept his voice calm.

"If you wouldn't mind doing that, I'll join you there as soon as I can."

Sebastian opened the front door of The Oaks, and stepped inside. No need for lights. Up the staircase. Into the bedroom. Behind the creamy walls Katharine had superimposed, he felt the old paper straining to push through.

The four-poster offended him. If he closed his eyes, he saw himself, coupling like a beast with his wife, and the sin welled up to choke him.

Out. Up the stairs to the attic. The top of the house. Under the roof, where the past was stored. Slabs of his life. Furry creatures and books and rocking horses and chairs to be sat in no more. By her. If he closed his eyes, he saw her sitting. Smiling.

Her trunk stood against one wall. He dragged it, making dark, straight tracks in the gray dust. If he closed his eyes, he saw himself pulling it out before, in the past. Heaving. When he was smaller, it was heavier.

He placed his hands, one on each side, on the handles, and lifted the lid. It creaked, the hinges groaned. The dust flew into the air, into his nostrils. He bent and, carefully, sank his hands beneath the layers of crushed fabric and lifted it out, tenderly. If he closed his eyes, he saw his father carrying it, his face pale and streaked with tears.

He lowered it gently to the floor and looked down into the trunk again. He took out the photograph, and the invitation. He looked at the photograph. And closed his eyes.

Raising her costume from the floor, the scent flowed freely all about him. He plunged his face into the dark, velvety blindness and inhaled deeply.

Out. Down the stairs. Into his nursery. Taking his leave, quickly. And down again, down the broad staircase, the costume heavy in his arms, stepping carefully. A moment in the drawing room. Looking up at her.

Ready now.

At a quarter past six, in the offices of Locke Mariner, Jeremy still waited. No sign of Sebastian and no word yet from Virginia. He and Elspeth had made excuses. The staff were anxious to leave, for the fog was rolling in, and they had their own New Year's Eve festivities to consider.

Jeremy sat, for a while, alone in his office. He tried calling The Oaks once more, tried the theater again. He thought about the things that the neurologist had said, and all his instincts told him that something was seriously wrong.

And he could no longer just sit there, doing nothing, so he went out and wished them all joy, health and prosperity, and then he left, heading for Hampstead.

Virginia arrived at The Oaks in a taxi, at half past six. The house was dark and unwelcoming, but she rang the bell twice before using her own key and letting herself in.

She called out Sebastian's name, then Ellie's, and then switched on the hall lights. She was instantly aware of the scent. A musty, stale, old fragrance. Virginia wrinkled her nose, peeled off her gloves and walked into the drawing room.

Turning on the lights, she noticed the photograph propped up on the mantelpiece right away. She crossed over to the fireplace and picked it up. It was a black-and-white picture, its edges curled and yellowish, of Diana, onstage, erect and aristocratic in a dark, high-necked, tightly waisted, long dress. Virginia turned over the photograph and saw the writing on the back. Andrew's writing.

Diana as Hedda Gabler. Dress rehearsal. May 20th, 1954.

Virginia stared, and turned the photograph over again. It quivered a little in her fingers, and she put it back on the mantelpiece. Her eyes turned to the invitation card beside it, cream-colored with age.

The pleasure of your company is requested on
May 21st, 1954,
to celebrate the first night of Hedda Gabler
in The River Suite, Savoy Hotel, London.

Virginia walked unsteadily to the telephone, sat down, and dialed the number of Locke Mariner. Elspeth Lehmann's voice, comforting and warm, answered.

"Still there, Elspeth?"

"I was just about to leave. How are you, Mrs. Locke?"

"Very well, thank you. Is Jeremy still there, by any chance?"

"No, he left a little while ago." Elspeth paused. "Sebastian called a few minutes after he'd gone, though."

"Thank goodness." Relief washed over Virginia. "Where is he?"

"He said that he'd been making arrangements for tonight, and that the fog had made it awkward for him to get back to the office."

"Did he mention what the arrangements were?" Virginia asked.

"He said that they'd be staying in town, to make it easier for Katharine."

"That's a kind idea," Virginia said. "Did he say where?"

"No, he didn't." There was a smile in Elspeth's voice. "I did ask, of course, but he was positively evasive. Wanting privacy, I imagine."

"I see. Thank you so much, Elspeth. Happy New Year."

"And to you, Mrs. Locke."

Virginia put down the receiver.

The relief had gone.

Shortly after seven o'clock, Jeremy's Morgan ground into the gravel drive. Virginia, waiting for him, opened the door before he had even reached for the bell.

"He called Elspeth just after you left," she said, without preamble.

"He's all right?"

"I don't think so."

Jeremy came inside and Virginia closed the door. She had made up her mind, even before she saw the fear in his eyes. They were not close. Virginia knew that Katharine had always felt uncomfortable with him, but there could be no doubting his friendship and loyalty to Sebastian.

"I have some things to show you," she said. Until now, the idea of sharing Andrew's books and notes with anyone had been unthinkable, but she was so afraid, so strangely, intensely afraid, that she knew she had no choice.

She took Jeremy into the study, showed him the books.

"They might, of course, have had nothing whatever to do with Sebastian," she said. "They're so inexplicable that they could be related to anything at all—a law case, perhaps. But Andrew was so unhappy before his death, and the change in him was so dramatic—" She broke off. "And then, there's the letter."

"What letter?"

"One of Sebastian's, from Marchmont. I'm afraid it's another link to *Hedda Gabler*. Your name is mentioned in the letter." Virginia handed it to Jeremy. "I'll leave you for a while. You'll need some time."

She sat alone, for about fifteen minutes, then made them both a drink. Whisky, with no water, no ice, something to brace them. And as she took the glasses in to him, she prayed that she would find Jeremy shrugging off the books in that ironic way of his, and that he would have an explanation for the letter that would prove that she had been overreacting, that she was a foolish old woman with an overactive imagination.

But Jeremy's face had grown pale, his narrow mouth taut, and when he looked up at Virginia, there was not a trace of irony in his eyes. Only horror.

"Here," she said, giving him a glass. "You need it."

He took a swallow.

"I'm not wrong, Jeremy, am I?"

He shook his head.

"There's more," Virginia said, and sat down in the leather chair facing the desk. "You and Katharine don't get on, I know, and I have to be honest and tell you that I believe you're mostly to blame for that."

"No doubt about it." Jeremy smiled slightly.

Virginia sat very straight. "So sharing her most intimate confidences with you is something I wouldn't dream of doing, unless I thought I had no alternative."

"I'm sure," he said. "But we all have one thing in common, don't we? We all love Sebastian."

By the time Virginia had told him about some of the problems Katharine had faced, lately, with Sebastian, and then, as she showed him, finally, the photograph and the invitation, both more than twenty-two years old, Jeremy had put it all together.

"Dear God," he said, softly.

"Now you," Virginia said. "Tell me what you know."

Jeremy shook his head. "It's quite a jumble. One of those jigsaws, with most of the pieces missing, and I don't understand at all how it's come to this."

"But you know something."

"I know that Sebastian's ill. Very ill." Jeremy licked his dry lips. "I know that he's obsessed. By his mother, perhaps. By *Hedda Gabler*, certainly."

"Because it was Diana's last part?"

"I was with Seb that day," Jeremy remembered. "The day Diana died. So was Kate." He paused. "And I was at Marchmont with Seb when the boy playing Hedda was injured with the acid." His mouth twisted a little. "They questioned me, as he said in the letter. I was a practical joker, so they wondered, for a while."

Virginia waited for a moment. "There's more, isn't there?"

Jeremy nodded.

"Tell me. Please."

"I went to live in the States in the summer of '67. Seb was at university up in Edinburgh. Before I left, I went to visit him. It was Festival time, and one night, we went to a Fringe production of *Hedda Gabler*." He drank the last gulp of his whisky. "It was dreadful, and we left before the end. I went on, it was early, and Seb said he was going back to his flat, but when I got back, he wasn't there."

Virginia felt that her heartbeat had slowed almost to a standstill. "What happened?"

"He told me next day that he'd seen a fire. I read about it in *The Scotsman*."

"The theater?"

Jeremy nodded. "It wasn't a theater, just one of those old, unused houses they used to take over for the Fringe. No one was hurt. I forgot all about it. Until today."

Jeremy had witnessed, but not understood, Sebastian's ironclad, inflexible determination to be involved with Peter March's Ibsen plays, and the uncharacteristically reckless investment from which Jeremy had tried, and failed, to draw him back, even a little. And he and Virginia had both observed Sebastian's relentless pushing of Katharine, from nowhere, into her acting career; and Jeremy remembered now, with clarity, that it had all begun in earnest here, in this house, a year before, after March had spoken to them both, during the New Year's Eve party, about his plans.

"Seb was furious when they cast Barbara, you know. He covered it up quickly enough, but I saw his face."

"Katharine told me, before Christmas," Virginia said slowly, painfully, "that she'd only just realized that he wanted Hedda for her—she'd thought he wanted Mrs. Elvsted. We both knew by then that it was because of Diana's connection with the part, but we didn't realize how obsessed he was."

"Barbara was perfectly cast, you know," Jeremy said, his face very white now. "She was one of his favorite clients. His anger made no real sense."

They both stopped talking. Their thoughts were loud enough, without speech.

Barbara had died. And Katharine had become Hedda.

Diana had not opened in the play. Nor had the boy at Marchmont. Nor had Barbara Stone.

Jeremy and Virginia were no longer afraid.

They were terrified.

At eight o'clock, in the theater, an air of gloom had set in. The cast sat, scattered through the first few rows of the stalls, awaiting Noël Harvey's notes on the final rehearsal. He was known to give extensive last-minute notes. He had even been known, on occasions, to give notes before the last night of a long run. He had said, this evening, that he would not keep them long, but no one believed him. Not that they minded. They needed the notes, they wanted the show to be perfect, it was vital to them all. Nothing else mattered.

After fifteen minutes, Katharine, feeling chilled, asked, apologetically, if she might run to her dressing room to fetch a wrap.

"Of course, darling," Harvey said. "All we need now is for your cold to turn to flu."

The note was in an envelope, tucked inside the pocket of the old blue cashmere cardigan she always used as a wrap in the theater. Quickly, she tore open the envelope.

> *Don't go home, angel. We have a room at the*
> *Savoy. I have everything you'll need. Love,*
> *S.*

Jeremy had left The Oaks at a quarter to eight. He and Virginia had agreed that he should drive to the theater, while she would leave word for Katharine that she was not to leave, that she was to wait until Jeremy arrived, and in the meantime, Virginia would wait in the house in case Sebastian came home.

The fog had formed a blanket over London. Jeremy had hoped to make the journey swiftly, but traffic was heavy and crawling slowly. What normally took five minutes was, this evening, taking twenty—the drive to St. Martin's Lane would ordinarily have taken little more than half an hour. He dreaded to think how long it would take him today.

At twenty past nine, Katharine, changed into jeans and pullover, her face scrubbed clean, called good night quickly through Sam's dressing room door and ran toward the stage door. She was anxious to be out of the theater, and after the strains of the past few weeks, and the desolate absence of feeling from Sebastian, the tone of his note had given her fresh hope. She might be a fool clutching at straws, after all that had gone before, but he was still her husband, and maybe tonight, if she told him about the baby . . . Maybe the New Year would stop the rot, allow them to start over—

"Miss Andersen!" Bill, the stage-door keeper, called to her as she hurried past him. "There was a message for you."

"Thanks, Bill," Katharine called back over her shoulder. "I've already had it."

And he nodded, crumpled up Virginia's message, and threw it into the wastepaper basket.

Jeremy had never known such traffic. He tried every trick and short cut that he knew, but nothing was working. At the back of Camden Town, a van ran into a taxi, tempers grew heated, details were exchanged, horns began to blow, and even when the vehicles were cleared, they hardly moved. The crawl continued. Jeremy saw the clock on the dashboard ticking by, switched on the radio, then pushed in a cassette, fighting to calm himself, knowing there was nothing he could do, not a damned thing on earth, for the treacherous, blinding fog would not magically lift because Sebastian was in trouble, and he had to creep forward, inch by inch, and pray that he and Virginia were wrong, wrong . . .

In Charing Cross Road, there was another accident, involving a bus and a bicycle, and everything ground to a halt. For ten minutes nothing moved at all, and Jeremy could stand no more. The street in which they stood had stringent parking regulations, but Jeremy was beyond parking.

He drove the Morgan up onto the curb, right up onto the pavement, turned off the ignition and started walking.

Five minutes if I walk, less if I run.

Running in fog was one of the worst things that an asthmatic could do, and though Jeremy had not had a really bad attack in years, he knew it was crazy. But Sebastian was in his mind, before his eyes, looming out of the fog, and he knew he had to find him.

He ran.

Sebastian stood at the big window, looking out through his own, shadowy, reflected image, watching the fog clouds looming and rolling and shifting slowly across the river. Far over to the right, over an invisible Parliament Square, Big Ben's face vaporized and then reappeared, seeming to bob, ethereal, disembodied.

In the sitting room, behind him, and in the bedroom beyond the double doors, all was ready.

The taxi bearing Katharine to the Savoy deposited her, at last, at the entrance. A doorman, trim in gray tophat and overcoat, hurried to her assistance.

"Thank you," Katharine said, a little wearily, paying the driver. "Keep the change."

She walked through the revolving doors into the foyer. The immediate and unmistakable waft of log fires, expensive perfumes, polish and all the other less decipherable scents that were the hallmark of a great hotel on a festive night, was balm to her fatigue.

She went directly to the reception desk.

"I'm Mrs. Locke," she said, pushing her hair back from her face. "I believe my husband has already checked in." She waited, allowing herself the anticipation of a long, luxurious bath.

"You have a suite on the third floor, Mrs. Locke," she was told, "with a river view."

A uniformed boy, already loaded with luggage, was directed to take her upstairs, but Katharine smiled and assured them that it was quite unnecessary, since her husband had her bags, and she needed only the suite number.

She strode toward the elevators, her cheeks flushed, her mink coat swinging from her shoulders, her pullover and worn working jeans incongruous in the throng of sleek dinner jackets, black ties and evening gowns, but Katharine hardly noticed. There was a knot in her stomach, of apprehension and excitement.

She pressed the call button, and waited.

In the sitting room of the suite, Sebastian sat in a deep, soft armchair. He was as cold as death, his breathing shallow. Until, at last, he heard the gentle knocking at the door.

He breathed deeply. Once, twice. The knocking came again, a little louder this time.

"It's open," he called.

He felt the blood beginning to flow again.

Katharine stepped into the room.

"Hello, darling," she said, and the door closed behind her.

"Hello, angel."

She blinked. The sitting room was aglow with candles. They were everywhere. On the tables, the sideboard, on the mahogany escritoire, on the mantelpiece over the fireplace, even on the parquet floor where the Persian rugs ended. All stuck fast with their own wax, their little flames dancing wildly in the wake of her entrance.

Sebastian sat opposite the door, his black rollneck sweater and black trousers making his body hardly visible in the depths of the big armchair, the skin of his face and hands glowing white in the soft, lambent light. He rose, and his shadow sprang, long and black, up the walls and over the ceiling.

"I'm glad you've come," he said. "I've been waiting a long time."

Katharine put her shoulder bag down on the sofa. She felt a desire to groan with exhaustion and disappointment. She had prayed for things to be normal tonight, for just one evening of ordinary affection and lucidity.

"Noël gave notes," she said, suppressing a sigh. "And the traffic's all backed up with the fog." She went to him, kissed him on the cheek. His skin was cold again, she noticed. As it had been on Christmas Eve, before he had attacked her. An eternity ago.

"Do you like it?" Sebastian asked, indicating the room.

"Lovely extravagance," Katharine said, outwardly composed. "And all these candles—romantic." She saw an ice bucket on the table. Dom Pérignon for the New Year.

Sebastian sat down again, and the big, black shadow folded behind him.

"And now?" Katharine asked, her voice falsely bright. "What's the plan? Are we going down for dinner or staying up here?"

He did not answer. The light from the candles closest to him struck his face, and she saw, with a new pang of uneasiness, the opaqueness in his eyes.

Outside the suite, in the corridor, laughter broke through the silence, and a group of guests moved past their door, voices chattering, skirts rustling. On the Thames, a foghorn penetrated the windows. Katharine sat on the sofa, near the fireplace, her hands nervous in her lap.

"Why don't you take off your coat?"

His voice startled her, but she slipped the fur from her shoulders and let it lie around her, not getting up.

"When did you leave the note?" she asked, after a few moments. "Did you see the rehearsal?"

"Some of it."

"It didn't go all that badly," she said, "considering. Does that bode well or ill for tomorrow?"

"Who knows?" He paused. "Why don't you have a look around?"

"All right."

Katharine rose, and the candles flickered and leapt. "Isn't this just a bit dangerous?"

Again, Sebastian did not answer.

"Sebastian, for heaven's sake!" Her nerves were too frayed to cope with his games any longer. "Why did you bother to arrange all this if you don't even want to talk to me? I'm tired and I'm hungry, and if you can't even be civil, then I'm just going to go straight to bed."

He stood up, and the giant shadow sprang over the ceiling again and slipped down the walls.

"Why don't you look at the bedroom?" he said, softly, as if she had not spoken.

Shrugging off her exasperation, Katharine turned on her heel.

"Why not?" she said, and opened the double doors. Her eyes widened, and she gave a little gasp.

The bedroom was lovely, oval-walled, high-ceilinged, with creamy, silken fabrics and delicate rounded cornices. But it had been transformed, by Sebastian, into a glowing, eerie chamber. The electric lights were all off, and the candles, scores of them, led in parallel lines, like a little flare path, to the bed.

The costume lay on the bedspread. It was spread out gracefully, like a negligee. A black mourning dress of velvet and silk, the hundreds of puckers and creases from over twenty years of folding, shining like tiny dark ripples in the candlelight.

Katharine let out a long, soft sigh. She knew, without being told, whose costume it had been.

"Hedda's," Sebastian said, right behind her.

Katharine's heart leapt high into her throat.

"Diana's," she said.

She did not turn around, but stepped, carefully, into the brilliant path, one pace nearer to the bed.

"It's beautiful, isn't it?" he said.

She felt his breath warm against her left ear. For an instant, she closed her eyes. The taste of fear, shocking and instinctive, was so strong that her desire to bolt, to rush through the candles for the door, was overwhelming. But she knew, intuitively, that he would not let her leave.

"Wouldn't you like to put it on?" His voice was a loving caress.

Katharine's breathing quickened. She knew that he sensed her fear and was glad of it, and that was so unlike Sebastian that she felt herself turning to ice.

"No," she said. She could not bear to turn and face him.

"Put it on."

It was a command. Flat and cold, the voice of a stranger.

"All right," Katharine whispered.

Moving closer to the bed, she reached for the dress.

The theater had been dark when Jeremy had reached it, the doors locked. He had run to the stage door, found it, too, locked and bolted, and had known then that the only place left to look was the Savoy. The old invitation had been left there for a reason; logic decreed that they must be at the Savoy. Though logic, God alone knew, had precious little to do with this.

Jeremy was out of breath and already starting to wheeze. He needed an inhaler, but he had not carried one for years. He looked at his watch, saw that it was already past ten o'clock.

He began running again.

"Take off your clothes," Sebastian told her.

"I don't want to."

"I want you to."

He was right behind her, the bed in front of her, the candles to right and left of her. Trembling badly, Katharine tugged the pullover up over her head, and unzipped her jeans. She wore no brassiere, and her nipples sprang erect, and the tiny hairs on her arms and legs stood upright as she stood naked, except for her lace panties.

"Put it on."

She fumbled with the fastening on the dress, sure that she would feel his hands on her at any moment, remembering the night in the nursery. But he did not touch her, only stood there, behind her, waiting.

She unfastened every hook and held it out before her, and the belt of the dress fell, when she had unhooked it, onto the bed. She stepped slowly into the skirt, put her arms into the sleeves, and it covered her, encased her. There was a musty smell of stagnant perfume absorbed deep in the fabric that revolted her, and her skin shrank from the scratchiness of the aged, cracked lining.

"Let me help you, angel," Sebastian's voice said, gentle again, and then his hands were around her waist and then at her back, fastening every hook until the costume hugged Katharine tightly, immuring her so that she could hardly breathe.

Jeremy was at the hall porter's desk. He was coughing badly, but in control. He needed the Lockes' room number, but the concierge would not give it to him.

"I can telephone the suite, sir." He picked up the receiver. "Your name, please?"

"Mariner." Jeremy was trying to catch his breath. "Please hurry—it's very urgent."

There was no reply, and the porter turned swiftly around to ascertain if the key was there, or missing, out of habit raising his hand to check in the pigeonhole in case it had slipped back.

"Thanks for trying," Jeremy said, having registered the number.

"Would you like to leave a message, Mr. Mariner?"

"No, thank you. I'll check in the bar, if I may."

"Certainly."

He located the suite, rapped several times on the door and, getting no response, turned away. He had to find a maid or waiter, someone, anyone with a passkey—either that, or break down the door, and he knew he was in no shape for that.

He found no one. It was late in the evening for maid service, and few people wanted room service on New Year's Eve.

Maybe I'm crazy, maybe they're sitting having dinner down in the restaurant or in the Grill—I didn't even look.

Jeremy hurried back to the elevator.

Katharine stood in the costume, Diana's costume, and felt Sebastian's hands on her shoulders, turning her to face him.

It was a little like looking at a ghost, she thought, with a new shock. Still handsome, but so very pale, the features still youthful, the features she knew so well, but the eyes seeming almost visionless.

"Sebastian."

Her voice trembled. She looked down and saw his hands. They were flexing and unflexing, their knuckles as white as his face, and they were holding the belt of the dress, a long, thickly twisted, velvet and silk rope.

"What are you doing?"

Katharine stepped back. The side of the bed was unyielding against the back of her legs.

The unseeing eyes were looking at her. *Not at me*, she thought. *At Hedda, or maybe his mother*. Perhaps she was no longer Katharine to him at all. Standing perfectly still, silently seeking her escape, she wondered if she, too, ought to participate in the bizarre charade— if she should *be* Diana Lancaster for now. *Anything to end this, anything to get out of this room.*

As if he had read her mind, Sebastian shook his head.

"No," he said, so softly that she could hardly hear him. "It's wrong."

"What's wrong, Sebastian?"

He twisted the belt in his hands, and Katharine looked down and saw the strength in his fingers, and looked back up at his face, and knew that he was beyond reason.

"No!" she said, and pushed at him, suddenly, hard. She ran toward the door, the gown weighing her down like lead, its hem sending candles flying, flames scattering, her breath a sobbing gasp in her throat, but he caught her easily, and one of his arms was around her waist and he was half carrying her, half dragging her back to the bed.

"No!" Katharine screamed, as shrilly as she could, and kicked at him, but he seemed not to feel anything. "Sebastian, *please!"*

She felt the belt around her throat, the rope, and one of his hands brushed her hair away from her neck with those icy fingers, and as she began to scream again, the belt tightened and the scream died within her, and she felt the blood draining out of her face, and she was fighting for her life, clawing at him, choking for breath—

A wind blew, suddenly, through the room, and the candles danced like dervishes as first the outer door opened, and then the bedroom doors were thrust wide, and Jeremy was standing in the entrance—

"Sebastian, what the hell are you doing?"

Katharine's eyes opened wide, and she fought the blackness that was smothering her brain, and she saw Jeremy as a dark, tautly poised silhouette, saw his smaller shadow on the walls and ceiling confronting Sebastian's.

"For the love of God, Sebastian, let go of her!"

She waited for the rope to loosen, for the grip to relax, heard her own gasping for air, stopped fighting, kept as still as she could, heard Jeremy's voice, clear and hard—

"What do you think you're *doing*, Sebastian? Take that away from her neck!" Jeremy's voice echoed in the room. "Are you killing Hedda? Is that what you're trying to do?" He spoke very distinctly, very loudly. "It isn't Hedda, Sebastian—it's Katharine—your wife, Katharine."

She felt herself swaying, knew that she was on the brink of fainting, and looking up into the crazed eyes, she saw them clamping tightly shut for an instant, then opening again, and blinking, fluttering, wildly, rapidly, before they flew open again, fully, and Katharine realized that this time he saw her, and that he suffered a split second's recognition of his own insanity.

The belt crushed tighter for an instant and then was released. With a grotesque wail, Sebastian stumbled back and fell against the wall, his hands bunched into fists, hammering into his own eyes.

Katharine, still struggling for breath, hampered by the long dress, backed away, and the velvet hem caught two candles, knocking them over, and tiny flames licked at the fabric—

"Oh, my God!"

The smell of burning shocked her into hysterical movement, rubbing, pummeling the flickering velvet even after the flames were out—

"Get out!" Jeremy hissed at her, harshly, pushing her clear.

Tears of shock spilling down her cheeks, Katharine obeyed him, moving sideways, slowly now, edging away. And then, close to the door, she stopped and looked back, and saw that Jeremy's face, the narrow eyes and mouth she had grown to dislike so strongly, was transformed into a mask of the most terrible grief. He stood quite still, staring at Sebastian, and he, too, was trembling, and there were tears in his eyes. He had already forgotten that she was there, now that her danger had passed, and all his attention was focused on the man now hunched on the floor by the wall.

With a great effort, Jeremy brought himself back under control, and walked across to Sebastian. Bending down, crouching, he put his arms around his shoulders, took one arm, and helped him to his feet.

"Come on, Seb," he murmured, gently. "Come and sit down."

He steered Sebastian past Katharine into the sitting room and, with the lightest of pressure, he pushed him down into an armchair, and she followed, keeping her distance, not daring to speak.

"I should have realized," Jeremy said, his voice so low that Katharine had to strain to hear him. "What the play meant to you. I should have known. About Charlie Grenville, at Marchmont. About Edinburgh." He paused. "About Barbara."

Fresh terror clawed at Katharine's spine.

"What about Barbara?" Her own voice was no more than a whisper.

"It was no accident," Jeremy answered, not looking at her, keeping his eyes on Sebastian. "I don't believe he planned to kill her, did you, Seb? Or maybe I just don't want to believe it. I don't know what happened."

"You're lying." Katharine's shivering increased, unable to bear it. "You're mad to say such a terrible thing."

Jeremy gave a small smile, half wry, half anguished. "I wish that were true, Kate, but it's about time we all understood. He's ill. There's something wrong, in his mind. We all knew that, you, Virginia, me —but none of us ever talked, so we couldn't help him, could we, Seb?"

Katharine looked at her husband, covering his face again with his hands. "It isn't true, Sebastian, is it? Tell me that he's wrong."

"He can't tell you that, Katharine. I don't even know if he knows how any of it happened, but it was there, lurking, even when we were children. He mixed acid with lipstick before the school production of *Hedda Gabler*, Kate, and later, at university, he burned down a theater—"

"Stop it!" Katharine begged. She felt violently ill. "I can't stand any more!"

"Why not?" Jeremy asked. "Why can't you stand it? Because you love him? You're not the only person who loves Sebastian—did you think you had a monopoly on love? I loved him long, long before you came back into our lives—I've always loved him."

Behind them, sitting in the half dark, Sebastian flinched, but Jeremy continued, unable to stop himself.

"He was always beautiful, even in those early days, a real golden boy." He shook his head. "He never knew how I felt, that I'd have done anything for him, still would. It's all right," he said, looking at Katharine. "You don't have to be afraid of that. Seb never returned my feelings. He always cared, of course, but if I'd told him how I felt, he'd have been revolted, and that would have ended our friendship."

"He's always known that you're bisexual," Katharine said, softly. "He would never have condemned you for that, not his best friend."

"It wasn't tolerance I wanted," Jeremy said. "It was love."

Sebastian groaned, a jarring sound in the room.

"You're listening, aren't you, Seb? Are you shocked, or does that groan mean you pity me because my life must have been so unbearable? Though it wasn't unbearable, until you met Kate. Before her, none of the girls, none of the women ever mattered to you, I knew that. Until Katharine." Jeremy's voice cracked. "She had everything. She was beautiful and gentle, and intelligent and refined, and she was so madly in love with you—"

"Jeremy, don't," Katharine said.

"I wanted to hate you, Kate. I really tried, but it wasn't all that easy to hate you, because you were always so damnably *nice*."

For several moments, no one spoke. And then Jeremy came back to the present.

"Why did you do it, Seb? Why did you kill Barbara? Because she was going to play Hedda?"

Sebastian's hands dropped away from his eyes.

"Why did you do it? Because of your mother? Because of Diana?"

The name hung in the air, blending with the smoke and the old, sickening odor of the costume, and in Sebastian's blue eyes the confusion was turning to hatred.

Jeremy bent over him, took his arms, gripped them.

"I'm not going to stop, Seb—I can't do that, not now, not anymore." His own dark eyes had become fierce with purpose. "You were going to kill Katharine, too, and I need to understand why. Because she tried to replace Diana, by loving you? She was the first woman you ever loved except for Diana, wasn't she? Kate made you love her, and then she moved into your mother's house and changed it, and you wanted to give her everything, and finally you gave her Hedda —but that was too much, wasn't it?"

"She told me."

For the first time, Sebastian began to speak.

"She said that no one else should play Hedda," he said. "No one but her. I heard her. She loved that part, it was what she'd always wanted, but then it killed her, it took her away from me."

The hatred had left his eyes again, and now there was bewilderment and fear. He had forgotten that, until tonight, had not really understood, but now, suddenly, the memory was so vivid, so clear that if he closed his eyes again, he could see his mother just as she had been that last time, onstage, dead in the black dress. And he could hear his father's voice saying that Hedda had killed her.

"I thought," he went on, softly, looking at Katharine, "that I wanted it for you more than I'd ever wanted anything in life. I thought you were so perfect for it, the only person alive who could play Hedda. But it all went wrong."

He got up from the chair, and looked directly into Katharine's face, and in a voice so faint that it was much less than a whisper, he said:

"Forgive me."

His face was gaunt and strained, with lines of pain that she had never seen before. Weary beyond belief.

"Forgive me, angel," he said again.

And then, moving very slowly, but steadily, Sebastian walked to the outer door, and his fingers were on the handle.

"Sebastian, no!"

Katharine's voice was torn with sudden dread. She stepped forward, but Jeremy gripped her arm, restraining her, and the door opened and then closed, and Sebastian was gone.

"What are you *doing?*" Katharine screamed at Jeremy, frantic now. "I want to go *with* him—he's in no condition to be left alone!"

Jeremy still held her arm, and he was very controlled.

"Look at yourself, Kate," he said, and steered her to the mirror.

Katharine saw the costume, half torn, the hem burned, her eyes red and swollen and anguished.

"You can't follow him like that, not if you want any shred of his reputation salvaged." Still, he gripped her arm. "I'll go after him, I'll find him, take care of him."

"Then for God's sake, *go*," she sobbed.

Jeremy released her and was at the door.

"It'll be all right, Kate," he said, quite kindly. "Wait here, and take off that dress. It'll be all right, I swear it."

And then he, too, was gone, and Katharine knew that he was lying to her, that it would never be all right again, and she had never felt more helpless, more desolate, in her entire life—

And then she remembered the child, the tiny embryo, and another new terror crept up and seized her, and she clasped her still perfectly flat stomach with both hands, and fresh tears began to fall.

Of grief.

Sebastian walked through the River Entrance out onto Savoy Place, and the doorman nodded to him, gray gloves touching his tophat.

"Happy New Year to you, sir."

"And to you," Sebastian answered.

He passed a huddle of chauffeurs, smoking together, and went on, through the gardens. Walking swiftly, hearing the quiet sounds of his shoes on the pavement. He crossed the wide street, looking right, left, right again. Carefully. One moment, he was a clear outline against the Embankment parapet. The next, he was one with the fog.

It was icy cold. He was burning hot.

There were hardly any people in the street. Just a few lonely figures, moving fast, heads down, breath steaming. No one to see.

He had never been down to the water's edge before, but he found the way easily, surefooted, silent. Down the narrow steps. A deserted stone jetty. Before him, around him, the Thames breathed rhythmically. Tiny waves, like rumpled black plastic, lapped greedy tongues at his feet. Above him, tall and incongruous, Cleopatra's Needle. Beside him, a sphynx, inscrutable, handsome. On the far side of the river, partly obscured, the Royal Festival Hall, a dim beacon, brimming with life.

Downriver, a foghorn sounded, muffled, then more strident, as the mists shifted and stirred. But Sebastian heard only voices—

Katharine's, soft and sweet, drifting past him, just out of reach. And he saw her face again, that first time, all golden and amber-eyed and full of sparkle and joy—

She didn't want another actress to have this part.

His father's voice, taking Katharine from him in a cloud of pain and bitterness, and another agonizingly clear memory from the deep, stabbing like thousands of needles—

Hedda killed her.

And he saw Diana, gazing down at him, her eyes tranquil and loving, flesh and blood on canvas, imprisoned in a wooden frame. Her voice, too, vibrant and alive and passionate, as he'd heard her so many years before.

No one else is going to play Hedda Gabler, she had said to his father. *No one, do you hear?*

"I *hear* you!" Sebastian answered her now—and his voice was beseeching, like a child's, as images smashed through him. The boy actor with his jagged, bloody mouth, lying at his feet, screaming. The burning house, the faces of the men struggling with the flames. Barbara, sailing down through the air, screaming, too—

He covered his eyes, cowering, arms flung over his ears, trying to blot them out, to obliterate the pictures and the voices, and his own cry passed away into the foggy night, a vain, bloodless whimper.

Just a few more steps.

The water was eager, clamping icily, shockingly, around his knees, like an insatiable woman, voraciously urging him deeper, grasping at his waist. For an instant, he was a child again, looking back through the fog toward the light, on the hill, reaching out through the dark, longing for something, yearning for something. That never came.

He tore his eyes from the light. For what he wanted was there, in the river. He knew that now.

And as the water closed over his head, Sebastian opened his eyes wide. And when he saw nothing at all, he tilted his head back into his welcoming, icy shroud, and laughed with the greatest relief that he had ever known. And the water rushed into his mouth.

Jeremy stood at the top of the steps. Watching.

There was a pain in his chest, in his lungs, and he heard his own harsh wheezing, and it was so like that day, long, long ago, at Aysgarth Falls, when he had seen his brother, Thomas, dying in the water, and he had stared and stared and been unable to move.

He had only loved two people completely. Thomas, who would always be ten years old, and Sebastian.

He looked down into the water and remembered that James, his father, had once told him that his great-grandfather had lost two sons and two brothers to the ocean and had uprooted his surviving family and moved hundreds of miles to escape from the water, to be safe from it.

He had reckoned without rivers.

"Sebastian!"

It was Katharine's voice, calling out through the fog, the desperation and the terror in the timbre and pitch of it, that brought Jeremy back, that forced him to move, at last, down the steps to the jetty, to the water. And it had seemed like an hour, a lifetime, yet it had been only minutes, perhaps even seconds, and as a boat passed by, its headlights captured a glint of white, and it was Sebastian's hair, and perhaps it was not too late—

Jeremy plunged into the water, and he had never felt such physical pain, but he found him, dragged at his arms, at his sleeves, pulled his head clear of the water. And Katharine was there, too, bending down, her arms outstretched—

"Take my hand! Jeremy, take my hand!"

And Jeremy thought that he would die of the cold, or that he, too, would drown, but then he felt her fingers reaching for him, and he had not dreamed that she could be so strong.

And then they were out of the water, and Jeremy laid Sebastian down on the stone jetty, and Katharine, the tears pouring down her cheeks, rolled him over, and Jeremy saw that she was in control now, that she knew what to do, and he concentrated, for the moment, on getting air into his own lungs, on surviving—and then he heard the sound of the siren, and after that there was nothing at all.

Until later.

I would have let him die. If she hadn't been there.

After I heard her screaming, I went through the motions of trying to save him. I even thought that I wanted him to make it.

But I didn't. I wanted him dead. I wanted it to be over for him. Because I loved him.

Kate would do anything for Sebastian. She'd see him a prisoner in some hospital, an institution, maybe, and she'd call that love.

I loved him enough to let him go.

I hope he dies.

c h a p t e r
30

S ebastian breathed, for a few hours, on a ventilator at St. George's
Hospital, until, knowing with certainty that he could not recover,
they turned off the machine and allowed him to die.

Twelve hours later, Katharine stepped out of the wings at the Albery
Theatre, and played the role of Hedda Gabler. It was only a preview,
and the critics were not present, but one man was heard to say, as
he and his wife were leaving the theater, that Katharine Andersen
was the most truly possessed Hedda he had ever seen.

Even Noël Harvey agreed that it was almost a tragedy that Katharine
had told them, before the performance, that it was the last part she
would ever play. She was not an actress, she had said, she had no
heart for it. She had played Hedda this afternoon for the sake of her
husband.

"Almost a tragedy," Harvey said, and March agreed, but they knew,
in their hearts, that they were both relieved beyond measure that
Rebecca Sykes, who had played Nora for them, had agreed to step
in.

Katharine's friends gathered round at Hampstead Cemetery, one
week later, in the early January snow, as they laid Sebastian beside
Diana and Andrew. Henrik Andersen stood on her right, Virginia on

her left, next to Ellie, and Sam, Laszlo and Betty, and Dixie, stood a little way behind. Jeremy stood on the far side of the grave, Elspeth beside him, and a crowd of theatrical clients and friends and acquaintances huddled under umbrellas.

And David, too, just yards away, watching Katharine's white face, his eyes never leaving her.

He stayed behind, at The Oaks, after everyone else had left, except Virginia, and she, tactful as always, had left them alone together in the drawing room.

A fire blazed in the hearth, but Katharine was cold, felt she would never be warm again.

"Would you like me to go?" David asked.

"No."

"Can I give you something? A drink?"

She shook her head.

"I'm sorry," he said. "We don't have to talk. I'm glad just to sit here by the fire."

"We do have to talk," Katharine said, softly. "At least I do." She paused. "There's something I have to tell you."

"When you're ready. Not before."

"I'm going to have a baby."

A small log fell sideways in the fireplace, sending hot sparks flying, and then there was silence.

"How long have you known?" David asked, at last.

"Just a little while."

"Are you sure? Shock can have some pretty strong side effects."

"I'm quite sure."

They were sitting apart, in separate armchairs. They had both avoided the sofa, both acutely aware that today, of all days, their own relationship, however it might, in time, unfold, was on hold. Was almost taboo. David longed to get up and go to Katharine, to hold her, but he sat quite still and waited for her to speak again.

"I'm so afraid," she said.

"For the baby?"

Her eyes met his. "You understand?"

"Of course I do."

"Virginia says that Jeremy told her he went to see a neurologist about Sebastian almost a month ago." Katharine spoke very quietly, had hardly spoken in a raised voice since her single performance as Hedda Gabler. "Her name is Joyce Osborne, and she couldn't tell

Jeremy much because all he knew was that Sebastian had had one fit, or what Jeremy thought was a fit."

"Jeremy didn't tell you about this fit?" David asked.

She shook her head. "We've never really communicated." She paused, and her eyes were filled with pain. "We all knew Sebastian was sick, David, and we all buried our heads in the sand. Partly out of loyalty, I guess. Mostly out of fear."

David said nothing, waited for her to go on.

"We might have saved him," Katharine said, chokingly, "if we'd shared what we knew."

"You might," David said. "Though I'm not sure, from what you've told me, that he would have wanted to be saved."

He went, without Katharine, two weeks after the funeral, to Joyce Osborne's consulting rooms in Harley Street. Painfully aware of her fears for the unborn child and anxious to protect her if possible, David had helped Katharine to assemble what evidence was available, to try to assist in what was now an almost impossible diagnostic exercise.

The meeting over, David took a taxi to Virginia's flat in Montpelier Square, where Katharine had stayed since the day after the funeral.

"I'll leave you," Virginia said, as they stood, awkwardly, in the hall.

"No," Katharine said, quickly. "I'd like you to stay."

"Let me get you both some tea then."

"Later, darling." Katharine was pale, but determined. "Right now, I need to hear what David has to say."

Virginia's sitting room was pretty and serene, with chintz fabrics and pale green silk wallpaper and family photographs on almost every surface. They sat down, in silence, and waited for David to begin.

"It's a bit of a jigsaw," he said. "Mostly guesswork. Dr. Osborne said right away that she doesn't like guessing, under normal circumstances, but she understands how you feel."

Neither woman spoke.

"They ran an EEG in the hospital, before Sebastian died. Do you know what that means?"

"Yes," Katharine said, and Virginia nodded.

"It showed an irregularity over one of the temporal lobes." David paused. "That could mean any one of a number of things, but one theory is that Sebastian may have sustained an injury at some time in his life."

"A head injury, you mean?" Virginia asked. "Wouldn't Andrew have known about it?"

"Not necessarily, if it seemed innocent at the time—a fall or a blow during sports, perhaps." David shrugged. "It could even have happened when he was born. Michael Adler, the old family doctor, passed on his records to Joyce Osborne, as did his mother's obstetrician. It was a tough birth, and a forceps delivery, and minor injuries have been known to happen."

"You're saying that Sebastian might have had brain damage? And no one knew it?" Katharine's voice was a disbelieving half whisper. "But he was a brilliant man."

"We'd be talking about a tiny amount of damage, sweetheart," David said, gently. "And there were contributory factors, too."

Dr. Osborne, David went on, had consulted a child psychologist, and they both agreed that the loss of his mother in what must have been—from a small boy's point of view—dramatic and traumatic circumstances, might have stored up future problems for Sebastian. The combination of such early trauma with a temporal lobe injury could have accounted for his illness.

"One of the symptoms," David told Katharine, "might have been a loss of awareness. He might, from time to time, have been briefly unconscious of his surroundings."

"Or of his actions," Katharine said, softly.

"You mean he didn't know what he was doing?" Virginia asked.

"Probably not," David said, steadily. "Or if he did, he may have blocked it out almost completely."

The room was hushed.

"And our baby?" Katharine asked, at last.

David's voice was very clear. "If those were the causes of his illness, then none of them are hereditary. You don't have to be afraid for your child, Katharine."

"Do you mean that?"

"Absolutely." David paused. "Joyce Osborne's message to you was that you should take what comfort you can from that knowledge." He sat forward, his eyes intent. "There's no reason why you should not have a perfectly healthy, normal baby."

Virginia was the first to react. She rose abruptly from her chair and went to embrace David. "God bless you," she said, her voice choked, and hurried from the room.

David looked at Katharine. She was even paler than before, and her eyes were shut.

"Are you all right?"

She opened her eyes, and he saw that they were full of tears.

"I'm fine," she whispered.

"You look like hell."

She smiled, weakly. "How can I ever thank you for this, David?"

"That's easy," he said.

"Tell me." A little color came back into her cheeks. "Anything."

"Let me see you happy again, someday." He looked at her steadily. "Perhaps let me share a little of that happiness."

Katharine never slept in The Oaks again. She put the house on the market and bought Ellie a flat close to her daughter's house in Aylesbury, and she stayed on, while their affairs were being sorted out, with Virginia. David telephoned from New York every day. Sam, his London engagement over, checked up on her regularly. Jeremy reported to her, from time to time, offers of acting roles, and Laszlo called frequently, urging her to let him escape from retirement so that they might work together again. But Katharine had no creative impulses left in her for the moment, except for the one that mattered most, and she did everything possible to make up for the terrible start to her pregnancy, ate healthy foods and exercised carefully, and thought, as much as she could, about the beautiful times with Sebastian, and about the last loving nights during which their child had been conceived.

"Is it wrong," she asked Virginia, one day, "for me to feel able to see ahead for myself and the baby?"

"How can that possibly be wrong?"

"Because I know that I'm burying the worst of my grief, and the shock. Maybe I'm just building up problems for the future."

"But you're burying all the terrible things, my darling," Virginia said, slowly, "for the sake of the baby. That seems quite healthy and sensible to me."

Katharine had felt a dreadful sense of guilt, in the beginning, but that had abated after a time, no longer consuming her, for she realized, as the weeks became months, that she could not, justifiably, blame herself, either for Sebastian's illness, or for his death. Jeremy said to her once, in a moment of particular misery, that it might have been different if she had left him, but Katharine thought that, eventually, someone else might have triggered the old nightmare again.

She had been with Sebastian, as an adult, for just two years and two months, and she often had the sense that their entire love affair and their marriage and life together had been a kind of fairy tale, a fantasy, with all its accompanying beauty and joy and tragedy. She had been spellbound by Sebastian. With him, it had all been fire or darkness, bliss or torment. She remembered, a long time ago—only three years—feeling too secure with David, too safe, and she realized now that although she was almost twenty-eight years old, it had taken her longer than most people to grow up.

Virginia went with Katharine to Heathrow in the first week of May. They parted with embraces and tears and promises to meet well before the birth, in New York.

"Will you be all right, Virginia?" Katharine asked, anxiously, for the fourth or fifth time since leaving the flat in Montpelier Square.

"I shall be fine, darling."

"And you promise you will go to Uncle Henrik soon? He wants you there so much—I think he'd leave Copenhagen and come to London if you wanted him to."

"I think he might," Virginia smiled, "but I don't think I'd let him."

Katharine held on to her hands and looked into her eyes.

"Do you think Andrew would have forgiven me?" she asked, her voice trembling. "I never really knew him, but I often felt both Sebastian's parents in that house—felt that they wanted me to look after him for them."

Virginia gripped her hands tightly. "Andrew would have loved you," she said, firmly. "And you know very well, Katharine, that there's nothing to forgive. You were the best thing that ever happened to Sebastian. He recognized that the instant he met you, and I'm sure he was aware of it even when he died."

Katharine felt numb throughout the seven-and-a-half-hour flight to New York and the landing at Kennedy, but then the turmoil struck her, first in the immigration hall and, directly afterward, in the customs area, and she experienced a huge surge of panic.

And then, emerging into the sea of passengers and relatives and baggage handlers and redcaps, she saw David, waiting for her, saw the undisguised happiness on his face, and the light in his eyes. And the panic died in her, and, as if taking its place, the child inside her quickened and kicked.

And Katharine picked up her bag, and, smiling at David, she walked back into her future.